Hiero's Journey

Hiero's Journey

A Romance of the Future

by

Sterling E. Lanier

CHILTON BOOK COMPANY
Radnor, Pennsylvania

First Edition   *All Rights Reserved*

Published in Radnor, Pa., by Chilton Book Company
and simultaneously in Ontario, Canada
by Thomas Nelson & Sons, Ltd.
Designed by Cypher Associates, Inc.
Manufactured in the United States of America

Library of Congress Cataloging in Publication Data

Lanier, Sterling E
Hiero's journey.

I. Title.
PZ4.L289Hi   [PS3562.A52]   813'.5'4   73-4999
ISBN 0-8019-5834-2

FOR PATTIE,

who does the work

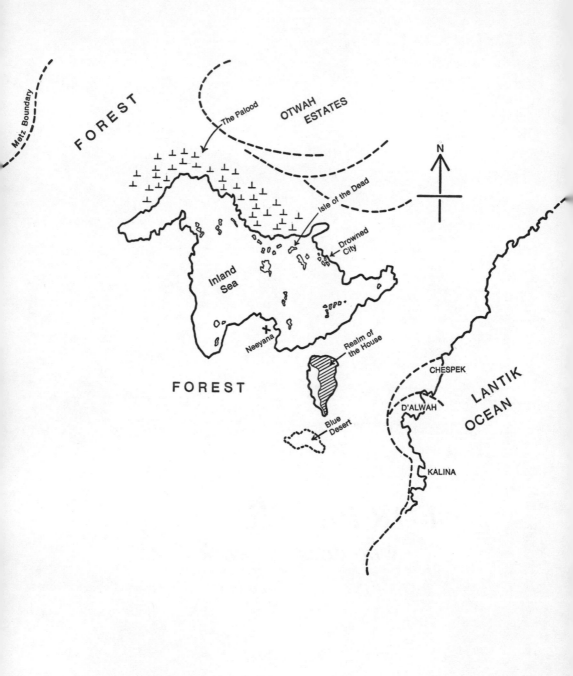

CONTENTS

I: THE SIGN
OF THE FISHHOOK

The Computer man, thought Hiero. *That sounds crisp, efficient, and what's more, important. Also,* added his negative side, *mainly meaningless as yet.*

Under his calloused buttocks the bull morse, whose name was Klootz, ambled slowly along the dirt track, trying to snatch a mouthful of browse from neighboring trees whenever possible. His protruding blubber lips were as good as a hand for this purpose.

Per Hiero Desteen, Secondary Priest-Exorcist, Primary Rover and Senior Killman, abandoned his brooding and straightened in the high-cantled saddle. The morse also stopped his leaf-snatching and came alert, rack of forward pointing, palmate antlers lifting. Although the wide-spread beams were in the velvet and soft now, the great black beast, larger than any long-extinct draft horse, was an even more murderous fighter with his sharp, splayed hooves.

Hiero listened intently and reined Klootz to a halt. A dim uproar was growing increasingly louder ahead, a swell of bawling and aaahing noises, and the ground began to tremble. Hiero knew the sound well and so did the morse. Although it was late August here in the far North, the buffer were already moving south in their autumn migration, as they had for uncounted thousands of years.

Morse and rider tried to peer through the road's border of larch or alder. The deeper gloom of the big pines and scrub palmetto beyond prevented any sight going further, but the noise was getting steadily louder.

Hiero tried a mind probe on Klootz, to see if he was getting a fix on the herd's position. The greatest danger lay in being trapped in front of a wide-ranging herd, with the concomitant inability to get away to either side. The buffer were not particularly mean, but they weren't especially bright either, and they slowed down for almost nothing except fire.

The morse's mind conveyed uneasiness. He felt that they were in the wrong place at the wrong time. Hiero decided not to delay any longer and turned south off the trail, allowing Klootz to pick a way, and hopefully letting them get off at an angle to the oncoming buffer.

Just as they left the last sight of the road, Hiero looked back. A line of great, brown, rounded heads, some of them carrying six-foot, polished yellow horns, broke through the undergrowth onto the road as he watched. The grunting and bawling was now very loud indeed. An apparently endless supply of buffer followed the huge herd bulls.

Hiero kicked the morse hard and also applied the goad of his mind.

Come on, Stupid, he urged. *Find a place where they'll have to split or we've had it.*

Klootz broke into a shambling trot, which moved the great body along at a surprising rate. Avoiding trees and crushing bushes aside, the huge animal paced along through the forest, looking deceptively slow. Hiero rode easily, watching for overhanging branches, even though the morse was trained to avoid them.

The man's leather boots, deer-hide breeches and jacket gave him a good deal of protection from the smaller branches which whipped him as they tore along. He wore nothing on his head but a leather skull cap, his copper helmet being kept in one of the saddlebags. He kept one hand raised to guard his face and mentally flogged the morse again. The big beast responded with increased speed and also rising irritation, which Hiero felt as a wave of mental heat.

Sorry, I'll let you do your own job he sent, and tried to relax. No one was exactly sure just how intelligent a morse really was. Bred from the mutated giant moose many generations before, although well after The Death, they were marvelous draft and riding animals. The Abbeys protected their herds carefully and sold their prized breeding stock with great reluctance. But there was a stubborn core of independence which no one had been able to breed out, and allied to it an uncertain but high degree of intelligence. The Abbey psykes were still testing their morses and would continue to do so.

Hiero swore suddenly and slapped at his forehead. The mosquitoes and black flies were attacking, and the splash of water below indicated Klootz was aiming for a swamp. Behind them the uproar of the herd was growing muted. The buffer did not like swamps although quite capable of swimming for miles at need.

Hiero did not like swamps either. He signalled "halt" with his legs and body, and Klootz stopped. The bull broke wind explosively. "Naughty," said Hiero, looking carefully about.

Pools of dark water lay about them. Just ahead, the water broadened into a still pond of considerable size. They had stopped on an island of rock, liberally piled with broken logs, no doubt by the past season's flood waters. It was very silent here, with the roar and grumble of the buffer only a distant background noise now, behind them and to the east. A small, dark bird ran down a lichened tree trunk and twittered faintly. Dark pines and pale cypress rose directly from the water, cutting off sunlight and giving the place a gloomy aspect. The flies and mosquitoes were bad, their humming attack causing Hiero to pull up the hood of his jacket. The morse stamped and blew out his great lips in a snort.

The ripple on the black surface was what saved them. Hiero was too well trained to abandon all caution, even when slapping bugs, and the oily "V" of something moving just under the surface toward the island from farther out in the open water caught his eye as he looked about.

"Come on up," he shouted, and reined the big beast back on its haunches, so that they were at least ten feet from the edge when the snapper emerged.

There was no question of fighting. Even the holstered thrower at Hiero's side, and certainly his spear and knife, were almost useless against a full-grown snapper. Nor did Klootz feel any differently, in spite of all his bulk and fighting ability.

The snapper's hideous beaked head was four feet long and three wide. The giant turtle squattered out of the water in one explosive rush, clawed feet scrabbling for a hold on the rock, the high, grey, serrated shell spraying foul water as it came, yellow eyes gleaming. Overall, it must have weighed over three tons, but it moved very fast just the same. From a sixty-five pound maximum weight before The Death, the snappers had grown heroically, and they made many bodies of water impassable except by an army. Even the Dam People had to take precautions.

Still, fast as it was, it was no match for the frightened morse. The big animal could turn on half his own length and now did so. Even as the snapper's beaked gape appeared over the little islet's peak, the morse and his rider were a hundred feet off and going strong through the shallow marsh, back the way they had come, spraying water in sheets. Stupid as it was, the snapper could see no point in following further, and shut its hooked jaws with a reluctant snap as the galloping figure of the morse disappeared around a pile of windfalls.

As soon as they had reached dry ground, Hiero reined in the morse and both listened again. The roar of the buffer's passage was steadily dying away to the south and east. Since this was the direction he wanted to go anyway, Hiero urged Klootz forward on the track of the migrating herd. Once more both man and beast were relaxed, without losing any watchfulness in the process. In the Year of Our Lord, seven thousand, four hundred and seventy-six, constant vigilance paid off.

Moving cautiously, since he did not wish to come upon a buffer cow with a calf or an old outcast bull lagging behind the herd, Hiero steered the morse slowly back to the road he had left earlier. There were no buffer in sight, but a haze hung on the windless air, fine dust kicked up by hundreds of hoofed feet and piles of steaming dung lay everywhere. The stable reek of the herd blanked out all other scents, something that made both man and morse uncomfortable, for they relied on their excellent noses, as well as eyes and ears.

Hiero decided, nonetheless, to follow the herd. It was not a large one, he estimated, no more than two thousand head at most, and in its immediate wake lay a considerable amount of safety from the various dangers of the Taig. There were perils too, of course, there were perils everywhere, but a wise man tried to balance the lesser against the greater. Among the lesser were the commensal vermin, which followed a buffer herd, preying on the injured, the aged and the juveniles. As Hiero urged the morse forward, a pair of big, grey wolves loped across the track ahead of them, snarling as they did. Wolves had not changed much, despite the vast changes around them and the mutated life of the world in general. Certain creatures and plants seemed to reject spontaneous genetic alteration, and wolves, whose plasticity of gene had enabled thousands of dog breeds to appear in the ancient world, had reverted to type and stayed there. They were cleverer, though, and avoided confrontation with humans if possible. Also, they killed any domestic dog they could find, patiently stalking it if necessary, so that the people of the Taig kept their dogs close at hand and shut them up at night.

Hiero, being an Exorcist and thus a scientist, knew this of course, and also knew the wolves would give him no trouble if he gave them none. He could "hear" their defiance in his mind and so could his huge mount, but both could also assess the danger involved, which was almost non-existent in this case.

Reverting to his leaf-snatching amble, the morse followed the track of the herd, which in turn was roughly following the road. Two cartloads wide, this particular dirt road was hardly an important artery of commerce between the East of Kanda and the West, out of which Hiero was now riding. The Metz Republic, which claimed him as a citizen, was a sprawling area of indefinite

4

boundaries, roughly comprising ancient Saskatchewan, Manitoba and Alberta, as well as parts of the old Northwest Territories. There were so few people in comparison to the land area that territorial boundaries were somewhat meaningless in the old sense of the word. They tended to be ethnic or even religious, rather than national.

The Taig, the vast boreal forest of conifers which had spread across the northern world at least a million years before The Death, still dominated the North. It was changed however, with many species of warm country plants intermingled with the great pines. Some plant species had died, vanished entirely, as had some animals also, but most had survived, and adapted to the warmer climate. Winters were now fairly mild in the West of Kanda, with the temperature seldom ever getting below five degrees Centigrade. The polar caps had shrunk and the earth was once again in another deep interglacial period. What had caused the change to be so drastic, man or nature, was a debated point in the Abbey classrooms. The Greenhouse Effect and its results were still preserved in the old records, but too much empiric data was lacking to be certain. Scientists, both Abbey and laymen, however, never stopped searching for more data on the lost ages in an effort to help shape the future. The terror of the ancient past was one thing which had never been lost, despite almost five thousand years. That The Death must never be allowed to come again was the basic reason for all scientific training. On this, except for outlaws and the Unclean, all men were agreed. As a good scientist and Abbey scholar, Hiero continually reflected on the problems of the past, even as now, while seeming to daydream in the saddle.

He made an effective picture as he slowly rode along, and not being without vanity, was aware of it. He was a stocky, young man, clean-shaven but for a mustache, with the straight black hair, copper skin and hooked nose of a good Metz. He was moderately proud of his pure descent, for he could tell off thirty generations of his family without a break. It had come as a profound shock in the Abbey school, when the father abbot had gently pointed out that he and all other true Metz, including the abbot himself, were descended from the *Metis,* the French Canadian-Indian half-breeds of the remote past, a poverty-striken minority whose remoteness and isolation from city life had helped save a disproportionate number of them from The Death. Once this had been made clear to him, Hiero and his classmates never again boasted of their birth. The egalitarian rule of the Abbeys, based solely on merit, became a new source of pride instead.

On Hiero's back was strapped his great knife, a thing like a short, massive sword, with a straight heavy back, sharp point, a fourteen-inch rounded blade and only one edge. It was very old, this object from before The Death, and a prize won by Hiero for Scholastic excellence. On its blade were incised in worn letters and numbers, "U.S." and "1917" and "Plumb. Phila." with a picture of a thing like an onion with leaves attached. Hiero knew it was incredibly ancient and that it had once belonged to men of the United States, which had long ago been a great empire of the South. This was all he or perhaps anyone could know of the old Marine Corps bolo, made for a long-lost campaign in Central America, forgotten five millennia and more. But it was a good weapon and he loved its weight.

He also carried a short, heavy spear, a weapon with a hickory shaft and ten-inch leaf-shaped, steel blade. A cross bar of steel went through the base of the blade at right angles, creating what any ancient student of weaponry would have recognized at once as a boar spear. The cross guard was designed to prevent any animal (or human) from forcing its way up the spear shaft even when impaled by the spear's point. This was not an old weapon, but had been made by the Abbey armory for Hiero when he had completed his Man Tests. At his saddlebow was holstered a third weapon, wooden stock forward. This was a Thrower, a muzzleloading, smooth bore carbine, whose inch and a half bore fired six-inch long explosive rockets. The weapon was hideously expensive, the barrel being made of beryllium copper, and its small projectiles had to be hand-loaded by the small, private factory which produced them. It was a graduation present from his father, and had cost twenty robes of prime marten fur. When his stock of projectiles was exhausted, the thrower was useless, but he carried fifty of them in his pack and few creatures alive could take a rocket shell and still keep coming. A six-inch, two-edged knife, bonehandled, hung in his belt scabbard.

His clothes were leather, beautifully dressed tan deer-skin, very close-fitting, almost as soft as cloth and far more durable. In his leather saddlebags were packed a fur jacket, gloves and folding snow shoes, as well as food, some small pieces of copper and silver for trading, and his Exorcist's gear. On his feet were kneeboots of brown deerskin, with triple strength heels and soles of hardened, layered leather for walking. The circled cross and sword of the Abbeys gleamed in silver on his breast, a heavy thong supporting the medallion. And on his bronzed, square face were painted the marks of his rank in the Abbey service, a yellow maple leaf on the forehead and under it two snakes coiled about a spear shaft, done in green. These marks were very ancient indeed and were always put on first by the head of the Abbey, the Father Superior himself when the rank was first achieved. Each morning, Hiero renewed them from tiny jars carried in his saddlebags. Throughout the entire north, they were recognized and honored, except by those humans beyond the law and the unnatural creatures spawned by The Death, the Leemutes* who were mankind's greatest enemy.

Hiero was thirty-six and unmarried, although most men his age were the heads of large families. Yet he did not want to become abbot or other member of the hierarchy and end up as an administrator, he was sure of that. When teased about it, he was apt to remark with an immobile face, that no woman, or women, could interest him for long enough to perform the ceremony. But he was no celibate. The celibate priesthood was a thing of the dead past. Priests were expected to be part of the world, to struggle, to work, to share in all worldly activities, and there is nothing worldlier than sex. The Abbeys were not even sure if Rome, the ancient legendary seat of their faith, still existed, somewhere far over the Eastern Ocean. But even if it did, their long-lost traditional obedience to its Pontiff was gone forever, gone with the knowledge of how to communicate across so vast a distance and many other things as well.

Birds sang in massed choruses as Hiero rode along in the afternoon sunlight. The sky was cloudless and the August heat not uncomfortable. The morse ambled at exactly the pace he had learned brought no goad and not one instant faster. Klootz was fond of his master, and knew exactly how far Hiero could be pushed before he lost his patience. The bull's great ears fanned the air in ceaseless search for news, recording the movements of small creatures as much as a quarter of a mile away in the wood. But before the long, drooping muzzle of the steed and the rider's abstracted eye, the dusty road lay empty, spotted with fresh dung and churned up by the buffer herd, whose passage could still be heard ahead of them in the distance.

This was virgin timber through which the road ran. Much of the Kandan continent was unsettled, much more utterly unknown. Settlements tended to radiate from one of the great Abbeys, for adventurous souls had a habit of disappearing. The pioneer settlements which were unplanned and owed their existence to an uncontrolled desire for new land had a habit of mysteriously falling out of communication. Then, one day, some woodsman, or perhaps a priest sent by the nearest Abbey, would find a cluster of mouldering houses surrounded by overgrown fields. There was occasional muttering that the Abbeys discouraged settlers and tried to prevent new opening up of the woods, but no one ever dreamt that the priesthood was in any way responsible for the vanished people. The Council of Abbots had repeatedly warned

---

* *Leemute:* corruption of ancient words, 'Lethal Mutation'. Now, in altered meaning, a creature lethal *to* humans, rather than to itself.

7

against careless pioneering into unknown areas, but beyond the very inner disciplines taught to the priesthood, the Abbeys had few secrets and never interfered in everyday affairs. They tried to build new Abbeys as fast as possible, thus creating new enclaves of civilization around which settlements could rally, but there were only so many people in the world, and few of these made either good priests or soldiers. It was slow work.

As Hiero rode, his mnemonic training helped him automatically to catalogue for future reference everything he saw. The towering jackpines, the great white-barked aspens, the olive palmetto heads, a glimpse of giant grouse through the trees, all were of interest to the Abbey files. A priest learned early that exact knowledge was the only real weapon against a savage and uncertain world.

Morse and rider were now eight days beyond the easternmost Abbey of the Metz Republic, and this particular road ran far to the south of the main east-west artery to distant Otwah, and was little known. Hiero had picked it after careful thought, because he was going both south and east himself, and also because using it would supply new data for the Abbey research centers.

His thoughts reverted to his mission. He was only one of the six Abbey volunteers. He had no illusions about the dangers involved in what he was doing. The world was full of savage beasts and more savage men, those who lived beyond any law and made pacts with darkness and the Leemutes. And the Leemutes themselves, what of them? Twice he had fought for his life against them, the last time two years back. A pack of fifty hideous ape-like creatures, hitherto unknown, riding bareback on giant, brindled dog-things, had attacked a convoy on the great western highway while he had commanded the guard. Despite all his forelooking and alertness, and the fact that he had a hundred trained Abbeymen, as well as the armed traders, all good fighters, the attack had been beaten off only with great difficulty. Twenty dead men and several cartloads of vanished goods were the result. And not one captive, dead or alive. If a Leemute fell, one of the great spotted dog-things had seized him and borne him away.

Hiero had studied the Leemute files for years and knew as much as anyone below the rank of abbot about the various kinds. And he knew enough to know how much he did not know, that many things existed in the wide world of which he was totally ignorant.

The thought of fore-looking made Hiero rein the morse to a halt. Using the mind powers, with or without Lucinoge, could be very dangerous. The Unclean often had great mental powers too, and some of them were alerted by human thoughts, alerted and drawn to them. There was no question of what would happen if a pack such as had struck the convoy found a lone man ready to hand.

Still, there had to be *some* danger anywhere, and fore-looking often helped one to avoid it if not used to excess. "Your wits, your training, and your senses are your best guides," the father abbots taught. "Mental search, fore-looking and cold-scanning are no replacements for these. And if overused, they are very dangerous." That was plain enough. But Hiero Desteen was no helpless youth, but a veteran priest-officer, and all this by now was so much relfex action.

He urged the morse off the track, as he did so hearing the buffer herd just at the very edge of earshot. *They are travelling fast,* he thought, and wondered why.

In a little sunny glade, a hundred yards from the trail, he dismounted and ordered Klootz to stand watch. The big morse knew the routine as well as the man and lifted his ungainly head and shook the still-soft rack of antlers. From the left saddlebag, Hiero took his priest's case and removed the board, its pieces, then the crystal and the stole; draping the latter over his shoulders, he seated himself cross-legged on the pine needles and stared into the crystal. At the same time he positioned his left hand on the board, lightly but firmly over the pile of markers and with his right made the sign of the cross on his forehead and breast.

"In the name of the Father, his murdered Son and Spirit," he intoned, "I, a priest of God, ask for vision ahead on my road. I, a humble servant of man, ask for help in my journeying. I, a creature of earth, ask for signs and portents." As he concentrated staring into the crystal, he kept his mind fixed firmly on the road and especially the area to the east and south, the direction in which he was headed.

In a moment, as he watched, the clear crystal became cloudy, as if filled with swimming wraiths of mist and fog. Thousands of years after western anthropologists had refused to believe the evidence of their own eyes when watching Australian aborigines communicate over hundreds of miles by staring into two pools of water, a man of the fifty-seventh century prepared to see what lay ahead of him in his travels.

As Hiero stared, the mist cleared and he felt drawn down into the crystal, as if he were becoming a part of it. He shrugged this familiar feeling aside and found himself looking down on the buffer herd and the road from hundreds of feet up in the air. He was using the eyes of a bird, almost certainly a hawk, he thought with a detached part of his mind. As his vision swayed to and fro over a wide arc of country, he fixed everything he saw firmly in his memory. Here was a lake, there to the south, a river next to a big swamp over which a distant road seemed to run on pilings (no mention of *that* in his briefings; better look out). The bird was not conscious it was being used. Hiero was not in any sense controlling it; that was a different business altogether and much harder, not always possible in fact. But his concentration on his route had allowed the mind of the creature which saw that route most clearly to somehow *attract* his, as a magnet draws a nail. Had no bird been overhead, perhaps a squirrel in a high tree would have been his lens, or even a buffer in the front rank of the herd, if nothing better offered. Hawks and eagles were the best possible eyes and there were enough of them about so that there was usually a good chance of hitting on one. Their eyes were not exactly the same as a man's, but at least they had a sort of binocular vision. This type of thing was easy for a man of Hiero's large experience, who could, if necessary, utilize the widely separated eyes of a deer which saw two images.

He noted that the buffer were moving at a fast, steady trot, not panicky, but alerted, as if some danger were coming but as yet was not too close. The two wolves he had seen earlier were most unlikely to have caused this feeling and he wondered again what had. Sitting up, he broke the trance and looked down at his left hand. Clenched in his fist were two of the forty small symbols which he had scattered about the shallow, dish-shaped board. He opened his own hand and saw another hand in miniature, the tiny carved Hand which signified "friendship." He dropped it back in the dish and looked at the other symbol. It was the miniature wooden Fishhook. He dropped that in too, and emptied the pieces into their leather pouch while considering. His subconscious precognition had found a curious combination, which needed thought. The Fishhook had several meanings. One was "concealed danger." Another was "concealed meaning" or, by extension, a puzzle. In conjunction with the open hand, one meaning could be "a friend approaches with a riddle." Another might well be, "beware of a seeming friend who means you ill." It had, curiously, nothing to do with either fish or fishing.

With only forty symbols, the precognition markers were often obscure. But as was pointed out to every beginning student, if they saved your life, or someone else's life, even once, they were certainly worth it, were they not? And a good, sensitive man or woman could do a lot with them. Hiero regarded his own ability in this particular area as only about average, not anywhere near up to his ability to use animal eyes as a concealed spyglass. But he had been helped by the markers before and he always felt better for having used them.

As he was repacking the saddlebag, the morse, who still remained on guard, snorted suddenly. Hiero turned, his heavy blade drawn out over his left shoulder and in a ward position as if by magic. Only then he saw the small bear.

Bears had changed over the millennia like everything else, that is, all bears had changed in some ways. This was a black bear and a twentieth century zoologist would have seen nothing odd about its body at first glance, except a larger and more rounded forehead. If he had looked not at, but into the eyes, more might have been glimpsed. Bears were never stupid; now they were, unevenly perhaps, approaching non-animal levels. It was alone, Hiero saw, and nothing else was around.

The bear looked about half-grown, and stood on its hind legs, front paws hanging limp in front of it. *It might weigh a hundred and fifty pounds*, thought Hiero. *It might weigh somewhat more, and not be half-grown at all, but a new type altogether.* His mind probed at the animal and he kept his guard up. The thought he got in return was strong.

Friend—human friend—food (a plea). *Friend—help—danger* (a feeling of heat). *Friend—bear* (himself—identity feeling)—*help—danger.* This was surprisingly vibrant and clear. Hiero was used to conversing with wild things, although with an effort, but this animal had almost the power of a trained human. What a lot there was in the world!

As the man lowered his short sword and relaxed, the bear settled on its haunches also. Hiero sent a thought at Klootz and told him to stay on guard, noting in passing that the big bull seemed to feel the bear was harmless.

Reaching into his saddlebags, Hiero brought out some dried, pressed *pemeekan*. The ancient travel food of the north, animal fat, maple sugar and dried berries pressed into a cake, still kept its old name unchanged. As he broke off a piece and threw it to the bear, Hiero sent another thought.

Who/what are you? What/who brings danger?

The bear caught the *pemeekan* between his paws in a very human gesture and snapped it up in one bite. His thoughts were confused for a moment, then cleared up.

Food (good/satisfying)—*more? Bad things come—hunt—hunt humans, animals—hunt this human—not far behind now—not far in front—Death lies all around—bear* (himself) *help human?*

There was a last blurred thought which the man realized was the bear giving his own name. It was unpronounceable, but Gorm was a fairly close approximation. Under the clear and obvious thoughts, Hiero learned more. Gorm was a young bear, only about three years old and relatively new to this area, having come from the East. But the danger was real and it was closing in

11

on all sides as they stood there. For a brief glimpsed instant, *through* the bear's mind, Hiero caught a flash of utter, cold malignity, an impression of something bloated and soft in a secret place, spinning a web of terror throughout the forest. The bear had shown him this deliberately, he now saw, to impress upon him the danger. Leemutes, the Unclean! Nothing else caused such horror and hatred in normal man or beast. Beside him, Klootz snorted and stamped a great forehoof. He had caught a good deal of what had passed between the two and didn't like it.

Hiero turned and finished packing, his back to Gorm. He was convinced there was no danger from the half-grown cub, and that the bear was both frightened himself and anxious to be of help. Civilized men seldom hunted bears any longer and the old enmity of pioneer and bruin no longer existed.

Swinging up into his high saddle, the man sent a thought of inquiry to the animal on the ground. *Where?*

Follow—safety—danger first—slow—follow came the answer as Gorm dropped to all fours and scuttled away from the clearing. Without even being urged, Klootz swung in his wake, maintaining a pace which kept him about fifteen feet to the rear. The fact that the morse trusted the young bear was a major factor in Hiero's own decision to do so. The morse stock was bred for alertness as well as strength and skill, and their mental watch-dog capabilities were considered quite as important as their physical qualities.

They went south, back the way Klootz had come, and soon recrossed the road. Here, the bear did something which made Hiero blink. Signalling them to stop, Gorm re-crossed the dirt track and then dragged himself back by his front legs, his fat rear end obliterating Klootz's broad tracks! Only the passage of the buffer herd and a smeared place now showed on the dust of the road.

Follow (Gorm)—*walk hard ground* (quietly)—*not leave mark* came the thought. Following it, there came one more: *Not speak—watch* (me) *only—others listen* (for) —*speak—danger.*

Hiero nodded to himself. The bear was indeed clever, very clever. There must be a nest of Leemutes or some center or other nearby. If mind-speech was used, it might well be picked up and some terror or other be sent on their tracks. He remembered that flash of shuddersome, gelid hatred the bear had shown him and a tingle ran down his spine.

For some time, Gorm moved at a steady pace which was no more than a good walk for the bull morse. The warrior priest kept a keen watch. A veteran woodsman, he noted that he and his mount were being led over underlying granite spines of firm ground and also that the woods were very quiet. The

12

great forest of Kanda, where undisturbed, was full of life, in the trees, on the ground and even in the air. Now, the land was silent. No squirrels chattered at the travelers, birds were few and shy, and not a trace of the larger creatures, such as deer, was to be seen. In the windless hush of the late summer afternoon, the almost noiseless progress of the three yet sounded very loud in Hiero's ears. A sense of oppression was in his mind, almost of pressure from outside, as if the atmosphere itself had somehow grown denser.

Hiero crossed himself. This strange silence and spiritual oppression were not normal, and could only come from the forces of darkness, from the Unclean, or some lair of theirs.

Abruptly, Gorm stopped. Through some signal that even his owner could not catch, the giant morse was given an order. Instantly, he too stopped, and just as instantly lay down, crouching beside a great pile of deadfalls. Klootz weighed just a trifle under a ton, but he sank to his knees with the grace of a dancer and without a sound. Ten feet in front of the morse's moist and pendulous nose, the bear crouched, peering around a bush. On the neck of the morse, Hiero too lay stretched out, peering forward and trying to see what had alarmed their guide so.

All three were looking down into a broad shallow hollow in the land, thinly planted with seedling alders and low brush. As they watched, from the tall forest on the other side of the dip and well to their right, a column of a dozen or so figures emerged.

Hiero had thought he was familiar with many types of Leemute, the Manrats, and Hairy Howlers, the Were-bears (which were not bears at all), the Slimers and several others besides. But these were new and, like all Leemutes, unpleasant to look at. They were short, no more than four feet tall on the average but very broad and squat, and walked erect on their hind legs, their bushy tails dragging behind. They were completely covered with long, dripping oily-looking fur, of a yellow-brown hue and their beady-eyed faces were pointed and evil. It would have been hard to trace their ancestry back to a genetic accident in a wolverine family after The Death, even for a contemporary expert, and Hiero simply catalogued them as a new and dangerous breed. For they had actual *hands* and their rounded heads and gleaming eyes indicated intelligence of a high if nasty order. They wore no clothing but each carried a long-handled wooden club, in the head of which was set glittering fragments of obsidian. A wave of evil purpose went before them like a cloud of gas, as they moved one behind the other, in a curious hopping gait, which still covered the ground at a good speed. Every few feet, the leader stopped to sniff the air, and then dropped to all fours to check the earth, while the others peered about on every side. The three on the knoll above them froze into immobility, trying not to breathe. The evil Furhoppers, as Hiero promptly named them, were perhaps two hundred yards off and if they continued their present course, would pass down over the shallow slope of the bowl and up the other side, moving off to the left of the three's position. But, when the line of crouching figures reached the center of the depression, they halted. Hiero tensed, one hand instinctively reaching for his reliquary and the poison it contained. For another figure had appeared and was advancing on the Furhoppers.

It was apparently a tall man, garbed in a long cloak of a dark grey, which was closely wrapped around him, and showed only his sandalled feet. His hood was thrown back and his naked hairless head was revealed in the rays of the evening sun. His skin was so pale as to appear dead-white and his eyes were a shifting color, impossible to see at this distance. On the right breast of his cloak was a spiral symbol, also difficult to see, etched in a dark scarlet, of interwoven lines and circles. He seemed to carry no visible weapons, but an aura of both spiritual power and of cold menace, radiated from him as the chill of a great iceberg goes out from it to warn seafarers.

This was an extraordinary chance, for good or ill, and Hiero knew it. The Unclean had been rumored and more than rumored for centuries to have human directors, a race of men totally given over to evil and wizardry. On several occasions such people had been reportedly glimpsed directing attacks on Abbey convoys or settlements, but the information was vague and contradictory. On two occasions, however, men had been killed trying to penetrate the secret training rooms and guarded files of Abbey Central in Sask. Each time, the bodies of the slain had almost instantly *dissolved* into piles of corruption, leaving nothing to be investigated save for ordinary clothing, which might have been acquired anywhere. But in each case, the Abbey guardians and priests had been warned by mental alarms of the spirit, not of the flesh, and in each case the man [or entity] had penetrated through many men on guard who recalled seeing nothing. This creature before him now could only be one of these mysterious men who were thought to rule the Unclean. No normal man, not even an outlaw, would or could associate with a foul pack such as this, and yet, as the man strode to them, the savage creatures cringed aside in evident fear.

The leader of the Fur creatures, crouching low, came up to the man and the two moved a little apart, while the others milled restlessly about, grunting and whining in low tones. Hiero could see that man's lips move and the yellow fangs of the Furhopper chief flash in answer. They were ac-

14

tually talking, not using mind speech, one to the other! Even as he inwardly shrank in loathing from the whole gang, the scientist in Hiero could not help applauding the feat. With normal speech, there would be no betraying mental currents, such as made him afraid to address Klootz more than was absolutely necessary and had caused the bear to impress mental silence upon them.

Now, the conversation apparently over, the man seemed to dismiss the pack of hideous creatures and turning about, simply walked away in the direction from which he had come. This was to the south and east. The Furhoppers surrounded their leader, who snarled something out which silenced them. In a moment they had formed their line again, and were tramping the dead leaves back on the way they had come, which was from the west.

As the grey-cloaked man disappeared in one direction and the Furhoppermutes in the other, all three creatures on the edge of the bowl relaxed a little. But no one used mind speech, they simply sat quietly and waited.

After what must have been a good half hour, Gorm the bear slowly rose and stretched. He looked around at Klootz and his rider sending no message, but his meaning was plain. The big morse arose as silently as he had lain down and from his vantage high on the great back, Hiero surveyed the silent forest before them.

The setting sun slanted down through the pines and maples and lit the patchy undergrowth in flashes of vivid green, turning various piles of dead leaves into russet and gold. Ancient logs glowed with color as green moss and grey lichen were caught in the last patches of sunlight. *How beautiful the land is* reflected the priest, *and yet how full of evil under its loveliness.*

But Gorm was all business and as he lurched down into the hollow, Klootz followed him, his great forked hooves making no more sound in the leaves than a mouse would have.

To Hiero's alarm, the small bear was headed for the exact spot on the far side of the depression into which the sinister person in the cloak had gone. While desperately anxious to know more about this dark being and his purposes, Hiero did not want a direct encounter with him. His mission, far to the East, came first above all else. He dared not send a mental message, not with the enemy so close about them that the sense of mental oppression was still a weight on his spirit, and could think of no way to halt, or re-direct, the bear except by physical means.

"Pssst", he hissed, and again.

15

Gorm looked back and saw the man gesturing violently to stop. He halted on a patch of leaves and let Klootz catch up.

Hiero, looking down at the bear, could think of nothing to do which would explain what he wanted. He was keeping a rigid mind-block on, and he had a more than strong feeling that loosing it would bring a pack of devils down upon them from every point of the compass. But Gorm saved him the trouble. Looking shrewdly up at Hiero for a moment, the bear bent down and swept aside some leaves with his curiously delicate paws. Exposing smooth earth, with one long claw, he made a line and pointed it with an arrow, just as a man might. The line led on the way they were going. On both sides of the line and behind it, Gorm carefully scratched numerous small circles or spirals. Irresistably, the priest was reminded of the spiral, interwoven symbol on the cloak of the enemy. The message was plain. Peril lay behind them and on either side, but despite the fact that they were following the sinister figure of the bald man, less danger lay on that route than on any other. The bear looked up and Hiero nodded. Gorm swept leaves over his artwork and started off again with no more ado. The man nudged his great mount and Klootz followed obediently in the bear's wake.

On his back, the rider turned over in his mind the way the bear had reacted, ever since he had first appeared. Why the creature was human! The Dam People were thought to be as intelligent as people, although with a different outlook on life. Many of the Leemutes, of course, were as clever as men, although altogether malign and dangerous to life and spirit. But here was another animal species rising to humanity. This would make a fine problem for the Abbey theologians, Hiero thought wryly. They still could not agree on the spiritual status of the Dam People, and a fresh species of creature for whom there was no scriptural precedent would start the doctrinal pot boiling all over again.

The sunlight under the big trees was fading fast, but Klootz could see in full dark like a cat and presumably the bear could also, so that Hiero felt no particular concern. He, himself, could see as well as many of the wild things when the light was dim, a result of a childhood spent in the forest as well as the cultivated ability of a trained woodsman. He was in no hurry to make camp, not being particularly tired and he badly wanted to get away from the artificial silence of the wood, the zone of mental oppression which he felt so strongly.

For a mile or two the little party moved under a pure forest of the great pines, the faint crackle of the deep-banked needles the only sign that bear and morse were passing. The light was very dim now, but an occasional ray of sunshine still broke through a gap in the foliage far above and illumined a patch of forest floor or a small clump of fern.

Suddenly, with no warning, Gorm was gone. One moment he had been padding ten feet in front, the next he vanished. Klootz checked, his big ears lifting and his great nostrils flaring as he sought for a scent of some kind. His rider reached smoothly for the holstered thrower strapped to his saddle, at the same time looking keenly about. *Is this treachery?* His mind raced. *The bear—had he been a friend or was this the sign of the Fishhook being revealed, a false friend and a traitorous guide?* The thrower was halfway from its scabbard and lying across the pommel of the saddle when the silence was broken by a voice.

Musical and deep, the note of a trained orator, it rang under the arched branches from their left, speaking in perfect Metz.

"An ugly beast and a still uglier rider. Who follows on the tracks of S'nerg? Is this the prey we have sought all day?"

One of the rare beams of last sunlight streamed down onto a flat boulder perhaps twenty feet from the morse's left side. Upon it, arms crossed on his breast, and a thoroughly nasty smile on his face, stood the man of the grey cloak, looking coldly at Hiero. Of the bear, there was no trace. Apparently the two men and the morse were alone.

"A priest and one of some rank in your absurd hierarchy, I see," the cloaked man, whose name as apparently S'nerg, went on. "We have seen few priests in these parts, having a dislike for such vermin. When I have made an example of you, Little priest, we shall see fewer yet!"

As he listened, Hiero had been slowly tightening his hold on the thrower, which lay across the saddle facing the other way from his enemy. He was under no illusions about his own safety despite the fact that S'nerg appeared unarmed. From the almost visible aura the man radiated, the electric sense of power, the Metz warrior-cleric knew he was in the presence of a great adept, a mental master, who in his dark way was perhaps the equal of a Council member or Grand Abbot. Against such, any physical weapons were a matter of luck.

Lowering his arms, S'nerg stepped from his rock and strode toward Hiero. As he did, Hiero whipped the thrower up and tried to fire. His finger could not reach the trigger. He was locked in a muscle spasm, the weapon's barrel halfway aimed, but unable to move further. Despite his best efforts, he could not move. He looked down in agony at S'nerg who stood calmly by his left leg, serenely looking up at him, the power of his incredible mind alone holding Hiero rigid. And not just Hiero. In a dim way the priest could feel the

17

giant morse straining to break a similar mental compulsion and no more able to do so than his master. The sweat of his effort streaming into his eyes, Hiero fought to break the bonds, using every technique he had been taught to free his own will from the dreadful grip which the wizard had laid upon him. As Hiero glared into the calm eyes of S'nerg, a shudder ran through his frame. The evil master seemed to have no pupils and his eyes were slanted, greyish pits of emptiness, opening on a nameless void. Despite all his efforts, Hiero felt a compulsion to dismount. He knew somehow that if he did, the control would grow even stronger, that the mere fact that he sat high on the saddle helped in a small way to limit S'nerg's power over him. Perhaps, mused a remote, absent corner of his mind, even as he fought, the morse's physical vitality somehow flowed into his master, helping him stay strong. As he stared down into the awful, pale eyes, he noted in the same detached way, that despite the smile on the cruel face, sculptured from sickly marble in appearance, that beads of sweat stood out on S'nerg's forehead also. The strain was telling on him too. But Hiero could endure no more. He began to sway in the saddle. "In the name of the Father," he gasped aloud, fighting with his last strength. The Unclean's adept cold smile deepened.

At this point Gorm suddenly returned. Even a smallish bear has very powerful jaws and they now clamped hard to a most sensitive portion of the sorcerer's anatomy. He screamed in pain and fright, a curiously high tremolo note, and his mental grip dissolved on the instant as he staggered and fell. Hiero's strength surged back and so did all his other faculties. While Klootz still shuddered from the strain, his rider was out of the saddle and on the ground in a second. As the writhing tangle of bear and man rolled over, the priest saw an opportunity and his long poniard flashed from his belt and was drawn once over the white throat, even as S'nerg tried to rise. A fountain of dark blood obscured the contorted features and then the cloaked shape lay still.

Hurry came from the bear's mind. *Made* (too) *much* (volume) *noise. Go now—quick* (run/gallop).

Wait, said Hiero to the other's mind. He was busy searching the other's body. There was a peculiar and heavy bluish metal rod, over a foot long, a dark-handled knife, with what looked like bloodstains on it, and a roll of parchment. Under the cloak, the dead man had worn a soft woven suit, all one piece of greyish neutral-colored cloth, with an odd feel to it, almost slippery. In a small belt pouch was a round metal thing which at first glance looked like a small compass. This was all. Hiero tossed the rod, knife, parchment and compass-thing into a saddlebag and mounted in one easy motion.

18

Go now, he said. *All done here.*

The bear set off instantly at a rocking canter, in the same direction in which they had gone before. In long strides the morse moved in his wake, easily maintaining the distance between them.

Looking back, Hiero could no longer see the still form of his enemy in the gloom. *At least,* he thought, *he didn't seem to dissolve like the others had. Maybe they weren't men at all.*

For several miles the three moved at high speed, despite the fall of night. Many bright stars provided some diffused light and a pale crescent moon promised more later. Also, to Hiero's relief, the terrible mental oppression was gone, the dull feeling of stifling which had choked him for the last few hours had been lifted. It must, he decided, have emanated from the monster they had overcome. He did not forget to say a soldier's brief prayer of thanks. He was under no illusions as to how close he had come to death and perhaps worse. He had been about to submit to the terrible mind of the thing who called himself S'nerg. Whether he would have been slain on the spot or taken elsewhere to some foul den for torture and questioning he did not know. But save for the young bear they all would have been destroyed, he was sure of that. It must have taken great courage, as well as high intelligence, to hide, wait and attack as Gorm had done, and Hiero felt a powerful sense of respect for his new ally.

Eventually, the bear began to slow down, his faint puffs of breath indicating that he had run about as far as he could. Klootz slowed his own pace and they now moved at about the speed of a man trotting. The dark was full of sounds, but they were the normal sounds of the Taig, a grunting bellow in the distance, which was the mating call of a monster hog, the Grokon, the faint squall of some cat or other, the chitter-chatter of the night squirrels high in the trees and the mournful tremolo of small owls. There was nothing about such noises to alarm. Once a large form, pale as a ghost, rose from the earth and flitted away before them in great, silent bounds which soon carried it out of sight. The solitary giant hares were a prey to everything and never left their carefully concealed forms until full dark.

At Hiero's estimation, they had come about five miles, moving steadily south and east, when Gorm signalled a halt. They were in a stand of great, dark firs, and rotting logs lay about them on the carpet of needles. It was very black under the trees and even the dim starlight was blotted out.

Stay—rest—now (safe)—*here (?)* came from the bear. Hiero dismounted wearily and walked over to where the black form sat in the dark. Squatting on his haunches, he tried to look into the eyes of his friend.

Thanks—help (us)—*danger—bad,* he sent. He had noticed that each time, the exchange grew easier. He now could talk to the animal almost as easily as he could to his roommate Per Malaro at the Abbey college, who was also his frater and bondmate, closer mentally than anyone else in the world. The exchange was on the same level of intelligence too, not the way he talked to the big morse, whose answers were simple and contained no abstract concepts at all.

Now the bear responded. He felt a flick of the long tongue on his own nose, and knew it for a greeting. Also, he sensed a wave of shyness, or some emotion akin to it and with it, a carefully buried element of humor. Gorm was amused.

(Almost) *killed us—bad thing—saw it* (felt it) *watching us, so I went away before it* (caught) *me—made me* (not alive) *stay—not move.* Then: *came back—bite behind—stop* (break—*bad think—think at us. Good* (luck?) The bear paused, his mind not readable.

Why, why have you helped me? asked Hiero bluntly. *What do you want?* There was another pause. Behind his back, the man heard Klootz snuffling in search of some dainty, perhaps a mushroom growing on a fallen log. Finally, the young bear answered, his thoughts perfectly clear, but untrained—as if he knew what he wanted to say but not as yet very well how to say it. Finally:

(To) *go with you—see new things—new lands—see what you see, learn what you learn.*

Hiero sat back, nonplussed. Could Gorm have guessed his mission? It seemed impossible. Yet he had told no one and his coming was secret.

Do you know what I seek, where I go? the man shot back, fascinated by the new mind he was meeting.

No, replied the bear coolly. *But you* (will) *tell. Tell now. Perhaps* (there will) *be no time later.*

The priest considered. He was under a vow to say nothing of his mission. But the vow was not absolute but conditional, merely for common secrecy's sake, not because it was holy, or even a secret in itself. He could at his own judgment, seek any aid he wanted. He made a decision and once more leaned forward.

The two figures lay, head to head, in outward silence. The great morse bull kept watch, nose and ears winnowing the night air for news, near and far, while those he guarded conversed, each learning many things under the dark of the firs.

2: IN THE BEGINNING . . .

"We are losing, Hiero, slowly but surely, we are losing." The Father Abbot's brown-robed form paced his underground study chamber as he spoke, thin arms locked behind his back. "Faith alone is not enough. Never was, for that matter. Again and again in recent years, we have become conscious of a will, or group of wills, working with the utmost secrecy and deliberation against us. The human-seeming things which tried to invade Abbey Central and almost succeeded are only a small part of the problem, though of great importance. But there is much, much more, which the Council in its wisdom has kept from the people. No agent of the newsletters has, or will, hear a word of it." He paused and his lined, dark face with its pointed, white beard and drooping mustaches softened into a grin. "None of us have even told our wives." In an instant he was serious again, and picking up a piece of white chalk, strode over to a slate blackboard. He had begun a most successful career as a teacher of the young, as had the Most Reverend Kulase Demero, and old habits die hard.

"Look here," he said crisply, as he began to write. "A large convoy two years ago was ambushed well north of the Inland Sea, on the main road from Otwah. Ten loads of old-time laboratory instruments taken and some found destroyed later. Those instruments came from an undamaged Pre-Death site on the Eastern Ocean, and we think were experimental matter involving advanced weaponry of which we now know nothing. We'll call that item number one." He continued, glancing over at intervals to see that Hiero, seated at a long table facing him, was paying due attention, just as he had done with a thousand pupils in the past.

"Two, we sent a complete regiment of soldiers, under a good sub-abbot, twenty priests, a construction crew as good as any we had, and full supplies for all for six months, to start a new fishery-based Abbey up on the Huzon Gulf, to the far northeast, in the cold woods. You have heard of that, I imagine, as it was too big to keep quiet. Despite all precautions, continuous mental communication with our own Comm chambers at Abbey Central and at other Abbeys, the whole force, roughly eleven hundred picked men and women vanished utterly. Our only warning was a total and sudden lapse of communication. A Rover team found the site deserted and most of the remaining supplies being plundered by wild animals a half month later. There were vague traces of some element of the Unclean, but nothing you could put your finger on. Eleven hundred of our best! This was and is a terrible blow. So I say, we'll call that number two." He paused and looked at Hiero. "Any comment."

"Not yet, Father," said Hiero placidly. Those who did not know him sometimes thought him phlegmatic, but the abbot had watched his man for years and knew better. He grunted and turned back to his blackboard.

"That was about eighteen months ago. Next, which I'll call number three, was the affair of the ship. Damned few members of the Council know about *that* so I'll assume you don't. About two months after we lost the Abbey colony, which would have become Abbey Saint Joan," and another look of pain crossed his face, "a great ship was reported to us by certain trusted persons on the Beesee Coast to the west, well to the north of Vank and the great dead zone there, in a nest of rocky, wooded islands called the Bellas. These people are not Metz, but older still, in fact—"

"In fact, pure-bred Inyans," agreed Hiero. "And there are quite a few of them scattered about here and there, but they live in small hunting groups and won't come in and amalgamate. Some are good people, others trade with the Unclean and maybe worse. Now let's stop the baby stuff, Father. I'm not a first year student, you know."

For a second, the Father Abbot looked perfectly furious, then he laughed.

"Sorry, but I'm so used to explaining things in this manner to the average village councilman or even some of my more elevated colleagues on the Grand Council that it gets to be a habit. Now, where were we? Oh, yes, the ship.

"This ship, a big, odd-looking one, much bigger than any fishing boat we have, was reported wrecked on one of the outer islands of the Bella group. And there were people aboard from somewhere else, probably the other side of the Pacific! The ship was breaking up on the rocks and the weather was bad. Our Inyan friends tried to get the people, who were yellow-skinned just as the records say the East Pacific people should be, and just as the few rare fishermen who get wrecked here are, off in their small boats. We were already sending a cavalry squadron from the east, at Abbey St. Mark, as fast as we could. There are fairly good roads to that part of the coast.

"Well, when our people got there, nothing was left. The wreck was utterly gone, not a trace of it left. Three small Inyan camps on the coast, gathered for the salmon fishing, were gone too, with only a few traces that they had been there. But we found an old man in the woods, or he found us, an ancient cripple who had been taking a sweat bath and thus had been missed when the attack came. A horde of Leemutes, some sort of Hairy Howlers, I gather, had appeared from out of the *water*. They were riding great animals which looked something like the really big seals we see once in awhile on that coast. They stormed the shore camps, killing everything that moved and hurling the dead and all their possessions into the sea. The old man did not know what had happened to the ship, which he had only heard of and not seen, but it must have met the same treatment. Who knows what new knowledge from the Lost Years we missed that time? Are you beginning to see a pattern?"

"I think so," answered Hiero, "We are being physically penned in, you feel, but more than that, we are being blocked off from knowledge, especially any knowledge which might prove dangerous to the Unclean, to the Leemutes. And the plan is concerted, is organized, so that when we do hear of any new knowledge, it is instantly snatched from our grasp."

"Exactly," said the abbot. "That's exactly what I think. And so do others. But there's more yet. Listen a moment.

"A year ago, twenty of our best young scientists, men and women both, who were working on problems of mental control, in a number of new and fascinating aspects, decided to have a joint meeting. They came here to Sask City from all over the Republic. Parment wasn't in session, but the Abbey Council, as the Upper House, was, and we received word of the meeting, and our permanent scientific sub-committee knew all about it, of course. A routine Abbey guard, two men for the doors, was provided. Now one of the two, a sharp fellow, thought he counted *twenty-one* scholars going in one morning, after the group had been meeting for several days.

"If it were not for him—! Even as it was, things were bad enough. The guardsman looked through a window in time to see the twenty killing one another, in total silence, by strangling, bludgeoning, pocket-knives, whatever was handy. He burst in yelling and broke the compulsion. There six dead and eight more badly wounded. As you might expect, those with the strongest mental powers of will were the least injured. We could prove that from their school records." The abbot sighed. He had ceased his pacing and now sat on a bench opposite Hiero.

"The scholars remembered little. They too had the vague feeling that another person was present at some point, but they could not describe him, or it. The guard at the back door had been conscious of nothing at all. But to us, what must have happened is clear. It should be to you. Is it?"

"A mind of great power, I suppose," said the younger man. "One of the legendary dark adepts of the Unclean I've heard rumored. Is it, or they, really something beside a fairy tale?"

"I fear so," said the abbot. "Look, you understand the mental powers as well as any young man of the Metz. To accomplish this very daring stroke, aimed, mark you, at our freshest brains, our own greatest asset and greatest danger to any foe, a mind of extraordinary power as you say, had to be close. Had to be physically close, that is, to the persons under the compulsion. There can be no doubt that the lad on guard (who by the way is now getting advanced training) had a good mind and indeed retained the memory of seeing an extra person enter. Once inside, while simultaneously holding an invisibility spell upon their minds, the creature worked on tiny, everyday resentments until they were built into murderous compulsions to kill. But there's another implication you may have missed as well."

"The silence," smiled Hiero. "No, I got that."

"Good boy," said his superior. "You do have brains, Hiero, under that lazy mask. Yes, the silence. What a mind! To compel them, twenty good minds, to slay one another in total silence! Noise would have spoiled the plan, so they had to be silent. I don't think there are four men in the Republic who could perform that feat."

"And you're one of them, of course," said Hiero. "Is there more, or do we now get down to specifics involving me personally?"

"You knew about the two who almost got into our inner files and research centers at Abbey Central," said his superior. "We may call them case number four, I suppose. What they were is beyond our present knowledge. If they were actually human men, then how was it possible for their very flesh and bone to dissolve into the substance of an amoeba? The Unclean is overreaching us, Hiero."

"There are many other cases of interest if they are considered as part of the whole thing. Small parties of trained explorers, men like yourself, ambushed or worse, vanished, in areas where no one should have known they had gone. Messengers with matters of unusual importance for the Eastern League at Otwah, or perhaps from them to us, also vanished, causing delays of up to a years on matters of common concern. And so on. It all adds up to one thing; a web, Hiero, a deadly, tightening web, is being drawn in upon us, even as we sit and wait to find out what is going so wrong!" The lean old man fixed his keen eyes on Hiero. "I still haven't heard any very searching questions from my prize pupil. But I need them: we all do. Hiero, you can't be mentally lazy any longer. You've been doing work any journeyman priest-exorcist could do, mixed with a lot of forest running and plain loafing. Your scores at Abbey Central, and you know it, were some of the highest ever achieved. And you're not even trying! Now listen to me, Per Desteen, I am addressing you as both your Godly and your temporal superior, and I want your attention at its peak! Those of us on the Council who know about you have been giving you rope for years, for two reasons, one, in the hope that you would develop responsibility by yourself, always the best way of course. The other reason, mainly advanced by me, young man, was so that you could get experience in many areas. Well, the time for idling is now, this minute, officially over. Am I plain? Now, sir, let's have some intelligent questioning, because I have a lot more to say."

Black eyes snapping with anger, Hiero was now sitting upright, glaring at his friend and mentor, any pretense of being bored gone forever. "So that's what you think of me, is it," he grated, "a sort of chartered ne'er-do-well and good fellow. That's not fair, *Most* Reverend Father, and you know it!"

Abbot Demero simply sat looking at him, his wise eyes sympathetic, but not yielding, and Hiero felt his anger ebb away. There *was* truth, a good deal of it, in the charges, and being an essentially honest man, he could not deny it.

"I apologize for anger and impudence, Father Abbot," he said heavily. "I suppose I'm not really much of a priest, or a soldier either, for that matter. What can I do for the Council?"

"A good question, Hiero," said the Abbot briskly, "but not really the one I wanted, because it comes last, or ought to, and I want more thoughts from you first. Look now, my friend, what are your conclusions about what I have told you. I mean strengths, weaknesses, reliability, for that matter, plausibility, and above all—solutions, remedies. Let's hear your own ideas now."

"Well," said Hiero slowly, "one thing hit me from the very first, and it grew as the tragedies you related mounted. There has to be treason, at least one highly-placed traitor, somewhere in the Republic and probably more. I don't like saying this, but I have to, to be honest. What about the Council itself?"

"Good," said the abbot. "You're still able to think. Yes, there's treason and it's being carefully, very carefully, searched out as we sit here. As for my peers, and your superiors, on the Council, you have no business knowing what steps might be taken if we ever should suspect a traitor in such an unlikely place. Therefore I shall tell you nothing about any such possible theoretical procedures."

Two smiles met across the table. The old abbot had refused information and (literally) told Hiero nothing. As well as everything, including the fact that the Abbey Council itself was *not* immune from suspicion.

"I can't argue against a conspiracy," resumed Hiero. "We are definitely getting a series of blows, savage ones, from someone. And what you tell me is the final word. It must be coordinated. Since we are meeting here at a sealed office and *talking,* at your insistence, you must be worried about some sort of betrayal even here. If our minds concentrate on a subject, even if we speak aloud, there are currents set up audible to an adept, especially one such as you describe. What are you doing to keep this from happening?" He folded his arms on his chest and stared at the abbot in turn.

"This," said the abbot simply. While they had been talking, the younger man had not noticed a plain, wooden box, perhaps eighteen inches high, at one end of the table. The abbot lifted its lid and exposed a curious mechanism, a small, flat pendulum of some polished, ivory-like material, suspended motionless from a delicate wooden crossbar. Close on either side of the pendulum, two oval discs hung from the slender supports.

"There is a core of a very curious substance, something out of the Lost Years, which I'll tell you about some day, in that pendulum. If any thought, power, or what have you, had come upon us, I think there is a 98% chance that tiny weight would have rung against a side support piece. We've been testing it for two years, and it hasn't failed yet. In fact, it or a duplicate is what trapped the two spies at Abbey Central. Needless to say, very few of us know about it."

"I see," said Hiero, eyeing the little signal device. "Very reassuring. Let's hope it works, sir. Now, you wanted more thoughts, I believe. I only have one. There must be a plan, something to reverse this steady constriction you fear, and I'm to be part of it. It must need a younger man than yourself, and so some physical hazard is involved. Perhaps a journey, a probe into some guessed-at area held, or thought to be held, by the enemy? A reconnaissance of some sort? Beyond that, I'm in the dark."

"Think a little harder," suggested Abbot Demero.

"All right," said Hiero, "a weapon or weapons, exists somewhere. As a result, one extraordinarily gallant man may barely manage to penetrate the Unclean enemy lines, relying on cunning, stealth and sheer heroism, where a whole army could not get through. Frankly," he added, "I'm getting a bit tired of the mystery. Beyond the sarcasm I just gave you, I really have no suggestions and I hardly think a children's romance of the lone paladin against overpowering odds is what you're after. Come on, Father Abbot," he said impatiently, "what on earth *are* you after anyway?"

The Abbot looked a little nonplussed before he spoke, which in turn gave Hiero a bit of a start.

"Damnation, Hiero, you must operate on a level we can't tap! You see, that happens to be exactly what I want. You and a few other highly-trained men are something of a secret weapon. We want you to go and try to raid some of the Lost Cities in the far South, in the hope, which I confess to be dim, that you will indeed give us some secret of the past before the Unclean overwhelm us."

Despite himself, the younger priest was instantly fascinated. He had been as far east as Otwah, and into many wild areas of the north, but the far south was a closed book to almost everyone. For every mutated plant or animal in the northern part of the Kandan continent, there were a dozen in the South. There were rumored to be monsters so awful that a herd of morse would be but a mouthful to one of them and trees so huge that it would take a man half a day to walk around the bole of one. Most of these tales could no doubt be relegated to fancy, rumor and trappers' lies, but Hiero knew enough to know there was a grain of truth in many of them. He himself had been just far enough to see the southern end of the Taig and its countless pines and the beginning of the monster trees of the southern forest edge, which had few conifers, but many deciduous trees of far greater size. The lost empire of the once fabled United States had lain there, and every school child knew that The Death had hit it harder than anywhere else in the world, causing horrible changes to all life, such as had barely touched northern Kanda. Endless marshes, inland seas and vast tracts of poisoned desert, the latter lit by the undying, blue, bale fires of the Dead Zones, were said to exist in the unknown area. And the Lost Cities themselves, the very places he was to go, they were the worst of all! Metz children were frightened into obedience with tales of the towering vine-hung cliffs of the ancient tottering buildings, even a glimpse of which was said to bring a horrid end. There were Lost Cities in the North country too, but most had long been either isolated or explored, that is if known at all. And on them, in any case, the terrors of The Death had been laid lightly. Daring rovers and free rangers occasionally risked the anger of

27

the Abbeys, political, not religious, and explored to the South, but few departed thus and fewer returned. All this flashed through Hiero's brain on the instant, as he looked into Demero's wise old eyes.

He sat back, for once effectively silenced, and the long, windowless room, let only by the fluors on the wall, stayed quiet while both men took thought. It was Hiero who broke the silence, at length.

"Do you have any idea what it is I am to seek for, sir?" he asked quietly. "Or is it anything, just something that may turn up?"

"Well, there's that all right," said the older man. "But we're a bit more hopeful and knowledgeable, mind you, *and* knowledgeable, than that. We're looking for weapons, obviously. Now The Death was caused by weapons. We don't want those again, certainly. The plagues, the nuclear poisoners, all those things ought to stay buried. Unless the Unclean revive them, and I fear that mightily, I tell you! No, we want none such. But there are other things of power which are more or less intangible, at least in ordinary terms." He seemed to change his thoughts and for a moment Hiero was puzzled.

"Did you ever reflect on our own central files, at Abbey Central, Hiero?" said the abbot, leaning forward eagerly.

"Of course, Father," answered the priest. "I mean, what do you mean 'reflect'?"

"What do you think of them, that's what I mean," snapped Demero. "Are they efficient, are they useful? They cover an area of over two square miles underground, and they employ over two hundred highly trained priests and scholars. Is it worth it?"

Hiero saw that his old master was leading up to something, but for his soul he couldn't see what it was.

"Why of course, certainly they're valuable," he said thinking hard. "Without their collected and collated information, we'd never be able to get anything done. Half our research effort is simply adding to the information in those files. What's the point?"

"The point is this," said Demero. "When I ask for information, information mind you, which I know to be somewhere in the files, it often takes days to get it. Then, perhaps I need to balance several facts against each other; let us say the rainfall in the east of Sask prov., the yield of crops in the south, the latest news of buffer migrations. So, it takes more time to get these. Then, with the help of others, I balance them, weigh them together and make decisions. But you know all this, right?"

"Of course," said Hiero, intrigued by the other's manner, "but what of it? That's what's done with information; it gets utilized. So what does that prove?"

"All right," resumed his elder. "Now, suppose, just suppose I had gone to the files and told the files, *not* mind you, the librarians, *the files themselves,* all I have just told you about our danger. Don't interrupt, Boy, I haven't lost my sense yet. The files *themselves* next put all known information on this subject together and in ten minutes gave me back a sheet of paper which said as follows: 'if you do *x, y* and *z* in that order the enemy should be totally defeated.' " He paused, a gleam in his eye. "What do you think of that, eh?"

"Talking files?" said Hiero, one eyebrow cocked. "I assume, of course, you're not joking. We have begun to re-explore this radio thing, I know, but that's just people and an instrument. You're talking about a—well, a machine, a thing, holding all information and dispensing not just odd facts, but *conclusions.* Are you telling me such a thing is possible?"

The abbot sat back, satisfied. "Yes, son, not only possible, but well-known at one time, in the years before The Death. The machines were called 'computers.' Some of the scientists doing research on the archives of the lost age are led to believe that certain computers existed that were larger than this building we're in. Can you begin to imagine the possibilities?"

Hiero sat staring at the wall behind Abbot Demero, his mind racing. If such things existed, and he knew the abbot would not lightly mention a possibility as a fact, the world could be changed overnight. *All* the knowledge of the past might very well still be in existence somewhere. It was a frightening thought, for it meant that all of secrets of the age of The Death were presumably hidden and available as well.

"I see you're beginning to reflect a little on the possibilities," said the old priest. "The Science Committee has picked you to go south and east, far to the East, where we have reason to believe these things may still lie buried in certain of their lost caverns. Five other men will go elsewhere. It's best none of you know the others' plans." He did not elaborate, nor need to. If any of the six should fall into the hands of the Unclean alive, the less they knew of their colleagues' venturings the better.

"Now come over here, Hiero, and I'll go over the maps with you. They have the latest information of these probable computer sites. You mustn't expect to find a vast sort of library, you know. The information was apparently coded in different ways and put in the great machines in ways we only dimly comprehend. You'll get a briefing from some scholars who've gone furthest into the field later . . . "

And so the tale had gone. Telling this all to the bear, clever as the animal was, was simply not possible if only because bears, even mutant bears, don't read or write. But Hiero patiently and steadily made certain facts clear. In the blackest hours, before the first light of dawn, the man finally relaxed and willed himself to snatch a little sleep. Gorm now understood that his friend was on a long journey, but to Hiero's gratification, he still wanted to come. Also, the bear had enough reasoning power to understand that there was knowledge he could *not* understand, in fact he may have been the first of his species to grasp the idea of abstract knowledge. He knew that the man was a foe of the Leemutes and that they were seeking something in a far land to hurt these evil things. With this knowledge he was content, and now he also rested, occasionally letting out the faint, puffing snore of a sleeping bear. Standing over the two, still saddled, his legs locked tight at the knee joints, the great morse kept his unbroken watch, in a state perhaps between dreaming and waking, but with all his magnificent senses alert for the first sign of danger. Klootz was not tired and his kind did not lie down to sleep in any case, although they sometimes rested with their legs tucked under them. But tonight he rocked and swayed, chewing his cud and missing nothing that passed in the night, a sentinel without compare.

At first light, Hiero felt a velvet touch on his forehead and looked up to see the great damp muzzle an inch from his. Satisfied that his master was awake, Klootz carefully lifted his huge hooves from either side of the man's body and moved out of the little grove into the grey dawn. In a moment the crunch of shredded bushes being devoured signalled that his breakfast had commenced.

Hiero rubbed his eyes. He was stiff, but not unduly so. It would have been better to have unpacked his bedroll and made a bed of spruce tips, but he had simply been too tired and too busy the night before. Besides, he was a seasoned woodsman and a night spent on dry ground meant little to him. He looked over and saw Gorm was also awake and giving himself a wash with a long, pink tongue.

Any water about? he sent.

Listen (you can) *hear it,* came not from the bear but from the bull morse. A mental picture of a small stream a hundred yards off came to the man and he rose and followed Klootz, who was ambling that way.

In twenty minutes, all had washed, eaten and were ready for their new day's travel. Hiero ruefully checked his *pemeekan* supply. The way Gorm ate, it would be gone in no time and they would have to stop and hunt. This, aside from carrying an unnecessary extra element of danger, would further delay them.

Gorm caught his thought which was unguarded. *Try and save the sweet food,* he sent. *I can find much of my own.* Once again, the brains and unselfishness of the strange creature who had appeared in his life out of nowhere made Hiero blink.

Hiero next rubbed Klootz down with a double handful of thick moss. He felt guilty for having left the big animal saddled and packed all night, but the morse seemed none the worse for it, and a roll in the little brook, which sent water cascading up the banks, put him in fine fettle.

The sun was now fully up and the forest was alive with sound and movement. Birds were everywhere and as they began to travel, the priest glimpsed startled deer and small rabbits, as well as a sounder of Grokon passing along a distant aisle of the pines, even the striped young hoglets considerably larger than Hiero himself.

Gorm, the night before, had attempted to explain the route he thought best to follow. The man could only grasp parts of it, but he gathered that a considerable marsh lay to the south and that it was necessary to cross it at its narrowest place. The road on which he and Klootz had journeyed for the last week was a place of great peril, watched by many unseen eyes. It was only luck that the two had come so far undisturbed, for no people had used that road in a long time, or if they had, they had not lived to go very far upon it. On no account must they return to it for any reason. The fact that so few human beings traveled alone through the wild may have dulled the watchfulness of the Unclean and allowed morse and man to come as far as they had. But now, surely the whole area would be on guard. And when the slain wizard was inevitably discovered, they could expect a hue and cry of massive proportions indeed to be set on foot by the enemy, so Gorm indicated. Once again, mind speech was to be halted, or at least understood by man and bear to be held to a minimum.

They had gone perhaps three hours from the night's resting place when they received proof that they were not to journey undisturbed and unsought. The three were fording a shallow brook, when Hiero felt the morse stiffen under him and at the same time saw the young bear come erect on the bank just ahead. A second later, his own, less alert senses were assaulted. He had never felt anything quite like it before. It was as if something strange clawed for his mind. A savage questing force somehow probed at his inner being. He drew on all his own years of training and managed to make no response, keeping the pressure and the *call,* for there was an element of that too, away, repelling it by not acknowledging it. For what seemed like a long minute and

31

was probably very little time, a mere instant, the searching presence seemed to hover over him in an almost physical way; then it moved on. He knew it had gone on elsewhere, but he was not absolutely sure he had managed to deceive or deflect it. He looked first at Gorm and in turn saw the bear's weak little eyes fixed on him.

Something bad hunts, came the message. *I was* (only) *a bear. It left me and did not* (see) *me.*

I (think) *it missed me,* sent Hiero. *And Klootz also, for it is not hunting four-footed animals, at least not yet.*

There will be other things (like the) *evil fur things of yesterday,* came the bear's thought. *This forest is full of many creatures who* (serve/hunt for) *the evil power. Many of them go on four legs and have good noses.*

The priest found less and less trouble understanding the bear. The whole exchange, plus a new decision, now to utilize the stream, was over in a split second.

All day long, they followed the brook, for it was little more, down its winding path. As much as possible, they stayed actually in the water, so as to leave as few tracks as possible. The force or entity which had tried to locate them did not reveal itself further. They saw fewer animals though, and none of the larger ones at all. Once a great, foot-long, water beetle sought to bite Gorm with its savage pincers, but he avoided it easily and Klootz, following close behind, brought a great, flattening hoof squarely down upon its armored back. Very few of the giant insects bred from The Death's radiation were much of a menace, since they tended to be slow-moving and clumsy.

They made an early camp on an island. The stream which Hiero had not been able to locate on his maps, probably because it was too small, broadened a little, without getting more than two feet deep, and the little willow-hung islet might have been designed for them.

While the bear went shambling off in search of food and Klootz, now unsaddled, wrenched succulent water plants from the stream bed, the man ate a frugal supper of biscuit and *pemeekan* while he tried to analyze what he had learned in the last few days. There was sunlight still, and Hiero had camped early because he needed light. He wanted very much to examine the various articles he had taken from the dead man and this was the first opportunity.

The metal rod came first. A little less than an inch thick and about a foot long, of a very hard, bluish substance, not unlike patinated bronze, at first sight it looked unornamented. A closer look showed Hiero that four tiny knobs, set in a curved line, were sticking out of the sides. Hesitantly, he pushed one. At once an extension of the rod's other end began. The thing was a cylinder, with many tubes beautifully fitting one inside the other. While Hiero watched, it extended itself until it was a slender wand about five feet long. He pushed the same button again and it began to retract into itself once more. He stopped it by pushing it a third time. Next, he tried another button, the central one of the three. Two flat, oval discs on the end of two delicate arms emerged from the supposedly featureless rod and each stopped at a six-inch distance away from the rod, forming a prong set at right angles to the rod's body. Hiero turned the rod over and examined it from every angle, but he could not fathom the purpose of the discs. He raised the rod's lower end to eye level to examine the discs better, but they were featureless. He tried to look at the rod's body again, while holding it upright, but he forgot the discs on their arms and they banged into his forehead, just over his eyes. Annoyed with himself, he started to lower them when suddenly he stopped and gently put them back where they had been. They fit! Excited, he held the rod upright and extended it to its fullest length, keeping the two ovals on their extensions clamped to his forehead. He was now beginning to get an idea of what he held, and with great care, he slowly pressed the third tiny knob.

A tremendous voice slammed into his mind with overpowering force, almost physically knocking him over. *Where have you been? Why have you not communicated? Some strange creatures or groups of them are moving through our area almost undetected. The normals may be assaulting us with something new.* There was a sudden pause, and the dazed Hiero could nearly feel the almost tangible suspicion in the other mind. *Who is this?* came the mind voice. *Do you hear, I*—click. The priest had managed to shut it off.

He leaned back against a tree trunk, both frightened and angry with himself. The strange device was apparently both a communicator and an amplifier of great strength, obviously increasing the distance over which mental speech could be sent at least tenfold. He had never heard of such a thing, and he doubted any Abbey scientist had, either. He must get this object back to the Abbey research centers if he did nothing else. The thought that the Unclean even possessed a thing like this was nerve-wracking. *No wonder the abbot has the jumps,* he thought. He looked at the rod again and then carefully made it shut and the two head pieces go back into the handle, noting as he did so that the machining was beautifully turned and that the metal was one he had never before seen. He was about to wrap it carefully and put it away when he remembered the fourth button. This was not next to the others but nearer the butt end and to one side. He considered it for a moment and then wedged the rod, extension end up, between two heavy rocks. Next he broke off a slender willow sapling about eight feet long and carefully positioned himself behind its parent willow tree, while reaching for the enigmatic button with his new pole. The thought that the sinister makers of this thing might have built in a self-destruct device was late in coming, he reflected, but might still save his life. He checked and saw that the morse bull was several hundred feet upstream and then, with only his hand exposed, probed for the button. Face pressed to the tree, he heard one swift metallic sound, as if a great spring had been released and then silence. He waited an instant and then looked cautiously around the tree. He got up at once and tossed the stick aside. The amazing rod's last trick was both simple and entirely unexpected. It had fully extended itself again, this time in a single instantaneous motion. But now, projecting from the end was not the blunt cap of before, but a two-edged razor sharp lance head. It was over half-an-inch wide and almost as long as the original, folded-up rod itself. Hiero bent the extended rod sideways, but the tough metal gave very little. He hefted the thing at shoulder height. It was a perfectly balanced javelin. Lowering it, he eyed the edges of the blade and confirmed his first impression that they were smeared with some sticky substance. *Undoubtedly not a face cream,* he reflected. He shut his new prize carefully up again and put it away.

Next came the knife. It was a short, one-edged thing in a leather sheath and had been used recently, being sticky with dried blood. There appeared to be nothing odd about it, and he cleaned it and put it away too, after ascertaining it bore no marks of any kind.

He now examined the rounded object which had looked to him earlier like a small compass. Many of his colleagues, indeed most people, still used compasses, but Hiero did not. He had a built-in sense of direction and while in school had won many bets by being blindfolded and always picking out the correct compass points.

It was obvious at once that if this was a compass, it was no compass he had ever seen before. There were no obvious compass bearings, no directions and their subdivisions. Instead, there was a thing like a circular wheel, or round track, under the glass plate on top. Set at intervals next to this track were symbols of some kind with which he was totally unfamiliar, for they were neither numbers or letters he had ever seen before. On the circular track was a round, fiery bead of light, which swayed gently as he rocked the case in his hand, just like the air bubble in a carpenter's level. Hiero examined the symbols again. There were four larger ones set where the main directions on a proper compass should be. He aligned the four symbols one by one to a map of his own and managed to pick the one near the loop end of the object as north. But the fiery bead was not fixing itself on north or any of the four points when so used! *If the damned thing isn't a compass, what is it?* he wondered to himself. Reluctantly, he replaced it in its pouch and stowed it away again, determined to re-examine it again soon.

Last of all came the rolls of yellowish, parchment-like material. He tried to rip a page corner experimentally and found that it tore, but with great difficulty. It was certainly not a paper, nor was it parchment either, but a synthetic material the like of which he had never before glimpsed.

Most of the papers bore writing, closely spaced and not printed, in a dark, reddish ink, which looked unpleasantly like dried blood, especially in the fast-waning light. Like the lettering or whatever on the compass thing, the symbols were totally unintelligible to Hiero. But one piece was mostly taken up by a large map, and this he studied with great care. It somewhat resembled his own map in general outline. The Inland Sea was there and, he thought, several familiar roads to the north. The main east-west Otwah road was quite clear. Most of the marks were obscure, though, especially many in the South. Rivers and swamps seemed to have been carefully drawn in signs he used himself, and he felt that the map might prove a useful guide. Many marks were thought-provoking. He was reasonably sure he had found some of the ruined cities of the pre-Death eras, for the few such sites marked on his own map were in the same places. But the alien map had many more of them, as well as much else that was strange.

Eventually, that too was put away and he prepared a bed, digging hollows for hip and shoulder and spreading his bed roll. Without being ordered, Klootz was feeding close to the island and his master knew he had nothing to worry about, at least that was physical, in the way of nocturnal danger. The bear had not returned, but Hiero had earlier agreed on a travel plan with him, and he was confident Gorm would be back when wanted. He curled up with a sigh and dropped off while the last light of day still lingered in the west.

He was awakened by rain, a light spatter on his upturned face. It was very dark and the damp clouds had rolled out of the east, bringing moisture from the distant seas. He was about to pull his hood over his face and go back to sleep when a wet reek of fur strongly assaulted his nose. Gorm was standing next to him and the bear's whole manner demanded attention.

Something comes in the night (perhaps) *many things, but one for certain* (emphatic)! *We must go the way we planned/discussed. Listen!*

Sitting up, the man did indeed listen intently. He was conscious of Klootz standing quietly nearby, his great ears also belled into the rainy night. For a moment the falling rain drops and the muted gurgle of the stream were all that was audible. Then, far away in the west, at the very limit of Hiero's hearing,

35

there came a sound.

It was a high keening shriek, rising to almost the level of inaudibility and dying away then into silence. Twice it sounded and then only the listening night could be heard. But no one, neither man, nor beast, needed to hear it again. There was a menace implicit in that distant cry which raised the hackles on one's back. It was a hunter and it was on a track. In the situation they were in, it was no time to debate on whose track was whatever had screamed. The long-expected pursuit was upon them and it was time to go.

For a seasoned traveller like Hiero, it was hardly more than a minute's work to break camp, including packing. Once up in the saddle, he loosened the great knife in its back sheath and, slouching comfortably, let the bear lead the way, Klootz ambling along in his wake through the shallow water. Hiero's time sense was not as good as his directional sense, but he had a fair idea of the present hour, about two P.M. Like many of the ancient mechanisms, clocks had been rediscovered, but they were large and clumsy. A woodsman of Hiero's caliber had no need for such things, indeed would have discarded a wristwatch if one had been available. Living in the wild for long periods gave you a built-in clock in your own body.

The rain lifted a little and became a fine mist. The animals did not mind getting wet particularly, although the bear liked to sleep in a dry place, and Hiero's tanned leather was treated with various water repellents which made him almost completely watertight. In any case, it was still warm in the last days of summer.

The little party travelled hardly any more slowly at night than during daylight. Hiero could rely on the sense of the two beasts to move without stumbling at a good pace, even when sight was at a minimum.

For two hours of steady and undisturbed travel, they followed the little stream bed, which still kept its same dimensions. Hiero eventually signalled a halt and swung down on the bank to stretch and do a few muscle-limbering exercises. Gorm flopped down next to him, also grateful for a rest. Bears can and do travel long distances, but steady marching, day in and day out, is not their habit. Klootz browsed in the shallows, adding more supplies to the many pounds of plant food he had already devoured that day. An eater of green stuffs never really stops unless asleep, since the nourishment is so much less than from a direct protein intake.

The priest now briefly said his morning prayers, a process the animals ignored as incomprehensible. The bear was mildly interested, but only mildly. Hiero however, had detected that casual interest earlier and made a note in his mnemonic files that discussing religion with an intelligent animal might prove immensely rewarding.

Prayers over, Hiero stood listening in the dark. As he did, for the first time since they had left camp on the island, the faint scream of the hunter broke through the misty night. It was unmistakably a lot closer than at first. With a smothered oath, Hiero mounted and this time sent a thought to Gorm as he did so. *Hurry up, you, or we'll be trapped!* The young bear led off again at a splashing gallop and spray fountained as the big morse lumbered after him through the shallows, his wide hooves coming down on the invisible water like dinner plates.

As he rode, listening hard, the man tried to think rationally and analyze their danger. He had no idea what followed on their tracks. Whatever it was, it seemed to be a night hunter of uncommon skill, and perhaps it was a pack of them. And whatever it (or they) were, it was moving incredibly fast. The bear and the morse had not been loafing, indeed for nighttime had been setting a good pace. But neither walking in the running water nor moving at a steady clip had thrown whatever pursued off their track. What could it be?

One faintly encouraging thought rose to Hiero's mind at this point. Anything moving that fast probably could not carry and certainly could not lead, any human master. Whatever atrocity was tracking them down almost had to be running unleashed and free. *At least,* Hiero reasoned, following this train of thought, *if I'm right, I won't have to worry about facing someone like S'nerg.* It was probably a purely physical danger.

Even as the thoughts came to him, the evil cry, clearly audible over the splashing, again welled up in the distance. The *near* distance, he observed. The hunter, whatever it was, could certainly move. Damn, the pursuit was going to catch up with them while it was still dark! This could be very bad. It was at least an hour to first light.

Leaning over, he fumbled in his left saddlebag and finally located by touch the packet he wanted. To a stranger it would have appeared no easy task, doing this blind while the morse's great body lurched along underneath him, but he had practiced many times in the past, and had little trouble securing what he wanted. Next, he loosened the strap on his holstered thrower, so that it could be whipped out in a hurry. As an afterthought, he reached into the saddlebag again and took out the murderous rod he had taken from S'nerg's dead body. As an emergency weapon, should he lose his regular spear, it might be of great use, and he tucked it into his belt. The spear itself was in its socket at the saddlebow, ready to his hand at need.

Now, he concentrated his mind on his steed and the bear. *Find an open place, close to the stream if possible,* he sent. *We must fight. Whatever comes is too fast to run away from.* In the back of his mind was the thought that Gorm, invaluable as he had proved in the recent past, must be tired now and probably not much use as a fighter. If the small bear could get even a few moments rest, it might make some fleeting difference. The Abbey Battle Code was never out of a trained Killman's mind. "Use *every* tiny advantage and perhaps the enemy will use one less," so ran one of the ABC rules.

The bear did not answer as he galloped on, but Hiero knew he understood. As for Klootz, the rapport between man and mount was so strong that he knew the great bull was already seething with rage and ready for a battle of any size, shape or description. An Abbey morse did not like being chivied over the land by anyone, regardless of what they were.

Behind them, the chilling cry broke out again, a hideous, thin screaming in the quiet moist night. This time Hiero thought he could distinguish several voices and he knew the distance was shortening. It was logical. A solitary hunter, no matter how powerful, might be immobilized by sheer accident. A pack was always more effective. But a pack of what?

Here, the thought came suddenly from Gorm. *A place of grass and no trees. Is this what you want?*

Yes, sent the man. *Lie down and rest until they come. Do not fight if you can help it.* He urged the morse out of the water and onto the sward of a natural forest opening. The very first faint light in the east had appeared, not enough for any detail to show but enough so that he could barely see they were in a natural clearing, one which sloped gently to the stream's edge. As Klootz stood silently dripping and the exhausted bear lay panting off to one side, Hiero considered tactics. The glade was perhaps a hundred yards wide at its tips by the brook. It was roughly shaped like a half-moon and the forest edge at its center was two hundred feet from the water. He urged the morse on until Klootz now stood almost exactly in the clearing's center, back to the trees, but fifty feet away from them, so that nothing could use the trees as cover to leap upon them from behind. Hiero reached into his saddlebag and extracted his beryllium-copper helmet, round and unornamented, save for the cross and sword on the forepeak. It fitted over his cap, and was his sole piece of armor. He put it on and tried to catch the minds of their pursuers. He found blind ravening appetite, more than one, coming fast, unreachable at any level he could influence!

Man and morse waited, alert and ready. They had done all they could. Gorm was silent now also, hidden somewhere in the black shadows and ready to pounce if possible.

They had not long to wait. The blackness of the dying night was still almost totally unrelieved when from up the shallow stream, the way they had followed, came the sounds of splashing water and many clawed feet striking on rocks. Sensing rather than actually seeing their attackers, the Killman-priest twisted the heads of the two objects he had been holding and hurled them away, one to the right and one to the left. As they hit the ground the two flares burst into life and a white, incandescent glow illumined the whole area.

At once, Hiero saw that he and his animal allies had made a basic, if un-avoidable, error in traveling down the stream and keeping to the water. The five, sleek, sinister shapes poised at the brook's edge resembled grossly enlarged mink or some other water weasels quite enough to indicate that a river bed was the last place in which anyone ought to try and elude them. *No wonder they came so fast,* thought Hiero as the momentary surprise of the lights froze the creatures in place.

Their undershot, shark-like jaws and vicious teeth glistened in the light as they blinked their beady eyes and then recovered. Each one, from wet muzzle to long tailtip was at least ten feet and could hardly have weighed any less than a full grown man. Collars of bluish metal glinted and betrayed their wearers' allegiance even as they scuttled out of the water and rushed to the attack, snarling as they came.

Hiero fired the thrower and dropped it all in one motion. It took too long to reload and these things were coming too fast. But the tiny rocket went true. The leading animal, head hit, simply blew up in a burst of orange fire, and the one next to it writhed aside, screaming shrilly and dragging a broken leg.

As the other three paused, shaken by the explosion and the death of the leader, Klootz charged with a bellow of fury. Spear couched, Hiero gripped the bull's barrel, ready to strike.

The wounded fury could not escape and the morse's pile driver front hooves crushed his life out in a terrible, smashing blow. Another one, leaping straight up at Hiero, took the heavy spear in its throat, right up to the crossbars. The savage brute fell back, choking on its own blood and Hiero let the spear go with it, whipping out his heavy sword-knife as he did so.

The remaining two fell back for an instant, but for true mustelids, like all weasels, the thought of retreat never occurred to them. Separating, their grin-ning masks of fury showing the white fangs, they attacked like streaks of dark, undulating lightning, leaping at the rider and not the mount, and from two sides at once.

Fortunately for Hiero, he had worked out such a development with Klootz many times over on the Abbey's training fields. Automatically, the bull took the opponent to his left and paid no attention to the other, leaving that

39

one to his master.

Rising in the saddle, Hiero cut down at the upthrust, rapid head in one terrible chopping blow. The solid bite of the ancient blade could be felt all the way up to his powerful shoulder. The giant weasel-thing was dead before it hit the ground, its narrow skull cloven almost in half.

But even as he recovered, the man felt a terrible pain in his left leg. Overconfident, Klootz had underestimated the speed of his enemy. Even as his great hoof had come dashing down, the last of the hunting pack had swerved aside and altered its spring in mid-air. A slash at Hiero's calf had opened the flesh almost to the bone and he swayed in the saddle from shock, as the animal leapt away.

The bull was not to be taken twice this way. Knowing his rider and master was hurt sent him stark mad, but with a cold fury. He advanced slowly on the surviving hunter, rocking gently from side to side, grotesquely mimicking the way a playful fawn minces up to another baby opponent.

A fury to the end, the last servant of the Unclean sprang from a crouch, again at the drooping rider and not the morse. But Klootz now on guard, was not deceived by the supple twisting spring. A great, cloven hoof shot straight out and the lashing blow caught the leaping death squarely in its midsection. There was an audible crack and the next instant, the sleek-furred monster was writhing on the grass with a broken back. Not for long. In one savage rush, the infuriated bull morse trampled the creature into a pulp even while it still snapped and tried to sink its teeth into its giant foe.

Hiero hung limp in the saddle while the morse lowered his own great body gently to the ground so that the man could dismount. The priest wobbled off Klootz's back and collapsed against one of the bull's huge, sweaty sides, breathing hard and trying to keep from fainting. Finally he looked up and saw the anxious face of Gorm looking at him from a few feet away.

I was ready but it was too quick, came from the strange mind. *Can I help?*

No, sent Hiero. *I must bandage/cure myself. Watch for any danger while I do so.* The bear padded off and left him.

Painfully, the priest removed his slashed leather boot, now full of blood, and examined the wound. It appeared clean, but any animal bite ought to be dressed quickly. He fumbled in the saddlebags, conscious of waves of blackness hovering over his pain-wracked mind. The flares had gone out long since, but they had served their purpose. Dawn light was flooding into the clearing and the chirping of the awakening birds seemed ironic after the blaze of sudden death which had heralded the morning, and the five grim shapes on the reddened grass.

40

Hiero finally got the medicine kit out and gingerly spread the healing salve thickly over the long, bleeding wound. He next bandaged it as tightly as he could. It probably needed stitching but in his present condition he simply wasn't up to it. When he was sure he had done all he could, he gulped a Lucinoge tablet. The mind expander was also a narcotic of sorts and as he sank into slumber he could feel his muscles relax. His last thought was a mild worry that something or someone might take over his mind while he was unconscious. Then he remembered no more.

3: THE CROSS AND
THE EYE`

Hiero woke in the dusk. The hush of early evening lay on the land of the trees and over his head a great balsam branch hung in the windless air. It was obvious he had slept the whole day away. Looking down, he saw that he was now lying on a pile of soft balsam tips and that his other boot was off. Instinctively, he reached back over his shoulder for the heavy knife. It was in place, as the sore part of his back testified.

He sat up, feeling no more than a bit dizzy and looking about, found Gorm lying a few feet away sound asleep. Listening, Hiero caught the sound of shredding plant matter from a position around a bend upstream. He sent a thought to the big morse and in an instant Klootz appeared, green fronds of pickerel weed still hanging from his blubber lips. Swaying over, he leaned down and a stream of cold water ran off his shiny neck and into Hiero's face.

"Phew, get away, you horror, before you drown me!" spluttered his master, but at the same time his strong hands were gently rubbing the great antlered head.

"Your spikes are hardening, Boy, which is just as well, because the way this trip is starting we're going to need them." Shifting from speech to mental rapport, he ordered the morse to remain still while he used the big beast's legs to try and stand up.

He found he could remain erect without too much trouble, although walking at all made his leg throb painfully. However, with an effort, he managed to unsaddle Klootz and lay out the saddle bags where he wanted them. Then he dismissed the bull but told him at the same time to stay close to camp and remain on careful watch.

Next, Hiero seated himself and turned to Gorm, who now also sat looking up at him. Reaching over, the man touched the bear's nose gently.

42

Thanks (warmth/ friend feeling) *Brother,* he sent. *How did you make* (the bed of) *branches? And why did you take off my boot?* This was actually the greatest puzzle of all. He could see that the young bear might well be clever enough to make a bed; after all they used them in their own winter dens, but how did the creature know enough to remove his other boot so that his feet could rest?

It was in your mind, came the astonishing answer. *I looked to see* (what) *must/could/should be done. Your mind does not sleep,* Gorm added, *all that is there can be seen if* (one can) *look. I can see only a little but what I saw, I did.*

Hiero once again got out his surgical kit and examined his wound carefully, at the same time thinking over in fascination what the bear had just told him. Incredible, but it must be true! He, Hiero himself, had known what ought to be done and the young bear had found what knowledge he could in the man's own unconscious mind. Incapable of surgery or even first aid, yet Gorm had made a rude but comfortable bed and managed to at least tease off one boot so that Hiero might sleep better. Resolving to look into this further, the rover priest bent to his task.

What followed was unpleasant but necessary. First Hiero cut off the blood-soaked stocking and the equally caked bandage he had applied the previous morning. Then, bracing himself by various forms of nerve-block training and a small further Lucinoge dose, he sutured the edges of the long gaping slash with medical gut. Fourteen stitches later it was done, again disinfected and re-bandaged. He hauled on his right boot and put a clean stocking and a moccasin, taken from the saddlebags, on the left. Then he directed the bear to take the bloody rags and bury them somewhere deep.

Doing this, he suddenly thought of something else and looked about. There were dark spots here and there on the grass but the bodies of their assailants were gone.

From the shadows, Gorm sent an answer. *The big* (horned/stick head) *and I buried them. Their bodies* (would have) *drawn other things to* (the) *hunt. But only small things have come* (easy to) *frighten away.* His mind sent a picture of jackals, bush cats, foxes and other little scavenging creatures.

So the bear and the morse could work together even when he himself was out of the picture! This was also fascinating, reflected Hiero. It meant, it had to mean, that the bear was the one giving orders, for Klootz, smart as he was, could barely think ahead to the consequences of any given action. More food for thought and future exploration, reflected the man.

Have you (felt) *nothing else hunting/danger to us?* he asked Gorm.

In the distance/far? (dimension problem) came the answer. The bear was not being clear and he seemed to understand this and tried again. *Long way, far off* (in) *many directions. But only once* (strong) *and that came from above/the sky?* (impression of something both nasty and winged).

The man probed but could get little more, beyond a vague and distant sight of something with wings but not a bird apparently, glimpsed (or sensed) far off in the sky earlier in the day, and from which had emanated a powerful feeling of evil.

Filing this as one more piece of information to be mulled over later and also making a mental note to avoid going out into open areas as much as possible, Hiero re-packed his possessions. Hobbling to the stream, he cleaned the blood off his weapons and sharpened both spear and knife. When he came back he also reloaded the thrower, which had been replaced in its saddle holster.

Sitting down again, he ate some more *pemeekan* and biscuit. When he offered it to Gorm however, the bear refused it and said he had been feeding on ripe blueberries all day. He showed Hiero where they grew nearby and he was able to limp over and gather several handfuls for dessert. He refilled his big saddle canteen and the small emergency one strapped to his belt, and then as the last of the light faded, took a quick bath in the brook, being careful to keep his wounded leg out of the water. Dried off and dressed again, he said his evening orisons and lay down again. There seemed nothing abroad in the night that could harm them and the sounds of the forest were all normal. The death cry of a rabbit sounded in a nearby thicket and the hum of many mosquitoes made Hiero unpack and draw a fine-meshed net over his upper body. Once that was done, exhaustion took over and he was asleep in a second.

The next day dawned hazy. The sun was behind wreaths of fog and low-lying cumulus clouds, and there was no wind. The air seemed damp and oppressive to Hiero, but only the normal result of a falling barometer, not from any other cause.

Once saddled, Klootz pranced a little, as if tired of simply standing around feeding himself. The man and the bear had decided to leave the stream. Their new route lay more to the south and after another brief meal, they were off, alert but confident. Hiero's leg was now only a dull ache and the rest had helped his tough frame almost as much as the medicinal salve of the Abbey doctors.

For five days they traveled uneventfully through the great pines and spruces of the Taig, always going south. They kept a strict watch, stayed under the trees and used mind speech seldom, but detected nothing of any menace or importance. Game was plentiful and Hiero was able to stalk and kill with his spear a giant grouse, as big as a child, while the foolish bird scratched away in the pine needles. He built a small fire and quickly smoked a lot of the breast, thus obtaining nearly twenty pounds of meat, which would feed both himself and Gorm for a good while.

On the sixth day, the priest estimated they had made perhaps eighty or so miles, and he began to feel a little easier. Whatever malignancy the Unclean tried to send after them now, if any, was going to have a fairly rough time in tracking them down, he thought. He had not yet learned the power and determination of his enemies, nor had he guessed at the fury over his deed in slaying one so high in their dark councils.

Toward noon, the ground became boggy and moist. It was obvious that they were heading either into a swamp or the margin of some body of water. Hiero called a halt, stopped on a patch of dry ground, and got out his maps, bringing the bear over to consult with him while Klootz was turned loose to browse.

Ahead of them lay an enormous area, roughly given on one of the Abbey maps as a vast marsh, called by some the Palood, and both trackless and unknown. The bear's knowledge also stopped here, although he agreed with the map in that he felt the Inland Sea or a great water of some kind lay to the south, beyond a wide expanse of fen. But he had never in his life, not a long one in Hiero's opinion, traveled so far down into the unknown. Most of his information seemed to be second-hand, as indeed was the man's.

Reflecting, the priest decided to try a scan with the crystal and also to cast the symbols. He got them out, said his prayers, put on his vestments and instructed the two animals not to disturb him. Fixing his mind on the route ahead and staring into the crystal, he sent his thoughts out in search of a pair of eyes.

His first vision was disappointing. He found himself looking at a desolate stretch of water, from very low down, apparently almost in the water itself. Nor could he see very well, since the frog, turtle or whatever, whose eyes he had borrowed, was lurking behind a clump of tall reeds and in addition, possessed short-range vision. Shutting his own eyes, Hiero willed a vision change, this time emphasizing height, distance and clarity of sight. Surely, he felt, there must be a hawk or some other bird of prey quartering back and forth over the open water and marshes ahead of them.

Once again the crystal cleared, and this time the mental emphasis on height had paid off, but not at all in the way Hiero had planned!

He was indeed very high up, perhaps a mile or more, and he had an instant to note the land spread out below, the pines of the Taig fading into the great swamp and far off the gleam of what could only be the Inland Sea. And his vision was now superb, much too superb! The highly intelligent mind whose eyes he had inadvertently borrowed was in turn aware of *him* instantly, and as it became aware, tried at once to find out who, what and where he was. He was somehow linked to a furious brain which, cold and repellent though it was, was nonetheless almost identical to his own, seeking with every ounce of its being to locate his present position.

Just as Hiero broke the connection with a wrench which hurt his head, a last, close-up look through the enemy eyes showed the rounded nose of a strange craft, a thing like a huge bullet, and the edges of his vision the beginnings of great wings, made of something like painted wood.

Flight by men was no more than a present dream of the Abbey scientists, but they were well aware that it had been a part of world-wide technology in the ancient past, and they had no doubt it could be and would be re-discovered when more urgent matters had been disposed of first. But here it was, in the hands of the Unclean! High in the blue sky of the Taig, evil and unsuspected eyes marked all the land below, and now sought to trace the travelers and pin them down. And Hiero had led a deadly watcher right to his present position, at least in a way which would allow more rapid pursuit to be organized! He sprang to his feet.

"Lie down," he vocally ordered the bull and led him under a dense clump of fir trees and with his free hand pushed Gorm the same way, urging them on as best he could himself. The bear understood at once, and made no effort to talk with his brain. The trained morse and the untrained bear both had got the feeling of immediate and pressing danger and needed little urging to do what they were told.

Lying against the bull's side, Hiero kept the thrower cocked and ready across his outstretched legs. It was really only accurate for about three hundred feet, but it could be used for double that, and it was the most powerful weapon he had. Straining his eyes up through the canopy of needles and branches, he sought for his enemy. Presently, he saw him. Quite far up, in lazy circles, a black shape like a great falcon, soared and sailed, now drifting out of sight and now moving back. The priest unpacked his seldom-used far-looker, a short brass telescope, and tried to see how much of the peril he could discern. The machine, in fact an unpowered glider, a thing Hiero could not comprehend, stayed too high however, and beyond seeing that the wings had a slight bend backward, thus simulating real bird's wings, he could learn little. *This, then, must be the thing the bear had tried to describe*, he reflected. The hunt had not been thrown off at all, but merely diffused, and despite the distance he thought he had put between them and himself, the forces of the Unclean were still on his track. He looked dismally at the ground and then at his left hand, still clenched into a brown fist.

A fist! He peered quickly out into the little clearing they had just left. The casting bowl and the pieces still lay there and so did the crystal. He had scurried undercover so quickly he had completely forgotten them. He was allowing the enemy to frighten him, to shake his inner confidence. He said a quick, mathematical table as a prayer and then looked down at his now open hand and the three symbols which he had unconsciously caught up while battling in the mind of the flier high above.

First, the little Fish, an unmistakable, fork-tailed carving. It meant water, any kind of water. It also meant, or could mean, boats, docks, nets, lines, salt and other watery concerns. It was also one of the symbols of male virility. The second symbol was the tiny Spear. It meant war, up to and including fighting of all kinds; also any dangerous hunt. The last sign was an odd one, and he had to think back to his early classwork for its various meanings, since it had never once before come to his hand, not in all his many wanderings. It was a cross, a tiny symbol of seven millennium old Christianity, but superimposed on its center, where the arms joined, was the oval carving of a miniature eye. The Cross and the Eye! He felt a shiver run up his spine. This rarely turned up symbol stood for the presence of a spiritual evil, something which menaced not just the body but the very soul.

He laid the three symbols gently on the ground and darted a look at the sky. The flier was still visible, but only just, now far way, at the limit of Hiero's vision to the north. The priest darted out into the open and retrieved the bowl and also the crystal on its wooden base. Not even an eagle could have seen a movement at that distance, he felt.

Repacking his apparatus in the bag while Klootz mumbled over his cud and the bear snored, utterly relaxed in an instant nap, the priest turned the three symbols over in his mind. He was heading for water. Even if he had tried to turn back it was almost certainly too late. The flier knew roughly where he was and the pursuit must already have been summoned. He dared not use his looted rod to listen, for fear of being detected himself, but he was sure the ether was thrilling with the summons and exhortations of the Unclean. Leemutes no doubt were pouring from various dens in the North. But what of the South? Was a trap being laid there, or perhaps many?

The Fish, the Spear, and the Eyed Cross! Water, battle and coming of some spiritual bane or woe. But was that the right reading? As always, the little signs were chancy to interpret. The last sign, the Eyed Cross, could mean a grim psychic menace but it could also mean a great sin upon the caster's own conscience, a mortal sin in fact. *Be damned to that*, said Hiero angrily to himself. He had confessed before leaving the Republic, to Abbot Demero in fact. And telling Leolane d'Ondote that she was going to be neither his first, second or indeed any other wife, and further that her talents were exclusively prone was *not* a mortal sin, even if more than a trifle rude. And that was the heaviest guilt currently on his mind.

Suppose, now, that the Spear meant a hunt and the Fish a boat? No, that was silly in his present condition. Well then, what about other possibilities? Through the long afternoon, he turned over and over in his mind the various combinations of the three pieces. But the Eyed Cross dominated his thoughts. Deep inside him was the certain knowledge that he was not in mortal sin and that he was instead approaching some dread encounter with a great evil of the Unclean.

Determined not to expose himself to the man, Leemute or whatever, which rode the sky machine, he waited with his two allies until the Sun was only a dim, red glow in the far West. Then they sallied out from the gloom of the firs and headed south into the muddy paths between the last straggling trees of the Taig.

Under the evening stars, gleaming pools of water began to appear and soon grew more frequent. The trees grew less in size and the pines now vanished at last. Great spatterdocks and overgrown marsh plants, looming oddly in the night, began to replace them. Strange and lovely perfumes came from pale night flowers growing on the surface of muddy pools and rank stenches came from other and seemingly identical pools. Ferns too, were increasingly large, often as high or higher than Klootz's head and they grew in great black clumps, some so thick that the travelers had to detour around them. The air had been growing steadily warmer for the last few days, but now it was suddenly both warm and damp, and even when perfumed, carrying a hint of fetid decay and over-ripe growth under the pleasant scents. They had left the Taig and its cool breezes for good and were now breathing the air of the Palood, the monster-haunted fen which for league upon league bordered the northern edge of the Inland Sea. It was a trackless, horribly dangerous waste, and only roughly defined on any map.

Even as Hiero recalled all this, a hideous croaking bellow rang out somewhere ahead of them. It drowned the normal noises of the night, the constant hum of the swarms of insects and the chorus of small frogs, by sheer vibration.

Klootz jerked to a standstill and ahead of them in the dark Gorm halted like the grotesque shadow of a distorted pointer, one foot raised dripping from a pool of dark water. For a moment they listened and then, when no other sound came, began to cautiously move onward. Hiero's face and hands were now smeared with an insect-repelling grease, but the cloud of bugs still penetrated his clothes, and it was a sore trial not to be able to curse wholeheartedly. They had gone only a hundred feet or so when the grunting roar again broke out in the moist dark ahead of them. With it came a prodigious "splat," as if some vast platter had been slammed down hard into soft mud. The myriad small animal voices of the marsh, the night birds, frogs and other things fell silent. Only the humming drone of millions of mosquitoes and gnats went on. The three again paused, but this time not for so long.

Behind them another awful bellow exploded in the night. The sheer volume of the second cry had to make the bulk of its owner simply enormous. And it seemed to be closer than the one in front.

Hiero looked desperately about. They were in shadows on the edge of a big patch of open, shiny mud, well lit by the bright stars above and the half-full moon. To their left and in front was only the mud, but to their right, some dark clump of other of vegetation rose against the stars.

Get to the right quickly, he sent to the bear and the morse. *Into those bushes or plants and lie down again. We can't face these things!*

They had barely begun to move when the growth parted on the far side of the mud patch and a face out of nightmare leered over and down at them from a hundred feet away. Dimly, Hiero could see, the scientist still operating in his mind, a frog or a three-quarter grown tadpole might have provided a possible remote progenitor. The great opalescent eyes were set ten feet apart on the blunt, slimy head. It squatted many yards off the mud on monstrous bowed forelegs, and horny claws tipped the giant toes. And the incredible gape of the jaws now gleamed with lines of giant fangs, teeth such as no frog ever had, like a forest of ivory needles, each a foot long, glistening in the moonlight.

The morse did not move, and Gorm, almost paralyzed with fear, shrank against one of his rigid forelegs. The priest raised the thrower and took careful aim, saying a silent prayer as he did so. Even the powerful charge of the small rocket-shells was simply not designed for this scale of being. Under his body, Hiero felt the bull gathering himself for an enormous leap.

Klootz's hindquarters tensed and sank down.

Wait! sent Hiero, just as Klootz was about to explode like a coiled spring. The man had seen the attention of the monstrosity suddenly waver. It crouched as he watched and its eyes and head shifted to the left and behind them.

Then suddenly, it just took off. The pillar-like hind legs, no doubt the legacy of some pre-Death ranid ancestor, hurled the whole bulk of the titan, long tail trailing, past and *over* the three shrinking mammals. Before they could even blink, the weight of what must have been fifteen tons hit the mucky ground well behind them. The shock wave made the mud rise in a mighty wave and at the same time an incredible flailing uproar broke out, great limbs kicking and tremendous bodies straining, while showers of plant matter and acres of muck were hurled into the night air. The vast creature had fallen upon another of its own kind, Hiero realized, suddenly remembering the second awful cry which had come in from their rear.

It took little urging to get Gorm and the morse away from the appalling sounds of the struggle. They galloped away through mud and slime, splashing recklessly through several shallow lagoons and over reeking patches of some evil-smelling herbage. Finally the uproar died away in the distance and Hiero commanded a halt. They now stood on a long, raised bar of packed, dried reeds jammed together by some flood of a past year, and listened to the night.

The insect and frog chorus reverberated, but otherwise nothing else sounded or moved beneath the white moon, save for the cry of a startled heron which they disturbed. They could see quite a way in several directions, the principle obstacles to viewing now consisting of great reeds, whose clumps had been steadily increasing as they progressed. Some of the smooth stalks were two feet around and the feathery tops towered up far over the soft upthrust points of Klootz's antlers. Between the reeds grew many huge mallows and stands of giant arrowweed, the triangular leaves of the latter dipping gently like fans in the gentle breeze. Lanes of still moonlit water stretched between the patches of mud and plant life, some opening into large ponds, others winding out of sight around distant corners. It was a scene of strange beauty and even the ever-present smells of the dissolving marsh gases and rotting vegetation did not really detract from it, Hiero thought as he gazed.

With an effort, he recalled himself to the present. They were very lucky, in the headlong flight from the amphibian collossi, not to have blundered into some other and possibly worse peril. It was definitely time to pause and consider the next step. The Abbey maps were quite useless here and Gorm was as alien to this strange country of mingled land and water as Hiero himself. What guides had they then? They knew in which direction they wished to travel, south, and where it lay. They knew the Unclean were seemingly somewhere still on their tracks, coming from the opposite direction, the North they had left behind. The great swamp stretched before them unbroken to the horizon. The limits of its existence, both from the maps' outlines and the brief glimpse the priest had caught through the eyes of the Unclean flyer, were shorter ahead of them than to either side. The marshes might stretch for hundreds of miles in the lateral directions but barely for fifty in front, southward, if his vision was any judge, the man reflected. There really wasn't much choice. South and through the narrowest part of the swamp the path had to go. There were sure to be dangers, but true to his training, Hiero had selected the route which promised the most for the least, in terms of rewards and perils.

Through the remainder of the night they slowly moved on south, wading through many shallow pools and avoiding equally many deep ones. It was necessary to swim on two occasions, broad channels which intersected their path and could not be circled. In the first one nothing occurred, but as they left the second, and the dripping morse hauled himself out on the mud bank, Hiero, looking back, saw the black water heave ominously, as if something large were moving off the bottom. He had been carrying his thrower across the saddle, ready for any action, but above all he dreaded an assault from below, in which all of them would be more or less helpless. The bear he had made swim just in front of Klootz's nose, so that he could at least attempt to defend him if he were attacked.

As they now stood looking at one another, the priest could not help smiling ruefully. All three of them were now soaked, and mud caked the legs of the four-foots. The clinging bog smell was vile and there was no way of getting rid of it, not until they got out of the swamps at any rate. One advantage the caked mud gave the animals was that it at least partially protected them from the incessant, droning attack of the mosquitoes. Slapping at himself, Hiero wondered if his protective ointment would last. He was used to bug bites as any woodsman had to be, but the legions which rose from the Palood were something else again! To make matters worse, huge brown leeches had to be picked off the two animals at almost every stop, filthy things which haunted every pool of water.

The first day was spent huddled in a thicket of the towering green reeds. Determined not to be caught out in the open muck or water by one of the flying enemy during daylight, Hiero had hacked a careful way into the reeds which he thought unlikely to be seen from above. By the time the sun was fully up, they were well hidden in the heart of the reeds, but little more, if any, comfortable than if they had been in the open. It was a cloudless morning, and the August sun grew steadily hotter as the day advanced. The mosquitoes, shunning the light, were overjoyed to find helpless targets buried deep in the shade and attacked in new armies. Minute gnats and crawling bugs, mercifully absent during the hours of darkness, joined the onslaught and helped make them all miserable. As if that were not enough, the leeches too, emerged from the water, and suckers waving, inched on to the three at every chance.

The man cut what he could spare from his own mosquito net and managed to rig crude muzzle screens for the two tortured beasts, so that they could at least breathe in comfort without inhaling clouds of flying, stinging pests. Beyond plastering themselves with as much mud as possible, there was little else they could do. At least, thought Hiero, there was no water shortage. Where the pools were not churned up or too shallow, he had found the water to be perfectly clean and needing only to be strained once to remove insects and other vermin before being added to his canteens.

Food was another matter. There was some grouse, quite a lot of *pemeekan* and even more of the biscuit left in the saddlebags, but he was aware that it really ought to be saved as much as possible. The morse would simply have to be allowed to feed before they started the night's journey; there was certainly enough succulent vegetation growing in or near the water. But what could the poor bear do but eat the dwindling rations along with himself? Aha! Aha!

He fumbled quickly in the near saddlebag momentarily forgetting the insects and the cloying heat. Sure enough, the fishing equipment was still in its case. *Let's see now,* he thought, *can I reach the water from here with a throw?*

Carefully trying a shiny weighted lure to the gut line, he threw it out into the channel which ran, brown and turbid, a few yards from the mouth of the tunnel he had carved for them in the road bed.

On the third cast a violent tug signified some luck and soon a fat, striped fish, a perch of some unknown sort, he thought, weighing about three pounds, was flapping its tail on the packed mud bank. Before his luck ran out, he had caught two more of them. He gave one to Gorm who fell upon it and seemed to find it excellent. The other two he cleaned and scaled, packing one away for later and eating one now himself. He had eaten raw fish many times before and examination showed these not to be infested with worms as was sometimes the case. Certainly lighting a fire would be the absolute height of folly, knowing that the heavens were no longer free of inimical eyes. He ate one of the dry biscuits with the fish and a small lump of *pemeekan,* since the fish contained no fat or oil. Then he curled up for a nap, doing his best to ignore the vermin, winged and legged and to endure as stoically as his two allies.

At nightfall, having seen nothing of the winged watcher during the day, he told Klootz to go and eat, and soon the steady maceration of waterplants added to the insect and frog drone. Some sorts of small birds appeared in quantity in the evening sky for the first time, and he could hear their many shrill calls as they hawked for insects over the marshland. He sourly felt that about 8,000,000 more of them would be needed to diminish the mosquito population in some degree. He shared two biscuits and the other fish with the small bear, who also had found and dug himself two whitish roots or tubers from the mud. Tasting one of them gingerly, Hiero felt the sting of some powerful acid, and knew that he would be unable to supplement his own diet with this particular plant.

Giving the big morse an hour to feed, Hiero decided, would be about all the time he could spare. The marshes had to be traversed and the sooner the better. As things were now, they could travel only during the night and even that time was cut into by feeding and finding shelter.

Klootz came willingly enough and his master noticed that he had not bathed, that only his head and legs as far as the hock were wet. Since the big morse loved water and wallowed at every opportunity, this was surprising.

Something (nature unknown) *in the deep water* (under/watching), came the thought when the priest sent a question. *Bad too/very bad (to) fight.*

This matter-of-fact statement from his mount made Hiero blink. He saddled hastily and calling Gorm, rode to the far side of the reed island they were on. Moonlit shallows stretched away before them, broken by many mud banks, and no deep open water was visible except far off and to one side. The man was very glad they had swum the other channel the night before, and wondered what the morse had sensed lurking out there. It never occurred to him to question Klootz's judgment or his keen senses. If he said there was something bad out in the water, then there was, and if he was afraid of it, it must be pretty horrendous. It could be anything, from a collossal snapper to one of the great frog monsters they had encountered previously. *Or something nastier still,* reflected Hiero. He had wondered earlier why the flying watcher had made no appearance during the day. Perhaps the answer was too simple. The great marsh was (rightly) thought so dangerous that the Unclean either could not believe he had entered it or if they did, were confident he would never emerge. Both conclusions made logical sense, he admitted to himself.

Once during the night they heard the vast bellowing cry of a giant amphibian, but the sound came from far away and to one side, in the distant East. Again, later, from a tangle of tall vegetation they were skirting, there came a mighty hissing as if the grandfather of all snakes were suddenly angry. They made haste to leave the area, and although Hiero was careful to watch the back trail for an hour or so, nothing appeared to be following them. Gorm was very cautious in the lead, testing all the mud patches they traversed to be sure that they were not some quicksand or ooze which would sink the whole party. Twice such areas were found, but the bear seemed quite able to tell them from the rest of the landscape and the man gradually relaxed his fear of being mired in some sucking bog.

The damp air was stirred by fitful breezes and ever stranger odors came to them as they went deeper and deeper into the watery waste. It occurred to the priest, watching Klootz's broad hooves flatten on the mud, that he might well be the first man to try the swamp with both a steed who was semi-aquatic and a priceless guide and outrider such as the young bear. This might mean that they would succeed and get through where others had failed.

They spent another miserable day, this time in the rain, which fortunately was warm. Gorm had located another mound of rotted plant matter from which reeds and giant docks were growing and once again Hiero hollowed out a cave into which they all had to crawl.

It was still raining at evening and Hiero had caught no more fish, despite repeated efforts. He and the bear shared some grouse, biscuit and *pemeekan* but the animal could discover none of the roots he had found earlier. Klootz, however, seemed quite pleased with the water plants near their mound and there was no deep water nearby, so that he was able to have a roll in the muddy shallows.

Eventually Gorm led off again, with a fine drizzle still falling and little if any light to illumine their way. Possibly as a result, they had to swim on two occasions, though fortunately without incident.

In actuality, they were all very lucky, if Hiero had only bothered to think for a moment. For three days, they had safely penetrated the great wilderness of water and yet had seen or encountered few of the monstrous life forms which inhabited it. And despite the swarms of noxious insects which caused them all such misery, Hiero, much the most susceptible, had caught none of the sickening fevers which made even the very borders of the Palood feared.

54

Once again, the priest hacked away into an island of partly growing, partly dead plant matter. After adjusting the mosquito masks on the animals, he put on his own and prepared for another soggy, leech- and bug-ridden day of itching and cursing. They were camped on the edge of a dark, deep lagoon, but he ignored the black water, his wariness for once strangely lulled.

The priest was so tired however, that he soon fell asleep, despite the bites and the steamy heat. As the day passed, he lay in a sort of drugged torpor and the two animals slept also, hardly moving and simply enduring while even the thick mud-plastered hides of the morse and the bear were drilled again and again by the sucking worms and clouds of waiting gnats and stinging flies.

Exhausted they must all have been, but there perhaps was more to it than that. Deep in one of the saddlebags a tiny bead of light glowed under a glass dial, brightened, dimmed and then grew bright again. Forces and currents, invisible to the eye, but nonetheless powerful, moved through the steaming fog which lay on the Palood. In dark places, unknown to normal mankind, consultations were held, fears explored and decisions taken. Curious things stirred under the slime and the Unclean concentrated their vast powers on the heart of the bog, where a tell-tale glow on one of their hidden control boards told them a deadly enemy of unknown power, a foe to their fell purposes now lay concealed. From drowned cities, lost and buried forever under the fens and mud of the marshland, came the flicker of strange movement and unnatural life.

The morning grew old. A pale sun shone through a watery fog and yellowish vapor rack. No wind disturbed the quiet pools and the tops of the tall reeds and docks hung limp in the mists and humid steams which rose from the surface of the great fen. Still the three drowsed on, occasionally murmuring or groaning softly in the trip of their overlong sleep. Afternoon passed and still they lay unmoving. The light died slowly as the sun sank into the cloudy west. Now the white fogs of night began to rise from the meres and dark waters, mingling with those left from the day, until vision shrank and one could only see in streaks where the veils curled aside before re-closing and forming new banks of haze and murk.

At this dree hour came the Dweller in the Mist. From what foul den or lurking place it issued, none may ever know. The ghastly cosmic forces unleashed by The Death had made the mingling of strange life possible and things had grown and thought which should never have known the breath of life. Of such was the Dweller. How it had found the three, only it, or perhaps the Lords of the Unclean, could have said. Perhaps the telltale in the saddlebag helped. It had found them and that was enough.

Some warning gave Hiero a fighting chance, some spark sent by the trained soul the Abbey fathers had taught, to the trained mind which they had disciplined. He woke, clutching the silver cross and sword upon its neck thong and saw before him the doom which had stolen upon them as they slept.

The vapors had parted briefly over the dark lagoon which lay before the entrance to their refuge. Around a corner of the next islet of mud and reeds came a small boat. It was hardly more than a skiff, of some black wood, with a rounded bow and stern. On it standing erect and motionless, was a figure swathed in a whitish cloak and hood. What propelled the strange craft was not apparent, but it moved steadily through the oily water, coming straight for the place where the priest now sat staring.

Before the shrouded figure in the pale draperies there came out a wave of fell power and evil intent which struck Hiero and piled over him like some vast and clammy net. Beside him, the two faithful beasts apparently slept on, unmoving. The force which the Dweller commanded held them in their places, if not asleep, at least numbed them into unconsciousness. The man knew that something had caught them all unaware which might, in truth, destroy the bodies of the two animals, but which was really directed at him, and the aim of which was the total enslavement of his mind and soul. Here, he knew on the instant, was the embodiment of the warning given by the little Eyed Cross.

All this flashed through his mind as he prepared to do battle and the black skiff glided to a halt, nosing into the soft mudbank not ten feet from where he sat. From the place of his inner being, Hiero looked into the shadows under that pale hood and from that caverned place the Dweller's eyes, two pits of ocherous evil stared silently back.

In one sense, though only the broadest, it was another mental struggle, such as Hiero had waged unsuccessfully against S'nerg. But there were important differences. The Unclean wizard, bad as he was, was still a man, and his control owed much to simple hypnotic techniques, amplified and strengthened by years of training and practice in telepathic control. That which was called the Dweller was not remotely human. What it was, even Hiero never learned and the powers it drew upon were somehow inherent and natural to it. It sought control by a form of mental parasitism, as a vampire sucks blood by instinct, rather than by any design. Its form of attack was nonphysical but two-pronged.

Hiero felt an intensification of the smothering, clinging feeling which had announced the Dweller's coming. His mind, his body, his inner processes, his center of being, felt steadily constricted and squeezed, as well as feeling a

56

constant drain of energy. In addition, however, a subtle feeling of *pleasure* was projected at the same time, a sense that the Dweller meant all that was good and beneficial, both to his physical and to his spiritual well being. There was a subtle biological side effect, sexual in nature, which filled Hiero's mind with mingled loathing and delight at one and the same time. The overall attack was very powerful. The psychic energy of the swamp thing seemed almost a visible aura around its shrouded head, the bulk and shape of which, even under its wrappings, looked all *wrong* and somehow not physically possible or proper.

One hand clutching the Cross and Sword on his breast, the priest fought grimly back. The part of his total being which was being seduced by the promise of unspeakable pleasures he concentrated on memories of strength and austerity. Such were the Abbey choir services of the motet evenings, the mental courts, where novices battled one another in silent struggles of the mind. He had obtained just enough time before the Dweller's net was cast to start reciting the table of logarithms with yet another part of his brain. Long ago, the Abbey masters had learned that the ancient mathematical formulas were a strong defense against mental attack. Based as they were on logic, repetition and disciplined series, they formed a strong barrier, when properly utilized, against the illogic and confusion which, of necessity, were the chief mental weapons of the Unclean. Yet it was a struggle which Hiero felt to be steadily going against Him. The draining power of the Dweller seemed inexhaustible. Each time the priest blocked off an avenue into his mind by which it tried to lure him into acquiescence, another similar attack would commence on some other flaw in his psyche. And the steady compression of what Hiero felt to be a net never ceased its remorseless constriction as well. The appeals to his gross senses and the black strangling clutch at his thought processes seemed more and more hopeless to combat.

Yet, even as his will seemed to him to weaken, his courage and resolution actually flared higher in response to the danger. And an unexpected help came, unrealized in fact at this time, from the dead mind of S'nerg whom the priest had slain. His struggle with the adept had given Hiero's own dormant powers a new strength of which he had as yet no conception. He battled on, therefore, no hint of yielding in his soul, determined that if this nightmare from the swamp murk were to conquer him, it would only be at the price of his death!

The physical world about him had completely disappeared. He was conscious of only the black foulness before him, the veil from which stared the twin pools of lambent horror, the eyes of the Dweller! And in those eyes, he saw, or sensed, for the first time, something change, some shift or evasion. So close now was his rapport with the thing before him that he realized at once what had happened. It was no longer attacking! The doubt, faint as it was, had interfered with the stream of projections and mental bolts which the Dweller had been using, and even the tiny hesitation had broken the flow of its concentration. To gain the victories to which it had been used, weakness and weariness must help and undisciplined minds must inevitably yield to the frightful powers it both controlled and lived by.

For the first time, Hiero's mind *reached out* and in a way impossible for a non-telepath to imagine, struck back at the Dweller. The stroke was not one of great strength, being both hesitant and clumsy. But the thing almost visibly staggered. It had never been challenged so in all its foul existence, prowling the swamp and its borders for prey. What became of its victims was best unthought. To what hell they had been lured and their subsequent fate there, no one would ever know, but Hiero always felt that some joint serfdom of physical pain and soul suffering was their fate.

Again he lashed out with a mental bolt and this time actually saw the horrid spots of spectral light which were its eyes blink in response. Gaining confidence with each probe he directed, he felt new strength surge through him. For the first time in a long while, or what seemed so, he became aware of the world about him and felt the night air on his face and saw the hooded shape before him and its place in the scheme of things, not as an inchoate force, but as a vile object to be destroyed. He next struck at the net of thought which the Dweller had tried to use to compress his mind in a cage, and one strong blow shattered the invisible bonds completely. Now, rejoicing in the clean surge of energy which he was using, he shaped a web of his own, willing the strands of psychic energy to form a pattern of power which would hold the living horror which was the Dweller enmeshed in its own turn. Remorselessly, calling on the Trinity and all the saints to aid, he began to choke the monster's mind and dark spirit as it had tried to do to him.

Neither one had moved a muscle during the encounter. But as the burning, almost tangible power of the warrior priest began to slay the Dweller, it let out one fearful cry, a mewing sound, as if some ghastly stringed instrument, some guitar forged in the nethermost pit, had struck an impossible chord. Then, grimly, it fought for its existence. And fought in vain, for all its shifts and evasions, its counter strokes and lurements were to no purpose.

Fending off each rally by the mere-thing, Hiero, by the power of his trained will and armed spirit, inexorably drew the strands of his mind trap tighter and tighter. When he had bent a last effort (he thought) and still found

58

the other's will unbroken, he breathed harder and using his new knowledge, concentrated a dart of energy, which went through the net he fashioned in some way without disturbing it.

Once more, and for the last time, that awful mewing, twanging cry, the death scream of something never meant to give voice at all, echoed over the lonely fens.

Then—there was an instantaneous vacuum, as if a soundless bubble had burst, perhaps somewhere in another alien dimension superimposed upon ours. And then, nothing more. There was only the soughing of the night wind in the reed tops, the hum of countless insect hordes and the rasping obligato of frog voices.

The black skiff still lay nosed upon the muck, just in front of Hiero's tunnel. But no hooded figure now stood glaring in at the priest. A heap of colorless rags lay spilled half over the gunwales and from the clothes, a sticky, oily substance was leaking, covering the now moonlit water with a foul stain. A charnel stench came from the rags, a reek which made the worst efforts of the marsh gases seem like perfume by comparison. Whatever had worn the hooded cloak had returned to its native elements, as foul in its strange death as it had been in life.

Choking at the vile smell, Hiero rose and putting one foot on the strange, little craft, gave it a hearty shove. To his amazement, the skiff did not simply glide off at the force of his push, but instead turned and moved away, in steady progress up the channel down which it had first come. He could see clearly now, for the mists had cleared while he had fought for his life, and he watched the mysterious boat, bearing the remains of its ghastly pilot, sedately turn a corner in the reed banks and vanish. In its strange going it kept the last secret of the Dweller in the Mist.

Wearily, Hiero looked up at the white moon. The incredible struggle had gone on for at least three hours and yet had seemed like only a few moments. When the Dweller had first appeared, the last sickly light of the fog-shrouded sun still lingered in the West. But the position of the moon showed that it now was not far short of ten o'clock.

He turned and looked down at his two partners in jeopardy. For the first time he smiled. The bear was swatting mosquitoes in his sleep and growling angrily as he did. Klootz was also asleep, but emitting gargantuan grunts and rumblings, while every inch of his great hide twitched and rippled in an effort to shake off the stinging bugs. Whatever spell they all had been under was completely lifted, that was certain.

The priest said a brief prayer of thanks while he watched the gibbous moon rise still farther. He was still somewhat bemused, and his nervous energy was a long way from returning to normal, while the tremendous dose of psychic strength he had utilized to fight the Dweller had taken a toll. He felt as if he had been riding for two days without a break, at a full gallop.

But it was not time to delay. The mystery of how the horror of the mere had found them was insoluble, at least at present, but one thing was clear, it had had help! That much he had been able to read from its anguished brain even as he destroyed it and sent it back to the nameless deeps from which it should never have emerged. Somehow, even though he had seen no flier, felt no follower of any kind, the three had been tracked. They must move on and at once, before fresh forces could be assembled for their destruction. Hiero felt fairly sure that the Dweller had not been able, even if willing, to summon any aid in its last moments, because he now knew the strength of the weapon which he had used to slay it. And it had been too preoccupied fighting for its unnatural life to send any messages whatsoever. But if it could find them, by whatever means, so could others. This was a matter on which he would have to take thought, but later on, not now.

He was amused that his new confidence seemed more than temporary. Beyond, and indeed underlying the amusement, was a hard-won feeling of mental power. Hiero knew without even wondering *how* he knew, that Abbot Demero or any others of the Council would now be hard-put to stand against him. He hastily put aside such thoughts as vainglorious and impertinent, but they were still there, buried but not dead, in the deep reaches of his mind. He was learning something the Abbey scholars of the mental arts were just beginning to conceive, the fact that mental powers accrete in a geometric, not arithmetical, progression, depending on how much and how well they are used. The two battles Hiero had won, even though the bear had helped decide the first, had given the hidden forces of his already strong mind a dimension and power he would not himself have believed possible. And the oddest thing was, he knew it.

Tired, but feeling somehow wonderful anyway, he roused Gorm and the morse. The bear rose, sniffed the air and then sent a message. *You have fought. It is in the air.* (But) *there is no blood* (and) *we have not waked. The enemy which strikes the mind?* (Doubt/fear)?

Marvelling at the bear's perceptions, not for the last time, Hiero briefly told him of the Dweller and the fact that It was gone forever.

Gone, that is good. But you are weary, very!! Weary and also troubled (as to how) *the enemy found* (smelled out) *us. Let us go. We* (can) *eat later.*

The big morse nosed him all over and wrinkled his lip in distaste at some smell he seemed to detect on the mud-smeared leather. Hiero saddled him, picking off some more of the big leeches as he did, and in a short time they were on their way again, under the bright moon.

The night's journey was uneventful. Beyond Klootz's shying at a small water snake and Gorm's frightened avoidance of a still pool covered with the scented pale blossoms of some giant nenuphar, nothing occurred.

Dawn saw them camped in yet another clump of vegetation. But it was not a reed bed, but rather a hollow in some large rounded bushes, with laurel-like, dark green leaves. Hiero guessed, and rightly, that the appearance of these woody plants and also the solid ground on which they grew, meant that at long last the Palood was coming to an end. He fell asleep as the sun rose in a clear sky. As he dropped off, he dimly heard the morse chewing his cud and very faintly, far off in the distance, the apparent raucous screeching of many birds.

That evening, after sundown, when the three had all fed, the man and bear sharing pack rations and Klootz thirty pounds of fresh green fodder, Hiero sat for a moment before leaving. All day, while nodding drowsily in the high-cantled saddle, he had ruminated over the problem of pursuit.

How had the Dweller been led to them? The bogs and pools swallowed any tracks on the instant. No hunters trailed them beyond earshot. The three were too sensitive now to allow any undetected surveillance of that sort. Could a flier be so high in the sky at night that they, the travelers, were visible to it? Perhaps a means of seeing at night lay open to the enemy of which the Abbey scientists knew nothing. But he had to dismiss the thought. If that were the case, there was nothing he could do about it anyway, but he did not believe it. No, the fragment of thought he had plucked from the dissolving mind of the living foulness which was the Dweller had seemed to say (or meant) that the creature had been *led* to its sleeping victims.

Led by what? The priest continued to brood as he saddled Klootz and swung up into the saddle for the night's ride. And as he rode along under the serene light of the moon and countless stars, he continued to dwell on the problem. The hunting pack of giant water-ferrets had simply followed their trail by means of their keen noses. Or had they? Had they, and perhaps the flier too, some better guide, some aid which allowed them, if not to pinpoint the exact location of the three, at least to know the general position where they might be found? "Damn it, how!" muttered Hiero aloud in vexation. "It's as if they had a string on me somehow, something on me they could follow, like a bad smell that never grows any fainter."

His thoughts shifted to the Unclean as he spoke and suddenly he grunted at his own stupidity. Quickly he ordered a halt. They were crossing a hard-packed sand bar at the time, and the instant Klootz and the bear stopped, Hiero was down on the ground, tearing open one of the saddlebags. His hand seized what he wanted and he pulled it out into the moonlight.

It was a moment of irritation, bitter and intense when he held the betrayer in his hand. He smiled grimly at the realization of how the possessions of the dead adept, S'nerg, had led his foul avengers upon the tracks of his killers. The tiny bead of light in the thing like a compass glowed steadily as it rocked back and forth on its circular track. The priest needed no more proof, he *knew*. Whatever else the curious instrument was, and it probably had several uses, it was also a "homer" of some kind, a fix which told the position of its owner to his friends, so that he would never be totally out of touch. Enraged at his own folly, Hiero crushed the instrument under his heel. He had no fear of the rod and the knife, since he knew the former's powers, and the knife was simply and only that, a knife. Once more he remounted and with a lighter heart, signaled his companions to lead off south.

Far away, in a place buried deep beyond the reach of the last, dimmest ray of the sun, a hooded figure turned from a great board of many-colored lights and pointing to one darkened bulb which was set in a vast wire frame, showed by a shrug that it had now gone out.

4: *Luchare*

By the time the next dawn that they made camp, well before the rising of the sun, Hiero and the two animals could see that the great marsh was at last coming to an end. All night the hard sandbars had grown more and more frequent, steadily replacing the mud and soft muck of the swamp. Huge logs, some still bearing leaves, showed that seasonal flooding or storm-driven waters came into this area at frequent intervals. Patches of higher, firmer ground now supported stunted trees instead of the great reeds, and occasional spines of rock protruded from the ponds and channels, forming craggy islets in the wider and more open stretches. Halting on top of one of these, whose ramp-like slope had tempted him to gain a better look about, the man glimpsed a number of great, domed shapes, black against the moonlit sand, moving on a beach below him. Their furious activity puzzled him until he realized that he had caught a group of snappers laying their leathery eggs in the churned-up sand. He dismounted and waited patiently, signaling the bear to do the same. After the moon reached zenith, the last of the monster turtles waddled back into the water and disappeared, their task of reproduction over for another season.

Keeping a sharp eye out for any stragglers, Hiero and the bear went down and dug up a nest they had previously marked in the moonlight as being in a shallow hole. Gorm gulped down three of the great, golden-yolked things, each an easy hand length in diameter, while Hiero spooned up one himself. But he packed the morse's saddlebags with eight more, all he could get in, and then the group had set off again, the bear moving rather more slowly because of his gorged stomach.

As they topped a small rise in the land, Hiero reined up. Ahead of them reared a row of dark hills, which shut off the view of the country beyond. Where these mysterious mountains had come from was a puzzle to him, since

63

they ought to have been visible a long way off and yet had not been. He decided to camp on the spot, selecting a handy cleft in a large rock, which was partly overhung by vines and bushes. The puzzle of the suddenly-appearing hills could wait for dawn and that was not far away.

As the sun slowly rose, Hiero peered out and started to laugh, in both joy and relief, making the bear look curiously at him. The "mountains" he had seen a few hours before were nothing but a crest of tall sand dunes and they were no more than a mile away, across a belt of scrub with a few streams trickling through them. He, or they rather, had conquered the great marsh!

For a long time he lay, the morning sun warm on his tanned brow and watched the dunes. A short distance beyond them could only lie the Inland Sea. A road led to the extreme western edge of this great body of fresh water, that is a road from the Metz Republic, far to the Northwest. But Hiero knew that he was nowhere near the place where that road reached the brawling port town of Namcush. He must be hundreds of miles further to the east, and what towns if any lay in this part of the sea or on its shores, no one really knew, beyond perhaps some few close-mouthed and suspicious merchants. The men of the merchant guilds sometimes voyaged for thousands of miles, but many of them were pagans with no love for the Abbeys, or the Republic either, or indeed any governing body save their own loose, mercantile federation. They were not men who gave up information easily and more than one of them was certain to be allied with, if not an actual servant of the Unclean. Yet it was necessary to deal with the merchants and some of them were good men who served as spies and secret messengers for the Abbeys, often earning themselves a horrible death.

It was mostly information given by trading merchants, sometimes filtered through thousands of miles of rumor, which Hiero had stored in his brain ready for mnemonic recall whenever he needed it. But any information of the Inland Sea's eastern, central or southern end was vague, out-of-date and apt to be inaccurate.

A number of ships sailed the Inland Sea, some of them mere rowing barges but most with sails. Pirates manned some of them and merchants and traders others. Sometimes it was hard to tell which was which, for like the Vikings of remote legend, an honest merchant sometimes found a colleague in trouble too easy a bargain to resist.

Also in the deep waters and among the many islands skulked the Unclean, in strange, seldom-glimpsed craft. And there were great beasts too, lurking in the open deeps, some of which came into shallow water to seize their prey. Other vast, nameless monsters were said to be plant eaters, but were nonetheless bellicose and easily aroused to fury.

The worst of the so-called natural disasters and perils though, were ancient, as old as the Inland Sea itself, which had once been five smaller seas, a thing the oldest of the Abbey's preserved maps clearly showed. These were the places of the cold Death, where the fires of the dreadful radiation of the last cataclysm still poisoned the air and water. Most of them had lost their once dreadful potency. Daring freebooters sometimes risked a horrible end to loot one of the Lost Cities which bordered the Inland Sea, and had been designated over five thousand years gone as First Strike targets. Some of these dreaded places were plague centers too, so that a man ran the risk of dying hideously of radiation poisoning, or, if he missed that, of some fell sickness and of passing that on to his neighbors before he died himself.

As a result, those who went to the Lost Cities, even those places judged to be cleansed by time and the elements, were apt to do so secretly, lest their fellows (unless pirates themselves) be inclined to kill them out of hand, for threatening them in turn with an unpleasant death by disease.

Around the shores of the Sea and on its surface too, roamed various groups of human nomads, some living from the water directly, as fishermen, others gleaning the refuse of the shore or doing both and living in semi-permanent camps. By all accounts, the Inland Sea and its environs was a lively place, where a man could get himself killed in a different way for each of the twenty-four hours, seven days a week, with no fear of repetition.

All this ran through Hiero's mind as he stared at the dunes and imagined what might lie on their far side. And so dreaming, he fell asleep, the sun beating down on his bearded face, tangled black hair, now stiff with filth and his mud-caked clothes. A piece of abandoned human refuse, he looked, as he lay under the hot sun, instead of a Per of the Church Universal and an Abbey scholar of good repute.

Anxious to push on, he allowed Klootz only a short time to browse that evening. The young bear had caught Hiero's excitement and was as eager to be off as he. As soon as they had gulped a meal of five-day-old grouse (now growing a shade high) and biscuits, they set off, all feeling a sense of release after the ordeal behind them.

The moonlit scrub area which lay between them and the tall dunes proved to be mostly berry bushes, intermingled with a few low cactuses of the pincushion variety. The ripe berries, a reddish brown, were tasted by the bear, who at once began to gulp hand- or rather, paw-fuls. The big morse wasted no time in reaching out and lipping in whole branches, and Hiero, after failing to identify the fruit, nevertheless ate a pound of the sweet things himself, and felt the better for it. When all three could hold no more, they ambled on, feeling much too full to set a fast pace.

The white sand dunes, soon reached, proved to be only about a hundred feet high and filled with gullies and other easy methods of gaining the top. In no time, the travellers stood at the summit of one of them and gazed in delight at the sight which lay before them, spread out clear and distinct under the soft light of the three-quarter moon.

They were gazing down at a great bay of the Inland Sea. Directly before them, below and no more than a thousand paces away, was a long white strand, blotched and partially covered with driftwood and flotsam. Straight out to the calm south, the water lay almost motionless until the gaze met the dark horizon of night. Faintly visible to both right and left, tall black promontories guarded the mouth of the bay, which was perhaps five miles deep and twice that wide. No breeze, but the faintest, stirred, hardly enough to ruffle the man's filthy locks. The water was as calm as a bath. The Inland Sea, whose savage storms were legendary, was in a moment of repose and slept, undisturbed by any wind or other atmospheric turbulence.

But all was not lifeless. From the shore below them, and out some few leagues into the bay, great leaves, round and many yards across, floated on the smooth mirror of the water. White flowers, blooms of some enormous lily, opened here and there, and the intoxicating perfume they gave off was so strong that Hiero could almost feel the fragrance as a material thing.

In the open water between the giant lily pads, great dark bodies noisily churned the water into boils of foam and then vanished, only to reappear and shatter the calm surface somewhere else a hundred feet away. A herd of some enormous, feeding animals were disporting themselves, wallowing and splashing in the relative shallows near shore, and as they rose and sank, small waves rolled up the gentle beach and the huge round leaves of the lilies dipped and rocked on the water, set in uneasy motion.

Hiero sat down with a sigh to watch. His hopes of a clean bath in the sea were obviously doomed to postponement. Even allowing for the distortion of night, any one of those things down there would make four of Klootz, big as he was. Gorm and the morse sniffed the breeze in loud snorts, excited at the smells of the night and the noise of the sportive behemoths. Hiero bade them lie down and wait with him.

Presently one of the creatures emerged from the water and waddled out upon the sand directly below the watchers. It was huge, long and low, balanced on four, short, sturdy legs, each with three wide toes. There was a great, blunt head shaped like a long-snouted keg. It yawned suddenly, displaying a pale gullet in the moonlight, which also glinted on huge tushes set at each corner of the gaping jaws. As the water ran off its great back in runnels, a short plush coat of fur began to dry and give the animal a lighter shade of color. Something in looks like a cross between a pre-Death hog, a hippopotamus, and even a Brobdingnagian seal, what its ancestors had been was a mystery. It began to graze contentedly on some short-stemmed plants and the contrast between its peaceable eating habits and otherwise horrendous demeanor made Hiero chuckle.

Faint as the sound was, the great beast heard it and its small ears flapped vigorously as it looked suspiciously about. Deciding the neighborhood was apparently dangerous, even though it could see nothing, it lumbered back into the water, twitching a tiny curled tail, and rejoined its fellows among the enormous lily pads.

Happening to glance beyond the herd and out to sea, the priest caught an even more wonderful sight, which left him dumb with amazement and awe.

From the quiet water out near the mouth of the bay there soared into the moonlit night the black outline of a monster fish, long and slender with a sharp-pointed head, identical in appearance with the pike Hiero was used to hooking in every cool northern lake. For a fleeting instant he felt himself back in his piney wilderness looking at a leaping catch, not on the unknown shores of the warm sea of the South. Then, as he shook his head to clear his vision, the *scale* of what he was seeing came home to him.

"God in Heaven!" he murmured aloud. The titanic falling shape hit the shining water with a crack which echoed like the noise of a colossal thrower shell and the sound echoed back from the distant cliffs. *The fish he had just seen could have swallowed one of the ponderous water beasts below him in two bites!*

He looked down in amazement. A few ripples stirred the giant leaves and tiny wavelets lapped the shore, but otherwise nothing stirred. Only streaks of iridescent oil on the dark water told him that he had not been dreaming. The advent of the Leviathan he had just seen had made the herd of great water hogs vanish as silently as if they had never been there at all.

He waited with his impatient allies for a few more moments, but since the waters remained silent and undisturbed, he decided the big animals must have dived and gone elsewhere. In any event, the dirt and filth accumulated during the journey through the swamps were too unbearable to stand any longer unless absolutely necessary.

Thrower cocked and the butt resting on his hips, Hiero urged his big mount down the white face of the dune. Klootz simply sat on his broad bottom,

67

braked his splayed-out front legs and slid, the bear sliding along next to him.

Once at the bottom, they all paused and looked about them, keen ears and noses testing the breeze for signs of danger. Seeing and hearing nothing, the calm bay before them still undisturbed, they tramped over to the water's edge. To the intense annoyance of the big morse, after unsaddling him, his master told him to stand guard. He stamped off up the beach, grumbling, and took a stance on a hillock of sand, shaking his still-soft antlers in anger.

Gorm waded carefully into water about six inches deep and then lying down, began to roll over and over, emitting 'whoofs' of sheer pleasure. Hiero painfully removed his filthy clothes, save for his linen and shorts, laid them in the sandy shallows, weighted down by a large rock, to soak. He next carefully cleaned his undressed leather boots with a knife and a stiff brush, the latter taken from a saddlebag. This done, he was ready for his own bath. He also did not go very far in. He was a fine swimmer, but the recent glimpse of the local wildlife had cured him of any desire to leap out into the depths. Even where he was, he kept a wary eye out for any suspicious looking ripples or surges. However, nothing disturbed his long-overdue wash and he finally had had enough and came out, bringing with him the bear whose sodden fur, pressed to his plump body, made him look a third smaller.

Grunting with joy, the big bull now rolled happily in the shallows, and chewed up several bales of the nearer lily roots and leaves when he was done, actually diving for some of them, which made Hiero very nervous. Not until Klootz too was out on the beach and drying off under the warmth of the August night, did the man totally relax.

Working by feel, Hiero shaved, a rough but adequate job, and even trimmed his short mustache and his black hair also, so that it hung less heavily over his ears. With a second set of clean leather clothes from the saddlebags and his old ones now drying over some stones, he was able to enjoy the feeling of content that comes from cleanliness after a prolonged spell of enduring compulsory dirt.

A little back from the beach, a spur of grey granite thrust itself out from the sand dunes which had flowed around it over the centuries. Here, the man thought, would be a good place to camp for a day. The rock furnished a shelter on its rearward face, away from the sea, where an overhanging shelf gave access to a narrow cave.

Soon all the contents of the bags were stowed in the cave, and Hiero and the bear were snoring away in close harmony, while the faithful Klootz, chewing his cud and belching comfortably at intervals, maintained an unwearied sentinel's position just in front of the cave's entrance.

Just as Hiero dropped off into a deep and untroubled sleep, he was conscious once again of the harsh, far-off screaming of many birds and mingled with it this time, a muffled resonance, a faint vibration of some kind which he could not identify. Even while his tired brain attempted to form a coherent thought about the distant sounds, sleep overcame him.

He awoke in late morning, feeling better than he had in a week. Had it only been a week since he had left the unused, dusty road far to the North?

He went out of the little cleft in the rocks and found a warm, fresh breeze blowing from the lake, which was a sparkling blue, flecked with many white-caps. Offshore, a great drift of swans were resting, honking and gabbling. They looked as if a great mound of soft snow had been sent down unseasonably from the High Arctic.

His two allies were so full of high spirits that they were playing a game out on the open sand. The small bear would charge at the morse, snarling in apparent savagery and the big bull would try desperately to hook him with his palmate antlers, always "missing" but at least a full bear length. When that happened the bear would tear around in circles trying to catch his stub of a tail, while Klootz would rear up on his hind feet and paw the air madly with his immense bony front legs and platter-like hooves.

Hiero was so amused at the two that for a moment he forgot the possible danger of the aerial spy they had encountered previously. When he did, he quickly scanned the sunlit heavens, but except for a few small, puffy clouds, they were empty of motion. Nevertheless, he was disturbed. They had escaped several unpleasant deaths only by the narrowest of margins, and only a good day's ride away had he himself managed to destroy the tell-tale instrument which he had so thoughtlessly carried in his saddlebag. A sudden feeling of euphoria could get them all killed just as quickly as a blunder into an obvious trap. It was when you were feeling at your best you were apt to relax, sometimes with fatal results!

He saw nothing dangerous, however, and could not help wishing he had four legs of his own so that he could join the game. As he watched, keeping a weather eye out in all directions, he thought about his further plans. For over four days the flying thing had apparently been absent. Why not try daylight travel? As they moved along the seashore, going east, it would be dangerous enough moving even in daylight, and they would need the extra vision time given by the rays of the sun. That was it, he decided. Unless he saw the flyer or found some hitherto unknown danger menacing them, they would travel by day from now on.

The two animals noticed him at this point and came gambolling over, sending up showers of sand.

Feeling good, eh, sent Hiero. *You're a fine pair of guards! I could have been eaten/caught/killed by now* (time past!)

They both knew he was fooling and paid not the slightest attention, except that Klootz bunted him gently with his antlers, making him stagger and catch hold lest he fall. He felt the horn, hard and getting sharper, under the soft velvet as he did so, and indeed, a piece of the latter peeled off in his hand.

Ha! he sent. *Stand still, you big oaf, and* (let me) *try to clean you* (up a bit) *scrape/peel/rub.*

The morse shook his head ornaments vigorously and then stood quietly while Hiero tested each section to see how loose the covering was. Like most male deer, Klootz had to grow new antlers each year, and it not only took a lot of energy but made him nervous and itched badly as well, particularly when, as now, the velvet was peeling and shredding to reveal the hard core beneath. The Abbey scientists had long ago discarded the idea of breeding the antlers out. For almost half the year they provided superb weapons of defense, and in addition they made their wearers feel tough and confident. It was decided that the energy saved by eliminating them would be a bad bargain, and anyone who wanted to ride or drive an antlerless cow, such as most farmers used, could do so.

Hiero peeled a small amount of the covering off with his fingers, but whenever he met any resistence, let it alone. He and Klootz both knew how much help was needed and when to stop, for it had been six full seasons since they had chosen each other at the great annual calf roundup. Hiero next got out a small steel mirror and touched up his face, shaving more carefully and repainting his rank badges, now almost obliterated. This done, he re-packed.

Soon they were swinging along up the edge of the beach, Hiero in the saddle and the bear lumbering over the hard-packed sand and shingle out in front. It was not long before they came upon signs that they were back in lands used by humans.

From a pile of rip-rap, sticks and dried weed, which lay on the shore in a little cove, a polished human skull looked blankly up at Hiero. He dismounted and examined it thoughtfully. There was a gaping hole in the occiputal region and a few faint shreds of dried tissue there indicated the thing to be not too old. He put it down reverently and mounting, rode on. It might be an accident, indeed there were a thousand ways of accounting for its appearance, but why a fairly fresh skull and no body at all, not even one bone? That hole looked like something (or someone) had gone after the brains. He suppressed a grimace and said a one-line prayer for the repose of the skull's owner, assuming charitably that the man (or woman) had been a Christian.

They rested briefly at noon in the shade of a large leaning tree of a variety new to Hiero. He recognized it as a palm of some unknown type, from pictures he had seen and realized that winter could hardly be too severe in these parts if such a plant could endure it. The scrub palmettoes of the Taig were able to grow only through buried trunks. He must be even further south than he had realized.

During the still heat of early afternoon they had one encounter with a foe, but it passed off without doing any harm. Rounding a shoulder of rock, and actually in shallow water, since the beach had briefly disappeared, they suddenly found a large, black-spotted, yellow cat tearing at a carcass on the next patch of open sand.

The big cat raised bloody fangs and snarled in angry warning.

Go! suddenly deciding to test something, Hiero used a bolt from his new armory of mental weapons. *Leave! out of our way or you will die!*

The animal cringed as if hit a blow by a stick. Its ears flattened and emitting a frightened "miaow", like a vast kitten which had been spanked, it left the beach in one huge bound and vanished into the dunes in a second. Hiero was thunderstruck at his own success, and then burst into laughter.

He got off and picked up the carcass, a small striped antelope of some sort, hardly touched by the cat. It must have just been beginning to feed. Here was easily-obtained food for himself and Gorm! He slung it carefully before him on the saddle. Klootz did not ruffle a long ear. Blood was nothing new to him, and he had carried far worse burdens than this one.

Some time later, the priest, idly glancing out to sea, reined his mount up sharply, making him snort with annoyance. *Sorry, an accident,* sent Hiero absently. Far out on the blue wave-flecked water, two small black triangles were outlined against the horizon. The ship was moving along in the same direction they were, the man decided after watching it for a few moments, but far faster. Also, it seemed to be going away as well as east, so that even as he watched, it sank below the edge of the sea.

As he rode on, he made a note to keep more of an eye seaward. A telescope could probably pick Klootz and his rider out at long way off, and he had no desire to end up in one of the pagan galleys he had read of, chained to an oar with a ship instead of meals. Also, the Unclean had ships too, of some curious types, and they were supposed to haunt little-used parts of the vast freshwater sea.

They were approaching a dark promontory of rock some hundreds of feet high, which projected out into the water for a short distance when the noise first came to them. It was late afternoon by then and they had seen nothing of note for a considerable time. Hiero was wondering how deep the choppy water was at the foot of the rock massif and whether the going would be safer, if more time-consuming, inland when the rattling, screeching cry, the noise of a bird redoubled tenfold, fell upon his ears. Again, and yet again, it rang out and then he saw it.

Briefly, over the crest of the towering, jagged rock in front of them soared a brown bird whose sail-like wing-spread could not have been less than thirty feet. Before it dipped down again on the far side of the peak, it opened its long, hook-tipped beak and let out a repetition of the scream he had just heard. Other echoing screams answered it, and told him that more than one of the great birds were aloft just out of sight.

Then mingled with the rasping cries of the birds, an unmistakable drum thundered out, a long roll of muffled thunder. When it ceased he heard the massed yelling of a horde of people mixed with the piercing cacophony of the birds. Again the great drum rumbled, silencing for a moment the other noises. This was the noise Hiero had heard the previous dawn!

By this time, at his master's urging, Klootz was racing for the seaward base of the jutting rock. Behind him, tongue lolling out, Gorm gallopped, laboring to keep up.

Not curiousity alone impelled Hiero to goad the morse on. The base of the rock was an obvious place to hide, should one of the huge birds sight him. The look of that immense hooked beak was dismaying, and the priest had no belief in his invulnerability from a flock of things that size.

Splashing through the shallows and circling the water-lapped boulders at the foot of the precipice, man and morse picked their way around the looming granite elbow and finally, both cautious, peered around the outer rim to see what had caused all the peculiar noises. Behind them, allowing them to first brave whatever danger there might be, the young bear paused, waiting on events.

The first thing Hiero was conscious of was the stake and the girl, the next the great birds, and last of all the spectators. He did not at first notice the shaman or witchdoctor, and his crew.

A short stretch of curved beach sloped gently away from the sea, up to a high and artificial looking bank of packed earth, which backed the beach, cutting off any glimpse of further inland. A sort of arena, or amphitheatre was thus formed, one side wall being the cliff around which Hiero and Klootz now peered, the other being a similar abrupt rocky hillock a few hundred yards away. The sea, lapping at the white sand, formed the fourth side. The little beach was swept spotlessly clean, only the tall, wooden stake in the center interfering with the symmetry of the smooth, white sand.

Tied to the stake by a length of supple, twisted rawhide perhaps fifty feet long, was a very dark-skinned, almost naked girl. A scanty rag about her loins was her only garment and her feet were bare. Her massed, tightly-curling black hair tossed freely in the vigor of her movements. The rawhide was tied tightly to another lashing which secured both her wrists together in front of her. As a result, she could run, leap, dodge or hide, turn or fall, but only in a fifty-foot arc around the wooden stake. She was doing all these things, her body a sweat-oiled blaze of dark movement, as she sprang and crouched, ducked and spun, in her hopeless battle against the winged death.

The great birds! There were about eight of them, Hiero saw in one glance. Somewhat like giant gulls, but brown, not white, and with savage beaks, they circled and wove, always slashing down at the leashed prisoner. Like gulls too, their great feet were webbed and thus they seemed only to use their murderous beaks as weapons. But that was enough. Despite her most desperate efforts it was obvious the girl could only hold them off a little longer. As he watched, she scooped fine sand into her bound hands and hurled a cloud of it at the head of a swooping flier, which shied off with a scream of rage. But a long, bloody wound on her glistening back showed that the girl had not warded off all the attacks from above.

As the bird sheered off, the crowd let out a yell of derision. They made Hiero look at them then, with more than a passing glance. They sat in wicker-roofed lines of dirt seats, arranged in tiers on the earth back at the rear of the arena they had so obviously created. The roofs were not because of the sun, obviously, but rather to keep the birds from selecting an impromptu victim from among the screaming audience.

They were very light-skinned, Hiero saw, an archaic human stock he had only glimpsed among the southern traders once or twice, or else learned of through the old books, and many of them had light-brown or even blondish hair. All, men, women and children, seemed to be half-naked and all were armed, no doubt as extra insurance against the birds. They were waving every type of sword, spear and axe as they yelled a raucous encouragement to the flying deaths.

To one side, a group of kilted men, hideously masked, and with towering plumes of feathers, presided over a bank of giant polished drums. These people had no protection from the birds, and apparently no fear of them either. Now, as Hiero watched, they bent to their drums and under the direction of the most gorgeously-masked and feathered, the obvious high priest, beat out

73

another rumbling roll of thunder on the tall black cylinders. The audience screamed anew, and their cries were taken up by the birds, who stooped again, their shrieks drowning out the human yowling. Then suddenly, all noise ceased and the arena was silent in shocked surprise at what they now saw.

Hiero had ordered Klootz to charge and unlimbered the thrower almost without thinking. He also held two more of the tiny rockets in his mouth, praying he might get a chance to reload. As the bull morse tore out of the shallows and around the corner of the cliff, his rider noted in passing that a group of swarthy men, in good cloth clothes and leather hats quite unlike the rest of the audience, occupied the seats nearest to his end. Like all the others, they were gaping in amazement.

The great birds, seeing the charging bull and his rider as some terrible combined beast, flared lightly up like great feathers from their attempted kill. All except one, which was so intent upon the girl that it noticed nothing else.

She had fallen in a wild leap, and in falling had apparently knocked all her wind out. She was crawling, but as the bird sailed down, she seemed to sense it and turned face up with her bound hands raised in front of her.

She's still trying to fight, the priest thought in admiration. *That's really a tough one.* He was aiming his thrower as carefully as was possible, to intersect the great bird's stoop. Practice over a long period of time in handling all of his weapons while mounted made this sort of thing a matter of trained reflex, but never exactly what could be called easy. One went through the proper motions and then simply prayed.

The prayer or the training, possibly both, worked. The propellant fired perfectly, and the rocket hit the bird monster smack between the shoulders. There was an incandescent blaze of white fire and the two great, brown wings, no longer connected to one another, sailed to the ground, a few charred rags drifting away from between them.

Hiero had slashed the leather thong connecting the girl to the post and puller her across the saddle on top of the stiffening antelope carcass before the still-stunned audience began to wake up. Circling high above, one of the great birds screamed once, fearful of coming lower or perhaps mourning the death of a mate.

As if the cry were a signal, an answering yell of rage broke from the flock's aroused patrons. Mounting in one movement, Hiero knew his spell was broken and that a shower of lethal missiles was next on the agenda.

"Travel, boy!" he shouted aloud, whacking Klootz with the wooden stock of his thrower. Only as he yelled did he remember the two shells in his teeth and the fact that in yelling he had to let them fall. He holstered the thrower, pressing the girl tightly to the pommel with his left hand. Fortunately she was either stunned or had good sense, for she made no move and lay absolutely limp, face down.

As they raced in the only possible direction, the water's edge at the far side of the arena to the east, Hiero saw the first spear hit the sand by one of Klootz's great legs. The next instant he heard the whistle of more, and worse, of arrows, one of which buried itself in the thick saddle with an audible "thonk."

But his chief attention was ahead. The tall plumed priest who led the drummers had abandoned his drums and followed by his gaudily-dressed followers, was rushing down to block their escape. As they neared him, the rain of arrows ceased, since the crowd did not wish to kill their own men.

The priest ran well in front of his men waving a long sword and Hiero made a very quick decision. The high shaman had discarded his mask; in the pale, narrow face and blazing blue eyes, Hiero read both fanaticism and intelligence. This was not a follower one needed or wanted. The man could have been avoided, but weakening the opposition was a better strategy.

Kill him, Klootz! he sent, even as he tightened his grip on the helpless girl, for he knew what was coming.

The great bull swerved slightly to the left and ran as if to pass just in front of the leader of the enemy. The shaman, fearful of missing his blow, ran a trifle harder. And as his arm went back for a hard cut, he died.

With hardly a break in his stride, the battle-trained morse lashed out in one of his awful stiff kicks, using his giant left foreleg. The terrible hoof took the priest squarely in the stomach and hurled him, broken-backed, and gushing his life blood away, back into the arms of his followers. The morse raced on and before the first yell of rage and despair had rung out, he was already in the shallows and thundering around the wall of the eastern cliff.

To his delight, Hiero saw that a long stretch of empty beach stretched for miles into the distance before them. Nobody on foot was going to catch them now, and he urged Klootz on, hoping to make the lead as long as possible. The only obstacle he could see was a small river, whose waters glinted in the late afternoon sun about a half mile off. It did not look particularly wide or deep, and he felt sure that only the middle would require swimming, if indeed any of it did.

He looked back and saw a few black figures on the sand near the cliff, waving their arms and leaping up and down, and he smiled in contempt. Then, as the act of looking back made his memory work, a sudden thought came to him. Gorm! Where was his friend and guide? Had he been slain? Even as he thought this, his mount caught the thought and answered, once again surprising the priest with the realization that he would probably never know just how smart Klootz was.

He (will) *follow/track/smell out* (later), came from the morse's mind. *He goes* (away) *not/near water*. Having delivered this message, the morse lapsed into silence and once more concentrated on running steadily over the long white strand toward the rapidly approaching river.

The shrill screech of one of the giant birds came to Hiero and he looked up quickly, wondering if they were going to attack or could be somehow controlled, perhaps by the priests. He could not take time off from his escape to concentrate mentally and probe the bird minds, or indeed any minds at this point. He had not forgotten the lonely skull and the hole in its back where a great beak had almost certainly probed. To his relief, the little flock of remaining birds was circling far above, and even as he watched, they flew out to sea, no doubt heading for some distant island rookery. The interuption of their routine of human sacrifice apparently had confused them and rendered them incapable of further harm.

A torrent of high pitched, angry and unintelligible speech suddenly broke out from the rescued prisoner and at the same time she began to kick and squirm vigorously. Hiero reined up, and looked around. The river was a few hundred yards off still, and the ant-like figures of their enemies were barely visible in the distance behind them.

"I might as well free you, young woman," he said aloud and hauled the girl upright, turning her as he did so that she sat facing him over the front of the saddle, the dead antelope serving as a seat for her. He had been reaching for his belt knife to cut the leather which still bound her wrists together, but at the first good look at her his hand stopped and he simply stared. Quite unabashed, she stared back.

She was totally unlike anyone he had ever seen before, but in spite of that, lovely, in a rather wild and untamed way. Her skin was far darker than his, a warm chocolate, as contrasted with his copper color, and her great dark eyes were no lighter in shade than his own black. Her nose was moderately long and very straight, her nostrils quite widely flared out, and her dark lips very full and pouting. The great mass of her hair was a tangled, uncombed heap of tight, almost screwed, black curls, each of which looked like black wire. Her firm, brown breasts were not large and gave the priest the feeling that she was considerably younger than he had first supposed. Metz women covered their upper bodies, but he instinctively sensed that nakedness meant nothing to this

76

one. He doubted somehow that the loss of the very short and ragged skirt she wore would have bothered her at all.

She had been studying his bronzed, hawk-nosed face, with its short, black mustache even as he had studied her, and now she held up her bound hands and said something impatient in her unknown language. Obviously, she wanted to be cut loose and Hiero did so, and then lifted her again and turned her forward so that she now sat astride in front of him, facing in the same direction. He noted in doing so that her slim waist seemed to be muscled with steel and leather.

Once again he urged Klootz on toward the river. For some reason he could not fathom, some thought at the very back of his mind, the sight of the not-very-imposing stream disturbed him. It was as if some important fact were tied to it which it was necessary to remember. Something to do with the people back there perhaps? *Now what the devil was it, anyway?* A feeling of guilt at risking the possible success of his whole venture at a moment's hazard for a girl he had never seen before? Could it be that? *No, not that, damn it, the* river. *Think of the river!*

The flash of mnemonic lightning hit his mind a bit late, in fact, just as they reached the river's brink and saw the long, log canoe, hard-driven by a dozen paddlers, sweeping down the muddy center channel at them. As the white-skinned rowers spotted them, a fierce yell rang out and they bent even harder to their paddles.

The village, of course! Hidden from any sea raiders, it must lie up this river, since he had not passed it earlier. What had been plaguing his mind was the buried realization that there had to be a village close by from which all those women and children could have walked. Now a message had been sent to the village guard, perhaps, indeed almost certainly by crude but adequate telepathy. This art was common not just in Metzland, but among almost all living people at least in some small degree. The savage priests were probably pretty good.

As all this flashed through his mind, he was feverishly loading the thrower, and at the same time kicking Klootz into the water. If they got trapped on this bank . . .! Better to now take a chance in the water. The channel was probably only a few yards wide and once across the level beach stretched on out of sight, empty and inviting.

In front of him, saying nothing, the girl reached down and lifted the broad spear out of its saddle sling. The casual arrogance of the gesture made Hiero grin in spite of their predicament. This was indeed a tough, young animal!

Hiero's luck with the thrower ran out this time, but it was partly his own fault, as he was the first to admit. He waited too long to fire, so that when Klootz stepped off into the channel at the exact instant the rocket shell ignited, the aim was hopelessly spoiled. Not only that, but the canoe was too close to allow a reload, its sharp prow thrusting down upon them in midstream, even as the morse swam mightily for the shallower water on the other side.

But they had never seen, let alone, fought a morse before, nor had they any conception of the deadly Abbey killer teams of morse and man. Hiero threw both arms around the girl, gripped tight with his legs and ordered Klootz to dive. *Down, boy, down!* sent his mind, *come* (up) *under them!* As the bull porpoised down under the surface toward the oncoming canoe, Hiero saw the slack-jawed surprise on the faces of the pale savages, several of whom had dropped their paddles and had lifted weapons for the kill.

Klootz, through cleverness or luck, Hiero never would learn, came up gently, though firmly, from off the river bottom, which was not far under. Hiero, eyes shut, crouching over his rescued prize in an effort to shield her, felt the bottom of the canoe slide off his own back, pressing him down even harder, flattening him on top of the girl and the dead antelope. When the sliding canoe hit his crupper though, which was the next thing to happen, Klootz abandoned gentleness and simply heaved up with all the enormous power in his great hindquarters.

The two half-drowned humans and morse erupted out of the water and into the light as the loaded canoe, hurled straight up in the air, broke and threw its occupants in various directions into the churning water. They could all swim and there seemed to be none dead, Hiero noted in relief, as Klootz splashed through the muddy shallows and out on to the eastern marge. The priest could be ruthless enough to enemies of decent humanity and the Abbey, but he disliked killing men and women whose chief fault was ignorance, for which they ought not to be blamed.

Amid spluttered cries and curses, whose nature was evident from the looks and gestures of those who made them, the morse again bore his two riders away down the strand into the east.

The long rays of the half-set sun cast gigantic shadows before them as they went, Hiero now had released his death-grip on the girl, and she sat firmly in front of him, apparently none the worse for the experience. The cut on her shoulder and back had begun to bleed again though, and he signalled the morse to come to a halt after a mile or two. Lifting her down, he smiled as he saw that she still clung to the spear.

"You can put that back," he said, pointing at the saddle socket in which it belonged.

She gabbled something, looked about, shrugged as she saw no visible danger and (reluctantly, he thought) restored the weapon to its place.

As Hiero got out his medical kit, she watched with interest, and when he indicated that he wanted to sew up the lips of the wound before bandaging it, she merely nodded. Whether this indicated native trust, ignorance of suturing or what, Hiero had no idea. Even with the Abbey's salve it was a painful process, but aside from tightening her lips once or twice, she gave no sign that it hurt. Finally the wound was stitched and bandaged, and the priest lifted her up on the morse again, while he re-packed his belongings. When he was through, he noticed that she was leaning over Klootz's long neck and scratching behind his flapping ears, something he loved dearly. Hiero gave her another good grade for liking and understanding animals.

Once mounted, he looked back, but he could see no sign of pursuit. Inland rose the same lines of dunes which had accompanied them all the way so far, except where the rock spines of the subsoil broke through, and he felt sure the swamp began and still stretched endlessly on, only a few miles beyond that.

It was late evening now, the low clouds red in the West and the sun's disk altogether gone. It was high time to look for a camp site, but they had only come a few miles and he had no idea how good the savages were at tracking. His decision to kill the shaman might have merely enraged them instead of helping to hinder pursuit by forcing them to ritually mourn the death of a leader. The girl too, ought to have rest and food very soon. She might be as tough as she appeared but what she had been through that day would have tired a strong man. The priest himself felt weary and he had endured far less.

Another hour's ride and in the full dark, more water loomed up. It was impossible to see how broad it was, and it would be insane to try swimming it in dark. Reluctantly, Hiero turned the morse inland, following the bank of the stream or inlet, and keeping double watch in case anything large came out of it and wanted dinner.

Their progress was necessarily slow and grew slower yet as cacti, vines and woody plants grew more common. Eventually, peering about on the side away from the water, Hiero caught sight of a dark hillock somewhat to their left. He steered Klootz that way and to his surprise found that the "hillock" was an enormous, rounded bush or low tree, about forty feet high, with a stout, central trunk. Its branches hung nearly to the ground and provided as close to a natural tent as one could hope to find.

Once "inside," after they had unloaded and unsaddled the morse, Hiero dismissed him to feed and mount guard, simultaneously. He decided to risk a very small fire of twigs, and after he had gathered them and got it lit, realized that no good reason for it existed, save to look at the girl. This discovery annoyed him.

She had sat quietly, arms around her knees while he unloaded and puttered. As he got food from the packs and water from the big canteen, she accepted a share in silence, but made no effort to talk. Eventually, the short meal over, she brushed a few crumbs from her lap and once again stared levelly and impersonally at him over the light of the wee fire. It was obviously time for some attempt to communicate.

Actually, it took only four tries. She did not speak Metz or Inyan of the western type, or understand the silent sign language. But when Hiero tried *batwah,* the trade language of the merchants, she smiled for the first time and answered. Her accent was very odd, if not downright bad, he thought, and many of her nouns were utterly strange to him. He guessed, rightly as it proved, that he came from a place at one end of a very long trade route and that she was from far off, either near or at its other extremity.

"What kind of man are you?" was her first remark. "You look something like a slaver, like those who sold me, but you ride that wonderful fighting animal, and you got me away from those pale-skinned barbarians. But you owe me nothing? Why did you do it?"

"Let's have a few facts first from you," he countered. "What's your name and who are you and where do you come from?"

"I am Luchare," she said. Her voice was rather high-pitched but not nasal. She spoke with pride, not arrogance, just pride. *I am who I am* was the unspoken message, that of one who valued herself. Hiero liked her, but kept that fact to himself.

"Very interesting, Luchare," he said, "and a pretty name, no doubt of it. But what about my other questions? Where is your home? How did you get here?" *And what am I to do about you?* was the unspoken one.

"I ran away from my home," she said. Her voice, like his, was now flat and emotionless, but she watched him carefully, her eyes bright in the firelight. "My home is far off, far beyond this sea, I think there." She turned and pointed unerringly to the northwest in the direction of the Republic.

"I think it unlikely," said the priest in a dry tone, "because that's where *I* come from, and I never heard of anyone like you before. But don't worry about direction," he added in a voice he tried to soften, "that's not important. Tell me about your country. Is it like this? What are your people like? You called those white people who set the birds on you 'barbarians.'

That's an odd term for a slave girl to use."

Their conversation, it may be added, was not at first this smooth and continuous. There were many gaps, fumblings for alternate terms, corrections of pronounciation and explanations of new words. But both were highly intelligent and quick at adapting. As a result, it went at an increasing rate of progress.

"My people are a mighty and strong one," she said firmly. "They live in great cities of stone, not dirty huts of hide and leaves. They are great warriors too, and not even the big horned one could have saved you as he did this afternoon if it had been they you fought."

Just like a women, thought Hiero bitterly, *give Klootz all the credit.* "All right," he said. "your people are great and strong. But what are you doing here, which I gather must be a long way off from wherever you started?"

"First," she said firmly, "it would be more correct if you told me who *you* are, where you are from and what rank you held in your own country."

"I am Per Hiero Desteen, Priest, Scholar and senior Killman of the Church Universal. And I fail to see why a barerumped chit of a slave girl cares what rank the man who has rescued her from an exceedingly nasty death!" He glared angrily at her, but he might as well have spared himself the effort.

"Your church can't be all that universal," she said calmly, "if I haven't heard of it. Which is not surprising since it just so happens, Sir Priest, that we happen to have the only true church in my country, and if someone went around looking like you, with silly paint on his face, saying he was a priest, they'd put him in the house for mad people. And furthermore," she went on in the same flat lecturing voice, "I was not always a slave girl, as any man with breeding, sense or manners, could tell who looked at me!"

Despite his Abbey training in handling people, Hiero found her very annoying. "I beg your pardon, your ladyship," he rejoined acidly. "You were, I suppose, a princess in your own mighty kingdom, perhaps betrothed to an unwelcome suitor and forced to flee as a result, rather than marry him?"

Luchare stared open-mouthed at him. "How did you know that? Are you some spy of my father's or of Efrem, sent to bring me back?"

Hiero in turn stared back hard at her, before laughing in a nasty way. "My God, you've grabbed up the fantasy of every girl child who has first heard the legends of the ancient past. Now stop trying to waste my time on this silliness, will you? I want to know about wherever you come from, and I solemnly warn you, I have my own methods of finding out, even if the manners you boast of, plus a little common gratitude, don't get me the answers I want freely given! Now start talking! Where in the known universe do you come from and if you really don't even know that, at least tell me the name of the place, what it's like and how you got here!"

The girl looked at him darkly, her eyes narrowed, as if in thought. Then, as if she had come to a decision, her face cleared, and she spoke reasonably and in softer tones.

"I am very sorry, Per Hiero (is that right?), I honestly didn't mean to be rude. I've made believe I was someone extra important so long that it's hard to be normal again. I come from a country which I guess is south of here, only as you saw just now I don't know where south is. I did really live in a city, and the country especially the wilds, are not what I'm used to. Oh, yes, my country is called D'alwah, and part of it lies on the coast, the salt sea of Lantik. What else did you want to know?"

"Well," said Hiero more cheerfully. "That's quite a bit better. I'm not really as nasty as I just sounded. Only remember that I'm fond of straight talk, my girl. Save the fairy tales for the kids from now on and we'll get along. To start with, how did you get into the fix where I found you?"

As the tiny fire grew dimmer until it was only an unregarded, winking ember, Luchare spun her tale. Hiero still believed not more than two thirds of it, but even that was interesting enough to hold him rivetted.

Judging from her description, she did indeed come from the far south and east, in fact just about where he himself wanted to go. Which made him listen to every word she dropped with extra special attention.

Her country was a land of walled cities and giant trees, a tropical forest which reached up to the very sky. It was also a land of constant warfare, of blood and death, of great beasts and warlike men. A church and a priesthood not too unlike that of the Abbeys, so far as he could gather, governed the religion of the people, and preached peace and co-operation. But the priests were seemingly incapable of stopping the constant warfare between the various city states. These states were socially stratified, with castes of nobles, merchants, artisans and peasants, plus autocratic rulers. There were standing armies, just as large as could be economically maintained without crippling their respective countries through taxation exacted from the peasants to maintain them.

Hiero was frankly incredulous. "Can your people read and write?" he asked. "Have they any of the old books of the past? Do you know of The Death?"

Of course they could read and write, she retorted. Or at least the priesthood and most of the nobles could. The poor were kept too busy to learn, except the few who got into the church. The merchants could do simple practical arithmetic. What more was needed? As for The Death, everyone knew about it. Were not many of the Lost Cities nearby, and some of the deserts of The Death too? But books from the pre-Death age were forbidden, except perhaps to the priesthood. She herself had never seen one, though she had heard of their existence and also that anyone who found one had to turn it over to the authorities on pain of death.

"Good God!" exploded the Metz. "Your people (and I'm assuming that most of what you've told me is the truth) have picked up all the discarded social junk of the dead past at its worst. I knew some of the traders down here had slaves, but I thought they were probably the most primitive people we knew about. The Eastern League at Otwah can't have heard about you either, because they're not far behind us, if any. Kingdoms, peasants, internicine warfare, armies, slavery and general illiteracy! What your D'alwah place needs is a thorough house-cleaning!"

His obvious disgust silenced the girl, who bit her full lower lip in anger at his open contempt. She was nothing near being stupid, and she knew that her strange rescuer was both a clever and more, a learned man. For the first time in a long while, Luchare began to wonder if her long-for homeland was quite as perfect as her dreams made it.

"I'm sorry," said Hiero abruptly. "I was rude about your country and you had nothing to do with making it the way it is. I've never seen it and it's probably a very nice place. It sounds interesting, anyway. Please go on with your own story. I'd like to hear what brought you so far from the Lantik Sea. I know how far away *that* is, at least up in the north."

"Well," she began, a little doubtfully, "I ran away, from my—my slave master, who was cruel to me. I really did," she said earnestly, her dark eyes large in the dim light.

"Oh, I believe you. Go on from there. How long ago was that?"

It had been well over a year, Luchare thought. It had been hard at first, and she had learned to steal food from peasant huts. Wild animals had almost caught her on several occasions, but she had got toughened up and had weapons too, also stolen, a spear and a knife. She had lived thus on the cultivated lands at the edge of a great jungle for several months, until one day she had fallen from a tree, breaking her ankle. While waiting for the inevitable prowling animal to find her, an Elevener had come instead.

"What, you have them too?" he interrupted. "I had no idea they went so far. What do they do in your society? Are they well thought of, do people trust them?" He was really excited, for here at last was an actual link between the two widely separated areas from which they came.

The "Eleveners," the mysterious followers of the so-called Eleventh Commandment, were a group of wandering men whose little-known order dated back to The Death itself and perhaps even before. They wore simple clothes of brown cloth, were strict vegetarians and carried no weapons beyond a belt knife and a wooden staff. They seldom appeared in groups and indeed were usually alone. They wandered from place to place, harming no one, occasionally doing some work for keep, teaching children their letters or watching flocks. They were skilled physicians and always ready to help the sick and injured. They hated the works of the Unclean, but sought no trouble with anyone, unless actually attacked. They had strange powers over animals and even the Leemutes usually avoided them.

No one knew where their headquarters was, or even if they had one, nor how they were recruited or where. They seemed to be utterly apolitical, but many of the Metz politicians and even some of the Abbey hierarchs distrusted and disliked them. When pressed such people could never say why, however, except that the Eleveners "must be hiding something." For they were no Christians, or if they were, they concealed it well. They professed a vague pantheism, in line with their ancient (apocryphal, the Abbey scholars said) commandment: "Thou shalt not destroy the Earth nor the Life thereon."

Hiero had always liked the ones he had met, finding them merry, decent men, who behaved far better than many of the self-proclaimed leaders of his own country. And he knew, too, that Abbot Demero both liked and, more important, trusted them.

He was leaning over, intent on further questions, when with a strangled cry, Luchare sprang over almost dead coals right into his arms, knocking him flat on his back in the process.

5: *On to the East*

"Look out!" she yelled, "a monster behind you! I saw it! Something black with long teeth! Get up and fight, quick!"

It had been over three weeks since he had even spoken to a woman, reflected Hiero, as he held her warm body tightly and made no effort to move. She smelled sweetly of girl, perspiration and something else, something wild and fierce.

"That's my bear," he said mildly. "He's a friend and won't hurt you!" As he spoke, his mouth was pressed against a mass of warm, scented hair and a soft cheek. Hiero had detected Gorm some ten minutes back and sent him a mental order to stay outside the tree's domed shelter, but the inquisitive young bear had wanted to look at the stranger.

Luchare pushed herself off him and glared down at his smiling face. "So, what they say about priests is true, eh? A bunch of lazy womanizers and sneaking skirt-lifters! Don't get any clever ideas, Priest! I can defend myself and I will, too!"

Hiero sat up and brushed himself off. Next, he carefully threw a few more twigs on the fire, so that it flared up, illuminating his copper skin and high cheekbones.

"Now, listen, young lady," he said, "let's get everything straight. I was the one jumped on just now, not the other way around. I'm a healthy, normal man, and regardless of what takes place down south in your peculiar-sounding country, Abbey priests have no vows of celibacy and are in fact, usually married, by my age, at least twice! However, we do have rather firm rules against rape and any similar forced consent. Also, I am not in the habit of making love to children and rather think you're about fifteen. Am I right?" As he spoke he was patting Gorm, who had now crawled all the way in and was lying with his head in the man's lap, peering short-sightedly at the girl across the fire.

"I'm seventeen, almost eighteen," she said in indignant tones, "and priests aren't supposed to go around with women, at least ours don't. Who ever heard of a married priest?" In a lower voice, she halfway apologized. "I'm sorry, but how was I to know? You never said anything about that new animal. And how did you know he was there, anyway? I heard nothing and I have good ears."

"I accept the apology," said the priest. "And I might as well interrupt your story briefly and spell out a few more things, since we're apparently going to be travelling together for some time, until I can figure out what to do with you. Does anyone in your country have the ability to speak with his mind? That is, send silent thoughts, so that without using his (or her) voice another person or perhaps an animal can understand him?"

Luchare drew back, lips parted slightly, her dark, brown skin reflecting the firelight in soft shadowed movements.

"The Unclean, the evil monsters from the days of The Death, are said to do this thing," she said slowly. "And there are many rumors (which I know now to be true) that they are ruled by the most wicked of men, horrible sorcerers, who also have this power. An old church priest who taught me my lessons, a good old man, said that such powers of the mind might not themselves be evil in theory, but that in actual practice only the Unclean and their devils seemed to know how to make use of them." Her eyes brightened suddenly. "I see! You knew that animal was out there by thinking to him! But you are not one of the——" Her voice failed as she realized that she might be in the presence of one of the nightmares of her childhood, a wizard of the diabolic enemy!

Hiero smiled cheerfully. "Unclean? No, Luchare, I'm not. And neither is Gorm here. *Gorm, go over slowly, lie down and put your head in her lap. She has* (never) *seen a bear* (I think?) *or believed* (been taught) *in thought speech/mind sending. We'll* (have to) *teach her like a cub.*

The slim, dark brown girl sat frozen, as the small bear ambled over and did as he had been directed. But when a long, pink tongue came out and gently licked her hand, she relaxed a little.

"You—you told him to do that, didn't you?" she said in a shaky voice. "You really can talk to him, just as you do to me?"

"Not as easily, no. But he's very clever, in fact, I'm not sure how exactly clever he is. He's really something almost as new to me as to you, and we've only been together a week. Now Klootz, my bull morse, the big fellow outside, has been my partner for years. I can talk to him easily, but he's nowhere near as clever as Gorm here. Still, he fools me at times too, and just

86

when I think I know the limits of his brain he tries something brand new and surprises me."

"Gorm," she said softly, stroking the furry, black head. "Will you be my friend, Gorm?"

"He'll be your friend, don't worry," said Hiero. "And he's also a very effective guide and scout. But now please be quiet for a few moments. I want to ask him how he got here. We parted when I went clumping out in the open to pick you up." He leaned forward and concentrated on Gorm's mind.

The bear, it seemed, had drawn back behind the rocky point as soon as he had seen where Klootz was heading. He had tried to make mental contact with the departing priest, but realized quickly that it would be hopeless in all the confusion. He had, however, picked up *other* telepathic minds, not Hiero's, although he could not make out what message they were sending.

I think that was our enemies (who were) *trying to get people to hunt/stop/attack us from in front,* sent Hiero. *How did you/Gorm smell/find* (us)?

Easy/cub/trick, came the answer. *Went* (back from) *big water, walked along - came down to big water - smelled - went back - swam small water above men's houses - came down* (again) *followed and smelled your trail.*

By that time, Gorm had come to the hut village of the white savages, most of whom were back from their bird arena, and were milling around and all making a fearful racket in the night. He had watched for awhile and then, seeing that the villagers had a large pack of yelping dogs, he had quietly swum the little river and gone on east, returning to the beach to pick up Klootz's tracks and then simply followed them until he found their present camp.

The priest decided that pursuit that night sounded very unlikely, and they could relax and trust Klootz and the bear to warn them. Settling himself once again, he recommended questioning Luchare where he had left off.

"The Elevener? Why, he looked like anyone else, an ordinary man of my people, perhaps fifty or so years old, except for those drab, brown clothes. Why?"

"That's very interesting," said Hiero. "In your country, it's obvious, the people are all as dark-skinned as you, have that curly hair and those dark, dark eyes, right?"

"Of course, why? Until I ran away, I never saw anyone of another color, except once or twice a white-skinned slave from the North, from around here I guess. But the few Eleveners I've seen have all been of my own people."

"Well," said the man thoughtfully, his eyes fixed on the tiny fire, "up *my* way, they all look like *my* people, that is with bronze or the Inyan reddish skin, straight black hair, high cheekbones, and so on. Which, I think, tells us something interesting about the Eleveners that the Abbeys hadn't known before. Now, before you go on with your own story, tell me one more thing about them. In our areas, they carry no weapons, teach children in school, serve as animal doctors, work on farms, eat no meat and never take any pay, except mere subsistence. Also, they hate the Unclean, but never seem to do much about fighting them. Is all that true down in D'alwah?"

"Yes, I think so," she said. "The church doesn't care much for them, but the poor people get very angry when there's any talk of bothering them, so they're generally let alone. You see," she added naively, "the peasants have so much to get angry about as it is, why stir them up over something that makes no real difference? That's what my—a teacher I knew, told me. They don't really mean anything one way or the other, just like the Davids."

"Who are the Davids?" asked Hiero.

"Oh, a funny group of traders, who call themselves People of David, who live in our big city and in some of the others, I guess. They actually don't believe in the church, they won't eat lots of ordinary things, and they don't marry anyone but another David. But no one bothers them either, because they pay their taxes promptly and always trade honestly. Also, they can fight like wildcats if anyone tries to molest either them or their church. They have a funny one with no cross and no Dead God at all, and at school once, one of them told me it's much older than ours! They're really peculiar!"

"Humph," grunted Hiero, thinking 'at school', eh, and trying to assimilate all he had learned. "Must be an odd heresy of some ancient kind we never got up our way. The last one in Kanda, a group called Prostan, I believe, re-united with our church over two thousand years ago. Since then, it's all been one Church Universal. You certainly have a lot of strange survivals in the far South. But go on with your own story now, and I'll try not to interrupt."

He fed the wee fire to provide a light and as the faintest haze of smoke rose to the highest level of shiny leaves under the round dome of the tent-tree, the girl talked on, her matter-of-fact tones seeming to emphasize her extraordinary story. Hiero had lived through many strange adventures, including the most recent ones, but he was spellbound just the same. The bear lay dozing, head in her lap.

The Elevener, a quiet, elderly man, had set Luchare's leg, and helped carry her to a shelter. He had then gone away, but soon had come back with a large, draft animal, something like Klootz apparently, but striped and light in color, with short, straight horns, which stayed on all year, unlike antlers. It was commonly called a kaw. Both of them had ridden the kaw away on a trail to the northwest. The Elevener, whose name was Jone, had told the girl that he was going to try and take her to a place of safety run by his order, but that it was a long way off, and that they would have to be very careful. He had asked no questions of her at all.

They had traveled for many days through the great, tropical forest, avoiding the main roads between the warring city-states, but using game trails and village paths where they could. The peasants and woodsmen were always glad to see them, gave them food and shelter, and warned them of migrating herds, rumored appearances of Leemutes and other signs of the Unclean. In return, Jone had helped the village sick, sat with the dying and distributed sets of little carved wooden letters he had made, so that the children could learn to read and write. This idea, interjected Luchare, was one of the tricks that really annoyed her church about the Eleveners, since they did not believe, and still less did the nobles, in giving the peasants new ideas.

"Some of my own church don't like them any better," admitted Hiero, "though everyone can read and write in our country. But conservatives dislike them as a rival religious group. I guess they are in a way, but if we're not doing the job properly, then they *should* take over, as better men, that's what my abbot says. But go on."

After some three weeks of travelling, in a generally western direction, tragedy struck. They were now far beyond the limits of any of the city-states and their appenaged villages. Jone had told her that another week or so would bring them to a place of safety. Actually, she had never felt more safe than with the gentle Elevener. Dangerous animals almost never came near them, and if they did, snorted for a moment and then went away. Once, she said, a herd of giant snakeheads, the lords of the forest, had simply parted to one side while the patient kaw had carried his twin burden down a lane in the middle of the huge beasts. Jone simply had smiled when she expressed awe.

Hiero thought to himself that the Eleveners must long have been in control of mental powers he now felt burgeoning in himself, though his were drawn out by the two savage battles he had fought with his mind. And the broad extent of their society, in physical terms, was also news of the first magnitude. He listened intently.

They had been ambling down a game trail in the jungle, said Luchare, no different from a dozen others they had seen and exactly where, she had no faint idea, when suddenly a man had stepped into the trail ahead of them and stood with his arms folded, facing them. At the same time, a score of hideous hair-covered Leemutes, things like enormous, upright rats, naked tails and all, but far more intelligent, and armed with spears and clubs, had come from the jungle on both sides of the trail. *(Man-rats,* said Hiero to himself). They were totally surrounded, though none had come closer than a few feet.

Luchare had been terrified, but Jone's gentle face had not lost its impassivity. The man in front of them was ivory-skinned, totally hairless and wore a grey robe and hood, the latter thrown back. His pale eyes had been cold and evil beyond description. She knew that a master wizard of the Unclean held them fast and she tried not to panic. There was a moment of silence, during which she had simply shut her eyes and hugged Jone around the waist. Then she heard his calm voice speaking in D'alwah.

"Let us speak aloud. There is no need to frighten the child. I offer a bargain."

"What bargain, Nature-lover, Tree-worshipper? I grip you both tight in my hand."

"True enough, oh Dweller in the Dark. But I can slay many of your allies, and even you yourself could be injured, or at least drained of power for days by the struggle. I am an Ascended One, as I think you are well aware. This trap was set with some care, and in an unlikely place."

Trembling, Luchare had heard the enemy's harsh voice ask again what bargain was proposed?

"Let the child and the animal go. If so, on my word and soul I will make no resistance to you and will submit myself to your wishes. Speak quickly or I will force you to kill us at once and it will not be an easy struggle."

"So be it, Tree-man. One of your rank, even in your weakling order, is a rare captive in all truth, since usually you skulk in safety in holes and corners. Let the child and the beast go, then, and come with us."

"In all your thoughts and deeds there are lies," was Jone's calm answer. "I will send her away, unfollowed by any of your dirty pack, and I can easily tell if that is so. I will remain here for an hour and after that time has passed will go with you. That is the unalterable bargain."

Luchare could almost feel the terrible rage of the Unclean adept, but in the end, as Jone apparently had known he would, he agreed.

Blessing her gently in an unknown tongue, the Elevener had also spoken to the kaw and the creature had at once moved rapidly away down the trail, now carrying her alone on its saddle. Her last sight of her friend had been the slim, brown-clad figure standing patiently facing the grey devil and his horrid crew of attendant monsters. Then a curve of the jungle wall of green hid them all from sight. At the remembrance of how Jone had saved her, Hiero could see Luchare was close to tears.

"He must have been a very good man," said the priest quietly. "I have met one of those wizards of the enemy myself, indeed, a man so like your own description that it might have been the same foul being, were the distance not so great. And he almost slew, or worse yet, captured me. Had it not been for the fat, clever one there, with his head in your lap, he would have done so." As he had hoped, the girl was distracted and forgot her sorrow in her interest. He gave her a brief sketch of his encounter with S'nerg and when he was through encouraged her to resume her own story.

The poor faithful kaw had been the first casualty a few days later. She had slept in a great tree one night, and some prowling monster had fallen on the kaw as he stood underneath and killed him. In the morning she had descended, avoided the bloody remains, on which scavengers were feeding, and had fled on foot, in which direction she hardly knew.

Great beasts, many of them things she had never seen before, constantly snuffed on her trail, and she only escaped death by inches on more than one occasion. Several times she had thought of suicide, but some tough strain or other had forced her on. She still had her spear and knife and had managed to feed herself, though mostly by watching what the birds and small monkeys ate. This had hazards though, and she had got very ill on two occasions.

Exhausted, her clothes in rags and close to starvation, one day she had heard human voices. Stealing closer to investigate, she had found herself looking at a camp of traders, swarthy, black-haired men, not unlike Hiero, she said, whose kaw-drawn wagon caravan was parked in a large clearing. Moreover, the clearing was athwart a broad trail, almost a dirt road, which entered one side of it and left by the other.

While lurking in the brush, hoping for a chance to steal food and clothing, she had been surprised by an alert sentry, who had with him a big watchdog on leash. She had tried to fight but had been knocked cold. When she woke up she had been brought before the master trader who had examined her carefully. She would tell them nothing, although they spoke some bits of her language. The trader chief had ordered some of his women (it was a big wagon train) to examine her physically, and on finding out that she was a virgin, had treated her well, but had her heavily guarded. It was made plain that she was valuable property, to be sold to the highest bidder.

She had ridden for several more weeks with them, always watched, but treated well enough. She had learned to speak *batwar* then, she said, and was

91

soon able to talk to the other women, who were not unkind, though making it plain that she was not on their social level. But she was not beaten or raped, and was allowed cloth to wear and given a riding kaw, though it was led by another.

They had crossed several wide expanses of open grassland, and once had avoided what they said was one of the deserts of The Death. One day they came to the Inland Sea, of which Luchare had only heard vague legends, and there found a walled harbor town and many ships, traders and merchants, inns and market places. Quite a large permanent population lived there, some of them farming the fertile land on the port's outskirts and selling grain and produce to the passing ships and caravans. There were people of all skin colors, including both whites, dark browns, like her own, and the traders, most of whom looked more like Hiero than anything else. She even saw some battered-looking churches, though none of the traders she saw were Christians and she was not allowed to go near the buildings or speak to a priest. She thought she had seen only one at a distance.

The town was called Neeyana, and was said to be very old. Luchare did not much care for it. The people were apt to be sullen, and she saw faces in the shadows which reminded her of the Unclean wizard. The Unclean were not ever mentioned there except under one's breath and after looking over one's shoulder first. She had the feeling that somehow the Unclean were *in* the town, woven into its fabric in some evil way, so that they both tolerated it and influenced it at the same time. The girl found this difficult to explain but Hiero thought he caught her meaning. It was obvious that just as the Eleveners' order extended far beyond 'his previous conception of their scope, so too did the power of the enemy.

Luchare had been sold, after several weeks in guarded seclusion, to yet another merchant, a man who was embarking on a ship with his company and his trade goods.

He had also had her well guarded, apparently also appraising her maidenhood at a high price, which made the Metz smile inwardly. What on earth was so valuable to these strange Southerners about female virginity he wondered?

She had never been on anything larger than a rowboat or canoe before, Luchare went on. The ship had great, pointed sails and seemed immense to her. But a storm came up after three days' fast, smooth sailing and there was a wreck. The ship was driven on to a small island of rocky precipices and cliffs at night. The following morning they had been discovered by a white savage tribe who came out in canoes, they being the same from whom Hiero had rescued her. They seemed friendly enough to the merchants and their chief priest had had a conference alone with the shipmaster. But in return for saving the traders and their goods, such as were not lost or ruined, they had wanted Luchare, whose skin color they had never before glimpsed, to sacrifice to the huge birds they worshipped.

"The traders agreed, the dirty lice," said Luchare. "They even came and watched. Did you see them, all sitting on one end? They were dressed a bit like you, but had hats." And the following afternoon, she had been stripped, and tied to the stake where the priest had first seen her, while the flock had come from afar, drawn by the summons of the tall drums. Those drums which Hiero had heard the previous day had heralded the previous death of a male prisoner, a captive from another tribe down the coast.

Exhausted suddenly as the events of the last few days caught up with her, and with her tale finally done, Luchare fought to stay awake. Hiero got up and gave her a blanket and a spare coat of his own from the saddlebags. She smiled drowsily in thanks, curled up and was sound asleep in seconds, the sleep of healthy youth, able to shrug off worry in a matter of seconds. A faint buzzing noise from her pretty mouth, her rescuer decided, was altogether too feminine to qualify as a snore. What a beautiful thing she was, even with that weird hair, like bunches of great, loose springs!

Hiero realized at this point that he was yawning so continuously his mouth was unable to shut, and hastily gathering up the other blanket, he fell asleep himself, quite as quickly as had Luchare.

Outside the shelter of the tree, the big morse browsed under the stars, the warm scented air bringing him many messages from far and near. Presently the bear emerged and touched noses with the bull, then turned and set off into the night on a hunting expedition of his own, while inside the tree's shelter the two humans slept, knowing they were guarded.

In the morning, Hiero awoke with a start. A strange sound caught his subconscious and made him sit up and reach for his knife in one and the same movement.

But a second later he stopped the motion and grinned sheepishly. The sound was a soft voice singing a little tuneless song, over and over in a refrain that wavered up and down in an odd, but pleasant way. It was enough like a lullaby in his own language for him to feel that it probably was one in Luchare's too.

When he pushed the branches aside and squinted at the sun, he knew it was mid-morning. He had slept over ten hours and must have needed it. A few feet away, with her dark back to him, the girl sat sewing something, using his own repair and mending kit, which she had discovered in the pack. Her gentle singing masked his approach, and realizing this, he coughed politely.

Luchare looked up and smiled. "You're a late sleeper, Per Hiero. See what I've made?" She stood up and before he could say or do anything had slipped off her ragged skirt. For a second she stood, revealed, a slim, nude statue in polished mahogany, then she slipped on the garment she had been working on. In another second she was laughing at him from a leather one-piece suit, with short elbow-length sleeves and shorts that came to mid-thigh.

"Well," he managed, "that's very neat. My spare clothes, I gather."

"Only part," she answered. "I left you the extra pants and under things, so this is only your other long leather shirt. You don't mind, do you?" Her face grew long at the thought of disapproval.

"Not a bit, You're a marvelous needlewoman. If I get any more holes in things, I'm going to have you fix them up for me."

"I only learned, well—after I ran away. I'd never sewn anything before. It's pretty good, isn't it." She pirouetted, arms held out a pretty picture in the sunlight. Behind her the big morse looked on, blinking, and Gorm, as usual when there was nothing else to do, slept under a small bush.

The water he had not wanted to ford the previous night lay a hundred yards off. In the glare of the day, he could see it was nothing but a small bay, not a river mouth, and that they could walk around it in half an hour.

They ate a brief meal from the pack. The grouse, even Gorm now disdained, and it was hurled away, but antelope steak, *pemeekan* and biscuit were a whole lot better than nothing, and five of the great snapper eggs were yet unbroken in their packing. The bear and each human ate one. Then Hiero and the girl cleaned the saddlebags, washed out the squashed egg, and aired the rest of the contents. A little before noon, they were on their way again.

All the rest of the day, they followed the shore eastward. Occasionally, a rocky outcrop would make them turn inland, but they seldom deviated much from their course.

Hiero was pleased with his capture, though at intervals his mind would grapple with the gloomy realization that he had no idea what to do with her, and that she was in no sense supposed to be a part of his mission. In fact, he thought in one of these moments of clarity, by distracting him, she was probably a positive danger! Still, she was from the very area to which he had been sent, she was a mine of information of the people, customs and political makeup of her land and beside—there was no obvious alternative!

Once they came to a place where a series of long sandbars, strewn with logs and other storm wrack, lay in the sea, just off the mouth of a small creek. On these bars, some of the great snappers, their dark grey shells crusted with growth and algae, lay basking and sunning themselves. They hardly blinked their evil eyes, however, as the little party went on by along the beach and splashed their way across the stream.

"Do you have those in your country?" asked the priest as they watched the comatose monsters warily.

"Yes, and much worse things," was the answer. It seemed that the very sewers had to be screened with great iron bars and grills of massive stonework, even in her own proud city. Otherwise, foul things, water borne and avid, emerged at night to devour whatever and whomever they could. Bridges too, had to be covered with strong barriers and roads near streams strongly stockaded when possible. Even with all that, heavily-armed, mounted patrols went continually about on regular beats, looking for intrusive jungle creatures, and repelling incursions of Leemutes. Hiero was used to a life of fairly constant strife, but he began to feel that he had always lived in peace and quiet after hearing about everyday existence in distant D'alwah.

That night they camped on a high, rocky knoll, from which, at early evening, Hiero could see well inland to the beginning of the Palood, its night mists rising in the still air. Far on the distant air as he watched, came the faint bellow of one of the monster amphibians, a grim warning not to venture back into the great marsh.

As they sat talking after their evening meal, which consisted of one of the last snapper eggs and some chunks of the cooked antelope which they had carried along, the Metz priest suddenly fell silent.

Very faintly, out at the edge of his mind, his psychic consciousness, he had felt something, a touch, a thought, plucking. It was hardly enough even to notice, but he was becoming more and more aware of his widening powers in this area. He now could "hear," without even thinking about it, the "voices" of little birds and small hiding animals they passed as they rode along. Luchare, he did not probe, out of courtesy and decency, but he felt sure that he could do so if it should become necessary.

The dark girl noticed his intent look and started to speak, only to have him wave her into silence with a peremptory hand.

Concentrating very hard, he tried his best, using all his new-found (and hard-won) knowledge to pinpoint and identify what he was "hearing," but it was useless. Yet he had a more than strong feeling that whatever it was, it

95

was finding *him,* albeit very gently and subtly!

Hiero got quickly up and went over to the packs. Coming back, face set, he carried the strange metal antenna-spear of the dead S'nerg, and sitting down, opening the thing out to its fullest length and drew out the two forehead contact rods. With these on his head he felt the power he possessed within himself expand suddenly, and almost felt something else!

Greeting, Enemy! came a surge of evil force. The priest felt at the same time a wave of power, as the person or entity on the "sending end" tried to use his strength to pinion Hiero and enclose his mind with an intangible, yet very real block. He had been incredibly lucky, he now knew, when he had first activated this thing. If the power on the other end of the communication band had then tried this trick at once, he would probably have been caught. But now, armed with his new-won strength and knowledge, it was easy to fend the other off, as a fencer wards a sword stroke, and at the same time keep open the message level so that he could either listen or talk.

You are strong, Enemy, came the next grudging thought. *Are you a renegade brother of ours or perhaps a new mutation we know nothing about? We have continuously watched and guarded this wave length since we realized that you had slain our brother and stolen his* (indecipherable name or symbol) *communicator.*

Hiero sent no answering thought. The other knew he was listening however, and he had a feeling that the Unclean, almost certainly one of their wizard lords, would not be able to stop talking. It was obvious that they had no idea who or what he might be. They were arrogantly sure though, that he must have their kind of twisted, sick mind, whatever he was, and the idea that one of their despised foes, an Abbey priest, had such power, was obviously alien to them.

You are not one of the disciples of the tree-worshippers, the soft Earth lovers, who call themselves the Eleventh Commandment Seekers, that is plain, came the thought. *We know their mind patterns and you are far more like us in power and cunning.*

A dubious compliment, recorded another section of Hiero's mind, at the same time making note of the fact that the Eleveners, while implacable foes of the Unclean, yet apparently were also in some kind of communication with them.

We lost you in the great marsh, came the cruel thought. *And we sent an uncertain ally, now also seemingly lost, so that perhaps, though he is very strange, even to such as we, you slew him as well. In any case, you found the* (undecipherable) *which you also took from our brother's body. And you silenced it*. There came a pause.

Will you not speak? The thought was sweet, now, with the evil persuasive sweetness of uncatalogued sin. *We, our great brotherhood, acknowledge you as a full equal. We wish you to join us, be one of us, share our power and our purposes. Do not fear. We cannot find you unless you wish us to. We wish only to exchange thoughts with a mind of such power as yours, and one so different.* The thought was soft, and honey, sickly sweet. *Speak to us, Our Enemy, whom we wish to make a friend.*

The priest held his mental barrier raised high, as a gladiator *secutor* once held a shield against the deadly net of the *retiarius*. He remembered the Elevener, Jone, who had died to save Luchare and his remark, "In all your words there are lies." Further, Hiero was by no means sure that the other and his crew could not locate him, should he try and speak to them as they asked. In fact, he decided, *maybe they can even trace me now, while I just listen to them. Who knows what they can do?*

He tore the contacts off his head and slammed the antenna back in and telescoped the main rod shut, all in one motion. The alien voice stopped abruptly. Yet at the very edge of his mind once more, he could feel the faint (and irritating) plucking and twisting as it still attempted contact.

He concentrated, thinking hard. Perhaps if he altered the basic mind shield he had been taught at the Abbey, *so*—then using his new powers, next activated another different, mental shield causing that one to overlie the other, *thus.*

It worked. As his new barrier fitted over the old, the voice or mind touch ceased abruptly, like the light of a snuffed-out candle. He was no longer conscious of any contact at all, and he was sure he had shaken off the enemy.

He looked up. It was full dark again, but the moon was bright and Luchare and Gorm sat together a few feet away, in silent companionship, waiting for him to return to them. The morse could be heard as he fed himself down at the bottom of the rock, as usual keeping an unsleeping guard.

Hiero rubbed his eyes. "Don't worry," he said. "The Unclean were just trying a few games. They can't do it any more and I'll be all the more ready next time."

"Are they following us; are they able to—to talk with your mind?" the girl asked hesitantly.

"No, now now. They don't know where, or for that matter, what I really am, and I think they are getting a bit worried about me. Anyway, they've been sending out a constant wide-band signal, somehow tuned to what they had learned of my personal brain pattern, trying to get into contact. I felt it, took out this thing," he kicked the communicator, "which belonged to one of them, the one we killed, and talked to them. You see," he went on, "they think I'm a Leemute or something, some new kind of evil mutation, or just a naturally evil human like themselves. My mind seems to be changing somewhat, and they can't figure me out.

"Well, I got worried and cut them off, and then I fixed their probe so that they can't annoy me either. I don't think they have a hope of locating us that way any longer."

He next repeated what he had said, only this time to the bear, using a short-range band, he felt no one could pick up or "home" on.

Gorm understood remarkably well, and even drew a surprising conclusion. *You are strong now, Friend/Hiero. It will be difficult/impossible for most* (of the) *enemy except for the strongest/oldest/most senior to overcome you.*

This was more of a statement than a query and it made Hiero feel sure that the bear actually understood something of his, the priest's new mental development.

They slept the night peacefully away, and after breakfast down on the beach the next morning, Hiero decided to cast the symbols and use the glass. He was almost certain that none of the Unclean were close by and it seemed worth a small risk.

He explained the process, got his equipment, robed himself, said the brief invocation and waited for events. The girl, the bear and the morse waited quietly on the sand a little way off. Luchare was fascinated, but wise enough to realize that there must be no distraction and that questions could always be asked later.

Hiero's first view in the crystal was precisely what he wanted. A large bird, probably a sea bird, with white wings (he could see them flash) and excellent eyes, was flying along the coast to the east, going exactly the way the man wanted to go himself. The view was superb.

He could see the seacoast sand ran, uninterrupted by river mouths, or even small streamlets, for many, many leagues. The great Palood followed the coast only a few miles inland, but separated by a more or less constant barrier of higher ground, on which grew rank scrub and palmettoes. Far off, in one place only, the marsh touched the coast.

Far away too, in the remotest distance, Hiero could see what appeared to be many islands, but they were hard to make out. As the bird dipped and wheeled, using the air currents to plane, he also saw plumes of smoke rising from a stockaded village on a small river far back in the West. Obviously this was the camp of their erstwhile foes, the pale-skinned bird worshippers.

Nothing else stirred, except that well out to sea, on the distant horizon, some great dark thing made a stir on the water as it swam. If it was a fish, it certainly stayed curiously high out of the water, but he could make out no details.

He willed the sight to end, and opened his eyes to examine next what he held in his closed left fist. First, before looking, he called Luchare and Gorm over. There was nothing really secret, or for that matter, sacred, about the symbols. The prayer which preceded the casting in the bowl was simply to ask God's help in making the choice, but the things themselves were not like a piece of Communion bread or a cup of sacramental cider.

The girl was eager to know more and the bear appeared interested too, although Hiero wondered how much of the abstract thought he actually grasped. The amount of brain in that fur-covered skull was still a mystery.

What now lay in the priest's brown hand were some already familiar signs, and also some not yet utilized on this particular venture. There were five symbols altogether.

The Spear and the Fish were both back. "War and water, battle and ships, fishing and hunting," said Hiero to Luchare, as he set those two aside. Next he looked at the Clasped Hands.

"That sign means a friend in need," he smiled at her. "A good sign, one of the best. It can also mean an old friend will appear soon, or that I will make a new one, one whom I can trust. There's another symbol quite like it, this Open Hand," He showed it to her. "That one showed up when Gorm appeared first. But the Clasped Hands are a little different." They meant a friend for life, among other things, but he somehow did not mention that fact.

"Could it mean me?" she asked. "I mean, I have so few friends of my own and I wondered...?"

"It almost certainly does mean you. I doubt if we're going to see many other people very soon, and those we do are most unlikely to prove friends. Let's assume we each have a new friend." They both smiled this time, the copper face and the dark brown one displaying twin sets of perfect white teeth.

"Let's see," Hiero went on, "what else have we? Two more? Well, first the Lightning. That has three meanings of which two are very uncommon. First, I could be hit, that is, actually struck, by lightning. I take leave to doubt that. Next, I could grow very, very angry. It sometimes means beware of anger. Possible, but I never felt less angry." He laughed and turned the little thing over on his palm. "No, I think the usual thing, the commonest of all its meanings is meant again. Just plain very bad weather, in fact,

99

a big storm. We'd better keep our eyes open for it." He placed the Lightning with the other three.

"Last, what have we? The Boots, or Shoes, as some call them. A long journey, and one which hardly needed an appearance, since I knew that before I set out. I guess it means that long as I thought it would be, it will end up being even longer still." He stared at the tiny, fringed boots in his hand and then gathered up all the five symbols and replaced them in the bag with the other thirty-five.

"Can you really make more sense out of it?" asked the girl. "It seems, well, a bit vague. Most of the stuff could almost be guessed, if you think about where we are, who we are, and what we're doing."

"First," said the priest as he finished unrobing and packing, "You're absolutely right. It *is* a bit vague. But I'm not a good talent at this particular form of foreseeing. I know men, friends of mine, who could get a lot more out of it, maybe draw ten symbols or even fifteen at one time, and make an extraordinary and detailed prediction. I've never got more than six myself, and I feel I've done well if I even get a modest clue as to what's coming."

They both mounted, Luchare in front as usual, and with Gorm ranging in front, he continued to lecture. "Now, we do have something to go on. The symbols are an odd mixture of forces, you know. Part of it is genuine prediction, part wish-fulfillment and part a subconscious (I'll explain that later) attempt to influence future events.

"So—we have the Spear, the Fish, the Clasped Hands, the Lightning and the Boots. A reading of the obvious answers might, I stress *might,* run as follows: a long journey, filled with battle impends upon us, or me. A true friend will help and the journey, or perhaps the next part, will be on, in or over, water. Now there are lots of other permutations possible. Oh yes, the journey will start with a bad storm, or in one or something. That's what I get, anyway. And I feel pretty certain that the storm is coming. That's the surest of all of the signs."

The prospect did not look much as if a storm were in view. The sun shone brightly, as it had for the past few days. The blue sea danced and sparkled, the tiny whitecaps not even indicating a stiff breeze. Rafts of small ducks and other waterfowl whirled out on the water offshore, rising in clouds and then settling as they fed and played.

Gorm, sent Hiero, *what weather is coming?* The animals could usually sense weather a day or two ahead, especially if the change were going to be drastic.

100

To his surprise the priest received a negative answer from the bear. *No bad wind, water coming. Sun, moon, quiet air is all* (that) *comes.*

"It may be," he said to Luchare, when he had explained his silent question, "that the weather is still too far away. The symbols are apt to be pretty uncertain about time, at least when I use them."

"Could I learn to use them, do you think?" she asked. They were so close, she riding only an inch in front of him, that she did not even have to turn her head. When the morse moved quickly, the scented, cork-screw curls blew in Hiero's face and he kept resolving to ask her to tie them up. Curiously, he never seemed to get around to doing it.

"Can't see why not. There are children, back in my country, who can use them more effectively than I. It's a talent, that's all. My own are a little different. I can do a good job of farseeing, I can talk to animals pretty well and now, just lately, I seem to be learning some new tricks, mostly about how to fight with my mind. But using the Forty Symbols to forelook just doesn't seem to be my best attribute. You might be a whole lot better. We'll try it out later on."

"What about using my own mind, the way you do. It would be wonderful to talk the way you and the bear do. Could I learn that too?"

"Well," said Hiero, "you could, I'm sure. It's just a talent and not a particularly uncommon one, either. But unlike casting the Forty, which is more or less instinctive, mind-speech and the other mind attributes, up to and including telekinesis, the manipulation of solids by mental force (that's a rare gift incidently), all have to be *taught*. And once taught, practiced, practiced constantly. I started at the age of ten, and many of the Abbey scholars started earlier still. Some actually get selected when they can barely talk, on the basis of some very complicated tests. So you see, it's not all that easy."

They rode in silence along the beach for a little way, and then in a small voice, she asked. "Do you mean I can't learn at all, that I'm already too old?"

"Good Lord, no," said the surprised Hiero. "I'll try to teach you myself when we have a moment. I simply meant it takes training, discipline, practice and time. You may be a marvel at it, and go extra fast."

Before he could even move, she had whipped around, eyes gleaming, and given him a tremendous hug. "Wonderful! Can we start now, right away?"

"Well, I, uh, well, that is, I hadn't...."

Most of the day passed quickly, in doing lessons. Actually, Hiero thought to himself, it was probably a damned good idea to have to recall all the basics

101

he had learned in the Abbey schools. Luchare was very clever and she was also willing to work. The one thing she apparently wanted above all else in the world was to talk to Gorm and Klootz, and this was the goal Hiero held out to her as a reward. But he spoke bluntly first.

"Now listen to me, carefully. The shield for your own thoughts is the most important thing you can learn, and it has to be learned first."

When she wondered why, he explained that with a decent mind shield, a child could evade the grip of the most skilled adept alive, so long as the two were not either very close physically to one another, or linked by an emotional bond of some kind.

"But if you start sending messages without any ability to defend yourself, why the Unclean could actually grab your mind, take control of it and either force you to go to them or else to do whatever they wanted, commit murder maybe, or anything! Even with a conscious shield, or the ability to create one, if you use the powers of your mind too widely, then another mind can "home" in on you, as if you were a target. That's what they've been trying to do to me for the last week, and it took quite a while to completely stop them annoying me. *Now* do you understand why what I say is important?"

"I'm sorry, Per Hiero. I'll let you be the guide. Only," she burst out, "Please hurry, that's all. Somehow, I feel it's very important! Why," she added, "don't the Unclean control everybody's mind, if they're unshielded?"

He laughed. "I'm sure it is important, at least to you. Now let's review what I just taught you. But first, the Unclean can't control an *unconscious* mind, one that isn't sending at all, unless they have the person in their physical power or in close contact. Now, to begin, the shield is to be conceived by your mind as an arc, surmounted by the Cross. Visualize this and then practice, with your eyes open, making it appear in your physical vision, so that the picture blocks out the horizon. Next—" He droned on, using his superb memory to simply repeat what old Per Hadena used to use as the basis for his lectures. This allowed Hiero to think of other things and to keep watch. He kept an eye out for the enemy flier, but no trace of it appeared. Many hawks were in the sky though, and he saw them diving on the countless waterbirds. Once they came to a place where a small herd of the great water pigs lay floating near the shore. At the sight of the travelers, the big, shiny creatures submerged in a welter of foam and vanished.

At another time they had to cross the marsh, previously glimpsed, where a long, skinny finger of the Palood thrust south and caused an oozing stream to drain into the Inland Sea. Hiero had Klootz and the bear gallop across the dirty shallows at the juncture of marsh and sea, while he watched the giant reeds carefully. Nothing appeared, however, and the whole area was only a quarter of a mile wide. Once through it, the pleasant sandy shore began again.

They camped that night under a rock overhang and Hiero allowed a tiny fire, first bringing a rock over to screen it even from the water which the girl thought amusing.

"There are ships out there, you know," he reminded her. "Probably very few contain anyone or anything friendly. You ought to remember; you were on one. And a fire might draw other unpleasant things too, not human at all." Having silenced her, he relented and after supper (the last snapper egg), he allowed the lessons to continue.

"I want you to realize something," he said next. "I could speed these lessons up considerably. The way to do it, and it's sometimes done in an emergency, is to go into your mind and do the teaching there. But I'm not going to."

"Why not?" she asked. "I don't mind and if it will help make things go faster—"

"You don't know what you're saying." He threw a tiny stick on the fire and poked it gently. The soft night breeze brought them many sounds. The muffled grunting from down the beach to the west, was probably the water pigs they had passed earlier. The squawking from offshore, which rose and fell, came from the sleeping flocks of waterfowl. Far away, so far as to almost be inaudible, a big cat screamed once. Little waves broke on the beach in front of their camp, a gentle splashing which never ceased.

Hiero went on gently, "To do what would have to be done, I would need to get into your mind almost completely. Do you want me to know your innermost thoughts, dreams, hopes and fears, many of which are in what the ancients knew as 'the subconscious'? That means the part of your mind which doesn't *think* so much as it does *feel*. Just reflect on that idea for a minute."

Her face was serious in the firelight. "I see what you mean," she said. "Thanks for being so patient. It's hard not to want to do everything quickly because it all sounds so marvelous. It's a new world to me. But I see what you mean. No one would want someone else to know *everything*. Unless they were,—or maybe not even then. I mean—"

"I know what you mean," he said in a firm voice. "And the answer is 'no', not even then. If two people in love open their minds to one another, they always shield something of the conscious mind and all of the subconscious. Now let's go back and review the techniques I told you to use in practicing. First . . . ."

The next morning, Hiero felt a bit tired but Luchare was as bright as ever. She wanted to work all day, and he finally had to call a halt, as much to give himself a rest as anything else. But when they rested at noon, he allowed her to try and call Gorm. To her inexpressible delight, the bear actually "heard" her mind voice and, as Hiero observed, seemed pleased too, almost as pleased as the girl herself.

The day was bright and clear again and neither bear nor morse could feel the tingle of any coming weather change in their sensitive bodies. This made Hiero worry a little, though he said nothing as they journeyed on. The Lightning was about as close to being an infallible sign as existed in the whole Forty. While the priest felt himself to be only a mediocre artist at the use of the symbols, still he was not *that* bad. Or was he? Still, perhaps the time element was the key. He turned to thoughts of other matters and allowed himself to forget his puzzlement.

Another night and day passed. Once they saw a flock of huge, running birds, apparently flightless, racing up the beach far ahead, but beyond noting that they were a dark green in color, could see nothing more. Whatever they were, they had excellent eyesight and were extremely alert and wary.

The next night, by the light of the now full moon, Hiero hooked a huge, round-bodied fish, weighing over a hundred pounds, he believed. Everyone helped, and once, when they thought its thrashing would break the line, Gorm waded into the water and walloped at it with an expert paw, which tamed it enough for Hiero and Luchare to haul it out. Even Klootz pranced around in excitement, although when they began to clean it, he snorted and went back to his fodder of bushes and his sentry go.

Everyone else fell asleep full of fried fish, the bear so round the priest thought he would burst. Lots of fish were smoked and packed for the future, something which always pleased Hiero, who had the true woodsman's feeling of not wasting the almost imperishable trail rations, the *pemeekan* and biscuit.

The next day dawned cloudy. As they set off, a very gentle rain, hardly more than a heavy mist, began to fall and Hiero got out his spare waterproof hood for Luchare. But it was not really uncomfortable, and the weather remained very warm. even at night.

The mild rain continued all night and into the next day. It was much too misty to see far. They paused briefly at noon and ate, then went on as usual.

104

The sea was calm, but the fog had increased and a vague malaise was growing in Hiero's mind. He now wished he had used another bird the last time it had been clear, and had looked ahead. Once again the thought of the Lightning came to him. A mild drizzle and a mist were hardly bad weather, at least in the sense of that particular symbol. It was most peculiar.

Luchare had been practicing her exercises very hard, which had made her unwontedly silent for the previous two days. She was now good enough to exchange mental "baby talk" with the bear and Gorm had also seemed to enjoy being told to *stop* and *go,* to *pick* (up) *that stick,* and in general be ordered about like a not very intelligent dog. But as the afternoon passed Hiero grew more and more uncomfortable and he finally told them both to stop using their minds, even at this close range. He could not see why he was disturbed, yet he trusted his instincts enough to believe there was a reason. Klootz and the bear seemed conscious of nothing out of the way, however.

Nevertheless, when disaster struck, the priest knew that it was his fault and that he had not been prepared or even alert, for that matter. In retrospect, the enemy had laid the trap with great care.

But if only Gorm had not been walking next to Klootz, if Hiero had not been laughing at the girl's mental efforts to make the bear pick up a dead fish. If—if—if!

At first glance, the little bay looked utterly empty. They had rounded another of the innumerable rocky points which thrust through the sand and out into the water when they came upon it. The mist partly shrouded some small islets just off shore. On the shore itself, a few hummocks of grey stone, their feet circled by olive-colored scrub palmetto, reared about the lighter sand of the beach. Only the lapping of tiny wavelets broke the silence of early evening as Hiero checked the morse, some evanescent doubt troubling his mind.

He urged Klootz forward, just as Gorm suddenly ran ahead of them, nose lifted high as he caught a rank scent. Luchare, unaware of any tension, laughed happily as she watched, finding the bear's pose ridiculous.

The rocks and bushes on the beach erupted leaping figures. A horde of fur-covered, bounding Leemute horrors, stub-tailed and with glistening fangs, resembling giant distorted monkeys, seen in a nightmare, came at them from all sides but the rear. As they came, their ululating, echoing cry, long familiar to Hiero on the northern marches, rang out in hideous familiarity. In their hands the Hairy Howlers bore long spears and clubs and brandished great knives.

Yet this was not the chief menace, bad as it appeared. From behind a small island of granite, a long, black vessel, bare of any mast, glided smoothly only a few hundred feet offshore. On its foredeck, hooded figures bent over a shining metal mechanism, whose short-pointed, solid barrel was aimed at the morse and his riders.

The priest reacted by instinct, the unconscious trained Killman taking over. His reflexes were thus even faster than either those of the bear or his own great steed.

Get back out! was his savage message to Klootz and Gorm as, thrower in hand, he slipped from the saddle. The girl, frozen in surprise, simply stayed fixed desperately in her place, as the morse turned about on his own rear end so to speak, almost squatting in his effort to obey the command he had been given. He was already twenty paces away in the first of a series of great bounds when his master fell.

Hiero had been bringing the thrower into aim, determined not to miss the boat and its menacing weapon when the Unclean gunner fired first.

There was a streak of blue fire and the stink of ozone. Hiero felt a terrible blow on his chest and a moment of intense cold as he blacked out. His last thought as he slid into darkness was *so this is what the Lightning meant!*

Then—nothingness.

6: *The Dead Isle*

Hiero's first sensation was of pain, the second of movement. Instinctively, the pain made him try to rise, but he found he was hindered, that he could not. This in turn made him realize that he was lying on his back on something hard which moved gently, heaving restlessly up and down, sideways and back, in a regular rhythm.

The pain was centered in the middle of his breast, a constant ache of tremendous proportions, which sent ripples of lesser pain throughout his whole body. His right hand was free and instinctively it sought his chest. It there encountered a hard object, of unfamiliar shape and fumbled with it. *That's wrong*, said his mind indignantly. *The Cross and Sword should be there!*

He realized at this point that his eyes were open and had been for some time. He was in total darkness, then, or almost total. A very faint line of light, a little below eye level, showed some way off. As he tried to concentrate on it and at the same time block off the pain by Abbey techniques, memory also returned.

The Lightning! Something very like real lightning had apparently been used on him. The meaning of the little symbol had been its rarest attribute, then, and it had tried to warn him that he would actually be struck by the strange weapon on the Unclean boat's deck. And he was on an anchored boat now, probably the same one. He had been on small vessels of the Republic many times and traders' boats too. The feeling was unmistakable.

The pain still a constant, but now rendered bearable at least, his mind began to work again. *What was this strange object that lay on his chest?* His free hands, left now as well as right, traced its outline in darkness until they came to a heavy thong which was attached to the object. As he realized what had happened, Hiero offered a silent but fervent prayer of gratitude. The

107

enemy weapon, the electric bolt or whatever, of the Unclean had hit squarely (or been directed: who knew God's will?) on the silver Cross and Sword medallion which was the badge of his order. Result: a fused mass of melted silver and a man alive who might otherwise have been dead!

His hands felt further down, to his waist, and encountered a broad band of smooth metal, whose very feel was strangely unpleasant. This was what held him firmly to the hard bed or table on which he was secured. Against his ear though, he now heard the surge and rush of water, and he realized that he must be imprisoned against the actual hull of the ship, apparently down in the hold, or a section thereof.

Eyes were now as night adapted as they would get and he could see slightly more. The thin line of light was indeed the bottom of a door. Hiero was held by the broad waistband, on a narrow bunk, and the band was secured at one side of the bunk by a massive lock. The room or cabin was small, about ten feet square and contained no furniture, except for a foul-smelling bucket in one corner, whose use was obvious although in his present condition his metal belt prevented his reaching it. Walls, deck, overhead, everything he could reach, were all of metal, featureless and blank, with no rivets or welds showing. Since all the vessels he had previously seen were of wood, with experimental iron hulls only being talked about, the priest was compelled to admire the workmanship. It was, he reluctantly conceded, well in advance of any type the Abbeys possessed, at least in the nautical realm. He remembered too, that the boat he had seen was mastless and no sign of smoke had shown either, eliminating both sails and the crude steam engines of the newest Republic craft as a means of propulsion.

As he listened now, he began to hear other noises over the faint groaning of the hull and the slap of waves on its outer surface. Voices came faintly to him and also muffled barking and grunting sounds, the latter all too familiar. Apparently some of the Howlers were on board. Underlying the other noises was a thin, whining hum, barely audible if one concentrated. This, he decided must be the ship's engine or whatever provided power, and he wondered how it operated.

Hiero had wasted no time in looking for any weapons. His belt dagger and his heavy sword-knife were gone and the rest of the things were on the saddle. Had Klootz and the girl gotten away? Had Gorm also escaped in the confusion? Poor Luchare, her protectors were always getting trapped by the enemy!

His musings were interrupted by the clink of a lock or latch. The door opened, sliding into a recess actually, and light flooded the little cubicle, causing the priest to blink and raise a hand to his eyes.

Before he put his hand down, a fetid stench warned him of one enemy, at least, a Howler. As he looked, his eyes adjusting to the new glare, he saw that his captors had turned on a fluor in the ceiling.

There were two men in the now familiar grey cloaks and hoods. One wore that mind-wrenching spiral on his breast, but this time instead of red, it was in a sickly blue. The same one, the obvious leader, had his hood thrown back and he so resembled S'nerg that Hiero had trouble in not gasping aloud. The subordinate creature kept his hood on, but the priest glimpsed a brutal countenance in the hood's shadows, bearded and with a broken nose. Against the wall near the door crouched the Howler, a pink-faced monster, well over two hundred pounds in weight, its dirty brown fur matted and foul. But under the brow ridges, the deep-set vicious eyes were alive with intelligence and malice. In one huge hand it carried a metal weapon like a great cleaver.

The keen eyes of the leading human had not missed the flicker of recognition in Hiero's, and it was he who spoke first. He used *batwah,* Hiero noted, not Metz.

"So—you have seen one of us before? All the Brotherhood are close kin, priest, and if you have glimpsed one, you have seen all."

Watching him under lidded eyes, Hiero could believe it. The man, if he was a human man, seemed a trifle older than Hiero's memory of S'nerg, and his throat lines were graven deeper. But the resemblance was still astonishing. Nevertheless, the priest said nothing.

The adept, for such he must be, spoke sharply in an unknown tongue to the other man, and the one addressed hurried to Hiero's side, bent and released the lock in the metal belt which held him fast. Hiero did not move, however, but remained lying there, watching the three attentively.

"Good, good," chuckled the adept. "A man of great control. Had you leapt up, even got up slowly, I should have had you knocked down, just as a beginning lesson in obedience. But we knew you were clever. Why else all this trouble? Still, I am pleased. Now pay attention, priest, if priest you are, and not something else.

"I am S'duna. The big one in the corner is Chee-Chowk and he does not like you. No, not at all. He had never seen a Metz priest, yet he knows an enemy, eh, Chee-Chowk? But actually, he's a delightful fellow. I only wish you could see him tear a man's leg off and eat it in front of the victim. Good sport, eh, my friend?" He smiled at the awful, grinning creature, and Hiero barely restrained a visible grimace of repulsion.

"Too bad humanity, or your weakling segment of it, priest, doesn't like the Howlers. Yes, we've adopted your name. It's not a bad one. You see, they're only mutated monkeys of some long extinct species. We think they were laboratory animals before The Death, but we're not sure. They're very clever now though, and they do hate humans, all except their good friends." His tone was light and bantering and he appeared in no hurry to move.

"We're going ashore now for a few questions. As you'll see, escaping is silly. And Chee-Chowk and his merry crew will be watching, waiting for a new kind of dinner, please remember that."

He leaned over until his white death mask of a face was thrust close to Hiero's impassive brown one.

"You're something a little different, priest, I'll give you that. We may just come to terms. Think that over, too. We don't generally use prisoners for anything except amusement. Ours, not theirs, I might say. But in your case, well, who knows?

"Now get up," he added sharply, "and walk behind us and in front of Chee-Chowk. And do what you're told. You'll live longer." He turned and left the cabin, followed by his silent acolyte.

Hiero got up quickly, but not quick enough to avoid a nasty cuff from the Howler, which shoved him through the door at the same time. He fell, still weak, to his knees, and a great paw next jerked him roughly erect by his collar and thrust him further on.

Ahead of him he saw the booted feet of the second man going up a narrow companion stair. The short corridor was grey and featureless save for a few doors like his own. He wondered if Luchare were behind one, but he dared not use his mind for a probe, not in this place.

When he crawled out of the foredeck hatch, pushed from behind by the Howler, he found the rain still falling, if anything, harder. As he tried to look about, two more grey-hooded men took him by the arms and half-led, half-dragged him to the side and thrust him down a ladder into a large rowing boat.

They were in a harbor, a hidden anchorage surrounded by tall spires of smooth rock, rising from the freshwater sea. Despite the rain and mist, the priest could see a few other craft, one of them with masts, at anchor not far away. None were large and there was no sign of movement on any.

Behind him, the huge Howler now crouched in the stern, while the horror's two masters stood erect in the bow. The two oars in the boat's waist were manned by a pair of half-naked slaves, white men, covered with scars and whose hair and beards grew rank and unclipt. They stank worse than the Howler if that were possible, and their eyes were vacant and apathetic. They stared at the water and made no sound.

As Hiero looked back, moving as little as possible, the boat turned under the oars' power, and he got his first good look at the ship which had captured him. It was sharp-bowed, long and slim, the hull of dark grey metal, and with a mid-ships cabin, also of metal. A curious short tower rose just aft the cabin, with a crowsnest full of strange rods and instruments on poles like giant fly swatters. On the foredeck, a cloth shroud of some sort covered the weapon which had felled the priest.

The rowboat turned further and the ship was lost to his view. Ahead of them, through the mist, Hiero saw a landing, a stone dock thrust out into the water from a rocky islet. On the islet above, half hidden under an upthrust crag, crouched a squat castle, a low stone keep visible in the center of massive walls, which lay open now to view through a great gate. The ponderous doors of the castle were flung wide against the grey walls, which rose up some thirty feet above the surrounding rock.

Nothing appeared to grow on the islet, and all was grey or black stone. On the walls' top, a few figures paced, but not in any regular order. The fortress of the Unclean seemed guarded not by arms, eyes, nor by regular sentries of any sort.

The Unclean leader, S'duna, turned from his place in the bow and stared down at Hiero. Then he pointed to the oily black water through which they were passing. "Look there, priest! We have many guards and many wards upon our island. Look and remember! None leave the Dead Isle of Manoon, save by permission!"

Hiero stared at the water to where the white finger thrust. Close to the boat and clearly visible, even in the mist and rain, a round thing, several feet across emerged, like a segment of greasy hose, magnified many times. As it turned and twisted, the Metz saw that it was an eyed head, a head of horror. It was some kind of giant worm creature, whose sucking, round, jawless mouth could not close, but gaped and contracted rhythmically, full of sharp fangs set in concentric circles. The thing dived under the boat as he watched, and he estimated the body to be many yards in length. It had made no sound.

He looked at S'duna and shrugged, very slightly, his face bland and unmoving.

The other smiled malignantly. "You appear a hardy one, I'll give you that, little priest. Let us see how hardy you remain when we go to visit in our order's house on Manoon. Is it not a heart-warming place?

Hiero was now paying little attention. As the boat drew in toward the desolate island, an assault had begun on his mind. He sensed that S'duna knew of it but had nothing to do with it. The forces which laired on the isle had been waiting for Hiero and their attack was the result of long preparation. It was both a test and an assault and also, in an odd way, a welcome. He knew that he was being subjected to enormous and increasing pressures, which were intended to destroy him if they could, yet which might allow him to defend himself if *he* could. And in the very nature of the onslaught there was an element of doubt. The Unclean rulers of Manoon did not yet know with what or whom they were dealing. They could have killed him while he slept. Instead, they were frightened enough to feel the need to experiment. And they still thought, apparently, that he somehow could be induced to join them!

He was helped or rather shoved, on to the stone quay, and with the Howler behind and the others in front, was marched up the path, paved and smooth, toward the gate of the Unclean castle.

This last physical exertion, while not especially strenuous, almost overtaxed his waning strength. He could not estimate how long he had been unconscious, but he was desperately tired and now felt the need of water and food as well. He expected none of the amenities, especially rest, however. The advantages to the enemy of questioning a weakened, half-exhausted prisoner were obvious. However, the process of holding his mind block against the mental assault, using his fast waning physical energy to do so, was wearing him out at a geometric rate. Halfway to the shallow steps of the fortress, he fell, and when Chee-Chowk's great paw wrenched him erect, he fell again. He made no effort to rise, concentrating only on holding the mental barrier, and at the same time nerve-blocking any unpleasant physical stimuli. As he lay, the Howler cuffed him but he felt nothing.

S'duna looked down at him thoughtfully. "Wait," he said, lifting a pallid hand to restrain the Leemute. "Lift him up. It will avail us nothing to have him die here. He is fast draining himself, and he is wanted for a long period of arduous questioning, if nothing more. Carry him gently, Chee-Chowk, as you would one of your dirty cubs, eh?"

The wizard certainly exacted obedience, Hiero had to admit. He was lifted gently in the great hairy arms and although the stink of the creature was appalling, he could block that out too. Carried, or rather cradled, he passed under the cold arch of Manoon. Few who entered that place left it and of those who opposed the Unclean in their purposes, none at all.

As he was borne into the court of the fortress, the mental assault ceased. Hiero felt that S'duna had signalled somehow, in a way he could not detect, that the prisoner was worn out and had best be allowed some respite. Whatever the cause, the pressure and probing ceased, and although he kept his shield of force firmly in place, with the rest of his senses he could look about, especially his eyes.

The fortress was not especially large. The whole extent inside the stone walls was perhaps two hundred yards square. Steps led up to the walls' angles and, as well as being low walled themselves, the parapets were broad enough to walk upon. A few hooded figures paced them, the same he had glimpsed from the boat. There were no armed men about and he saw no obvious weapons in evidence, save for Chee-Chowk's cleaver.

The square stone keep which lay before them was low, only about three stories high and had few windows. Those it had were narrow, and set in no obvious order. The roof was flat, making the structure look like a great, grey blank cube, its shape in some way an affront to any kindly softness or indeed the human condition. The pavement on which they walked looked like the same stone slabs as the walls and the fortalice. All seemed to the priest to have been made with one purpose, an arid and sinister efficiency, one which denied beauty or taste or even life as being necessary. Inwardly, far, far inside, he shuddered, but none knew or saw it by his actions or appearance. And too, his curiousity could not be quelled entirely, even here. No one had ever penetrated the lives of the enemy as he was now doing. He *must* observe, despite himself.

They passed through a narrow door, and went silently along an ill-lit, stone corridor. The dim blue glow of an occasional fluor provided the only light. Hiero looked back over the hairy shoulder of his carrier and saw the grey light of day in the door vanish as they rounded a corner.

Presently, after many baffling turns, the corridor began to go down. At the same time, the hollow echoing voice of S'duna reverberated back from in front.

"Manoon lies truly below, priest. We of the Great Brotherhood find the depths a relaxant, a shield against the silly clamor of the world. Only in the bowels of the earth is there the complete silence we crave, the spiritual emptiness we seek to encourage the growth of pure thought." His words echoed along the stone corridor in diminishing tones, "Thought, thought, ought, ought."

When the silence had returned, save for the pad of the three sets of footsteps, he added, gently, "And the dead, of course. They are here too." The echoes sighed, "too, too, oo, oo."

Eventually, the two ahead came to a halt. A small, metal door had been opened and the great Leemute stooped and entered. He laid Hiero on a pallet of straw, not ungently, and then backed out of the room, snarling as he did, to indicate his true feelings toward the captive.

"Farewell for a time, priest," came the voice of S'duna. "Rest and prepare yourself. You will be summoned, never fear." The door of heavy iron slammed shut with a clang and a lock clicked. Then there was silence.

Hiero looked about him. The room, or cell, a better description, had been hewn from the living rock. There was no window in the rough walls, but a small slit high in one corner, too small for a man's arm, brought air from the distant surface. A small fluor, set in the ceiling, protected by a metal grill, gave a dim but adequate light. The cell was about ten feet square and furnished with nothing, save for the straw mattress and a covered pail, the latter obviously for sanitary purposes. There was also an evil-smelling drain in one corner, again with a heavy metal grill covering its opening.

Next to the pallet was a wooden tray, on which was set an earthenware jug of water, another of some sweet dark wine and a loaf of ordinary hard bread. One sensing taste, an art taught in the Abbey schools, told him the wine contained some unknown substance, but the bread and water seemed pure enough, if a trifle flat in taste. He poured the wine down the drain, ate the loaf, drank all the water and lay down to rest. The air was damp, but not especially cold and he was not uncomfortable. The pain of the great bruise on his chest, where the lightning gun's blast had struck him, was still vivid but perfectly bearable. He now began, very cautiously, to try a previously thought-out experiment.

He lowered the mental guard on his mind a tiny, the smallest, bit. Imagine a man weakening a wall of rough stones from the inside, in order to see if an inimical force or a dangerous animal, is pressing on it from the *outside*. Bit by bit, careful to make no sound, the man removes first the larger stones, then the smaller ones, which fill up the chinks. He pauses and listens at frequent intervals. He is careful to leave the outer face of the wall unchanged. But until he is able to make at least a tiny hole all the way through, he cannot communicate with the outside world and get help. This is what Hiero did with his brain, slowly dismantling his invisible wards and guards, one by one.

The very last step was not needed, so delicately attuned had his mind become, and so sensitive the warning devices that he felt the Unclean outside waiting! It was a weird experience. He knew they were waiting, on constant watch, waiting in what numbers he could not tell, for him to relax his barrier. And he could feel them without so doing, feel them waiting to invade his mind, hoping he would be lulled into letting his inner fences down for even one split second which was all they needed. Give them that and he would be in an instant a mindless thing!

As carefully as he had dismantled his shield, so he re-built it. A few moments later and he could relax again. The wards were up once more and the whole thing had been put on "automatic." Invade the cell and kill him with a sword thrust, they could do easily at any time but invade his brain and spirit not at all.

He lay back, considering. He was sure of one thing, and that was that he must have frightened the Unclean adepts badly. Had this not been so, he felt sure he would now be writhing on some torture rack to give pleasure to one of their feasts. But they wanted desperately to know more about him, that was obvious. They wanted to know who and what he was and, (Hiero was certain this lay uppermost in their thoughts) were there any more like him! As long as he kept them guessing, he had a shrewd idea they would handle him with great care.

How on earth could he use his mind, since his body seemed trapped here? The mental communication bands were sealed off by the necessity of keeping up the wall between their minds and his. Yet he could never escape unless he could explore, could learn more about his prison, and the only way to do that was to use his unfettered mind. And he knew he had better hurry, for God knew alone how long he would last under the Unclean brotherhood's idea of an examination. The problem was a snake devouring its own tail. Relax the defenses and be overwhelmed. Don't relax them and die, through inaction, a little later, but just as surely. The mind's "doors" were all locked since no one could communicate except on the known wave lengths, not the Unclean, not the Abbeys, not the animals, not anyone.

Or—could they? Like many revolutionary ideas, Hiero's came partly through his subconscious. It was slow emerging into the conscious, and then suddenly it was there. *Or could they?* Where had he got that idea? Was it possible there were other bands, perhaps on another part of the mind's spectrum, one nobody had yet chanced upon? He began to probe, sending his thoughts out on a "wave length" neither he nor anyone else had ever tried before. It was a thought channel which had long been deemed blank, or rather too full of "static" to be useful. The only thing it had ever been demonstrated to carry was the mass mind of a bee hive or wasp nest, for the channel was so "low" or "coarse" that it was very close to the inaudible *sounds* of certain communal insects.

Once again, analogy is necessary. Try to imagine a specialized electronics expert, who only has knowledge of microwave amplifiers, forced to use a crowded police call band, and use it with the microwave equipment which is all he is accustomed to. In addition to adapting his unsuitable equipment, he must operate through the police calls which are already apparently using that particular band to capacity!

This is what Hiero now managed to do. Lying on his straw heap, eyes shut, to outward appearance sleeping, he began to tap the minds of his guardians at a level they had never suspected anyone capable to utilizing. It was hard at first but the new wave length had fantastic possibilities. For one thing, he found he could easily maintain his shields at the same time he explored with it. The two "bands" were totally different and one had no relation to the other.

First, he looked for the source of the pressure which never ceased to beat, although without any effect, on his outer, automatically maintained shield. In passing, he noted that he was now using his mind at *three* separate, quite distinct, levels, at one and the same time.

The enemy who watched him and kept up the thrust on his brain surprised him. It was only one man. But he had help. He sat before a curious machine, whose low humming and buzzing varied in a rhythmic pulse as it went up and down a scale. Above a board, covered with lights and buttons, hung a clear glass tube filled with some opalescent fluid, suspended by wire at both ends. The fluid, oily and shimmering, seemed to move in keeping with the wavering rhythm of the board below. The man, another adept, apparently, hood thrown back and eyes shut, sat with his hands fitted into two depressions on the front of the board, which were shaped to receive them. In appearance, he was another duplicate, Hiero saw, of S'nerg and S'duna.

Saw! Even as the word rang in his mind, he closed that channel off and mentally retired into his own skull again, safe behind his shields. *Saw!* Without the benefit of an animal's eyes, he had somehow *seen* the room and the man. There was only one possible explanation. On this new level, he was in the other's mind, undetected, and using the other's sense of perception. Could he use more than sight?

Cautiously, he eased himself back along the line to the mind of the Unclean adept who, in turn, was supposed to be observing *him*. He found to his amazement that he was occupying the other's brain and tapping the other's sensations all at the same time. The sickly scent of an unpleasant incense filled the control room in which the adept sat, coming from a small smoking brazier. Hiero guessed that it had an effect like *Lucinoge* and enhanced the mental powers. But the key fact was that he, Hiero, was *smelling* it, using the olfactory sense of his unconscious watcher! And he could *feel* the cold metal of the instrument board, where the other's hands now rested. The next step was one he was reluctant to take. But he could see no way out of it. The strange machine was undoubtedly tuned to the other's brain, was in a combined mental and physical contact with him. The priest wanted to know more about the machine, indeed felt it vital that he know more. The Abbeys were only beginning to consider mind enhancement by mechanical aids and the enemy was obviously far ahead.

Slowly, as slowly as a person with poor sight threads a needle, Hiero began to use his new ch nnel of observation to tap the adept's links with the machine. The experience was uncanny. Through the machine, he began to feel the mind of the adept beating remorselessly on his own, Hiero's, mental barrier! A feeling of ntense heat began to overcome him and he withdrew again, hastily. This sort of circular mental polarity was obviously not without danger. It was not necessary to kill himself to test his new powers and what he had just tried was something that obviously needed lots of lab work first.

When the sensation of heat, a feeling not physical, but none the less dangerous for all that, had vanished, Hiero set his mind to explore elsewhere, and sent it roving, to seek other intelligences nearby. He was doing now, he realized, in a conscious way, what his subconscious had always done when he wanted to see and put himself in a trance with the crystal.

He "knew" S'duna's personality from observation, both physical and mental, and he set himself to find that particular master of the Unclean Brotherhood. He touched several other human minds, and one non-human fleetingly. This latter he took to be Chee-Chowk or some other Leemute, but he went on without investigating. Ah! He touched the mind of the man he wanted.

The adept was apparently resting, his mind under the influence of some strange drug. Hiero was able to see part of the room, a large one, hung with dark draperies and containing many strange instruments laid out on tables. S'duna lay upon a bed and beside him another small brazier emitted a thin trickle of bluish smoke which he was inhaling. One brief look into the thoughts of the enemy was enough for Hiero. The man's plans for imaginative relaxation involved much that was bizarre and sensuous and more that was hideous, foul beyond belief. Hiero withdrew his mind, sure now that he could find the other again whenever he wanted.

What next? The time element he was being allowed in which to plan was uncertain, but must be decreasing. The fact that S'duna was under some drug seemed hopeful. A mind of that power would probably be involved in any interrogation. What more could now be done with this new attribute he had acquired?

He concentrated as hard as he could on *distance*. That is, he began to use the new band in an increasingly wide arc. Whenever he tapped a mind or even touched one which could be identified as Unclean or as being on the island, he thrust further *out* and *beyond*.

Soon, he knew he was sending his thoughts far beyond the physical scope of Manoon, as ripples from a far flung stone grow larger and larger. Now, he concentrated on Gorm and the girl. He knew their mental identities well and he began to search for them.

He encountered many minds, but all were animal, the brains of birds, intent on prey, usually fish, and the minds of fish and other aquatic creatures. Once he touched upon a cluster of human minds, all in one area, like a group of blips on an ancient radar screen. This, he guessed, must be a ship and he knew he was still *over* water in a physical sense. Wider and wider yet he cast his net of awareness.

Just when he was about to despair and abandon the process for some other, more hopeful, line of endeavor, he found them.

Gorm! The mind of the bear lay open to him, or at least partly so. To his surprise, which he momentarily put aside, there were some areas he could not penetrate. Using the bear's weak eyes, he could see that he was looking at Luchare. The two were on a lonely stretch of beach, in what seemed to be late afternoon from the way the light appeared. A shift of the bear's glance now revealed a huge foreleg blocking part of the scene. Klootz too, was still with them then!

Now, could he communicate? *Gorm, Gorm,* he called, using the new wave length as hard as he could. He could feel the animal shift uneasily, but he was not getting through. At best, he was making the bear uneasy, acting as an irritant. He tried again, this time not so *hard,* but using a narrower "needle" of thought. It must be remembered that the soldier priest was trying something utterly new. The full capabilities of his recently won system were unknown to him.

Mainly by luck, he made a fleeting contact. *Hiero!* He felt Gorm literally jump as the message hit him, then he lost the bear again. He tried Luchare next, but got nowhere. He was not surprised. She was a novice at mind speech and the bear was not. In fact, he thought, recalling the sealed elements of the ursine mind he had just noticed, the bear was still an unknown.

There was no time for such speculation however. Patiently, he went back up and down his odd channel, trying to relocate the precise point at which Gorm had been jolted. There it was again, a flood of thoughts! *Hiero,* the bear sent. *Hiero/friend, where are you? How do we speak, this* (strange) *way?*

The priest finally managed to quiet the animal, and began to slowly explain what he was doing and how. This time Hiero was not too surprised to observe how quickly Gorm understood. He had thought previously, it came to him now, that the young bear owned a brain not far short of a human's in power. It was now apparent that the estimate was far too low. The bear was quite as intelligent as Hiero, only in a somewhat different way, that was all.

I am a prisoner of the Unclean, sent the priest. *I am on an island in the sea, where I do not know. I am going to try and escape very soon, since I feel sure they will torture me. Where are you and how are you?*

As Gorm developed practice, the story of the three unfolded. The brief fight which had left Hiero dead, they thought, on the beach, had left them untouched. They had evaded all missiles and galloped away west. Easily losing the few Howlers who pursued, they had next gone a few miles inland to the very edge of the Palood, and headed east again. Now they were camped some half a day's eastward journey from the place where Hiero had been captured. The enemy was not apparently seeking them. It was supposed that they were thought to be mindless brutes and a stupid slave girl, not worth bothering about. They had been trying to frame new plans when the wonderful message had burst upon them. It was now a day and a half since the battle, if it could be called such. What did Hiero want them to do?

The priest reflected for a moment. It would be silly for the girl, who knew nothing of boats or deep water, the bear who knew even less and the morse, too big for most vessels, to try and reach him. He must escape in his own way and seek them out instead. The problem was where to tell them to meet him. But it was not insuperable.

Go, he sent, *to the east. Find a cove where a small boat can come in secretly. Wait there in concealment. The Unclean know nothing of this channel of the mind we use now.* He told them to send him a mind picture through Gorm once they had found such a location, and estimate how far it lay from the site of the battle. He would surely be able to direct himself to it with that help. He added a prayer, a message of comfort for Luchare and broke communication. A plan had been growing steadily in his mind and he felt he could no longer avoid trying it. Who knew how much more time he would be allowed?

Once again he mentally sought the nameless adept, the same who, by the help of the curious apparatus, was maintaining the combined watch and pressure upon him. Once again he had the weird experience of invading the Unclean wizard's mind and senses and seeing them focused on himself!

He began to insert a thought in the normal mental pattern of the adept, a thought which would simply appear as a subconscious command! The thought was simple *The prisoner was too quiet. Turn off the machine and go and check on him. Too quiet; go and check.* Over and over the thought was built, Hiero increasing its strength by degrees, his concentration never faltering as he tried not to let the pressure mount too rapidly so that the adept, himself a master of mental science, would suspect he was being tampered with. On and on, up and up, went the pressure. All the while Hiero watched the instrument board before him through the eyes of the man he was trying to mislead.

Suddenly there was a click. The priest felt his enemy's worry plainly as the light in the peculiar hanging tube dimmed and went out. The board's lights too were now shut off. The pressure on the other part of Hiero's brain vanished. And at the same time, before the Unclean adept could even rise from his seat, Hiero struck. The mental barrier he had erected to defend himself was swept down and he lashed out at the dark mind of the adept before the other could even think of guarding himself. Using *both* channels now open to him, Hiero captured the enemy's brain before any warning even could be formulated. Now Hiero paused, keeping a tight vise on the other, and waited to see if anyone else had been around. There was nothing, no thrilling of the ether, no alarm, no sign of awareness of what had happened.

After a moment, Hiero ordered his captive, bound no less strongly than if he had been loaded with chains, to come to his cell and release him. It was a risk, for the adept might have no key, but Hiero was gambling that anyone of that rank must have the ability to set him free.

He watched through the other's eyes as he left the chamber from which he had kept watch and headed for Hiero's distant place of imprisonment. Nor were the adept's eyes the priest's only aid. With the prisoner's *ears,* Hiero heard footsteps coming at a cross corridor and made the other stand in an alcove until they had passed.

All this time he could feel the enemy's own mind raging against its restraints. It was a strong mind and it battled desperately to free itself and the body it was attached to from the strangling embrace of the priest's brain. But in vain: so quick had Hiero been that the entire forebrain was completely under his power, all senses, all locomotor ability, everything. The Unclean could only rage futilely in the dark recesses of his mind, helpless to intervene actively.

Through a maze of dark corridors they went, passing closed doors at intervals and using the occasional dim bulb of a fluor set in the ceilings for light.

Once as they passed a door, Hiero caught the sound of a faint moan. But he dared not tarry to see what foulness of the enemy lay behind it. It would be all he could do to escape alone and it would serve no one to have him die here in the course of a hopeless attempt at rescue of some other of Manoon's captives.

Presently they were before his own door. He could feel himself *inside* and themself *outside* at one and the same time. Under Hiero's mental orders the adept was forced to release a tiny hidden catch in the stone corridor wall just outside the door. The door lock clicked and the adept opened it and entered. As he entered, Hiero forced him to his knees. The door closed by itself behind the Unclean. At the same time, Hiero clamped down on every neural synapse he could reach in the adept's body. With a muffled exhalation of breath, the enemy passed out cold, completely unconscious, even as the Metz left his mind completely and reoccupied his own in full.

He rose from the bed and crouched by the body. Hastily he stripped the other, finding a nasty-looking dagger belted on under the robe. This he took and drew on the grey robe and hood over his own supple leather clothes. He listened for a moment and heard nothing. He built again his "ordinary" mind shield, simply as a precaution lest a snooper try a chance probe at him. A sudden stillness made him glance down. There would be no need to tie the Unclean master up now for he had ceased to breathe. The ferocious nerve shock must have stopped the evil heart, Hiero realized and promptly forgot the matter. The sooner such creatures as this were exterminated, the better, was his only feeling.

Before he had "led" the adept to his own cell, the enemy's memories had been extensively looted. Hiero knew now where his cell lay, where the various entrances were and the whole maze of Manoon's underworld down to the last broomcloset. He shut the cell door behind him, locked it, and went on his way down the corridor, his hood over his bent head, to all appearances a master of the Dark Brotherhood intent on some problem as he paced along at a steady rate.

He was not heading for the surface by the way he had entered. It was not the closest way out for one thing, nor the most private. Also, there was something he wanted to get before he left. He kept his mind always on the warning pulse of the mental wave length he had found the Unclean to favor. Any human being within range would be detected before he ever saw him and either avoided, the best method, or taken over mentally if necessary.

He had crossed several hundred yards of dusty corridor, listening intently, his new knife held firmly up a sleeve when he thought he caught a faint sound.

121

He paused, his ears straining. The noise, if it were a noise and not the blood beating in his temples, was a soft scuffing and it had seemed to come from behind him somewhere. He heard nothing now. The buried world of Manoon was utterly silent. Far behind him, a dusty blue fluor glowed in the corridor roof and equally far ahead, another.

Once more he went upon his way. Soon he slowed his pace even further. He heard footsteps ahead and saw the glow of a stronger light. He was approaching, as he had meant to, a more used part of the dungeon-fortress complex. The footsteps died away again and he moved on. It had only been an underling, whose mind radiated nothing but vicious stupidity.

Hiero saw that the light came from a strong fluor set at the junction of his corridor with a much broader one. This was also as it should be and no Unclean minds were in close proximity. Hood drawn down, he stepped into the new hallway and turned left. In a short time he was before another door and finding it unlocked, he quickly entered. The small storeroom was empty. Having mind-probed first, he would have been greatly surprised had it been otherwise. On a shelf, shoulder belt, scabbard and all, lay his beloved sword-knife, flung there carelessly by hands disdainful of mere physical weaponry. In a second, he had his robe off and was belting the beloved weapon on. Only moments later he was out again and moving off up the corridor outside, back the way he had come, storeroom door shut behind him. It had been luck that the dead man back in his own cell had known where his sword was stored, but it had been forethought which had led the Metz to probe for the information. He wasted no time looking for the thrower. It already had been taken apart for examination, he had learned, and besides he had no shells.

Hiero met no one and sensed nothing on the way to the little-used corridor from which he had come, but he was nonetheless nervous. A feeling was growing that somehow he had been detected. Once into the corridor, he quickened his pace, moving at a dog trot. All of Manoon seemed unconscious of his escape but that feeling persisted.

The passage floor grew rougher, the jagged walls dripping cold water now and then, and the fluors were set even further apart. This was a path to a seldom-used exit, one originally designed in the far past to serve as an emergency escape route in the event Manoon should suffer a siege. When Hiero had ransacked the now dead Master's mind, this way had been the one which the Unclean himself had regarded as the most secret and the least likely to be either searched or guarded.

The passage floor now began to slope upward at a slight angle, which reassured Hiero who had been wondering if he had made a mistake. But the floor was even rougher and bits of rubble and even a few large rocks littered it. Also, it twisted, cutting down the dim light of the occasional fluors even more. His pace slowed to a walk.

The priest paused. Had he caught another faint sound, the rattle of a stone far to his rear? Once again he "swept" the airwaves for an Unclean human's presence and detected nothing. If anything, a rat or some other vermin, he decided and went on. No human mind stirred in the fortress.

At length the passage straightened. It ran up now at a fairly steep angle, and a tiny gleam of light far away heralded its end. Encouraged, the Metz loped on, breathing evenly. He was beginning to feel the strain of all the mental effort, even more than the physical exertion, but he still had reserves to draw on.

He had passed the last dusty fluor and gone into the darkness beyond, when the rattling scrape of claws on stone made him turn, freeing the heavy sword-knife and dagger together from the folds of the robe as he did.

One fluor's light beyond the near one, a great dark bulk filled the tunnel from side to side, rolling along at a terrifying speed. At the same time, realizing somehow that he had been detected, the monster gave forth with a ghastly ululating bellow which filled the tunnel with deafening noise.

Chee-Chowk! Somehow the giant Howler had sensed Hiero's escape and tracked him down. And the priest's watch for Unclean human minds had made him forget they too had allies who thought in a different band altogether! But there was no time for self-recrimination.

As the Leemute passed under the last fluor just in front of him, Hiero caught the glint of the cleaver-like weapon the filthy thing carried in one great paw. Then the priest attacked.

He had transferred his sword, letting it droop from his dagger, or left hand, while he stooped and then hurled a fist-sized piece of rubble as hard as he could, straight into the fang-lined maw which shrieked at him. Straight and hard went the missile and the chunk of limestone smashed into the hideous mouth, silencing the cries on the instant and making the brute halt in sudden agony, pawing the air with his free hand.

Behind the rock raced Hiero himself, sword now in the right hand, dagger in the left, using the downward slope of the tunnel to lend force to his charge.

Chee-Chowk tried to raise his own weapon, but using the long dagger as a *main gauche,* the defensive poniard of the forgotten *Cinquecento,* the priest beat it aside and struck a terrible blow at that awful, bleeding face which reared above him. The short, heavy blade, backed with utter desperation, for Hiero had no doubt as to the ultimate outcome if he should miss, came cleaving straight between the staring red eyes. It drove into the skull beyond and split it with a "chunk" sound, as when a man splits a heavy tree knot with an ax.

That was all. The Howler's giant body fell slowly forward, eyes glazed in death, and Hiero had to twist himself sideways to avoid being crushed. Even so, his sword was wrenched from his weakening grip, so deeply was it embedded in the head of his monstrous foe.

There was silence, broken only by the priest's panting breath. As soon as he could think again, he tried to tear loose his sword and while doing so, to use his brain to see if any general alarm had been given. But he could detect nothing. No mental clamor, no alert, nothing at all. The minds he was able to spotcheck back in the main fortress were unconcerned, set only upon their own routine business. S'duna still lay in drugged slumber, a prey to evil visions.

Finally, Hiero tugged his weapon loose, and stooping, wiped it more or less clean on the dirty fur of the Leemute. He stood looking down at the huge bulk, whose muscular spasms went on despite death. "A pity, Chee-Chowk," he mused aloud. "Perhaps if decent men had raised you, you'd have been just another kind of man, not a foul, night-haunting ogre." Moved by the tragedy of the Leemute's mere existence, he said a brief prayer, and then turned and resumed his march up the tunnel. Already he could smell the fresh breezes over the dank airs of the tunnel and the stench of the dead Howler.

The light was much further than it looked however, and it was more time than he cared to lose before he climbed the ramp to the end of the tunnel. His legs now really ached and he had a strong feeling that a Chee-Chowk one-year-old would have been too much for him.

The emergency exit from the buried world of the Unclean was not barred by any door. The tunnel walls made a double zig-zag, that was all, so that no one could see out or in. The last portion of the zag was a narrowing slit, through which one squeezed.

The Metz priest peered out cautiously. He had to shade his eyes, even though the sun was setting, until they grew accustomed to the normal light of the outside world. The bolt hole from which he peered was set high up, on the left arm of the bay to which the ship had come bearing him as a prisoner. He now faced east and the light of the setting sun was coming from above and behind him. While underground, he had come a long way out on to one arm of the two which guarded the harbor of Manoon.

124

Down a tumbled slope of rock and scree, on which nothing grew, the harbor lay before him. The few ships still rested silently at anchor, including the thin black craft which had captured him. A slight chop stirred the waters of the harbor, and looking to his left, the entrance, he could see white-caps outside where a brisk breeze was blowing. And he could see something else.

There was only one wharf, the one to which he had been taken, below the road up to the castle. The castle glowered at him across the silent harbor and the bare rock which surrounded its walls. The gate was shut. No one paced the walls and no sound came from the edifice.

But just to the right of where Hiero now crouched, a path led down to a tiny cove with a bare shingle of pebble beach. Spread out upon this were a couple of fishing nets, and near them two small wooden boats were drawn up on the shore, held by anchors tossed up into the rocks at the end of their ropes. The priest decided that the rulers of the Dead Isle occasionally wanted fresh fish and made some of their servants go out and get it. Whatever the reason for those boats, they represented a chance. Their oars were plainly visible, simply shipped inside and one of them even had a collapsible mast lying across its thwarts, a sail wrapped tightly about it.

Hiero had been maintaining a watch on the massed minds of the castle and its underground world. Still nothing stirred. Chee-Chowk apparently had followed his intended prey alone, not wishing to share what he no doubt thought of as a free dinner! But this could end at any time. Nevertheless, he decided to wait. The light was failing rapidly now and it must be very close to sundown. Nightfall would aid his chances enormously. It was a risk worth taking.

The shadows rapidly grew longer. No lights came on in the squat bulk of the castle and its sinister outline grew harder and harder to make out. Nor were any lights visible in the harbor. *Not even an anchor watch,* thought Hiero, who had some experience of the Beesee coast and its seamen. These people were overconfident, he decided, too arrogant to believe anything could challenge them or their fortress. Their very lack of apprehension would be a shield to one of God's servants. Or would it? He remembered S'duna's comment in the boat, about Manoon having "many guardians." Best to go cautiously.

A few stars had glimmered through the flying clouds, but no moon, and soon even the stars were invisible. The wind was making up now and it moaned among the empty barren rocks of the Dead Isle. The voices of the countless dishonored slain, the tortured victims of the Unclean, thought

Hiero, and resolved that come what might, he would not be among them.

He felt his way slowly down the slope, all senses alert, but heard nothing and sensed nothing with his mind.

Soon, he made out the outline of the small boats. He felt his way around the one with the mast and freed its anchor. Then, with the anchor rope over his shoulder, he began to drag the boat into the water. It was a sturdy little thing and it took some doing. Twice, he had to pause and rest, each time checking the dark mass of the fortress for lights.

Finally he got the boat launched and climbing aboard stepped the mast, though leaving the sail furled. Then he went back and smashed a hole in the other boat with a heavy rock, first transferring its oars to his own in case he needed spares. In another moment he was afloat, had two oars in the tholes and was pulling along the shore for the harbor mouth.

He rowed carefully, glancing ahead for rocks and not trying to make any speed. His little craft was almost invisible in the black shadows of the overhanging rocks and he followed each dip and twist of the shore with precision. At one point he had to pass quite close to one of the larger moored vessels he had glimpsed earlier but it was soon past and nothing stirred aboard it; nor could he detect any mind. His greatest problem was the increasing chop of the short, stiff waves as he neared the harbor mouth. Spray was already coming aboard but he was grateful for the fact that at least he would be in no danger from thirst.

Two oval flat pieces of wood, which sat on pins secured to the sides of the boat near the tholes for the oars, had caught his eye. Though he had never seen leeboards before, for his own people did not use them, he quickly grasped their purpose. The round-bottomed little boat would go faster sideways than forward under sail and might even turn over without a steadying influence. The leeboards rotated on bolts secured to the boat's side, and one of them could be dropped on the side away from the wind when the sail went up. The priest had been in enough craft with sails, even though they had had fixed keels, to understand what tacking into the wind meant, and he could see what he had to do to make use of the fishing boat's best powers.

Even though he was prepared for it, the full force of the wind at the entrance caught him by surprise. Actually, it was not gale force or anything like it, but in the tiny boat, only a dozen feet long, it felt far more severe than it was. A capful of water, caught from a wavetop, slammed into the back of Hiero's bare head and ran down his neck under the cloak, making him shiver momentarily. But it was not really cold, little less than blood heat, and he

126

pulled stoutly into the crests pounding up and down, quickly developing a rhythm which allowed him to avoid shipping much water.

He was squarely in the middle of the entrance, fangs of black rock rearing up on either side when all his mental alarms went off. Instantly he slapped on his own new spy-proof mind shield and simply listened to the clamor, while continuing to row his hardest.

He could hear S'duna's mind, almost incoherent with rage, as he was awakened and told the news. The minds of other adepts, how many he could not now tell, also tuned in and he felt the mental search pattern they established at once. But he also felt that it was harmless. His shield was impervious, giving him a mental invisibility the Unclean could not even detect, far less crack. He was much more worried about purely physical means of detection and pursuit, and he felt sure the cold minds in Manoon would think of them too, before very many more moments went by!

Luck, or something else, thought Hiero, mentally apologizing to God, was with him. He had barely rounded one of the corner rocks of the entrance when lights burst out on the walls of the castle. At the same time a flare hurled up by a rocket, cast a spectral blue light over the harbor. Not two wave lengths to the left of the boat, Hiero saw the harbor's mouth almost as brightly illuminated as if it were day. But a wall of stone, the outer bastion of the Dead Isle itself, shielded him from view.

Nevertheless, he was under no illusions about his safety. Once there had been time for logic to take over, the Unclean search would discover the missing boat. After all, how else could he leave the Dead Isle save by water?

He shipped his oars and freed the sail from its lashings. It was a simple type, a kind called a "standing lug" in the Lost Millennia and Hiero had seen similar rigs before. Next, deciding that he wanted to run along the island's coast in an easterly direction, he lowered the right leeboard into the water. Then he took one oar and locked its thole pin into a hole in the stern, so that he had a crude, but adequate, rudder.

It took a few moments to get the feel of the boat, and some of them were bad. Once he let her head fall off so far a bucket of water poured over the stern, but he managed to bring her up again and get her settled. Fortunately the wind was steady from the west and did not blow in gusts. Also, the little craft was well balanced, and once given a chance, sailed stoutly along.

Hiero had been so busy mastering the boat and watching for rocks that he had let his mental probes slip, though not the shield, for that he had put on "automatic." Now he felt something new, a strange, unpleasant thrilling of the mental communication bands. It meant nothing to him and was not actively harmful, being merely a minor annoyance. Since he had no idea what it meant however, it worried him.

Then, from the white-capped water off to his left, beyond the shadow thrown by the island, an enormous coil of glistening rope, as thick around as his body, rose from a swell and sank again, clear in the light of the dying flare.

The worm things of the harbor! Manoon had called new and awful pursuers from the slimy depths of the Inland Sea.

7: THE FORGOTTEN CITY

Luchare sat cross-legged and stared at the tiny, red fire in front of her. She shivered. But she was not cold, far from it. The young bear lay next to her, his head in her lap, and made faint woofly noises in his sleep. Beyond the mouth of the little gully, she could hear Klootz methodically chewing his cud even over the noise of the waves breaking on shore, and she knew that no unannounced danger could steal upon them in the night.

No, it was Hiero. The wonderful burst of communication had restored them all to life and purpose again. She herself had seriously contemplated suicide just before the priest had managed to reach their minds. Not that he had actually said anything to *her,* she thought illogically and quite angrily. No indeed, she was too stupid to hear him, a bear, a four-legged animal, was the only one smart enough, not a woman who—she shied away, even in her own mind, from the unspoken and unwanted thought. She, Luchare, daughter of Danyale IX, bothering to care about whether a common foreign priest, a low-born, painted-faced nobody, talked to a stupid bear rather than to her! Ridiculous!

Overcome with sudden remorse, she stroked Gorm's shaggy head. "Clever bear," she whispered. "Clever bear, bring him back safely."

Their camp was set back in a pocket of a rock outcrop only a few hundred feet from the sea. As Gorm had told her, they needed to find a little bay or cove where they could lie undetected and to which Hiero could aim. Open to the sky, but otherwise walled except in front, it was a good location. Luchare, mindful of Hiero's warning, had built a screen of brush on the beach side, so that the fire was invisible unless you came within a few feet.

The bear awoke suddenly and sniffed the breeze. *Wind, stronger, Girl* (identity Luchare symbol). *The sky is dark. Hiero may have good luck* (?) He lay back and shut his eyes again.

But he's in prison! she thought. The Metz priest himself would have been surprised at how well Luchare had learnt to use her mind. She and Gorm could conduct a regular conversation with very few breaks now, and she could even give the big morse intelligible orders, although she usually asked Gorm to do this for her. Klootz accepted Gorm's commands completely, as he would have Hiero's, another thing the priest would have found worth pondering. The bear had been very careful too, when planning their next moves.

Do not try (negative emphatic) *to talk to Hiero!* He had made the order plain. *Talk only to me or Klootz and when we are close together.* Being clever herself, she realized that he knew what the dangers were far better than she. She ought not to try and mentally locate Hiero, lest she unwittingly draw the enemy down upon them instead.

But damn this waiting and wondering!

An hour or so later, she felt the bear rouse himself again. This time he rose and stood, dark pointed head erect, as if trying to see through the racing clouds about them. Somehow, she now was attuned enough to know, he was in communication with the priest again. If only she could understand, and were not so stupid! There must be some way she could help, if she could only think of it! Then she realized with a thrill, that Gorm was now talking to her.

I cannot describe this place properly. You must tell him what it looks like. He cannot see well with my eyes.

Then, into her mind like a flood, came Hiero! But there was no greeting, no warmth, only commands!

Quick, girl, where are you? Try to tell me what this place looks like from the sea if you can imagine it. And hurry! There was a pause. *I am pursued; I cannot keep this mind path open for long. Hurry!*

Luchare was terrified. She had wanted so much to help but now she was unable to even think. Anything she thought might kill Hiero, if the information were incorrect. But she came of fighting stock and managed to rally.

Wait, she sent clumsily. *I will try. We are less than a day's journey east from where you were taken. Offshore is a lone rock, with two palms growing at the east end. The rock is high in the west, low to the east. Behind it is a small cove with a beach. We are there.*

That's enough! snapped Hiero. *No more until you see me or they will use you. Don't send any more messages until you actually see me, understand! Now wait!* There was a sudden blankness, a "silence." Luchare burst into tears. Here he was, in deadly danger, maybe about to be killed and not one kind word for her, not even a 'hello' or 'how are you'! The next moment her tears increased as the thought of her own selfishness. Even as she stormed at his coldness, he might be dead!

Wait, be calm, came the thought in her mind. Looking down through her tears, she saw that Gorm lay on his stomach, head on his furry paws, looking up at her.

He will come back, the thought continued. *And he thinks of you too. Only now he must fight for his life. Be patient.*

Luchare blinked back the tears and then reached down and hugged the bear. How had he known what she was feeling?

Your mind was open to me, he sent. *When Hiero spoke to you it was through me. Your own mind is not yet strong enough for such a task. Now sleep while I keep watch.*

Soothed, but still apprehensive, she lay down on her waterproof cloak, staring at the black sky above, and listening to the small breakers hitting the beach and the rattle of the wind in the palmettoes. She was sure she could not possibly sleep and the bear observed with satisfaction that she was asleep in hardly any time at all.

These humans, he thought. *They take their affections so hard!* Then he resumed listening to the night.

His face calm, but his mind racing, Hiero watched the coil of the great water worm disappear below the surface. He was braced against the lee side, gripping his steering oar in one hand and the sheet, the line holding the sail, in the other. The little craft was tearing along the rocky coast of Manoon, the wind on her quarter and he was keeping her as close to the cliffs as he dared. Something told him that the danger would be greater out on the open water. Soon, however, he would have to leave the shelter of the isle and strike out for the mainland. He knew by his internal "compass" and the glimpse of the land at sunset where he wanted to head, but keeping an unfamiliar small boat on course in this stiff breeze was something else again. And now the haunters of the depths were being lossed upon him. He could still feel the vibration in his mind which he had decided was the hunting call sent out from the Dead Isle to the monster worms. He strained his eyes through the black night to see if a worm or a sharp rock would appear first in the murk and destroy him.

Once a great swell broke two boat lengths to seaward of his little craft but he could not see whether something was lurking below or a wave crest had simply toppled over naturally.

A vagrant fleck of moonlight pierced the wind-driven banks of clouds and helped give the priest his new bearings. He was leaving Manoon at last. The farthest, most eastern, headland, gaunt and windswept, towered up to his right, blacker than the clouds, and beyond its point lay nothing but windswept open sea. Somewhere off there, how far it was hopeless to guess, must lie the mainland and his friends.

At this point, in order to head the boat around the island, he was forced to jibe and cross the sail over to the other side. This meant raising one leeboard, securing it, and lowering the other. Somehow it got done. Fortunately, the standing lug is one of the simplest rigs ever devised, which may account for its continual re-discovery throughout history. Bringing her around on the new course, Hiero looked back and instantly stiffened.

Out of the tossing sea, three waves back, caught in a ray of the fitful moonlight, the hideous round mouth, pulsing in horrid motion, of a giant worm appeared. To the priest, then and later, these dreadful brutes were 'worms', but in actuality, their origin like much else, dated back to The Death. In the past only foot-long sea lampreys, the scourge of the local white-fish and trout, forced mutation had turned them into mindless, ravening collossi, capable of overwhelming a small boat. The Unclean wizzards of Manoon had found a mental wave length which stimulated the hideous things into a simultaneous rise to the surface and quest for food. Only the adepts could then control them enough to keep them away from their own vessels and they thus formed a most effective guard around the island, many of them always lying on the bottom near it.

As the creature bore down on him, clear in the persistent moonlight, the neck arched and cut through the water like that of a giant snake's. The small, round eyes, set on the sides of the head, were visible as it swayed from side to side following each movement of the boat. Almost, it seemed to Hiero, the thing was toying with him, for it advanced at a very slow rate, far slower than if it had been coming in earnest. Probably it was only instinctive caution, for the tiny brain was incapable of any thought. At length it seemed to decide this thing was prey. The motion through the water suddenly increased tenfold and the head-mouth, barbed fangs all palpitating, struck down at Hiero as he sat in the stern.

The priest had never felt he had a chance once he saw the worm come, and he was very, very angry. To have come through so much, only to be dragged down by a hideous, mindless thing like this! But he was trained to battle and the first rule was never to give up.

He had taken a turn with the sheet to a rude wooden cleat and as the horror struck down at him, he in turn stood up, the tiller-oar held between his knees. At the same time, he thrust stoutly into the yard-wide, sucker mouth above him. He used the butt end of one of the spare oars, snatched off the boat's bottom, and he drove it home down the foul gullet as strongly as he could.

There was a shock which threw him to his knees, but he never lost control of the steering oar and he saw the great worm fling back its head in agony at the hard morsel so suddenly jammed in its throat. The wash of its recoil helped drive the boat forward a trifle faster. As he watched in fascination, the monster churned the water to foam in its efforts to expel the unwanted tidbit. Soon it was out of sight in the murk, but he dared not relax his vigil. There were assuredly many more of the things and he could not always count on such luck. Besides, he was fast approaching exhaustion. The strain of the two recent combats and the necessity of keeping a constant watch on the mental air waves had worn him down to a shred of his normal vitality. He had not had anything like a rest since his capture and he was not sure how much longer he could go on.

The island had long since been lost to view, and the now increasing gleams of the moon's rays on the dancing wave tops showed nothing but empty water as far as the eye could reach.

Tired as he was, Hiero decided it was time to try and get more information. He had no belief in the powers of good triumphing so easily. S'duna's rage alone had come clearly to his mind as he was leaving the harbor and the other adepts could hardly be less furious. S'duna had said himself that no one had ever yet escaped the Dead Isle. Pursuit would be coming and the sooner Hiero contacted his friends the better.

It was then that he called Gorm. If Luchare could have known his thought when he broke the mental contact with her, she would have slept with a smile on her face. Slowly, reluctantly, the priest was finding that dark face and dancing corkscrew ringlets were somehow always coming between him and any other work or thought, even in times of crisis. Almost physically, he shook off such feelings. *If he got out of this mess . . . .*

His brain was now tuned to the island behind him again and using his new wave length, he was able to separate several sets of minds from what must be the main group back at the fortress. Using his new-found powers, he was able to locate no less than three separate "groups" of mind pulses, apart from the central one which had to be Manoon itself. These three pulse groups were stronger than the other, and that meant closer! They lay, physically, that is, in an arc, between the island and himself. The pursuit could thus be pinpointed as being in three vessels, all more or less on his track. The Unclean lords had quickly guessed which course he would take, that was obvious. Now, how far away was the mainland?

The priest strained his eyes, staring ahead through the night, but the fleeting moon gleams, though they came at closer intervals, revealed nothing but more of the great freshwater sea. He tuned his mental energies to the subband again. God Almighty, the shore could not be too far distant, from the strength of the signals he had caught from his own friends. He must have come five miles at least, since leaving the Dead Isle. On and on he sailed, up one wave and down the next, the wind steadily from the quarter, the little boat's best point of sailing. But she was not designed with speed in mind and behind him the three clumps of mental force which he knew represented three enemy craft grew remorselessly more powerful. He knew too that they were seeking his mind and not finding it, which was his sole consolation.

As the night drew on, the light grew better. The clouds began to thin out and the moon and stars appeared in greater and greater frequency. This was bad, but there was nothing the priest could do except hold his course and pray.

What was that? A dark line ahead, glimpsed in the waning moonlight? There, it came again, and yet again as he rose to a wave top. It was land, a little to the left of his bearing. He trimmed the small sail and the boat bore up, while his heart pounded. Once again there was a chance and he was going to take it. Now once more he reached out for the bear's mind.

Wake up, break camp and wait! Be ready and don't answer, or you'll be detected. Three times Hiero sent this on his new low-level wave length and then ceased. He had done all he could.

The wind still drove him on with the same strength. But the clouds were almost gone now and even his small sail must be visible for some distance in the moonlight he knew. He sought the enemy minds and marvelled at how close their "images" were. Yet, when he looked back, he could not see them.

He could begin to make out details of the land now, but to his disappointment saw nothing but a line of light-colored beach and dark scrub and whiter dunes behind it. No island such as Luchare had described appeared, indeed no islands of any sort. Had he overshot them? No matter, getting ashore was the first step, away from those pursuing boats. He aimed directly for the nearest stretch of beach, now no more than a half-mile away.

As he did, he sensed the sudden surge of emotion in the minds of his nearest foes as they glimpsed him for the first time. Alerted, he looked back and saw them. Two dark triangles rose from the shining waters, rose and fell back, then rose again. The sails of the pursuing vessel were about the same distance from Hiero that he himself was from the beach and safety. It would be a close race. But he had been lucky and he knew it. He had struck the westernmost boat, the one at the left end of the line of three, and it was not one with an engine. But he could feel the thrilling of the communication bands as the Unclean sent out word that he was in sight and sure enough he felt the other two mind "clumps" begin to close up towards his position. He readied the long knife in his lap, this time for himself. He would receive no second chance to escape, he knew, and the enemy were going to get no live prisoner this time. He looked back, calculating his chances, estimating the speed of the two-masted vessel. It was gaining on him fast and he could see the black outline of its hull now, and even a twinkle of light as some edged weapon caught the moon.

But the beach was also very close. He heard the breakers rolling ashore, and could make out the black outlines of individual palm trees behind the sandy margin, ethced in chiaroscuro by the moon.

There was a "zzzup" sound and then another. Round holes magically appeared in his sail, but the tough cloth from which it had been woven did not fray or tear. With a sharp thud a heavy bolt of some kind, *probably from a crossbow,* he thought, in a remote corner of his mind, buried itself in the gunwale a span away from his hand. There was nothing he could do and he did not even bother to look back, but drove on straight for the creaming surf. Shooting at one small boat from another at night and in a wind was as much luck as a matter of skill and hence not worth thinking about.

Now his boat was rearing up in the first breaker and he hastily dropped the sail and steered her in. He had no time to raise the dropped leeboard, but he managed to loosen it so that it at least swung free on its pintle.

Down went the blunt bow as the wave caught the boat and hurled it at the beach just ahead. Crouched amidships but keeping the boat steady with the steering oar, Hiero rode her in, in a long sweeping rush.

As sweetly as if the little craft had tried to come to rest, the leeboard and then the bottom grated on the sand. The priest, free of his stolen cloak, now tucked under one arm, was running through the ankle-deep water and up the sandy slope beyond almost at the same moment.

The zipping of more of the enemy missiles over head and along side did nothing to slow him down. Now, an enraged ululating yell rang out behind him and as he toiled up a gulley in one of the high dunes, he knew the boat had a complement of Howlers aboard. He stumbled to the dune top and as he did, looked back for the first time. His little craft lay on her beam ends in the breakers, white water pouring over her side. He felt a moment's regret, for she indeed had saved him. Just beyond the outer waves the enemy lay hove to and in the moonlight he could see black figures dancing with rage on her deck and hear their redoubled shrieks of fury. He smiled wearily and wondered how long he had before they put a company ashore to try and run him down. *God knows at this stage it wouldn't take long,* he thought, rubbing his eyes, his breath coming in pants.

He lay down now on the crest of the sand hill, hidden from his foes by some grasses, but able to watch them. Time enough to run for it inland if he saw a boat being lowered. The enemy vessel was bigger than he had imagined and there might be fifty souls aboard; plenty to spare for a landing party.

Then over the waves, he saw the outline of the slim, engine-driven vessel which had captured him. It came fast from the southeast, a white curl of foam at the sharp bow, slicing through the waves like a knife. In a few moments it was resting bow to bow with the sailing ship, rocking up and down in the waves. He could see a cluster of dark figures on her foredeck and he knew the "lightning gun" again was seeking a target. He crouched quickly and slid down the back side of the dune. As he did he saw the the dune grass burst into orange flame a few yards over his head.

Idiot! I never moved sideways from where I ran up the slope! He trotted slowly away from the dunes through the palmettoes and scrubby bushes, picking a way around patches of growth too dense to cut through. Behind him, he heard more fires crackle. A stitch began to cause a sharp pain in his side and he had to slow to a walk. All the while he tried to monitor the enemies' minds, but a new difficulty had come up. Apparently there were *too many* minds and they were all trying to shield themselves and concentrate on him at the same time. He found it almost impossible to separate their thoughts, even on the new wavelength of which they were ignorant.

Suddenly a clear message came to him, standing out, so to speak, above the jumbled thoughts of the others, like a mountain above hills.

Priest, I think you can hear me! You have some new tricks, Priest, and I want them. You have slain another Elder Brother (sacrilege!) *and made away with the chief of our Howler allies in some manner, this too we know. Now listen well, Priest! I, S'duna, a Master of the Dark Brotherhood and Initiate of the Seventh Circle, swear by our most sacred bond to slay you, yes, and by the most horrible means we can devise. And I will never rest until I bring this about. I go now, but you will see me again!*

Hiero sat down under the shadow of a large bush and stared dully at the moonlit vegetation before him. He felt so tired that further physical effort would probably kill him, but he also felt marvelous in another way. He could *feel* the enemy minds and they were not coming ashore! And there was only one answer to that. They feared him, alone and worn out, feared him desperately! Only this could make a heavily armed pack of over a hundred (a guess)

136

furious Unclean, including their acolytes and Leemute allies, abandon so hard a chase. They had no idea of what he was really capable and their leaders feared an ambush! The priest giggled weakly at the thought. I was all he could do to stay awake and keep his mind shield up and the Unclean feared a superhuman one-man ambush!

He roused himself at length. What little store of strength he still possessed must be used before it too gave out. He concentrated in the new channel on Gorm. The bear must have been waiting, his response was so quick.

I'm ashore to the west of you, I think, Hiero sent, striving to keep his message coherent. *You'll have to find me. I couldn't see your island, but I'm back in the scrub about a quarter mile from the dunes. I can't stay awake much longer and my mindscreen will be on lock. You'll have to use your noses and ears. The enemy is near, just offshore, so stay behind the dunes and guard your minds! Repeat, guard your minds!* He fell forward on his face in the sand, the last trickle of energy leaving his body. Anyone passing by would have had to look hard to see that one patch of shadows cast by the moonlight under a certain large bush had a solidity that the others lacked. A child armed with a rock could have slain him.

He awoke to find it dark. Water dripped down his face and for an instant he thought it was raining. Then he felt the canteen spout against his teeth and realized that he was leaning on something soft which smelled wonderfully of girl. His head was on Luchare's breast and he now saw the young bear a few paces away in the moonlight, and heard his snorts as he sought for a scent. The giant morse loomed in the background, dark against the star-filled sky.

With an effort, for he was terribly stiff, Hiero pushed himself up on his elbows and took the canteen from the girl's hands. She squeaked in excitement and surprise and started to babble.

"Are you all right, we looked all day, and just found you a few minutes ago, that is, Gorm did. He smelled you and I don't wonder, I can myself, where have you been, you need a good bath and I—"

Hiero had freed one hand and pressed it firmly over her mouth while he drank again from the canteen. When he had had enough, he put it down and released her lips.

"I need food," he said firmly. "While I eat I'll talk. But we're by no means out of the woods. Have you seen any of the enemy, either at sea or here on shore?"

She sprang to the morse's saddlebags and was back with food on the instant, but her voice now tried unsuccessfully to be indifferent.

137

"How—how are you, Hiero? We were hiding about three miles down the coast in a bay. I guess you couldn't see it. You look terrible and smell worse." As she spoke, she handed him some smoked fish and biscuit.

Between ravenous bites, he told her briefly what had happened to him since his capture. At the same time, he was telling Gorm the story, only with his mind linked to the bear's. It was tiring, but saved repetition. The mental history only took a minute or two, so fast is mind speech, and Gorm wandered away when he had heard all he wanted.

Hiero finished his meal with a chunk of *pemeekan* explaining he wanted some sugar. Then he stood up and stretched, breathing deeply.

"You don't know how good this feels after those black dungeons," he said, inhaling the scented night breeze. "Manoon is really indescribably horrible. Even the air smells dead, and nothing grows there, not even weeds or cactus."

She shuddered appreciatively and he looked her over. She was still neat and immaculate-looking in her leather suit, the mass of dancing curls shining in the moonlight. Something in his eye made her hand go up to her head and attempt to adjust her hair, while she rose nervously from where she had been sitting in front of him.

"I missed you, you know," he said quietly, first sitting down and then leaning back on one elbow.

Luchare now had her back to him and she seemed to be staring at the dunes, white in the distance under the moon. "Did you?" she said, her voice uninflected. "That's nice, because we missed you too."

"I said I missed *you*," returned Hiero. "I thought about you a lot. I was afraid you'd be hurt, much more afraid than I was of my own troubles, surprisingly."

She turned and he could see the great dark eyes clearly in the moonlight. For a moment there was silence, then she spoke.

"Hiero, I'm not really a runaway slave girl," she began, hesitantly.

"Now really," said he, suddenly annoyed for no reason he could think of. "I'd already come to that fascinating conclusion. And I don't give a damn, either, even if it seems so important to you. I was talking about how I felt about a-a-well, friend, a girl I liked, and who and what you are in your own benighted, barbarous country is of no conceivable interest to me at all!"

"Oooh!" she gasped. "You selfish, arrogant *man*! I was trying to tell you something important, but as far as I'm concerned, you can go get in a boat and go back to your Dead Isle as fast as possible! You're half-dead yourself, and you look like a dug-up body and stink worse!" Furious, she stamped away into the night, leaving the equally angry priest glaring after her.

His annoyance left him quickly and he scratched his head ruefully. *Now why did I get so angry?* he wondered. *I was the one who blew up first.* He could not see the growing fear of personal involvement and other even stronger emotions were clashing within him.

What news? he sent Gorm, rubbing his dirty, unshaven face.

Nothing stirs in the night, came the answer from nearby. *I can feel nothing, smell nothing but the ordinary night creatures. The enemy has withdrawn, perhaps to the island you were on.*

Wait here, he sent, *and all keep watch. I'm going to bathe and get clean.*

He walked slowly to the dunes and climbed them even more slowly. The Inland Sea lay empty and beautiful once more, under the bright moon. Only a light wind riffled the waves. His thoughts ranged far beyond his eyesight as he sought for news of his enemies. Up and down the coast went his mind. Never once did he encounter anything but the brain of a beast or bird.

Then he gathered his new strength and his mind ranged far out, miles away over the water to where he knew the Dead Isle brooded. The new mental wave sought for the evil minds it knew to be there and found—nothingness!

Shocked, Hiero tried again. It was no use. There, out in the distant fortress, the Unclean had built a mind shield of their own. He could locate the island and even sense minds there, but he could learn nothing. He was in the position of a man who tries to peer through the dirty glass of a neglected aquarium. Behind the barrier he can sense dim shapes moving, but what they are and what doing remains a mystery.

That was quick, he acknowledged grudgingly, as he slid down to the beach and stripped. Behind him he heard Klootz also coming down the sand hill. The big morse was not going to risk losing his master again, and was determined to mount guard.

As he washed himself, and shaved with his gear from the saddlebags, the priest brooded over the new enemy shield. Obviously, they were unsure of his present powers. But S'duna and his crew must have felt certain that a new mind power existed and they had managed to nullify it in a very short time. They could not prevent Hiero from sensing where they were, but they had completely stopped any penetration beyond that.

The moonlight was strong enough so that he was able, after washing his clothes and changing to his set of spares, to retouch his badges of rank with the paint stick. Feeling a hundred times better and only missing the weight of his medallion, for he had thrown the remaining lump away, he headed back for the dunes again, Klootz falling in behind.

As he topped the crest, he found the girl and the bear climbing the other side. For a second the blood beat in his temples as he looked down at her, then he controlled himself with an effort. *God in heaven, what is the matter with me?* he wondered.

In her turn she stared coldly enough at him, then merely smiled politely. It was an almost overwhelming temptation to invade her mind. *What in the nine Hells was she thinking? Why do I care?* repeated his mind, warding off the answer which made him so nervous.

"I'm sorry I was impolite back there," he said stiffly. "Please put it down to being tired." His voice sounded artificial even to himself, and he cursed his own clumsiness as he spoke.

"Not at all, Per Hiero," she said lightly. "I'm sure I overtaxed your strength and was being silly. Please forgive me!"

They glared at one another from behind frozen masks until Hiero mounted Klootz and held down his hand for her to take and then lifted her up before him. With Gorm ranging in front, once more they were a team.

After a while, the tension went out of both Hiero and Luchare. They did not speak again of the curious and disturbing exchange which had just taken place, but common sense made them both talk naturally of other things. The strained feelings were put aside by mutual and unspoken consent, buried but not forgot by either party.

As Klootz carried them along at his mile-eating amble, Hiero explained what he thought might be the next order of occurances.

"They must know fairly well where we are," he said. "Now they're somewhat scared of me, but that won't last too long.

"Still, here's how it would seem. We must go on, round the end of the Inland Sea or even across it, and get to the shore on the southeastern edge near this Neeyana place you went through. The Unclean will have alerted all their groups and allies ahead of us, you can be sure of that. My maps, even *their* maps, show nothing ahead on this coast but a complex of marking which apparently mean Dead Cities. Now I'm supposed to hunt certain Dead Cities, but these particular ones, no. For one thing, they seem to be half-submerged. The Unclean map I took from the man I killed up North shows the Palood coming south again and touching the Inland Sea for the last time, just where the city markings are. I'd hoped to cut north before this, but we haven't time now or the thrower either. I'd need that to fight the big marsh animals."

They rode on beneath the moon until dawn, always on the landward side of the dunes, which necessarily slowed their pace. Klootz had to pick his way through thickets and palmetto scrub and also avoid cactuses and he could not move at the speed he used on the open beach. But Hiero dared not expose them in the open, not with S'duna and his evil company ready to pounce from offshore. All the time he monitored the mental bands, looking for any trap or signal, but the mind waves were silent. Evidently the Unclean had developed some inkling of his powers and were lying low, and not communicating. This was all the more dangerous. But, as the night drew on, he lost the ability to detect the Dead Isle at all, and this made him feel a little better. If his new powers could not reach out to them, the reverse was probably true. Also, though he could not prove it, he had a feeling that their newly-developed shield was linked somehow to the fortress, to Manoon itself. Perhaps it was an actual physical device of some sort such as the one he had seen his Unclean warder use, a mechanical amplifier of the mental powers. In this case, his thoughts went on, it might be too cumbersome to move. He would only have to avoid fortresses and concentrations of the Unclean. If he could find them, that is!

At dawn, they sheltered under a dense clump of some squat palm. Hiero had once again become wary of observation from above, though he had seen no Unclean flier since entering the marsh far to the West. This was no assurance that none was above however, and he dared not try and use the eyes of a bird lest the enemy be able to get on their track. He did not even want to cast the Forty Symbols, though that was mainly because he was depressed.

They ate quietly and drowsed through the long, hot day.

He occupied himself with searching the neighboring trees and shrubs until he found one he liked, a low, tough thing, whose shiny black wood met his chopping blade with a resounding 'clang' when he cut at it. Off and on, he worked at securing some heavy pieces of this wood all day, and by nightfall and the recommencement of their journey, he had what he wanted. He had been forced to resharpen his sword and his belt knife many times, particularly the latter.

"It's for a crossbow," he explained, when Luchare questioned him. "A Killman, a trained soldier, that is, ought to be able to make a complete set of weapons out of almost anything. I have no thrower any longer, and a heavy crossbow is the next best thing I know. I may use animal horn later, if I can get any, and I need metal and feathers or something for bolts. It will take a while, but I've got nothing better to do."

"Could you show me how?"

"Why not? I've got more than enough wood for a second one here. The better we're armed, the more chances we have. Look here, I'm whittling on this stock. The butt end runs so—"

It was hard to explain at night while they were riding, but during the next day he was able to sketch on sand so now both of them whittled away on their weapons, chatting companionably as they did. Long spells of outward silence usually meant that they were talking to Gorm who lay and watched them as they worked. Hiero had outlined the route ahead as he saw it, and warned the bear that the area seemed to be very dangerous and filled with the Dead Cities. To his surprise, Gorm seemed somewhat contemptuous.

I have been in some of them to the north, the places of your human past, he explained. *They are evil; Unclean things there, what you call the Man-rats and others, but they are clumsy and do not use their noses and ears, almost as bad as you two,* he added. *I am not afraid of such places.*

Hiero learned that the young bear had indeed ventured into several of the ruined towns of Kanda at one time or another, though he became evasive when asked why. *The Elder folk have us do it,* he finally sent, and would say nothing more. But the priest gathered that it was some kind of test, perhaps an emergence into adulthood.

He was quick to tell Gorm that the vast Dead Cities of the south were nothing like the abandoned places he might have seen in most of Kanda, being far larger and apt to be ten times as dangerous. Luchare chimed in to add her views.

"There are several of them in D'alwah," she said to Hiero. "Tell him plainly, you're better than I, that no one, save for the Unclean, goes there at all. Strange things, horrible things, are said to lurk there, creatures which are not found elsewhere."

Perhaps, was the bear's calm answer. *I am always careful. But we must go there anyway, so why worry?*

"My people have a few strange instruments," Luchare offered. "They are either very old or copied from very old ones, made before The Death, it is said. The priests and a few nobles whom they trust keep them. When it becomes necessary for someone to go near a Dead City, or one of the Deserts of The Death, one of these is taken out of safekeeping and sent along. It tells you when the invisible death is still there, the flesh-rot."

"Yes," said Hiero absently, eyeing the grain of the wood as he whittled

142

at his crossbow. "I know what you mean, We have them too. What you call the 'invisible death' is actually lingering atomic radiation. We can't produce it but we know about it up North." He laid down the bow and watched the setting sun a moment before continuing. "As long as you're with us, you won't need one," he smiled. "Klootz and I are trained to detect it with our bodies. And I suspect our fat friend can do it too." A question to Gorm elicited the fact that he knew well the danger of hard radiation and could detect its sources easily.

Luchare marvelled inwardly. She would rather have been flayed alive than let it show, but every attribute Hiero demonstrated seemed to put him on another and higher plane from herself. In her heart, she felt that her pride in her exalted origin was simply a last defense against admitting a foreigner of no particular birth was too good for a girl from the barbarous South, no matter how lofty her social position.

Both too preoccupied and too honorable to probe her mind and a prey to conflicting emotions himself, Hiero saw nothing on her face to indicate any of them.

"Let's take another look at the maps," he now said. "We are fast getting into what seems a very nasty area. Did you hear the frogs last night?"

They had all heard the increasing racket of the amphibian chorus and all knew what it meant. The Palood was angling toward the coast again. The soggy world of fen and marsh met the symbols of the half-drowned cities on the Unclean map, and could not be far ahead.

"Look, if we can get through here," he went on, "this symbol down the coast might well be your Neeyana, Luchare. Now, I can't read the peculiar script they use and knowing them, it may be in code as well. But see," his finger indicated a wavy line going away east from the southeastern corner of the Inland Sea. "This looks as if it might be the trail you came over with the people who took you captive. This blob here then looks like a good bet for a desert of The Death. See, it has the same mark as these circle things just ahead that must be Dead Cities.

"Now then, beyond that desert, here to the south, are three more cities, Dead Cities. One is very close to the desert marking. Those three are marked on my own maps too, the first more heavily. They are among the few that are. This is where I'm supposed to start looking for—what I need." He rolled up the set of maps and carefully restored them to the saddlebag.

Again they set out in the half light of evening. Not only were the frogs growing louder, but the buzzing, biting insects had made an unwelcome reappearance also. Hiero's salve was now exhausted, and there was little they could do but grimly endure, slapping when the nuisances became unbearable.

Once more, Klootz began slopping through puddles and mires. The great reeds and giant dock leaves now looked up in the dark again, replacing the dry land growth through which they had marched for so long.

All through the night they moved on at a walk. Twice they had to circle broad pools from which bubbles of marsh gas rose and burst. Once Klootz stamped a great hoof down on a pale snake, an adder of some sort which made the mistake of striking at him. Hiero roved the night with his brain, searching for danger, but he was too unfamiliar with his abilities to be very sanguine. An amphibian mind is the same whether the creature is twenty yards long or three inches, and it gives off much the same emotional values and neural reactions. No true "thought" occurs at all. Thus, if the priest were trying to see if the thing he was inspecting was one of the huge frog monsters which had almost attacked him before, he had only the view from the animal's own eyes, dim at best, to give him a scale of reference. Once indeed, they heard one of the great creatures bellow, but the sound came from far away.

The first faint glimmer of dawn was barely beginning to lighten the east when they came to a halt. A few moments earlier, Hiero had ordered Klootz to stop and had got down himself to test the surface on which they were travelling.

"Thought so," he muttered half to himself. "There's only an inch or so of muck here. I heard the hooves strike something hard quite a ways back." He raised his voice so the girl could hear. "I think we're on a road, or at least something once constructed, a thing artificial." *Gorm, come back and tell me what you think.*

Man-built, very old, was the bear's verdict. They stood listening to the frog and insect chorus on the warm night, while clouds of gnats and mosquitoes descended on them. Hiero felt the bite of a leech through a tear on his ankle, and looking down saw that the morse's legs were covered with the black, worm shapes, clearly visible in the waning of moonset.

"Day's coming," he said. "We'll have to find cover." He instructed the bear to look for shelter and began to walk by the morse's head.

The decision was soon made for them. With no warning, they rounded a clump of the big reeds and found a still expanse of open water before them, broken only by dark hillocks and peculiar, tall peaked islands, fast taking shape in the dawning light. Looking about, Hiero spied a low mound not far away to one side, which had some vegetation growing on it. He remounted and Gorm and the morse floundered through muck, for they quickly left the firm surface, until they reached the place.

Klootz heaved himself out of the mud, which would have been up to a human neck, with a sucking noise and the two humans quickly dismounted. They were on a flat-topped island in the mud, about ten yards square. Thick bushes and even a small palm grew on it and none of the marsh plants, proving that it was solid ground. While looking at its curiously regular edges, the priest unsaddled the morse and began to pick leeches off his mount's body.

"This is an ancient building, I feel sure," he said at length, yanking the last rubbery body off Klootz and hurling it out into the marsh. "We're standing on a flat roof. God himself knows how much is sunk below us. This building could have been tall enough to reach, well, the height of a hundred men. The muck might be easily that deep."

They covered themselves against the insects as well as they could, and then all crouched down under the cover of the palm tree and bushes, to pass the day as best they might. Hiero made sure that they were covered from above by cutting a few branches and laying them over the four bodies. They would be hot, dirty and uncomfortable, but also hard to see.

As the day flooded the landscape with light, their spirits sank, at least those of the humans did. Klootz ate steadily at every piece of browse within reach and Gorm managed to sleep, keeping his bearish thoughts to himself.

But the landscape, or rather waterscape, which now lay before them could hardly be considered inspiring even with a clear sky above and a warm sun.

The Inland Sea had vanished. As far as the eye could reach, there was water, but it was brown and still. From it, stretching equally far out of sight, thrust the ruins of a vast and ancient metropolis, the hecatomb of a vanished race. Some of the buildings were higher than tall trees. Their original height made the imagination boggle, for now they rose from the unplumbed water. Smaller ones, or perhaps those which simply had sunk further into the surrounding mud, were only domed islets, covered with vegetation, like the one on which the travelers now lay concealed. Others were between these two types and they made up the majority, rising a few stories from the water, their tops alone heavily laced with plant growth. Even through these clustering plants and the wear of millennia, the destruction by some inconceivable force was still visible. Many of the ruins were shattered and broken, as if by some titanic blow, one which combined both fire and shock. Water plants, huge lily pads and arrow weed, others like great floats of green bladders, covered much of the still water. Here and there, great piles of logs lay tumbled, many overgrown with vines and creepers, the wreckage hurled in by past storms.

The brown and black buildings had dark and gaping windows showing in many places, where vegetation had not obscured them. Here and there amazingly, a fragment of incredibly ancient glass still glinted in the sun and occasionally even a scrap of some rustproof metal. It was a drear and sad prospect to see, a world of death and old ruin, old beyond memory.

The voices of the frogs had died down with the coming of the sun, but the insects still buzzed and stung, although mercifully in far lesser numbers.

Other life there was little, save for a few scattered flocks of some small dark birds, which flew silently about the roofs of some of the buildings. Large blotches of white stained other buildings, looking to Hiero like the marks of nesting birds of a larger sort, but the birds themselves were absent. Perhaps the season was over and they had gone elsewhere.

The priest probed the area with his mind and found nothing. In the waters and under them, there was much life, but it was not of a kind he could reach or understand, having no intelligence, only appetites and fears.

Yet he did not like the place. Even in the sun there was a brooding presence to it, a feeling that all was not well.

All day they watched the buildings and the water, but saw nothing beyond the movements of small creatures of mud and pool. The afternoon drew on and the sun sank lower toward the west. The first frog voices began to sound, hesitantly at first, then louder. The insect voices also restarted and their humming battalions attacked in new numbers.

"Let's get out of here," choked the priest, spitting out a cloud of bugs.

They repacked Klootz and mounted. Hiero saw nothing for it but to try and move around the shoreline, muddy though it was, and circle the forgotten city. The water between the buildings, he felt sure, was too deep and also too extensive to try swimming. Who knew what lurked under the surface?

Hardly had they started, indeed Gorm had barely put a front paw off the islet, when they all froze.

The insect and batrachian chorus ceased. Over the still lagoons and through the ruined towers of the ancients, there rang a long, echoing wail. As they listened, it came again. "Aowh, aowh, aaaaouh," it sobbed, rising and falling on the evening air. Three times the mournful notes hung suspended, their place of origin a mystery. Then there was silence.

As the four listened, a frog spoke hesitantly, then another. Soon the full croaking orchestra was in full swing again.

"Could you tell where it came from?" asked Luchare.

"No, and neither could Gorm. It seemed to be some distance away, out in the water, but I don't like it. There is an intelligence here, I feel it in my bones. Something malignant, evil, watching and waiting. We must stop a while longer while I think. I don't like this plunging into the night with no protection. The Unclean may be here, hidden perhaps by a mind shield."

Full night was almost upon them. Only a red line showed the sun's last light. Hiero dismounted, his brow wrinkled. *Ought they to turn back? But where?* He felt he was being stupid. There must be some plan, some more sensible method of doing things that he was missing. *Damn!* He slapped at the swarming mosquitoes, more in frustration than anything else.

"I wish we had a boat," said the girl, looking about. "But it would have to be a big one to hold Klootz. Then we could get out of this mud, at least."

"Up north we build—Holy Mother, forgive my dumbness!" he exploded. "We build *rafts*, rafts for our animals when there's no bridge! And I've been sitting all day staring at a thousand log piles, logs all but covered with long vines! The only thing I haven't been given is someone to step up and kick me awake! Come on down from there and we'll get to work!"

It was true. The storm-brought drifts of logs lay everywhere. All about their islet were numbers of them, a few with leaves still left on their branches.

Even Gorm was a help now. Klootz was hitched to a vine rope and tugged free the ones they wanted, while the bear helped untangle branches and vines. Hiero hacked off limbs with his sword-knife and generally supervised while Luchare bound the big logs tightly together with cut lengths of tough vine.

At length they had done all they could. The priest had cut two twenty-foot poles and also made a couple of crude paddles, the latter in case the water grew too deep for the poles. The whole raft was about thirty feet long and fifteen wide. It was incredibly clumsy, but absolutely necessary, Hiero felt.

I (can) *swim*, Klootz sent, gingerly testing the structure with a huge foot.

No, Stupid, came back his master. *Danger under the water. You ride.*

It took every ounce of everyone's muscle to get the great thing off the mud and into water deep enough to float, especially with the big morse aboard. He finally had to leap on to it from the islet and the shock drove the raft momentarily under the surface. But he landed neatly and stood carefully and it rose again, spilling water, and floated.

The priest took the stern pole and Luchare the bow. The bear crouched next to Klootz, who had been told to lie down, and each watched his own side for any danger.

Hiero shoved hard and the queer craft with its strange cargo of passengers slid off into the insect-haunted dark. It was pointed straight for the broken towers of the dead and ruined past.

8: *THE PERIL*
AND THE SAGE

The huge raft was even clumsier than Hiero had feared. Still, with patience, it was just possible to move it slowly along. The chief problem was the vast tangled mats of vegetation which lay entwined on the water's surface. He had to lean over and cut them aside with his sword and he finally sat down and lashed the sword firmly to one end of his pole. He used leather thongs from his repair kit and tied everything twice before he was satisfied.

From then on he could cut more easily, and without having a fear that something would seize his arm as he leaned far over the raft's edge, and also without having to put down the pole.

Something bad near! suddenly came the bear's mental voice. *Not a human, something else which thinks and not-thinks.*

Hiero rested on his pole and so did Luchare. The great raft moved sluggishly forward for a few yards on momentum alone while all strained to hear the night, both with physical senses and mental ones. But there was nothing, nothing save the almost deafening chorus of frogs and insects, a medley of croaks, trills and stridulations which made ordinary speech almost inaudible.

It is gone, sent Gorm. *It was quick, like a moving fish. Now—nothing.*

The priest did not delude himself into believing the bear might be mistaken. Gorm's alertness had saved them several times already. If his quick mental perceptions, which after all were not human, had detected something, then something was there!

Thinks and not-thinks! There was no time to try and find out what the bear meant, not now. Worried and frustrated by the intangible menace, Hiero looked all around, taking in the still, dark water, the nearer buildings and the patches of floating plants. He noted in passing that Klootz' huge, flat antlers were hung with the last shreds of velvet and were now almost ready for use as weapons.

But under the pale moonlight nothing stirred. At last Hiero signalled to Luchare and thrust his pole deep in the mud again. Once more, the ponderous raft slid forward, headed for the wide opening between two towering ruins. Frogs blinked and fell silent, their cold eyes goggling from huge lily pads and bladderworts as the cumbersome thing went by. Once it had gone, the renewed chorus broke out in its wake.

As they passed into the first shadows of the shattered monoliths, the raft met with its first major check, a tangled mass of some floating weed. Hiero ran to the front of the raft (it had no real bow) and began to hack with his pole-knife while Luchare aided him by thrusting the cut portions aside. Fortunately there was deep water under the weeds and once cut they were little trouble. Still it was arduous work for the raft had to be poled a few yards and then the cutting had to commence again. It was to be only the beginning of such work.

Through the night the raft's slow progress continued. Black windows and gaping rents in the rotted, ancient masonry leered down at the wayfarers as they struggled on. Once, a cloud of bats issuing from one such ruin and swirling up across the face of the moon made everyone jump, but beyond that, nothing happened but hard work.

On two occasions they encountered a bank of thick mud, risen up invisible under the water plants ahead, and were forced to backtrack and seek another opening through the maze of the old city. Fortunately, there was one available each time. Again, while crossing wide stretches of water (perhaps, Hiero reflected, the remains of ancient squares or parks), they had lost touch with the bottom entirely. He blessed God's aiding his forethought in cutting the crude paddles. The silt-laden water was so calm that even these were sufficient to move the raft along until the poles could be brought into use once more.

As the first light of dawn came into the eastern sky, the Metz looked forward at his human partner and somehow both managed to grin. They were both filthy, drenched in sweat, palms blistered by their pole work and it seemed that not an inch of their bodies was unbitten by gnats and mosquitoes. But they were alive and healthy, and they must have come quite a distance, which was some satisfaction.

"I don't want to travel by day, not in this place," said Hiero aloud. "Look, over there, a sort of sloping place. We can spend the day there, and still be at least partly hidden."

The rapidly growing light revealed them to be in one of the numerous squares, as Hiero had come to call them. On three sides vast and rotted stone

150

structures loomed up far above their heads, pierced with countless windows and ancient scars and rents, black openings on nothing. Long vines and twisted lianas hid many other places.

The fourth side was more hopeful, however. Some huge building had evidently collapsed under the weight of the countless years, and in the not too distant past. The result was a great pile of rubble and broken stone, thrusting up in an irregular mound from the quiet waters of the lagoon. A few large bushes grew in one place, probably survivors of the original structure, but otherwise it was quite bare of vegetation.

Soon the raft lay in a shallow cove next to the island mound. Leaves covered it and to casual inspection it was one more tangle of drifted logs. The travelers, two and four legged, soon were huddled together under the clump of bushes, waiting in sticky irritability for the sun to rise even higher and add another dimension to their discomfort.

Gorm - what was the thing that frightened you? sent Hiero. *The mind touch you caught as we started, I mean?*

Something new, admitted the bear, as he tried to cover his sensitive nose from the crowding mosquitoes. *Only one, whatever it was; a bad mind, quick, sly, full of hate for everything not like itself. But not a human, not any animal I know either. Maybe*—there was a pause as the young bear reflected—*maybe, a little like a frog, but one that thinks!*

While the others absorbed this, he added, *it went away. Perhaps to find more.* With this parting message he covered his nose completely with his forepaws and fell asleep. His thick black fur saved him from most of the other bites and he seemed to have the ability to sleep anywhere, at any time.

"We'll have to keep watch," said Hiero to the girl. "Try and sleep, and I'll take the first one." He wiped the sweat from his eyes with a filthy hand and managed to get dirt in one of them. As he rubbed harder, Luchare pulled his hand down and from somewhere produced a damp and (relatively) clean cloth with which she sponged his face, cleaning his eye out in the process.

"There," she said in tones of satisfaction. "Now keep your dirty fingers out of it. What do you think Gorm felt, Hiero? Could he be imagining things? This place is enough to make anyone have bad dreams, even a bear." She looked out at the brooding land, or rather waterscape, before them. Even under the now completely-risen sun, the silent hulks of the past were not a pleasant sight. The green vegetation mats of water plants, the vines crawling up the buildings' shattered faces, the trees and bushes on their pinnacles, all added to the feeling of desolation.

"He doesn't imagine things," said the priest. He was trying to ignore the dirty, but enchanting, face so close to his and concentrate instead on what he was saying.

"There's something here, maybe a lot of somethings. I can't tap the mental channels, but I can *feel* thought going on around me, do you understand. Maybe several kinds of thought. We're going to have to be careful, very careful." *And lucky, very lucky,* he added to himself.

Another long day passed. They ate and drank sparingly. The canteens were running low and though Klootz and the bear did not seem to mind the lagoon water, Hiero tested it and it was foul, full of green matter and with a sickening smell. He did not intend to drink of it except as a last resort.

The sun reached zenith and the afternoon began and slowly waned. Luchare finally slept, and so did both animals. Save for the humming insects, which never ceased their myriad assault, no sound broke the silence. The towers were empty of bird life and none appeared in the blue, cloudless sky. Listening on all the mental channels known to him, the priest could detect no coherent thought. Yet all around him, intangible and in stealth, some spying, probing presence seemed to glare at them. A busy undercurrent of activity was at work; he felt it in his bones, but neither could actually locate or identify it.

They had just repacked the raft and were easing the big morse aboard when they froze in their tracks. The light of late evening still let them see the buildings around them clearly, but their eyes could detect no movement. The frog chorus had barely begun.

From out of the distant east, the direction they themselves wanted to travel, there came the same strange cry they had heard the previous evening. The frogs fell silent.

"Aoooh, aoooh, aaaoooooouh," it wailed mournfully. Three times it came and then there was silence once more, save for the insect buzz. Slowly the frogs began again while the two animals and their human friends stood in the gathering dark, each immersed in his or her own thoughts.

"Oh, I hate this place!" burst out Luchare. "It's not like the rest of the world at all, but some dead, wet, horrible wasteland full of moaning ghosts! The City of the Dead!" She broke into tears, buying her face in her cupped hands. Her long-held control had finally given way.

Hiero moved to her side and put his arms around her and patted her back, until at length her wet face was raised to his, a question in the great eyes which he had no trouble answering. He lowered his head and drank in the wild sweetness of her lips for the first time. Her strong young arms rose and tightened around his neck and when the kiss finally ceased, she buried her face in his jacket. He still stroked her back, saying nothing, his eyes staring sightlessly over her head into the gathering night. The bites of a dozen midges and mosquitoes were unfelt.

"What was that for?" came a muffled voice from his shirt, "a present for a frightened child?"

"That's right," he agreed in cheerful tones. "I do that to all the scared brats I meet. Of course, sometimes it recoils on me. I might even get to like it."

She looked up at once, suspicious that he was laughing at her, but even in the last light of day what she saw in his eyes was so plain that her face was jammed back into his chest once more, as if what she had read in his expression had scared her. There was another short silence.

"I love you, Hiero," came a small voice from his chest.

"I love you, too," he said almost sadly. "I'm not at all sure it's a good idea. In fact, I'm fairly certain it's a bad one, a very bad one. I have been set a task so important that the last sane human civilization may fall if I should fail to carry it out. I need a further distraction like a third leg." He smiled down at the angry face which had popped up again.

"I seem to be helpless, however." He tightened his grip around the firm body. "Win or lose, we stay together from now on. I'd worry more if you were somewhere else."

She snuggled closer, as if somehow she could bind herself to him. They stood thus, the world forgotten until a mental voice whose very flatness made it seem sardonic broke in.

Human mating is indeed fascinating. But we are in a dangerous place to study it. That is something of which I feel certain.

This acted like a pail of cold water. They almost sprang apart. Studiously ignoring the bear, who sat looking up at them from the middle of the raft where he sat next to Klootz, they seized their poles and pushed off into the humming, croaking dark. The moon had not yet risen, but the stars were out and both of them had excellent night vision.

Once again, a night of toil and discomfort lay before them. Yet they detected no signs of an enemy, though there were moments when the appearance of one would have come as an almost welcome distraction. On and on through the drowned city they poled, hacked and paddled their way. Hiero fell overboard once, but popped back up in a second, streaming foul, muddy water, at least cool for a few seconds.

The moon rose and made their task a little easier. The silent black buildings stared down from a thousand ruined eyes as they struggled past. Perhaps they were following boulevards and esplanades which had once echoed to the tramp of vanished parades. All were buried now, forgotten and lost under the weight of centuries of mud and water.

Luchare and Hiero had become so inured to their toil that the first light of dawn was a surprise, brought to their notice by the fact that they could now see one another's faces clearly.

"My love," said the priest wearily, "if I look half as dirty and tired as you do I must be the worst looking thing around."

"You look much worse," was the answer. "I may never kiss you again, at least not until I can scrape you off with a knife first." Tired as she was, the girl's voice was buoyant with love and happiness.

"Look at that damned morse," grunted Hiero, changing the subject. "He's getting back at me for all the riding, galloping, spurring and general hard labor I've put him through."

Klootz was indeed asleep, only his great ears twitching under his antlers, giant legs tucked neatly under his barrel. Beside him, the bear also slept on, as usual allowing nothing to come between him and his rest.

"They're supposed to be on watch. We could have been eaten by now with guards like that!"

"I know, Hiero, but we haven't been. I'm so tired and dirty it would almost be a relief, anyway. Where are we, do you suppose?"

The raft was drifting slowly along what once must have been a mighty avenue. The close-packed buildings on either side were so tall, even in their antique ruin, that most of the sunlight never reached the water lapping at their sides. As a result, few plants grew here. The water too, seemed much deeper. The two had been using the paddles for the last hour or so.

They could see light far ahead and equally far behind, but great ruined structures hemmed them in on both sides. There were bays and gaps in the looming, moss-hung cliffs and walls of stone, shadowed niches and caves, but the general effect was that of being in the bottom of some vast canyon. As the daylight grew, this effect was heightened, rather than the reverse.

Hiero looked about him carefully. Then his eye returned to one spot; he saw something which sent a cold chill up his spine.

Luchare! His mental voice jolted her as no spoken word could have. *Don't make a sound. Look at that opening to the right, at the water through the big hole in that building.*

The gloomy light was nevertheless quite strong enough to delineate the place Hiero was staring at. A huge masonry wall, or possibly a vast gate, for it

154

was hard to tell, had collapsed in a distant age. The water flowed through the wide gap and into a still pool, hundreds of yards across, completely surrounded by more shadowed and lofty structures as far as the two could see.

In the middle of the pool, directly opposite the entrance to the watery "street" on which now rode the raft, a tall thin object rose directly from the surface of the quiet water. At first, Hiero had assumed that it was some inanimate structure of an unknown type, perhaps a spire of some long-sunk house. But his eye had strayed back to it, warned by a physical sense he could not define and with a thrill of horror he saw that it was ever so gently moving. Then, the shape, like that of a giant amber leaf, complete with ribs, or vanes, became clear. They were looking at a colossal fin, whose owner lay just under the turgid surface of the water. The sheer bulk of the creature defied the imagination.

It must lie there in ambush, sent Hiero, *waiting for what passes. If we stay still, there's a chance.*

Indeed, a gentle current was taking them past the opening, although at a rate which seemed absolutely leaden. The two animals still lay in the center of the raft, apparently asleep. Yet both were not.

I heard you, came Gorm's thought. *What is the danger? I can see nothing.*

Something very large, just under the water, came Hiero's answer. *Do not move. It watches. It could eat this whole raft, I think. I will try to reach its mind.*

Try he did, on every mental band he knew, including the new one he had learned to use while on Manoon. But as the raft lazily drifted on, he had to acknowledge defeat. Whatever monster lay embayed back there, it sent out nothing he could distinguish from the thousands of other life essences in the waters around them. The size of the thing was no clue to its mental activity and sheer bulk gave off no mental radiation, at least any that he could perceive.

They drifted until even the buildings around the place where they had seen the fin were out of sight. Then and then only did Hiero signal to Luchare to resume paddling. And both did so with great care, being careful to splash as little as possible.

They had still a very long way to go down the gloomy canyon when Hiero exclaimed aloud, "Push her over to this side, I see something we badly need."

Between the two of them, they got the raft wedged into the angle of a great building which jutted out a little beyond its fellows. Hiero told Luchare to hang on and hold it there.

155

"Look," he said, "we're in luck, a copper band around this level of windows."

He had glimpsed the sickly verdigris of the copper as the raft approached it and remembered their three-quarters-finished crossbows. Using his belt knife and the pole's butt end, he managed to pry a strip weighing several pounds loose and on to the raft. Under the coating of verdigris the metal was untouched.

"I think it's bronze," he said, looking carefully at it. "Better than copper too, lots harder. We have enough to tip a hundred arrows here. Lucky it lasts forever."

Luchare shivered. "I'm glad too, but let's get moving. I still find this place makes me sick. All those old windows seem to be watching us. And where are we going to spend today? The sun's all the way up now, even if it looks so gloomy down here."

"I don't know. We'll have to keep paddling, that's all. Maybe we'll find an island or a cove or something. Perhaps an opening in the side of one of these buildings. One without an occupant," he added.

Despite the steady increase of light, they had little choice save to keep moving. The gentle current was growing stronger for one thing, and for another, no more large breaks in the walls of stone occurred. The eddying stream helped now though; the opening at the far end of the long line of buildings drew rapidly closer, far more rapidly than if they had been forced to propel themselves unaided. And the current also had prevented the formation of any mats of vegetation, so that no more cutting was necessary.

Still, it was almost noon when the raft shot from the darkness between the lines of towering ruins and out into the sunlight. For a moment the passengers were dazzled by the light, but when they saw clearly, Luchare let out an exclamation of delight and dropping her paddle, clapped her hands together.

They had emerged into, and now were drifting in, a small lake, whose clear blue water indicated great depth and a probable close connection with the Inland Sea. Around its fringe, many buildings formed a ring, save in one direction, the south, where a wide gap was evident.

But it was the middle of the lake that held their attention. A small, green island, covered with bushes and palm trees and showing patches of grass here and there, rose out of the lake's waters. Bright colored flowers, yellows and blues, glowed amid the herbage. And flocks of small birds circled here and there, while a raft of mingled geese and ducks, brown and white, fed in the shallows on the side facing the raft. After the days and nights in the gloom and stench, the insects and frogs, the fear and the labor, the place looked like Paradise.

156

"Come on, Hiero," she urged. "Let's get over there quickly. That place is big enough to even have a spring. We can get clean. Those trees may have fruit, and we can probably get a few ducks. Hurry!"

But the priest stood immobile, holding his paddle. True the island did indeed look inviting. Perhaps too much so! He had not forgotten, tired though he was, the stealthy sensations of the past few days, the weird calling in the twilight, the feeling that the party were somehow being kept under observation. This place was still surrounded by the drowned city and its ravaged buildings, attractive though it looked.

But fatigue won over caution. They had to rest somewhere, and both he and Luchare were nearly at the end of their respective ropes. Also, the need for food, fresh food, and clean water was urgent. And the animals needed them both as well.

"Come on then," he said and began to paddle. "At least we can hide there for the rest of the day. But don't talk so loudly! This place is no Abbey home for the aged and unwell! I still sense some strange mental undercurrent that scares me, that I can't pin down."

A gentle sloping beach on one end made the little island almost perfect. And there *was* a spring, or rather a dew pond, filled with clear, sweet water, set in the island's center and surrounded by tall ferns and sweet-smelling flowers. To make matters complete, Hiero found a bed of fresh-water clams in the shallows of the beach and the three carnivores feasted on the raw, juicy shellfish until they could hold no more. Klootz paid the clams no attention but began to put away pounds of grass and shrubbery at once.

By mid-afternoon, washed, cleaned and with full stomachs, all were fast asleep, save for Klootz who still roved the island selecting the finest bits of leaf and twig, while mounting an alert watch at the same time. Even he had rolled in the clear water and now he was engaged at intervals in rubbing the last of the soft velvet off his great rack of gleaming, black antlers. At times he paused and looked about, then, seeing nothing, fell to eating again.

So exhausted were the two humans that they slept through the afternoon and most of the entire night that followed. Hiero awoke in the darkness before dawn, and realized at once what had happened. Before he could even form a self-reproach, the bear's voice echoed in his mind. *You needed the rest. Nothing has come near. But still—something watches. I know it, just as I know the sun rises.*

We must be alert, Hiero replied. He stretched, feeling so stiff that he could hardly move, although the sleep had done him a lot of good.

Luchare awoke at the movement from her place nearby. "Is that today's new sun, that dim glow? We must have had a long sleep. But I still feel like sleeping again, Is that wicked?"

"No, it's not. We're both still exhausted. I'm going to declare a rest day. I think we can finish those crossbows and cut some bolts for them too, which will make me feel a lot better. We're going to need some missile weapons for hunting, if for no other reason."

The day began more pleasantly than any in weeks. Hiero managed to finish his own crossbow and to cut some bolts from seasoned dead saplings washed up on the island's shore.

Luchare was no help for she spent most of the time arranging her hair, bathing and pelting Hiero with bunches of flower petals whenever she caught him looking "too serious." At mid-afternoon, he gave up on any further work to simply lie with his head in her lap while she gossiped about her past life and speculated on their future together.

"I hope we have a long and happy one, Love," he said at last. "But we're a far and distant way from it now. And you've never mentioned, in all your gabble, just what led you to run away from D'alwah. An arranged marriage, one might guess?"

She gasped in astonishment. "I knew it! You too were peering into my mind!"

"No," He smiled up at the indignant face and with his finger transferred a kiss on the end of the dark aquiline nose. "You admitted you were no slave once before. You're the daughter of one of your great nobles, I imagine, because by your own admission, only the priesthood and the nobility get a chance to learn as much as you have. So it was a fairly easy guess. How great a noble is your father, in your own country's terms, I mean?"

"The greatest," she said in dull tones. There was a silence.

"The actual king, eh?" Hiero no longer smiled. "Now that's a pity. Are you the only child! It might be important."

"I had one older brother but he was killed in a battle with the Unclean. My father wanted me to marry and cement an alliance with the next most powerful state. I knew, everyone knows, all about Efrem of Shespek. He beats and tortures his concubines. His first queen went mad and he had her blinded, divorced her as not being legally married, since the kings cannot marry people who are physically maimed, you see, and put her in a nunnery. That's what I was running away from."

"Can't say as I much blame you," said Hiero, chewing a grass stem. "I rather was hoping to establish contact with various countries, especially yours, so that I could open a trade route and more important, we could start to re-civilize your area. Stealing a princess, the only princess, is a bad start."

She bristled. "What do you mean 're-civilize?' I'll have you know, Per Desteen, my bearded priestling, D'alwah is a great and powerful nation, with two walled cities and countless churches and other big palaces and buildings of stone. To say nothing of a great and brave army!"

Hiero smiled affectionately at her and said nothing. He rolled over on his stomach and still said nothing, his chin pillowed on his arms, apparently staring away off over the lake.

"I see," she said after an even longer pause. "Those things aren't enough to be called civilized by themselves, are they, Hiero?"

"Well, what do you think?" he asked. "They go along with a basis of chattel slavery, a strangle hold on wealth and education by a small propertied class, crushing taxes, a state religion which seems to have degenerated, at least in part, into sheer superstition, and finally incessant, bloody warfare with your neighbors. That last would be too silly and meaningless in any case, but it weakens your society terribly just when it needs its strength the most, to fight the Unclean and the ravening monsters of your own forests. Now you tell me if that's civilization. I'd call it pretty advanced barbarism and a plain path downhill to complete ruin."

"I suppose you're right," she said. "It's just that having been raised as the royal princess of D'alwah, and flattered and lied to by everyone from the time I could talk, I had no way of knowing anything could, or should rather, be any different."

"I know," he said, patting her shoulder. "The amazing thing, little princess, is that you turned out the way you did. Not only lovely but smart, smart enough to admit you don't know everything. The only kind of brains worth having, that is."

Her face bent over his and he pulled her down. The tall grass hid them from any observation and he breathed into her ear, "now?"

"I'm afraid," was the husky, low-voiced answer. "I'm a virgin. That's one reason I was supposed to be so valuable."

"You'll be my wife when we can find another priest. As far as I'm concerned, you're my wife right now. And my love. For ever and ever, until God calls us home. That's what our marriage service says."

Her lips came down on his then and silenced him. The grasses waved gently in the afternoon sun. Once there sounded a small cry, so soft and brief that even the bear could hardly hear it.

These humans! he thought. *At least, that's over with and we can concen-*

159

trate on other matters. He drowsed too in the warm sunlight half-listening to the grinding sounds of Klootz remorselessly demolishing his cud, over and over. The island slept, the silence broken only by the muted call of birds and insect hum.

They both awoke in early morning, or rather were awakened. Neither one said a word as they quickly drew on their clothes. The messages from Gorm, *Awake! They come!*, had hit their two sleeping brains like a thunderclap. In the instant that this took, the terrible wailing cry which had grown so familiar to them came again, louder than they had ever heard it, and this time it did not cease.

"Aoough, aaaouugh, aaaoooough!"

Now, in great volume, it came from all around them. In the half-light over the twilight lagoon, their island no longer seemed a haven of safety, but a tiny morsel of helpless sanity in a chaotic and implacable world. Hiero himself spared a brief and regretful thought for their first love-making, sandwiched between perils and duties, a moment already pre-doomed to evanescence.

With the morse and the bear, they rapidly took station in the center of their island. Around them the booming, menacing wail grew louder still. "Aoough, aaaoooough, aaough!"

Now, clearly outlined in the yet strong light, the travelers saw their enemies, and all knew at once that they had been watched from the beginning of their voyage through the drowned metropolis.

From every side but the open south, they came, in small, narrow craft, half raft—half canoe, apparently made of tightly-bound reeds, pointed at either end. From out between the encircling buildings, across the quarter mile of open water around the island, the strange craft surged, propelled by their owners' webbed hands, as well as paddles. And the white heads in the water between the boats showed where many more were coming fast by simply using their native element.

A new Leemute! Take a frog, thought Hiero, *and stand him up; give him a high-vaulted skull and a pallid skin, white and sickly looking. Give him evil black eyes, like huge bubbles of sparkling, vicious jet. Give him almost man size. Give him knives of bone, as white as his skin and spears of fish bone and bleached bone clubs. And give him hate!* As the things came steadily on, the priest thought of Gorm's first impression, *a frog that thinks. Must have been a scout and we've been stalked.*

The wailing, sobbing cry which had filled the air suddenly ceased. And only then did Hiero realize that the frog things themselves were utterly silent. The strange noise had come from the buildings all around them but not from the creatures themselves. Was it a signal to attack? Who had made it? Many other questions filled his mind, but there was no time for any of them. The first attackers had reached the island and were swarming ashore.

The priest's first instinct had been correct: get away from the lagoon and meet the frog creatures on dry land. They ran awkwardly, half-hopping, half scuttling and were obviously far less at ease with solid dirt under their great webbed toes than the swamp ooze or water. Still, there were many of them and only four of the travelers. But now, Hiero had lapsed into the cold killing fit of his Abbey training. Defeat was not even a consideration.

Luchare got the first one. Her long lance, the extendable javelin Hiero had taken from the Unclean priest, licked out and a frog thing's throat opened in scarlet. A shower of the barbed bone spears came whistling and everyone ducked. One struck Hiero full on the breast and he gasped. It had hardly penetrated the skin! The amphibian Leemutes were no spearmen. Apparently, their skinny arms were not shaped for throwing. Even so, though this was a boost to morale, quickly communicated to the others, there were apparently hundreds of the ugly creatures swarming up the gentle slope from the water. *And they will be getting harder to see,* thought Hiero, for the light was now fading fast.

But again, the things' own physical characteristics worked against them! As the light died, they became more, not less, visible! A strange, spectral glow emanated from their dank, squamous skins, and they were thus outlined in their own luminescence. A weird and frightening sight no doubt, but not to trained fighters and by this time Luchare was one too!

Klootz! sent Hiero. *To me.*

The big morse had been guarding the left flank as the bear did the right, keeping his ground and scything with his great antlers at any Leemute who ventured near. They were afraid of him and few of them tried that side.

Now he lunged forward between Hiero and Luchare, and at a word crouched. Both swung up into the big saddle, one spear couched to the left, the other to the right.

"Charge!" shouted the priest. *Around the island, you big clown,* sent his mind. *Clean up on them! Follow us, Gorm!*

Hiero had suddenly seen the best, indeed the only, method of attack. Once the strange characteristics of the frog things became apparent, it was obvious. Individually no menace, they yet swarmed in such numbers that they yet might pull down an immobile foe if allowed to. But if attacked, and on solid earth where their weak land legs made them doubly vulnerable, things might be different!

The giant bull morse was a creature such as they had never seen, and he was almost invulnerable to their feeble darts, which could barely do more than annoy him. The low bushes, and the few trees were no impediment to his charge at all and he simply tore through the glow of the crowding frog creatures as if they were not there. Their gaping mouths, rimmed with needle fangs, opened voicelessly in terror and rage. But save for the stamping, snorting and grunts of the morse, the growling of the bear, and the gasps of the humans, the strange battle was fought in utter silence. Even as he thrust savagely with his spear, Hiero wondered at the creatures. He had been able to detect no mental activity at all, and since they seemed voiceless, how on earth did they communicate? Twice around the islet they charged, scattering havoc through their phosphorescent foes.

Suddenly, they had won, at least for the present. With no signal that either human could see or hear, a scuttling, shambling rush back to the lagoon began. One instant they were surrounded by a hideous, glowing pack of nightmare demons, the next, innumerable blobs of living light were ebbing away to the water's edge. Even as Hiero signaled a halt, he observed that the dead and wounded were being taken too. *Probably to eat,* he thought sourly, unwilling to concede any decent values to the squattering Leemutes.

"They're gone," breathed Luchare, bloody lance resting across the saddlebow in front of her.

"Yes, but not very far; look!"

The island now was surrounded by a ring of cold fire! The amphibian horde lay in the water, aboard their reed boats or simply floating; it was hard to tell in the dark. But one thing was obvious, that they were not going away. "I think they'll be back all right, come first light probably," continued the priest. "Anyone hurt here?" *Are you all right, Gorm? Klootz, any wounds?*

Their weapons are weak. I thought they might have poison on the points, but there is nothing. I am not even scratched.

Klootz shook hs great antlers angrily. Drops of dark, evil-smelling blood flew back and caught his two riders in the face.

"Phew! I guess you're all right too!"

The man and woman dismounted and stood looking through the night at the weird cordon of light for a moment.

"Come on," said Hiero at length. "Let's clean our weapons and get some food into us. Then we can rest again. I'll take first watch. I've almost finished my crossbow and I want to start to cut and trim some quarrels and bolts. The moon's rising again, and there should be enough light."

"I'm not staying asleep while you work!" his young lady stated flatly

"Maybe we can finish both of the bows between us."

The love and trust in her voice caused a pang deep in Hiero's breast. He had not admitted how forlorn it all looked, even to himself. What could the morning bring but another attack, one in overwhelming numbers this time? His ideas about completing the crossbows were only to avoid having to face the inevitable. Ringed by water and countless aquatic foes, what help could they count on in escaping? None.

A true Killman never gives up, said one part of his training. *A priest trusts in God,* said another. *You've been stuck before; look at Manoon, now,* said a third. He laughed, a quick, short bark and Luchare looked curiously at him. But she said nothing. She was learning that her strange lover was a man of moods.

"All right," he said, "let's get busy them. Our two fur people can keep watch."

It must have been well after midnight when Hiero suddenly stiffened, his sensitive hands pausing, immobile over their work of cutting vanes for the crossbow bolts. A strange mental signal had come to him. Something inimical moved in the night, but behind a shield he could not penetrate. Yet he was conscious of it coming, like a menacing cloud, which still conceals whatever lies within its heart.

Quickly he woke the others, for Luchare had long since collapsed, exhausted, despite her earlier boasts.

I feel it too, came from the bear. *What it is I cannot tell, but you are right; it comes through the dark in our direction. It comes from there.* He indicated the south, where lay the open water.

"Unclean!" burst out Hiero in despair. "These damned frog Leemutes must be more of their allies. The feeling hung around them like an evil stench and I couldn't put two and two together!" *We should have tried to leave earlier, even if it meant fighting our way through the line out there. At least the danger from those things only hits at the body!*

Patience, was the bear's calm reply. *You chose the best way you knew. You are our leader. We have escaped other traps.* There was a pause, as if the strange, literal, ursine mind was considering something new. Then, there came a note of something surprising to Hiero—a touch of humor. *Let us not die before we truly are killed.*

Hiero probed the star and moonlit night, using all the new power of his own mind. The inchoate force continued to approach steadily and at last, just before dawn, he too, was able to pinpoint its direction, the same as that which the bear had found. With the coming of daylight, he guessed what he would

163

see. The familiar "feel" of the enemy, even masked and hidden, was unmistakable. Quietly, he gave his instructions to the others, not even excluding Klootz.

Luchare stared at him, wide-eyed. "Must we die, beloved? Is there no way out, no other hope?"

"I see none, dearest. They took me alive before and they will make no mistakes this time. From my brain, from all our living brains, they could force knowledge, a knowledge which would probably ensure their ultimate triumph. The ancient weapons I seek would be an irresistable force in their hands, plus whatever the bear knows and my own new skills in mindfighting." He smiled sadly down at the dark, haunting face, ringed by its tight, black curls. "I have two death pills," he went on, "here is one. Klootz will not be taken alive. *"Gorm, can you die fighting? Will you?"*

If necessary, was the answer. *My Old Ones laid that on me, just as yours did. When you give the word, that is enough. Still, let us wait for the dawn.*

Luchare understood him. "A false dawn," she said bitterly "And one which means only night and death."

Hiero mastered his grief for her, so young and lovely, and spoke calmly, concealing what it cost him. "Gorm is right. Let's not die before our time. Who knows what may happen?"

His arm over her shoulder, they stood on the highest knoll of the islet and waited for the morning light. The two animals waited patiently by their sides, the giant morse "snoofing" loudly at intervals as he tested the dawn breeze. The phosphorescent glow of their enemies' bodies faded as the East grew pale and the sun rose. Their ring of reed skiffs and slimy white shapes still covered the water however, and they gave no sign of moving.

For the last time, the four now heard the awful wail which for them had come to symbolize the city.

"Aaaough, aaaooough, aaaooough," it rang out, from all about, its source as mysterious as ever. Far over the ruined towers it sounded, seeming to defy the very day itself. At last it fell silent and the red disk of the sun appeared down one of the distant avenues of far-off buildings.

And those who had hunted the four so long also came with the morning. Out of the opening in the south came the hated black shape of that strange vessel which had caught Hiero. Perhaps, thought the priest, it was another like it, but it made no difference. In that black hull lay their destruction, sure and incscapablc.

The pallid Leemutes, their slippery, pale forms gleaming in the morning light, paddled and swam away from the prow of the oncoming ship. A

164

channel formed in their ranks and the black vessel came slowly through it until, its speed diminishing, it coasted slowly toward the island. The guardian circle of monsters reformed behind it. And all the other frog creatures followed drawing in from all sides, until they occupied only one, massed in deathly white on the side in which the black vessel lay and a hundred yards beyond it.

Hiero had never ceased sending mental darts at the ship, indeed had continually done so, even before it actually appeared. Now, as it came to a halt only a few hundred feet offshore, he ceased and merely held his own defense ready, waiting on the faint offchance that the Unclean might drop their barrier. He knew well the chance was infinitesimal. He could feel Luchare's body trembling, but he shot a sideways glance and noted proudly that her high-cheekboned face was impassive.

The adept who stood on the open bridge, surrounded by human aides and several Hairy Howlers spoke aloud in *batwah*. He was not S'duna but again the physical resemblance was uncanny. Yet Hiero was not fooled by the shaven head and the close approximation.

"Priest, we have you fast and your grimy crew as well, including your wench. Are you ready to yield without a struggle?" The voice, like S'nerg's and S'duna's was resonant, ironic and powerful. Its purpose was to intimidate, to weaken confidence, to inspire fear. It succeeded in none of its purposes. Instead, Hiero laughed.

"Still want my brain, eh, Baldy?" he said. The distance was so close that he hardly needed to raise his voice. With relish, he saw the pale skin of the other redden, while the Howlers started to chatter angrily. Hiero spared a glance at the foredeck. He frankly hoped the lightning gun he saw there would be used on them. The silver amulet which had guarded him before was no longer in place and that had been a million-to-one chance anyway. It would be a quick end and they would feel nothing.

But the two hooded men who manned the contrivance were well disciplined. They simply stood at its controls waiting for an order from their master.

The adept waved a hand negligently and the noisy Howlers fell silent. The shining head inclined gracefully toward Hiero and the priest was surprised.

"You are bold, priest of a forgotten god, courageous too. Qualities the Brotherhood values. We have you in our grip, but we need not close our hand. What if we still offered alliance? I confess it freely, we could indeed use your mind, one of power and indomitable will. S'duna sent me, S'carn, one of scarcely less authority, to reason with you, though why you still cling to the animals, especially that stupid bear, I utterly fail to see." There was genuine puzzlement in this last.

The Metz hesitated not a second. "You lie, S'carn, and so do all your dirty tribe! S'duna even now fears me, or else he would have come himself, to see my capture or to watch my doom. You have a machine in your ship to keep my mind from slaying all of you. Well, come and try with your weapons! I defy your Unclean crew, your filthy, perverted brotherhood and above all you, shave-pated master of foulness. If you have us fast, come and take us!"

For a second, staring over the calm water at the ship, only a stone's throw distant, Hiero thought he had succeeded. S'carn's face became a livid mask of horrid rage and his hands twitched on the rail of the bridge. But, to Hiero's intense regret, the adept controlled himself and did not order the instant death the priest sought for himself and his friends. His voice was now low and grating, filled with venom and hatred.

"You seek a speedy death, Priest, and when we have you on Manoon, you will pray to your foolish, non-existent god for it. And it will not come, no it will not come!" He turned to his swarming followers, who had stood in silent obedience behind him. "Put the ship's bow on the beach and take them! Take them alive!"

Hiero freed his right arm and raised his crossbow which had hung from the left, a new-made, bronze-tipped quarrel in its slot, the bow cocked. He drew aim on S'carn, who with his head turned saw nothing of his doom. But he never loosed.

"Peace!" The new voice speaking in *batwah* was so strong and vibrant that in comparison that of the evil adept seemed weak and sickly. With one word, the voice took the whole situation under its control.

Hiero lowered his bow and frankly gaped, amazed at what he saw.

Around a corner of the islet,unseen by anyone, there had come a small wooden canoe. In its stern there sat an aged man, a paddle in his lap, his long, white beard and hair flowing over his plain dress of brown cloth shirt, pants and soft boots. He seemed quite unarmed save for a small belt knife. His skin was very dark, as dark as Luchare's and his long. snowy-white hair was also just as much a mass of tight curls as hers.

The Unclean leader seemed as stunned as Hiero by this appearance. It was a second before he could gather his wits. His glance darted about as he sought for other enemies. It seemed impossible that one ancient had come alone into his power, as if out of thin air.

"What are you doing here, Elevener?" he hissed. "Are you mad to

166

come between me and my prey? Even your bands of crazy sentimentalists know what we can do to those who oppose us!"

Elevener! Of course! thought Hiero. *One of the Brotherhood of the Eleventh Commandment. But what was he doing here? Was he indeed mad, to thrust himself into his enemies' power?* A thousand questions jostled in his mind.

But the old man was speaking again. "Servant of evil, you and your brute horde are summoned to depart. Go, at once and cease molesting these wanderers, two-legged and four. I, Brother Aldo, tell you so, on penalty of your immediate death."

This was too much for S'carn. Indeed, Hiero himself was becoming sure the old fellow had lost his wits. To threaten a huge ship full of devil's weapons, Leemutes and Unclean warriors, while sitting alone and unarmed in a canoe was certainly madness at its peak.

"We are favored by fortune, dotard, for we have you in our net as well as these. Cease your senile maunderings and approach at once to surrender, lest I lose my patience."

Brother Aldo, as he styled himself, rose and stood erect in his canoe. He revealed himself as being very tall and lean and despite his age he balanced easily.

"We slay no one gladly, child of the Unclean, not even such as you." His arm thrust out, forefinger extended. "For the last time, I tell you, begone, lest I loose a destruction upon you! Can you not see your allies have fled, summoned by that which rules them?"

Hiero stared in fresh amazement. It was true. As the talk had taken this new turn, with the sudden appearance of the old Elevener, the frog Leemutes were gone! Stealthily, silently, their living ring of bodies had vanished. Not a reed boat or leprous white shape remained. The black ship and the tiny canoe, a hundred yards separating them, were alone on the blue dancing surface of the lagoon.

Even S'carn seemed taken aback. His crew too, began to mutter audibly and one of the Howlers let out a piercing wail. But the adept still ruled.

"Silence, you chattering cowards! And as for you, you old troublemaker, enough of your lies and Elevener gibberish! Approach and surrender or I will slay you!" Yet a new, sudden fear showed in his ivory face, despite every effort to control it. The old man had frightened him.

Brother Aldo dropped his hand and an expression of sadness crossed his dark, lined face. "So be it. The One knows that I do this unwillingly." With that he sat down quickly in the canoe and raised his paddle.

And the black ship rose in the air!

Rose up, held in the pointed jaws of a fish of such bulk that it dwarfed the imagination. The thing's gleaming, ivory teeth, Hiero saw in numb fascination, were each as long as his own body! Not a sound came from the crew. It was too quick.

For one second the ship hung ten spans above the heaving, foaming surface, then the incredible monster shook its vast head once and the big vessel simply broke in half. As the two fragments struck the surface, the leviathan vanished in a boil of water. From out of this there emerged a forked tail easily a hundred feet across! With a smash that almost pierced the eardrums it came down on the lagoon squarely on top of the broken pieces of the Unclean ship and the surviving men and Leemutes who now struggled and screamed in the water.

Brace yourselves; hold Klootz's legs, sent Hiero, seeing what was coming. A great wave rushed up the islet's beach and in an instant the two humans and the bear were waist deep in the surging water. The priest's warning had come in the nick of time, for the big morse held firm and they with him. Gorm had flung his strong forepaws around a leg as well, and Hiero had held on to both a leg and Luchare.

The water raced back as swiftly as it had come and the travelers stared out at the transformed lagoon. There was a long smear of oil, a growing slick and vast rings of racing, foaming ripples, all coming from the place where the Unclean ship had been. Of the ship and its sinister crew nothing remained. In less than thirty seconds they had been totally obliterated, as if they had never been. Only the small canoe, now half full of water, lay rocking on the surging water a few hundred feet away, its solitary occupant staring sadly at the fouled area of lagoon.

Hiero let go of Luchare and strode down through the soggy grass and shrubbery to the water's edge. As he reached it, he saw the canoe shooting in toward him, propelled by vigorous strokes of the paddle. In an instant its prow grated on the sand and its tall occupant stepped on to the beach, his vigorous movements belying his apparent age.

The two men stared at each other in appraisal. Hiero looked up at a face so strong and yet so calm, that it seemed to have grown almost beyond what could be called human. The very dark brown, almost black, skin was lined by a thousand wrinkles, yet the skin itself was clear and healthy. The broad snub nose surmounted a sweeping curly mustache which merged into the white beard imperceptibly. The frizzy white locks evenly fell to the old man's shoulders and were neatly combed.

168

But the eyes were the clue to the whole countenance. Black as night, dancing with light, they seemed to bubble with humor and yet to be grave as a granite monument one and the same time. They were eyes which loved life, which had seen everything, examined everything and were still searching for, and finding, new things to examine. In them could be read great age and wisdom and also the gusto and joy of healthy youth.

Hiero was won over on the instant. He extended his right hand and a long, lean hand met it in a grip as firm as his own, met it and held it.

"Per Desteen, I believe, of the Kandan Universal Church," said the deep voice. "A man currently much sought for, by many sorts of people, for good and ill."

With a shock, Hiero realized that Brother Aldo was speaking Metz, fluently and with no accent at all. Before he could say anything, the old man smiled sheepishly.

"Showing off again, Per Desteen. I used to be good at languages and I learned all I could long ago. And whom have we here?" He turned and gave Luchare a stare as frank as that he had given her lover.

She smiled and held out her hand. "You have killed our enemies, Father, and we thank you for saving us."

"Yes, Princess of D'alwah, I had to kill." He sighed, taking her extended hand in his own left, for he still kept Hiero's in his right. He ignored the girl's gasp at his knowledge of her.

"Killing is sometimes necessary," he went on, in the same *batwah,* now looking keenly at both of them. "But it ought never to be a pleasure. We do not need to kill for food each day, as do the lower animals. A burden on my mind, all those souls, weary with vice and evil though they were." He released their hands.

"We have much to talk of, we three. Or rather, I should say, we four." *Greeting, friend,* came the thought directed at Gorm, who had ambled up and now sat gazing at the old man.

Greeting, Old one, the bear brain answered. *We have much to thank you for. A debt is incurred. It will be repaid.*

If you feel so, a debt there is, was the courteous reply. *Now let us speak to one another. I am, as the two humans have heard, Brother Aldo, an elder, albeit humble, of the Brotherhood of the Eleventh Commandment. I was sent to find you if I could, and bring you to a place of safety.*

Why? It was Luchare who asked, her thought pattern ragged, but quite intelligible, evidence of her increasing confidence.

Why? Brother Aldo looked hard at her. *Have you forgotten one who promised you safety long ago, and passed into the enemy's hands to save you?*

"How could I?" She broke into speech in her agitation. "You mean Jone, don't you, father? Is he alive? Did you save him too?"

Yes, I meant Brother Jone, child. And I did not mean to sound so reproving. And although I am indeed vastly older than any of you and probably all of you at once, call me "brother." The fur-man here, and he indicated Gorm, *knows me as an "Old One." So I am. But being a father implies responsibility of a kind I don't have or want. A father directs; I guide, at best.*

"Per" means "father" in an old language, sent Hiero in somewhat truculent meaning.

I know and I think your church makes a mistake using it. But why do I wander so? I must be getting dim-witted. Let us sit and exchange thoughts.

When they were comfortably arranged on the fast-drying sand, Hiero asked the next question.

Are we still in danger, immediate, I mean?

No, or I should not sit here. My brother out yonder will wait if I choose. He nodded his head toward the still water. As they looked, first one battered piece of wood broke the quiet ripples and then another. As they watched a growing collection of flotsam continued to surface.

How do you control that thing? I never dreamt a creature that size existed or that if it did, that a level of intelligence that low could be mastered.

You have a few things to learn then, Per Desteen, was the almost dry answer. *It would take a lot of training to teach you and I don't mean to disparge your own powers. But it happens, in this case, to be neural rather than cerebral. And it's not always reliable. But let's say that control of our younger brothers and communication with them are and always have been specialties of ours. We are continually seeking contact with any life form we can reach.* Brother Aldo wrapped his arms around his knees before continuing.

Look—time is important. Before we go further, I need information. This whole part of the world is in a turmoil, mental and physical, and all because of you four. Now then, Per Desteen, you lead this party. Suppose you tell me briefly what you are doing here and the recent history of this group. I'll try not to interrupt.

Hiero considered briefly. The question was, how much could he trust the Elevener? He had always liked the men of the order he had met, but this was no quiet teacher or animal doctor, but a most formidable old man, whose mental powers were of an order which made the Metz awe-struck. While he ruminated, Brother Aldo waited patiently.

At length Hiero looked up and met the dark, wise eyes.

"I don't know what the Abbey Council would say, Brother," he said aloud in Metz, without thinking, "but I think you are honorable and trustworthy. I will keep one secret, the reason for my mission, if you please. The rest is yours."

I appreciate the compliment, was the mental answer. *Use your mind, please, for it saves time. Also, we must all listen and understand. Do not worry about a mind search by the enemy. That which lairs in the dead city was withdrawn both itself and its creatures, the frog Leemutes, as you call them. Nothing else is left to hinder us, at least nearby.*

So, as the morning climbed into the sky, Hiero related the history of his journey with Klootz, adding the others as they had joined him. He started at the Abbey with old Abbot Demero, and hid nothing save exactly what it was he had been sent to find. On and on went the story, through the Taig forest, the Palood, the shores of the Inland Sea, the Dead Isle of Manoon, and at last, the coming to the drowned city.

When he was through, Hiero looked at the sun and was amazed that he had only taken about a quarter of an hour, for it had hardly moved.

Brother Aldo sat quietly and stared at the sand. At last, he looked up at all of them. *Well, a good tale. You should all be proud of yourselves. Now I have a tale, less exciting and more historic. But one you should know, indeed, must know, before we go further. And it starts, not two months ago, or even two years, but five thousand and more, in the ancient past, before the coming of The Death.*

9: The Sea Rovers

You look about you, children, came the message from Brother Aldo's mind, *and you see in the world, green forest and glade, blue sea and river, yellow prairie and marsh. In them today lurk evil things, yet they also hold uncounted sorts of beauty and wonder. The singing birds, the breathing plants, the shy animals, the savage hunters, all have a place. Alone and unhindered, they change slowly, one kind yielding place to another over the centuries and millennia. This is the ordered course of nature, the plan as the Creator designed it.*

But before The Death, things most rapidly were changing, yes, and for the worst. The entire world as well as simply here in what was once called Northamerica, was dying. It was being choked, strangled in artificially-made filth and its own sickly refuse. He pointed a lean hand at the ring of ruined towers glaring across the lagoon.

See there! The whole planet, the good round Earth, was being covered by those things! Giant buildings blotted out the sun. The ground was overlain with stone and other hard substances, so that it could not breathe. Vast man-made structures were built everywhere, to make yet more vast structures, and the smoke and stench of the engines and devices used fouled the world's air in great clouds of poison. He paused for a moment and looked sad.

This was not all. The Earth itself trembled. Monstrous vessels, to which that Unclean ship of yesterday would be a skiff, fouled the very seas. Overhead, the air vibrated with the rush of great flying machines, whose speed alone, by its vibration, could shatter stone. Along countless stone roads, myriad wheeled machines carrying ever more goods and people, charged madly along, their poisonous wastes still further fouling the already wearied air.

And then, there were the world's people. The warring, breeding,

172

struggling, senseless people! The peoples of the planet could not, or rather would not, be brought to reason. Not only did they refuse to see how they were killing the life of the world, they could not even see how they were killing themselves! For they bred. Despite vast poverty, great ignorance, disease and endless wars, humans were still tough! Every year there were more. And more and more, until the cataclysm was inevitable. Wise men warned them, scientists and humanists pled with them. God and Nature are one, they said, and hence neither is mocked and defied with impunity.

A few listened, indeed, more than a few. But not enough. Certain leaders of religion, men ignorant of any science and any learning but their own outdated hagiography refused to heed. Other men, who controlled the world's wealth and soldiery wished more power. They wished yet more men both to make and to consume what they sold and still more men to wage the wars which they fomented in the name of one political creed or another. Races warred against races of other colors, white against yellow, black against white.

The end was quite inevitable. It had to come! Men of science who had studied many species of mammals in laboratories of the ancient world had long predicted it. When over-population and crowding, dirt and noise, reach a peak, madness remorselessly follows. We today call that madness The Death. Across the whole world, by land, water and air, total war raged unchecked. Radiation, hideous chemical weapons and artificially-spawned disease slew most of the humans then in existence, and much of the remaining animal life, too.

Nevertheless, a few had taken forethought. When the poisons had partly dissipated (they are not all so yet, even now), a few remnants of our Brotherhood emerged. Most were scientists of the day, specialists in a science called "ecology," which is the interaction of all living things. The Eleventh Commandment, as we call it, not in mockery of the Immemorial Ten, but in succession rather, was formally promulgated. It is simple: Thou shalt not despoil the Earth and the life thereon.

For five thousand years and more we have watched as humanity climbed upward again, trying our best to aid and guide a natural, decent re-ascent, one this time in harmony with nature and all life.

We have seen much that was good and much that was not. Many of the pre-Death beasts now have become wise, as wise as humans (if that is wisdom). He sent a thought at Gorm alone and Hiero could "feel" the bear's mind shift nervously. Brother Aldo's tale continued.

But long ago, a certain few survivors of other ancient sciences, principally psychology, bio-chemistry and physics, also banded together. They sought nothing less than to regain the ancient human domination of the world, which The Death had finally ended. All the machine-made horrors of life which had passed away, to them were beautiful. They took many of the more dangerous, non-lethal mutations (although you call them Leemutes, Per Desteen, that is an error of language corrupted by usage) and bred them to their service and to a hatred of normal humanity, any, that is, not yet under their own evil sway. And these other groups from the past, we call, collectively, the Unclean. A fitting name.

It is the main business of these foul remnants of the past to destroy any rising groups of humanity which they do not themselves control. If they cannot easily do so, they strive to pierce their ranks, to become hidden councillors or secret allies of any who desire to rule over their fellows. Per Desteen, you no doubt guessed as much. But you, princess, have you ever thought why our people, for I am indeed one of you by birth, continually war against one another to no end but evil?

For a long while, our Brotherhood watched these evil groups, unseen and unknown to them. There is a basic weakness to most wicked people of this sort. No matter how clever and determined they are, each wishes absolute rule of all the others. Hence, cooperation is always difficult for them, a fact to bear in mind. We hoped, I say, that this flaw, this lack of cohesion, would rot them from within, and cause them to destroy themselves. They were few, as were we, and it seemed possible, nay, probable.

Regrets are vain. We were mistaken. A twisted genius appeared in their ranks a thousand years or so ago and managed to forge a political device which allows them to cooperate without rending one another.

Now they form a dozen or so groups, each independent within its own geographic area. Promotion within each group lies in that group. But the Grand Masters of each group are also a permanent council, which can override any one group or minority in the interests of the whole. A sort of vicious but permanent oligarchy, well-suited to evil, is the result.

It sounds like the Abbeys' organization, Hiero could not help interjecting.

It is. A good idea can usually be perverted to evil, you know. But let me go on. The old lose their patterns of concentration easily. His humor flashed at the thought.

There are several rising groups of humanity on this continent, he went on. *The Kandan Confederacy, including the Metz Republic of the West and their confederates in the East, the Otwah League, are the most advanced, in both politics and science. The city states of the Southeast, such as D'alwah, are*

174

strong in human potential, but crippled by social archaisms and rotted from within by agents of the Unclean. They must be purged before they can be of use in the struggle.

In the far west and south and elsewhere too, are others. With them we are not here concerned, though I can tell you that Eleventh Commandment Brothers try to watch over them.

So then, we come to the here and now. In the last fifty years, a concerted attack on the Kandan Confederacy has been steadily building. We had hoped it could be warded off unaided, without our direct help.

For I must make one thing very plain. The Brotherhood I speak for seeks to guard the whole biosphere! We are concerned with LIFE primarily and humanity only secondarily, indeed mainly as it affects all other life. I trust this is clear.

Now then we come next to minds, minds and their powers, their powers and their abilities and even structures! Minds!

We of the Brotherhood have developed mental powers over several millennia, which had aided our purposes, indeed, made them possible. We grew overconfident, feeling that we alone had these secrets. As we here all know, this was folly! For the Unclean developed them too, although not in the same way, and they made curious machines and devices in their secret laboratories, devices which expanded their mental powers. And thus they became aware of us for the first time and were filled with fear and rage as a result, knowing very little but guessing a good deal of our long scrutiny of them. Ever since, they have sought to destroy us wherever they could. A number of good men and women have died to protect our secrets.

"Brother Jone," breathed Luchare aloud.

Yes, Brother Jone. But he died swiftly and in silence, as we Eleveners know how to do. And he told us of you first, princess, so that we have sought you ever since.

A new factor to consider, for you, that is, since we have long studied it in fascination, is that of the radiation-spawned growth of higher intelligence in non-humans. Our friend here (he indicated Gorm with a mental dart) *belongs to a new civilization. They are still observing humanity, we think. We have extended a welcome to their rulers or wise elders, but they distrust us as well as all other humans. So we wait, hoping that they will decide to aid us, eh, Gorm?*

I am young, was the quick answer. I go on my journey of Youth, where I will, as I will. The Bear folk, the new bear folk, are hidden and wish to remain so. Yet, much of what I have seen will make them think. I cannot speak for the Old Ones.

Good, I hoped, we all hope, for no more than a fair look. I cannot think that the Unclean have won, or will win your people, over to their side. And there are the Dam People, too, of the northern lakes, neither friendly nor unfriendly as yet. The Unclean have their Howlers, and their Man-rats and others still. Then, there are things stranger yet, if that is possible. These frog creatures you have just routed obey a different master again, something I cannot reach, which lairs in the depths of this sunken city. What it actually is I don't know, but it is both old and malignant, at least an ally of the enemy, if no more.

Stranger things yet, offspring of the atom and genetic frightfulness, alien and mysterious, lurk in the forests and marshes. Perhaps you have met some? Hiero thought of the Dweller in the Mist and shuddered.

I see you have. But not all are malignant. Some are merely indifferent to humanity, others even benign. The world is full of pulsing, seething life and many wonders still remain, undiscovered.

At last, I am coming to my presence here. We knew you were being hunted down the coast. I have an idea, by the way, Per Desteen, what it is you look for in the south. But of that, more later. He went on quickly before Hiero could even react in surprise.

At any rate, it was decided to aid you if we could. We have come, we Eleveners, to the conclusion that the Unclean are gaining great power, mental and physical, too fast for us Brothers of the Eleventh to hope we can stop them alone. Our powers primarily are of the mind and spirit. We need physical strength, mechanical strength if you will, though we dislike yielding to the necessity. I can tell you, Man of the Metz, that even as we sit here, Elevener emissaries are seeking to join formally with your Abbey Council and offer our help for the first time in battling the common enemy. This is a great concession for us, the greatest in our whole history.

I myself volunteered to come and try and help you. We did not know of the lady Luchare, though, as I said, we have long sought her elsewhere. We feared she was dead. As such things go, I have a good deal of authority in our councils. I ask you to let me join your party and go with you from now on. Two nights past, I sensed a converging of mental forces in this place, as I came up from the distant south. I struggled to reach you and was barely in time. Now, we have a brief, a very brief respite until the Unclean rally. They are terribly shaken by your mind, Per Desteen. You hardly understand your new powers as yet, but I can tell you that the aether was disturbed by you, half a continent away! The Unclean guess you seek something important. They are determined you shall not have it, and that they, in turn, shall.

What does the group say? I do not ask the good deer, for though his heart is great, his mind is not on a level with ours as yet; though that too may come in time. Thank you for enduring the rambling of the aged. His thought ceased abruptly and he sat back, looking from one to the other of the three with his sparkling black eyes.

All this tale had taken no more than a few moments. The mental pictures and concepts succeeded one another so rapidly and so clearly, that no ambiguity was possible. The bear understood quite as well as the man and woman. Despite his asides about age and accompanying decrepitude, Brother Aldo's mind messages were as lucid and sharp as any Hiero had ever encountered.

Luchare spoke aloud, looking directly into the old man's eyes. "I go wherever Hiero goes, now and always. But if my word means anything, I think we are very lucky".

I agree. I am grateful for our rescue, too, but more, I think we have a great source of strength in our new friend. The future may prove worse than the past. Hiero smiled at the Elevener and met an answering smile.

My own Old Ones told me that the Brotherhood were men we might seek help from if necessary. Also, I can "feel" that this man is a friend. This cannot be a lie. Gorm stared at Brother Aldo with his weak eyes. *Yes, he is a friend, this human Old One. And he is very powerful. Let us not anger him.*

The priest could not tell whether this last thought was simply a sample of bearish humor or not, but Brother Aldo apparently could, for he suddenly reached out and tweaked Gorm's nose. Gorm promptly fell over on his back, paws over his muzzle, and gave a superb imitation of a mortally wounded bear, complete with gasps, tongue hangings and pitiful moans.

The three humans laughed in unison and only when his sides ached, did Hiero suddenly remember where they were and what had recently happened here. His laughter ceased abruptly.

"Yes, humor and death make odd companions," said Brother Aldo. "Nevertheless, the chemistry of life itself is compounded of both." He stared out over the sunlit water.

Really, thought Hiero (behind a shield), *too much empathy can be unsettling!*

"If I may suggest a change of air," went on the old man's deep voice. "I think we ought to eat and leave this area. I have a ship a few leagues down the coast, waiting for me, and us, if I were lucky enough to find any of you. The enemy will be wondering at the sudden cessation of signals from their party. They may be in communication with that which rules the frog-creatures over there in the drowned city too. And I can sense very little of its purposes, save hate alone."

I can sense nothing at all of it, nor can Gorm. I marvel that you can. The priest's thought was envious.

Remember, both, or rather all three of you, are very young children compared to me. Even a stupid man can learn a lot if he has enough time granted him. This time, all three minds "smiled."

In no time they had eaten and set off again, on the far side of the island, their faces to the east once more. They took the little canoe and the old Elevener's small supply of provisions, mostly dried fruit, aboard the raft as well, and he lent a hand with the clumsy paddles. Not surprisingly, he was both strong and agile.

The sunken city came to an abrupt end not far ahead, he now told them. Another half day's travel would have brought them to it and to dry land. The Palood curved away back to the north at this point and no longer strayed down to the Inland Sea. Instead, wide lands opened out, prairie and great forest, sweeping to the far distance and eventually the great salt ocean, the Lantik.

But they were not to go east for a long while yet; rather their route lay south, across the eastern arm of the Inland Sea itself. Somewhere to the east of Neeyana, the trading port from which Luchare's captors had sailed, Brother Aldo hoped to strike a certain forest trail, without alerting the enemy.

That evening, on dry land, around a hidden campfire, buried deep in some brush, they again sought to plan for the future.

"If you have no objection, I should like to try the Forty Symbols," said Hiero to Brother Aldo. Gorm had vanished on some private errand and they were using speech.

"Why should I object? Precognition is an art, if that is the right word, of which we Eleveners know little. Our teaching lies in other areas of mind and spirit. But I cannot for the life of me see why it is wrong to use such a talent in a good cause. Save for the fear of becoming skilled enough to read one's own death. That might deter some people."

"You may watch if you wish," said the priest as he drew forth the box and the alb of his office. "There is nothing secret about any of this. We don't regard it as being hidden although we do think of it as a service."

When Hiero eventually came out of the brief trance, he saw Aldo watching him closely and next to the old man, Luchare, her eyes gleaming with suppressed excitement.

"There is some danger to your method, some that I had not quite foreseen," said Aldo. "Your mind was quite open and the power of the thought more than enough to reveal you to a mental listener close by. I cast over you a net of surface thought, a sort of mental screen, simulating the local small thoughts of animal and plant (oh yes, plants have "thoughts", though perhaps not the kind you are aware of) to deceive any spy who might be about."

"Thanks," grunted Hiero. He opened his hand and peered at the symbols now exposed on his palm.

The Fish lay uppermost. Water again! "That's no surprise," he said, after explaining it to the Elevener.

Next, there were the familiar little Boots. "Half my life has been a journey. Now we have a journey involving water. Well, we knew that too." The hawk nose lowered over the small third symbol. It was the House.

"What's that one?" said the girl eagerly. "Is it good or bad?"

"Neither," was the answer. "It's the House. The sign itself is a peaked roof. Its meanings are various and unfriendly. You know, or I guess perhaps you don't, that the Signs are very, very old. Many of the instructions and meanings of their first makers are obscure, open to several interpretations. This is one of them. It can mean simply 'danger indoors'. Or it can mean 'get under cover'! Or it can mean an enemy building, or even a town or city, is near. Not much help, really."

Hiero looked at the fourth symbol. It was a minute Sword and Shield interlocked. "That means personal combat for the one who casts the symbols." He looked at Luchare and smiled at the worry in her eyes, "I've drawn it three times in my life so far. I'm still here." There was no more to say. He put the signs away and called to Klootz to come and be rubbed down.

All three of them had been riding the morse, albeit at a slow pace. It was no great strain on him and he had been feeding fairly well. Even at his deceptive amble, he covered the ground faster than a man could walk, and went straight through things a man would have had to walk around.

Two hours jog the next morning along the shore brought them to a small cove, set deep in one side of a towering headland. As they appeared on the beach, Brother Aldo cupped his hands and let out a ringing shout, startling both the humans and the bear who had been sniffing some tracks beside the path. Klootz twitched an ear.

To the surprise of Hiero and Luchare, a section of low woodland on the far side of the cove began to move. Out from a shallow indentation in the shore pushed a stout little, two-masted ship. Tree branches had been lashed to her lateen-rigged masts and more branches and bushes woven into a great net which covered most of the hull.

Perhaps a hundred feet long over all, she was painted brown, and rose high at both bow and stern. There was a tiny deck cabin amidships between the masts, and various bales and bundles lying about here and there. Men moved briskly on deck about various tasks and a small rowing boat now pushed off and came shooting in to meet them as they came down to the water.

They dismounted and the two sailors who were rowing splashed out and pulled the boat up on the beach. This allowed the man in the stern to step out dry shod. He did so and came swaggering up to them. Luchare put her hand to her mouth to suppress a giggle.

"This is Captain Gimp," said Brother Aldo gravely. "He has waited for me patiently and has been of great service, both in the past and recently as well. No more renowned captain of merchants sails the Inland Sea. Captain, let me introduce my friends and your new passengers."

Captain Gimp bowed profoundly. He was extremely short and very wide, a washtub of a man thought Luchare. His original color was hard to make out for he was so brown and weathered it might have been anything. He was bald, or perhaps shaved, for a short, smoke-blackened pigtail thrust straight back like a bow, or rather, sternsprit. He wore a kilt of dirty greased leather, boots of undressed hide and a green coat of wool, much stained and worn. He limped a little, hence his name, guessed Hiero, and his black eyes were beady with impudent humor. His hands, at the end of long arms, were surprising, being as dirty as the rest of him, but with long, delicate fingers. He carried no visible weapon.

"Glad to make yer acquaintance, all," he said in understandable but accented *batwah* when the introductions were complete. "The Brother's word is good enough for me. Now turn your dear pets loose and let's get aboard. Wind's fair for the southard and it may shift." He spat something he was chewing in Gorm's direction even as he spoke and started to turn away.

The bear, who had been sitting up on his haunches sniffing the warm morning breeze moved like lightning. One broad paw shot out and intercepted the wad of spittle. Next the young bear rose on his hind legs and advanced on the dumfounded sailor, who stood only a few feet away. Reaching him, Gorm peered solicitously into his face from an inch away, snorted loudly and then wiped his paw down the dirty green coat. The coat now bore a new stain, as well as several leaves. Gorm sat down again and looked up at

Captain Gimp.

The Captain finally emerged from his trance, his face now a shade paler under the accumulation of smoke, dirt, and weather. Surprisingly, to Hiero at any rate, he crossed himself.

"Well, ride me under," he exploded. "I never see the half of that. That animal can talk! Who's he belong to?" he said, swivelling on the others who were all smiling. "I'll buy him! Just name your own price! I'm as fair as any master afloat, ask the Brother here now, if you don't believe me!"

It was some time before it could be brought home to the little sailor that Gorm was not for sale, and that he could think as well as a man. The Captain was still muttering to himself when Brother Aldo asked him to warp his ship in near the beach, so that a plank could be run out and the bull morse taken aboard also. This, however, seemed to be altogether too much.

"Look now, brother," he said to the old man, "I've carried those kaws on occasion, back when I had an old storeship, on local journeys, mind you, a day here or there. But I can't take that great ox of a thing. What would people think? My ship, *Foam Girl*, the finest thing in the trade, a dung barge? I ask you, now? It's not considerate of you, brother. Talking bears, women who ain't proper slaves or wives, that funny-looking northerner (no offense, mister) and now this animal mountain. No, it's too much; I won't do it, my mind's made up."

By the time they were aboard it was almost noon. Once his arguments had been beaten down, the squat little captain proved both helpful and extremely efficient. A log pen was quickly built next to the deck cabin and Klootz was secured by broad straps so that he could not slip.

The crew, Hiero noticed as the ship eased out of the cove, were a wildly varied lot. There were dark men, who with their curly hair, could have been Luchare's or Brother Aldo's cousins. But there were men in appearance like himself, though he heard no Metz spoken, and also there were others. He saw two, half naked men with pale skins and high cheekbones, whose eyes were an icy blue and whose hair was fiery red. He had read of red-haired men in the ancient past, but had no idea that they still existed.

"They come from an island in the far north, from what used long ago to be called the Green Land, I believe," said Brother Aldo, who had followed his glance. "They were probably outlawed, to be so far from home."

"Do your Eleveners reach so far?" asked Hiero. He clutched the rail as the *Foam Girl* emerged from the cove and a strong wind in the great triangular sails made her heel sharply.

"We do reach there, though we are called something else, a habit of ours in many lands," said Aldo. "One of the assistant witch doctors of the white savages who were trying to kill Luchare was an Elevener. That's how I got on your track, my boy." He smiled sadly at Hiero. "Yes, he would have let the birds kill her. He had no choice and he was next in line to be chief wizard or shaman. You see, that then he could have influenced the whole tribe, to who knows what good end? The enemy works on such primitive people, too, and we cannot neglect such chances. I am sorry, but that's the situation."

"In other words," said Hiero bitterly, "you'd turn on me if you had a change of mind about how much good it would do you. Not a very inviting thought when we're so dependent on you."

"I'm sorry," said Brother Aldo. "I was trying to be honest with you, Hiero. I openly allied myself to you and gave my word. Now the man I just spoke of made a calculated decision to remain silent in pursuit of a long-held purpose. Can you see no difference at all?"

"Possibly," said the Metz priest in a curt tone. "I am not trained as a casuist or debator of legalisms. It sounds a bit cold-blooded. Now I think I'll rest. I haven't slept in anything like a bed since Manoon." He nodded and walked off to the little cabin, whence Luchare had already retired, taking the bear with her, for Gorm, surprisingly, was seasick and wanted to be shut up, away from the sight of the wind-tossed whitecaps.

As Hiero, moved away, he missed the pain in Brother Aldo's eyes, which followed him until the cabin door closed.

The following day and for several more, the weather held fair. The travelers, even Gorm, grew accustomed to the wave motion and enjoyed roaming the little ship. Klootz fretted but Hiero spent a lot of time grooming him and keeping him soothed. Also, the old Brother seemed able to calm him at will and Hiero actually felt a bit of jealousy at the morse's fondness for Aldo.

The bear became a prime favorite with the polyglot crew, who considered him merely a very clever, trained beast, and fed him sweet things such as tree-sap candy and honeycakes until his furry sides bulged.

Luchare and Hiero had a marvelous time. The small cabin at last gave them some privacy and they made love constantly, with the fire and passion of superb health and no complexes. Hiero was worried at first, since the Metz Republic had a universally-known drug used to prevent childbirth and he had none with him. But a quiet word to Brother Aldo about his fears produced some of it or a workable substitute. In fact, the old Elevener had quite an extensive pharmacopeia stowed away in a small sea chest, and Hiero and he discussed various medicines by the hour.

Captain Gimp also proved an entertaining companion. Despite his funny face and bow legs, the little freshwater mariner ran a taut ship. *Foam Girl* was as clean as her Captain was soiled, and her strange mixture of a crew, though noisy, and ragged, were also well disciplined. Most of them carried long sheath knives and stores of boarding pikes and swords were racked in lockers around the cabin. A portable arrow engine, a device like a huge bow firing across a grooved table, could be mounted on the little poop abaft the wheel. It shot six long arrows at once and looked to the priest-warrior like a useful weapon.

"Never know what you'll need, not in these waters," Gimp said, while discussing his ship's armament. "There's giant fish (and sometimes we go after 'em with harpoons) and great beasts and pirates out for loot. There's slavers as'll turn pirate in a trice if given a chance. And then there's the Unclean. Been more of them about in the last few years. And some of their boats go by magic. No sails, nothing. You can't outfight *or* outrun them, not if what I hear is true." Reflecting on the lightning gun and his stay on the Dead Isle, Hiero silently agreed.

Life abounded in sun-flecked waters of the Inland Sea. Schools of fish leapt from the surface, driven by larger predators surging up from the deeps. Once, as the *Foam Girl* passed a small rocky islet, a half dozen sleek giant flippered forms, great toothed jaws snapping at the end of long necks, roared at them from the shingle on which they lay basking. Gimp's name for them was *Ot'r* and he kept a wary eye on them until the island was out of sight.

"They have good fur and meat too," he said, "but it takes a whole proper flotilla and trained harpooners to go hunting that gentry."

It was the fifth morning, a grey one, windy and full of scudding cloud, since leaving the northern coast. Hiero lay sleeping, his tousled head pillowed on Luchare's dark, gleaming breast, when a sailor's horny hand beating at the cabin door aroused them both.

Hurrying on deck, they found Brother Aldo and the little captain standing near the wheel, staring back beyond the wake. The reason was obvious. A great, dark, three-masted ship, all her square brown sails set, was coming up behind them with the calm inevitability of Fate. Even Hiero, no trained mariner, could see the newcomer was eating up the distance between the two vessels. Her decks were black with men and an ominous twinkle showed among them. She bore a huge black banner at the main truck, and gaudy red and white animals, monsters and human skulls painted on her sails.

Hiero looked at the nearest streamers on the mizzen rat-line. These showed the wind to be dead astern, and growing stronger. The day was an overcast one, with a promise of coming rain, but visibility was at least a good mile. They were seemingly trapped.

Next, he stared at Aldo, their minds meshing as he did so, but on a "closed circuit," limited to the two of them alone.

Unclean?

No, I think not, was the answer, *at least not directly. But a pirate, evil, yes, and cruel. And I think also, searching this part of the Inland Sea, perhaps on orders. The Unclean net is wide. When their own ship did not come back, they must have sent out new instructions, some to those they totally rule, others to those whom they merely influence and lead as yet. Their pawns rather than their servants, it appears to me. Try your own mind. Some of them seem not unprotected, which makes me even more suspicious.*

Hiero closed his eyes, gripped the taffrail and concentrated. Captain Gimp peered through a battered telescope, mumbling oaths through his quid. On the deck below, the first mate, a saturnine black-skinned man with one eye, served out weapons in silence to the little ship's crew. The team of three men who manned the arrow engine were setting up their contrivance only a yard away.

Brother Aldo was right, Hiero realized at once. The crew of the strange ship, a large one, were indeed evil through and through. But it was the human evil of wicked men, the scum which has always infested unguarded seas since the first pirate robbed the first trader, five thousand years before the coming of Christ.

Yet their leader's minds were guarded! All the Metz could get was an individual aura radiating from each one, an aura of power and evil. But the thoughts themselves were warded, even against attacks on the new band he had taught himself to use on Manoon. The Unclean truly learned quickly! For only they could have provided the devices and training which made his mental weapons useless. *But not quite useless,* he reflected. Only four of the minds on the ship were shielded from him, and the crew were totally open.

He felt for the steersman of the pirate, for such he now knew it to be without any question. The man's name, he learnt, was Horg, and his life had been evil, his mind a reeking cesspool. *Turn the wheel, Horg, my boy; edge off now, that's it, away a few points, now quick! Yaw, the ship's in great danger! Hurry!*

An exclamation from Captain Gimp made him open his eyes. Astern of them, the square-rigger had come up into the wind, her sails all flapping, the ship in irons. Hiero shut his eyes and simultaneously felt Horg's mind die, as the life went out of the man. The enemy wasted no time, though they had lost a quarter of a mile.

184

But as the big ship came around and back on course, a groan went up from the *Foam Girl's* idle sailors, who had been watching in fascination. A torrent of oaths from the square little skipper drove them back to their work and cleared the poop again, save for the helmsman, the arrow engine crew, Aldo, Luchare and Hiero.

Once again, the priest probed for the helmsman. But whoever was the master of the great ship was a quick thinker. One of the four shielded minds now steered the ship. Undaunted, Hiero found a nearby sailor. His name was Gimmer and his mind, if possible, was more repellent than that of the dead Horg.

The helmsman is your deadly enemy. He hates you. He is taking you into danger. He will kill you. You must kill him first! Quickly! Now! Coldly and ruthlessly, Hiero drove the craven will to the assault. Ordinarily a sensitive and kindly man, he had no compunction about slaying creatures such as these sea-lice. Wasting false sentiment over the truly wicked was no part of an Abbey warrior priest's training. The world was harsh enough on decent folk without coddling vermin.

But this time he was frustrated. The mind he had overpowered was not allowed to consummate its fell purpose. As (watching through Gimmer's eyes) he crept upon the helmsman, a sudden pain in the captive chest, a blazing weakness of the controlled limbs, halted him in his, or rather Gimmer's, tracks. Then as Gimmer too died, Hiero saw the arrow protruding from the sailor's chest.

Again he opened his eyes to the world as seen from his own body. He felt drained of energy. "It's no good," he shouted to Brother Aldo over the noise of the rising rain. "They had good archers stationed about the ship in key positions. Unless I can get one of *them* under control, I'm licked. They must have orders to shoot down anyone who even looks suspicious. And it's tiring me out. I can't keep taking these people over in this rough and ready way, forcing totally unknown minds to do whatever I want. It's drawing too much nervous energy out of my own body. I'll try again, but it really doesn't get easier. Just the reverse."

Actually, although he didn't want to admit the fact, Hiero was a bit ashamed. He had been sure he could do a lot more than he was able to in fact. He had felt that taking over a whole ship all at once would be easy. And now in mere moments, he was half exhausted and seemingly frustrated as well.

Captain Gimp chose this moment to try a maneuver of his own. He bawled an order and the two big lateen sails slatted as the wheel spun and *Foam Girl* came up into the wind, pointing as high as she was able. Instantly the ship's motion changed into a steep up and down chop as she began to attack the waves instead of riding with them as she had on the previous reach. She now was heading almost due west, seeming to charge the grey clouds racing down from the northwest.

"Square-riggers no good at pointing," shouted Gimp to his three passengers as they clung to the heaving rail. "Maybe we can get above him." He was seeking the protection of the wind itself, trying to move *Foam Girl* closer to the wind than the enemy vessel. The wind would provide an invisible barrier if the trick could be worked.

It could not. The great lean hull of their pursuer came around beautifully in line with their stern. The square yards, tiny figures scrambling along the yardarms, lay almost flat and the trysails and stunsails set fore and aft between the masts now showed as they took the weight of the wind. With the help of these sails and a huge gaff spanker on the mizzenmast, the big stranger began to overtake them even more easily than before, for her hull's length and height out of the water made far less of the steep wave action than the little *Foam Girl*.

"She's really unprintably lovely," shouted Captain Gimp in admiration. The squat sailor instinctively responded to the beauty of the other vessel's design even though it might mean his own destru tion He bawled another order and *Foam Girl* paid off, back on her old course to th southeast, with the wind in her quarter. At least this way she did not have to fight the seas as well, but could ride them. Behind her, close enough to see her black hull lift and the white bow wave, the pursuer came back too. She was less than half a mile away. A white figurehead, looking like a woman's body, glistened with wetness.

Can you do anything? the Metz asked Brother Aldo, once again mind-to-mind.

I am seeking what large water creatures are found here, was the old man's answer. *So far, I have found nothing. But I sense motion not far away. However, it is uncertain and I need a little time. Can you reach one of the archers you spoke of or are you too tired? Any delay will help.*

"I thought so!" shouted Gimp. His one-eyed mate had come and whispered something to him before slinking back to his control of the lower deck.

"Bald Roke is the man we have to deal with," the captain continued. "We can't be taken alive. His crew are cannibals and worse (Luchare wondered to herself how you got 'worse' but said nothing). That ship's *The Ravished Bride,* and she's manned by men, and other things, worse than any afloat. Bald Roke would skin his own sister alive for two coppers and a belly laugh. A good sailor, though, rot his dirty bowels, and that ship's a bloody marvel."

Hiero only half heard him. Once again he was seeking the unguarded minds of the enemy. He passed two non-human minds, one a Howler's, the other something new to him and then found what he was seeking. In a lower crosstree, crouched an archer armed with a crossbow, his gaze sweeping the deck as he watched for any sign of mutiny or other dangerous behavior. Hiero did not seek his name or anything else. With the utmost of mental strength he had left, he simply went after the man's own nerve endings, using the captive forebrain like a pair of pliers. The archer screamed in horror as his weapon rose to aim at *Bride's* helmsman despite his passionate attempt to force it down.

Once again, Hiero failed, though not by much. The bow went off and the quarrel sped on its way to bury itself in human flesh. But not the helmsman's. Instead, the bolt drove into the brain of a man standing nearby. At the same time the archer himself died as three arrows and a thrown spear struck him in turn. Hiero clearly saw the captain of the enemy who gave the order through the archer's fading sight, even as the man pitched from his lofty seat into the heaving sea. Tall, gaunt to emaciation, dressed in fantastic orange velvet, covered with jewels, his brown skull gleaming in the half light, Bald Roke was a strange and repellent figure. His thin clean-shaven face was disfigured by a scar running across it at the bridge of his nose, a crooked weal marking some past scuffle. Hiero felt him staring even as the priest withdrew from the dying body of his unwilling ally. Something else he saw too. Around the enemy leader's neck was a heavy chain of familiar bluish metal, and from it hung a massive, square pendant of the same, almost a shallow box. This was the source of the other's protection, the priest knew, a mechanical mind shield. He felt even wearier as he opened his own eyes again. Was there no weapon he could command against the hidden skills of the Unclean adepts?

But he was mercifully given no time to waste on self-pity.

"In the name of Blessed Saint Francis the Ecologist, they come!" shouted Brother Aldo. "Behold the children of the great waters!"

As he spoke, Captain Gimp ordered *Foam Girl* again into the wind and simultaneously had the sails lowered. They came down with a crash and all ran to the starboard rail to gaze at the new arrivals.

Protruding from the water between the two vessels, for the *Ravished Bride* now also came up into the wind and brailed her sails also, were two great heads. For a moment Hiero did not realize what he was seeing and then he gasped, for they were birds, although of monstrous size. The sleek, giant bodies were almost invisible under the tossing waters, but each was at least two-thirds the length of the *Foam Girl* herself. The beautiful heads and thick necks were not apparently feathered but almost scaled and a lovely soft green. The titanic beaks were straight, rounded javelins, each at least twelve feet long. The great bright eyes darted nervously about from one ship to the other, but the enormous invisible paddles kept the two avian monsters in place, responsive to the old Elevener's will.

"I won't have them attack if we can scare the other ship off," said Brother Aldo to the priest. "Even the Lowan are not invulnerable and that ship is full of weapons."

For a moment the two vessels hung, bowsprits to the wind while the crews simply stared at one another and the birds, each seeming to wait for the other to take some action. Then a human voice speaking *batwah* rose above the wind and carried easily over the two hundred feet of foaming water.

"Ahoy, there, is that you, Gimp, you little tub of rat puke? Speak up, lardguts, if you're not afraid to."

Bald Roke, his orange suit glittering even in the grey light of the cloudy sky, hung rakishly from one of his ratlines, leering across at the *Foam Girl*. As he shouted, his crew exploded in a storm of laughter and obscene jeers, glad to have a relief from the strain of watching the great birds, whose appearance seemed sheer magic to them.

"I'm here, Roke, you dirty corpse-eater!" yelled Gimp in reply. "Better get your carrion barge out of here, before we turn our little friends loose on it!"

"Will you indeed," said Roke, smiling gently. He seemed to ignore the giant birds and Hiero silently gave him credit for possessing his share of nerve. Roke went on.

"Tell you what, fatty, I think whoever runs these two pretty chickens would have turned 'em loose already, that is, if he dared. What do you think of that, now?" Again his crew screamed in delight, and a sea of edged weapons were brandished as they did. Roke waved one skinny hand and they quieted instantly.

"We could take you, birdies and all, you little blubber bag, but it might cost me some paint," continued the pirate, staring hard at the silent group on the poop of *Foam Girl*. "So being inclined for fun, I'll make you an offer, a generous one. Give us the dirty-looking rat with the paint on his nose and the whiskers, and the girl. In return, you're free to depart. What say you, short pizzle?"

Gimp answered instantly, but not before spitting into the sea. "Go fry your crew of maneaters in human grease, Roke. You'll get nought from us. But you brag, don't you, about how tough you are, skinhead? I dare you to fight *me* for a free passage, under Inland Seas Truce, man against man, hand weapons of choice. What do you say to that, you boney bag of slave girl's gauds?" This time it was the *Foam Girl's* crew who shouted and brandished weapons while the *Bride's* crew were silenced. The wonderful birds still held their place, as if they were mere ducks on some farm pond, thought Hiero absently.

After a brief colloquy with two of his subordinates, Roke swung back into the rigging, a vicious look on his face, the smile gone.

"All right, you little blot of slime weed, I take you. Anchor, and so will I. But not us two alone, see. Me and one of my mates will meet you and that brown-skinned savage with the painted face. Otherwise no go, and I gives the order to attack. What do you say, now, turdhead?"

"They're determined on you, Master Desteen," said Captain Gimp in a low voice. "They want you somehow, and what's more, Roke'll risk his whole ship and crew to get you. Can you fight? Are you game?"

"Try me," said Hiero, slapping him on the back. In truth, he was tired, but he saw no way out of this. "Will these dirty rogues keep such a bargain if they lose?"

"Oh yes!" Gimp was shocked. "Even the worst sea scum will honor a Seas Truce for single combat. Oh yes, have no fear. But Roke is a notable fighter. And who knows whom he'll bring with him? We'd better get ready." Captain Gimp turned and waved assent to Roke, who left the rigging at once.

Hiero now saw a ship's boat launched from *The Ravished Bride*, and while Gimp armed himself, he explained that the challenging vessel was always the scene of the combat.

"We have nought to lose," he went on. "All of the others will be slaves if we two are killed. But at least not killed and eaten. And if we win, we get their cargo or a good part of it; all we can carry at any rate."

Luchare helped Hiero strip to his pants and soft boots. Daughter of soldier kings, she said nothing and did not need to, but he could feel her body trembling through her hands. He knew she would not survive him by a minute, should he fall. Brother Aldo simply patted his hand and then turned away, back to his control of the birds.

Hiero weighed his short sword. He then turned and from a pile on deck, selected a heavy square brass shield, curved from side to side, for his left arm. His poniard was thrust, unsheathed, into his belt. With his bronze helmet on, he was ready. Gimp was now stripped to his kilt and was barefoot as well. He bore no shield but a long, gently curved sword, rather slender, something on the order of an immense sabre, save that the point was slightly angled. It was designed obviously, for both hands. His arms were very long and rippled with muscle as he waved the big sword delicately about. He no longer appeared comic and his square jaw was set.

The boat of the enemy grated alongside. Over the rail first came the bald head of the pirate captain and behind him came his partner. Hiero shuddered inwardly. A Leemute, and one of unknown type! And it also wore a mind shield about its neck.

The creature was as tall as a man and, Hiero realized, might really be descended from men. It wore only a short leather jerkin, but its natural skin was a mass of tiny dull grey scales. It had no visible nose or ears, only holes in both places and its dull eyes were lashless under massive bony brows. In one powerful arm it carried a single-edged, heavy axe, in the other a small shield. The crew shrank away from it.

Bald Roke still wore his orange finery and numerous rings glittered on his hands. Brooches and necklaces spangled his stained jacket, which had slashed sleeves for easy movement. He carried a slender, straight sword with a basket hilt and in the other hand, a long two-edged dagger.

The men of *Foam Girl* now scattered to the extremes of bow and stern, with a good few hanging on to the ratlines, but all well out of sword stroke.

"We fight around the ship, Skinny," said Gimp, "up to the forepeak line and back to these steps. No holds barred, no survivors. You get forward now, we'll stay here. At my word we'll start for each other, you and Corpseface there against me and my friend."

The creature with Roke snarled, displaying a mouthful of sharp, yellow fangs, but Roke laughed jeeringly.

"Suits me, Low-pockets. But you and your mind-twisting magician here ain't met a Glith before. Loaned to me he was, by good friends up north and west of here. We'll she how funny you think he is in a minute."

Hiero spoke for the first time, in a calm voice which nevertheless carried easily. "I know your fine friends, Captain Roke. They are among the living dead. The grave yawns for all of them and for this creature and for you as well." His vibrant tone seemed to carry flat certainty.

For a second Roke appeared to pale. If the horrid thing with him, the Glith, was new to the company of *Foam Girl*, the Metz priest was equally so to him, and despite his new amulet's protection, Roke was unsure of himself. But he was a hardy scoundrel, and rallied.

"Glad you found a voice, Whiskers. We'll mark your pretty paint in a few seconds. Come on, Daleeth, let's get forr-ard."

In a moment all was ready. The ship fell silent, save for the creak of timbers and straining cordage as her anchor line sawed the hawsehole. The two rogues, who had rowed Roke and the Glith over, clung to shrouds above the rail by their boat's painter, eyes glittering with excitement. A seabird called far off, a faint piercing cry.

From his place to Hiero's right, Gimp shouted "go!" and marched forward. The four, two and two, one to each bulwark, advanced cautiously toward one another. This care alone would have told anyone of experience that trained warriors were meeting. There would be no headlong rushes and novice blunderings here. All four of them knew their business.

Hiero faced the Glith and the two captains, tall and short, each other. They met on either side of the little cabin, almost exactly amidships. A vagrant gleam of sunshine momentarily pierced the racing clouds and illumined the foul creature's axehead as it advanced, but aside from that, it was a thing of dead hues, grey-scaled skin, grey garment and lustreless eyes. Yet it was alert and every rippling muscle revealed power and agility. Nevertheless, it advanced slowly, very slowly. As it came cautiously on, Hiero heard the clash of metal to his left where the other two had commenced. As any trained swordsman does, he watched fixedly his foe's eyes for a sign of its intentions.

Those eyes! Great, sombre, empty pools, seeming to have no bottom. Even as he watched, they grew larger. Larger! The Glith was no more than a few yards away, its axe poised on its shoulder, shield lowered. And all Hiero could see were the eyes, the round, lightless caverns of emptiness, which seemed to swell and grow until all else faded. Far off, he heard a woman scream. Luchare! The eyes vanished, shrunk to normal size and the consciousness of where he was returned. Almost too late!

Reflex and training saved Hiero. The old retired Ranger Sergeant who had first trained him had always stressed one point in the Abbey school of all arms manual. Close in! "Look," the old veteran had insisted, "always try to close in quick, particularly if your opponent looks better than you. There's no monkey tricks with sword or spear at someone's throat from two inches away, boys. Give luck and plain meanness a chance!"

He felt the wind of the heavy axe as he dove under it, not trying a blow, but simply shoving with his shield's boss at the Glith's body. Until he was ready and again unshaken, he wanted no more of those eyes!

Hypnotism! No mind shield guarded against that! Roke, or perhaps the creature itself, had been very clever. Almost, Hiero had been lured into the axe, like a calf to the slaughter, helpless to avert the deathstroke. Had not Luchare screamed, he would now be dead.

He wrestled now with the scaled thing, his shield arm holding off its axe above him, its own shield keeping his sword arm locked in turn. It gave off a mephitic foulness and its skin seemed to radiate a chill. Its hissing breath was a charnel stench but he kept his head lowered to avoid the eyes. God, but it was strong!

Hiero summoned all his own strength and simply shoved, at the same time springing backward. The axe fell again, but he was beyond its reach. For a second he faced his enemy, panting slightly, watching the pointed chin and the shoulders, but never seeking the eyes. He crossed his shield over so that it hid his body and lowered his short sword so that it hung at the end of his arm. Dimly, he was conscious of the clash of arms continuing on the other side of the cabin, but he kept his attention riveted on his foe. He heard Klootz bellow hideously, knowing his master was in peril, but he paid no heed.

It advanced again, axe held high. Was it inviting a low thrust, he wondered? He had trouble breaking the habit of years and never looking at the enemy's eyes, but somehow he managed it.

Then the Glith charged. As it came, the axe came down in a sweeping stroke and Hiero sprang back, ready to spring in again as the axe struck the deck. He had fought few axemen and it was almost the death of him for the second time. The Glith's powerful arms straightened and the blade of the axe swung, cutting a sideways arc with all its speed undiminished, straight at Hiero's knees.

This time, instinct took over and the priest leapt straight up in the air. Even so, the follow-through of the Glith's shield arm struck his thigh, a second after the axe itself hissed by under his feet. The impact sent him reeling backward. The downward heave of the deck now caught him dead wrong as he went and he stumbled away, fighting for his feet, fetching up with a ringing crash against the mizzenmast. With a grating cry as hideous to ears as its appearance was to the eyes, the Glith charged again, axe on high, clawed toes raking the planks of the deck.

But Hiero had never quite left his feet, though now he was crouching. And this was the chance he had been waiting for. As the Glith leapt forward, the edge of the square brass shield, like some strange quoit, came spinning at its legs with all the force the Metz could put behind it. When he had crossed the shield over his torso moments before, Hiero had also freed the arm straps which held it, in preparation for just this maneuver.

The skimming shield now took the brawny legs out from under the alien creature as neatly as if it had been tripped. The Glith crashed to the deck, prostrate, arms outflung, its noseless visage striking the wood with an audible thud. Even as it struggled to rise, the heavy, short sword came down on its scaled head, splitting it as a crow splits a cobnut. There was a rush of dark matter, the great limbs twitched once and then the foul life departed.

The priest managed to recover his shield and he ran clumsily forward past Klootz's pen, ignoring the morse's bleating as he went to where he could still hear the clash of steel. The strained silence of the crew and their eyes glued to the scene up there told him that the issue was still in doubt.

It was indeed. As Hiero arrived, winded but with shield up, he saw Captain Gimp block a high thrust of the pirate's sword and barely miss being skewered by the long dagger held in the other's left hand.

"I'm coming," Hiero yelled. "Hold him a second, and I'll help take care of him." This was no matter of chivalry. In a stark, four-handed duel of this sort, it was expected that the survivors should have won by any means possible, saving only illegal weapons such as bows. No quarter!

But Hiero's voice breathed new life into the little merchant skipper. Although his hairy torso was covered with blood from a dozen minor slashes, he still possessed plenty of energy. He stood, eyeing his equally bloody foe for an instant and then ran in with a great whoop, the long, two-handed sword held high over his head. Nothing loath, Roke came to meet him, his eyes mad with rage and disappointmcnt.

As they both charged, Gimp proved what his long, curved blade could do. Amazingly, he seemed to fall forward on his face, but his left hand caught the deck and held him off it. At the same time his long right arm, clenched fist now holding the long hilt by itself, swept out in a flashing backhand arc, like some monstrous scythe.

It was too late for Bald Roke, seasoned battler though he was, to check himself. He tried with his own sword to deflect the terrible blow, but all the force in Gimp's squat frame was in its onward rush. The razor edge of the great sword cut in below the pirate's elbow and severed his sword arm in turn as neatly as a scissor cuts a thread. Passing on through, it drove deep into his orange finery until checked with an audible sound by some bone. A shower of blood sprayed out, as Roke strove to keep his feet, even while life faded from his glazing eyes. He took two tottering steps toward his enemy, who never moved, spread out like a four-legged beast on the pitching deck. One arm still gripped the bloody sword which had now slipped from the now scarlet tatters of Roke's dress.

Then with a choked sigh, all ended. One instant Roke towered up, his poniard raised in a last defiance, the next, he lay a crumpled heap of blood-soaked rags, his severed forearm lying near him, still clutching his basket-hilt sword in its death grip. There was silence again.

Then the crew exploded. The shouting almost deafened Hiero, but he managed to lurch over and help the captain to his feet before embracing him. Then a dozen pair of hands tore them apart and carried them in triumph to *Foam Girl's* poop; there Luchare, her eyes blazing in triumph, waited for her lover.

Even as he hugged her in turn, forgetting Gimp's blood and the dark ichor of the Glith, Hiero suddenly began to laugh. For out of the ship's cabin, unbidden, had come a peevish thought.

What's all this noise? Why can't I get some sleep?

The lazy bear had slept through the whole night and the entire chase and subsequent battle. Now he was demanding to know what on earth was happening!

Still holding Luchare, Hiero watched in silence as the two bird giants, the Lowans, dived suddenly into the curling seas and disappeared, their vast bodies as easily handled as if they were dabchicks. He saw that Brother Aldo looked very weary, as weary as he himself felt, and he realized that the old man must have greatly exerted himself to have held the two bird things obedient to his will for so long.

Gimp was now everywhere, personally looting Roke's corpse, bellowing orders and calmly warping the *Foam Girl* alongside the *Bride* as if the latter were some peaceful barge be dealt with for hides every week in the year.

But his confidence seemed quite justified. Aside from some haggling over the worth of the *Bride's* cargo, there was no apparent animosity between the crews. The pirates were as villainous a crew of unhung ruffians as Hiero had ever imagined, but not even the single, dirty-looking Howler offered so much as an insult. Indeed, various scurvy wretches bawled coarse praise of Hiero's skill with weapons along with sundry odious compliments to Luchare's appearance and probable amatory skills. These latter drove that young lady quickly into the cabin, her ears burning.

While Gimp checked *The Ravished Bride's* cargo along with a burly thug who was now her temporary new master, Hiero sat on a bench and expressed surprise to Brother Aldo that such utter scoundrels would honor anything at all, let alone freely give up valuable goods.

194

"A pirate ship did violate the Inland Seas Truce in my lifetime, Hiero, long ago, long, long ago, but I can still remember. Everyone, pirate, raider, and armed merchant sought her for a season and eventually she was found and trapped. The crew, such as were not killed outright in the battle, were first impaled, then flayed alive. The captain, who had caused it to happen, lost a joint of each finger and toe, arm and leg, every day until he died. The same severed joints, broiled, I believe, were his sole sustenance until then," added the old man thoughtfully. "If a captain even suggested such a thing now, I suspect his crew would kill him before he succeeded in drawing his weapons."

"But how about the Unclean? Surely they honor nothing? And where are those other two men with the mechanical mind blocks? I can't detect them any more. Have they somehow escaped?"

"That's interesting," said Brother Aldo, his eye brightening. "Only one answer I can see. They're in the drink, my boy, put there by their own fellows for some foolery or other such as suggesting a truce violation. Or maybe just simple fear of the Unclean devices by their shipmates. No, they haven't escaped."

"We'd better get the two mindlocks that Roke and my friend, the Glith, had, in fact right now, while I think of it," said the priest, starting up with a groan. His side bore a great, blackened bruise where he had struck the mast and he ached all over.

Brother Aldo chuckled. He patted the leather pouch which hung over one shoulder and something within clinked musically. "I had Gimp take care of that right away. None of the common sailors wanted to touch them anyway. We'll have a look at them, you and I, when a little leisure presents itself." As he spoke, something stirred in the depths of Hiero's memory. Whatever it was could not rise to the surface, however, and he dismissed it with a sigh. Other matters came more easily to his attention.

"Would those birds really have attacked the pirates?" he asked.

"I'd have hated to do it, but yes, I think so. I think I could have made them." The chocolate skin of his face had lost its usual glow and Hiero saw that Brother Aldo was a very old man indeed. *How old* he wondered? Now as they watched the two crews transshipping boxes and bales of goods from the large ship down a gangway to the *Foam Girl,* the Elevener went on. "Who knows how it would have ended. Six tons or so of squawking, flapping Lowans would make even that big ship look smaller, especially if they were trying to come aboard! They're not at all common, you know, I've only seen them three or four times in my life."

"It was a great feat, to both summon and control such vast things," said

Hiero in honest admiration.

The old man shrugged off the praise. "My business, Hiero, and I think you have learnt more in a few months about such things that I in a great many years. But something else is troubling you."

"Yes," said the Metz, his voice lowered, so that no one nearby could hear him. "That thing I killed, the Glith, Roke called it. It was a mighty hypnotist, you know, and damned near got me under a spell. Only Luchare's shriek brought me out. What was it? The crew threw its body overboard quickly and I never got much of a look. Surely it belongs to the Unclean."

"I got little more of a look than you, but I did try to examine it when I took the mindlock from its neck. Gimp got the other one for me." Aldo paused.

"We have heard rumors of new mutations, what you'd call Leemutes, new and more dreadful ones, which did not grow by accident from ancient genetic damage. No—these new creatures have been *bred* and trained from birth in the Unclean laboratories and fortresses. This Glith thing could be one such. Certainly I never saw anything like it before."

"It was like a loathsome reptile crossed with an even more wicked and repellent human," said Hiero.

"A very typical concept of the Unclean it sounds, doesn't it?" asked Brother Aldo. He seemed to expect no answer and simply continued to stare blankly away over the grey and tossing seas.

10: *THE FORESTS OF THE SOUTH*

Night lay over the ancient port of Neeyana. A few small craft moved on the surface of the moonlit harbor, mostly skiffs taking crews out to sailing ships at anchor. No cargo had moved on any of the long piers and wharves since sunset. In the narrow murky streets leading to the harbor a few dim lights glowed where a street held a few taverns for late roisterers. Now and again a furtive, solitary shape moved in the shadows bent on some dubious errand or other, but no honest man ventured out at night in Neeyana unless well guarded or simply desperate. Too long had evil had its way with the old harbor town and now only those under the protection of that same evil could walk unchallenged save in broad daylight or in well-armed company. Yet cargo had to move and no other sea port served this southeastern corner of the Inland Sea. Hence the east-west trade passed through Neeyana, in haste and fear on one side and grudging reluctance on that of the other, which ruled. A greater tribute could hardly have been paid the mercantile instinct of the human race in the fact that the trade continued and in some sense even flourished.

From high in a tower, indeed the actual highest point in Neeyana, two dark shapes watched over the nighted harbor below and the moon-rayed expanse of sea beyond, out to the black line marking the northern horizon.

"All seems useless against this fantastic crew of intruders," said a harsh voice. "Whatever we do, whatever weapons we use, it seems to make no difference. The chief enemy bursts our bonds, evades our strokes and destroys our ships without trace. Nothing seems capable of arresting his progress, even momentarily. A pretty pass we've come to!"

"I agree," said a second voice, as like the first as a twin. "But consider. They, or he, for we have no idea what his allies actually represent, has now

197

passed through two Circles. The Yellow, ours, lies before him, unless he turns back or goes elsewhere on a tangent. And both ideas seem to me unlikely. He has always moved in this direction since we first had word of his coming. And the Blue Master, S'duna, is also coming here!

"So he too will come here, our foe will, or at least near to here. In fact, I have news. He *is* coming. I just came from the instrument room. Two of the new Vocoders registered by the Blue Circle are moving this way across the sea. We have established that the Blue Brothers gave out four! Three to shipmen in this area, men we know well, led by Bald Roke. And one, mark you, to a Glith! The Glith was along to keep Roke under control if necessary."

"And now?" the first harsh voice was eager.

"Two of the instruments are gone, destroyed at a guess. Two are turned off but of course still registering on our screens. I would hazard the four original owners, the Glith included, were now dead and that the enemy, unwitting, has pocketed the two remaining instruments, perhaps for study. A guess, but I think rather a good one." There was a pause.

"Now, I believe, we can start to summon some of our own forces. The Yellow Brothers at least will not fail the cause!"

There was silence again as the two dark shapes, their hoods drawn in the moonlight, stared out over the old town. The stone parapet on which they leant had long ago encircled the belfry of an ancient church, but the tall tower now housed only nightmare evil.

Far off in the east, a faint light gave promise of coming dawn. The figures turned and vanished from the tower.

"We will have to trust to our wits, at least as much as any Unclean chart, Hiero." Brother Aldo's long, dark forefinger pointed to a line on the map spread out before them. "For one thing," he went on, "we can't read all of it."

The bear drowsed in a corner of the little cabin's heaving deck, the flickering lantern light making him look larger than he was. At the round table, its base clamped to the deck, sat the Metz, Brother Aldo, Luchare and Captain Gimp, all trying to interpret the secrets of the strange map.

"We Eleveners have learned to read some of their symbols, over the years, that is," went on Brother Aldo. "But things such as these maps have seldom fallen into our hands in my lifetime, which is not a short one. This must be a precious chance.

"See here!" His finger traced a thin, crooked line from the Inland Sea, which inclined roughly southeast by east. "This is a trail I have not used in many seasons. It lies to the north of the track over which you were brought, Princess. That particular one is the major route between the Lantik coast and this sea of freshwater on which we now ride. It goes to Neeyana, *here.*" His finger indicated a circle.

"Now, as you felt in your bones, child, Neeyana is wholly given over to evil. This mark I know well, an enemy mark, unchanged for hundreds of years. It means 'ours' and see here, it overlies the whole city. Still, trade, some of it quite innocent, passes through. The Unclean suffer it, taxing it not too heavily, but gathering a good deal of information and also using the traders as a cover for their own agents and schemes.

"Well, so do we! And I would wager we generally know more of their plans than they do of ours.

"But I wonder." Again his gnarled finger traced the narrower line of the northern trail. "This goes through the forest, and Hiero, my friend, you have never seen our southern trees! Look here, now, look, a patch of another circle. Blue it is. Without trying to figure out the enemy color chart, I can tell you what that means. A desert, and a deadly one for it was caused by the radiation of The Death. These blighted deserts and similar strange radioactive spots are generally shrinking, but they still exist, and a few even spread, so long was the life of the deadly cobalt bombs, and the stranger life they engendered. Hence the blue. For on our own maps these places are colored blue also, 'cobalt' being an ancient pre-Death word for that color.

"So, Hiero, the large dead city you seek seems to lie near to that waste, or on its northern edge. In the distance are other lost cities, but much further on to the east. Still I would feel better if I could see the map the Abbey rulers gave you. If you will trust me."

There was a brief silence. The lantern creaked at the end of its short chain. No one spoke.

"Surely you trust the good Brother, Master Hiero?" burst out Captain Gimp. He banged his fist on the table. "Why, he's saved all our lives a dozen times over in the past, and yours twice I knows of!"

Hiero laughed, his swarthy, hawk face clearing on the instant. "Sorry, Brother Aldo. You're quite right, Gimp, I apologize. But Abbot Demero laid it upon me to keep this secret. My mission, I mean, or at least its ultimate goal. I find it hard to trust anyone at all. The Unclean have so damned many disguises!

"Still, if I can't tell my real friends by now, I'd better give up! And I mean you too, Captain! Here's the map then. What do you think, Brother?"

199

"Ah!" For a minute or so, the curly white beard almost touched the surface of the Abbey map as the old man pored over it. Then he straightened and looked at the others, dark eyes glowing, the whites like new ivory.

"I thought so. This is a very old map, Hiero, or rather a new copy of an old map. There are things on here I did not know still to exist and others which I know for a fact not to exist at all, at least for many centuries."

"In other words," said the priest, "a quite unreliable guide?"

"Yes and no. Alone, with no other aids, definitely yes. But with me and with the Unclean's own set of maps, perhaps, not. For as I said, there are things on here, on your map, which are now covered by ancient forest and evil waste and yet which could perhaps now be found again."

They pondered this for a while as the even rhythm of the *Foam Girl* never changed, rocking up and down, up and down, as she rode the long swells running to the south. Above their heads the lantern smoked and swayed in tune with the shifting motion. It was two days after their battle with the pirates.

A discussion of routes continued. Hiero had still not mentioned what he ultimately sought and he had no intention of doing so. The fewer people who knew, the better, even if utterly trustworthy. He could always kill himself if trapped, in which case the enemy would still be left uncertain as to his true goal. He knew more strongly as each league rolled under *Foam Girl's* keel, that the Unclean would lay a nation in ashes to gain one of the ancient computers. With such a device they would be literally invulnerable.

He saw that Brother Aldo was looking at him expectantly and brought his attention back with a start.

"Sorry, I missed that last remark."

"Well, Gimp knows of no harbor, at least none inhabited, on that coast where the northern trail comes down. He says it's untouched forest right down to the edge of the sea. But we'd better try and find that trailhead all the same. Even overgrown, I feel it is our best chance, and it heads straight to that desert. And one thing about the great woods is that there we will be on *my* ground. The Unclean do haunt the forests at times, but even with their beast and Leemute allies, they do not *know* them, not as we do. And Hiero, you are a woods ranger too, even if only of the smaller woods of the Taig, which we southerners know to be stunted and shrivelled." His laughing eyes made the others smile at the jest.

"All right," said Hiero, folding the maps and stowing them away. "How far from Neeyana is that trail end do you think?"

"If that map, or rather all them maps, are right, not much more'n fifty miles up the coast," said Gimp. His small eyes stared beadily at them.

"There's sometimes a few savages in the woods around there, mostly a wee kind of red dwarf man with poisoned arrows, that likes to shoot at ships when we come in for wood or fruit. I'll do my best to get you in to where that line there ends, but how you'll find it in them trees is beyond me. And the animals! Whew!"

"Good," said the old man. "Never mind the beasts, Gimp. You'll be safe enough in our good ship here. The high forest does not reach out into your beloved waters. Hiero, we have a little time now and we should make land in only a few hours more. What do you say we examine those mind locks which we captured from the enemy? I have them right here."

In a moment the two strange devices were laid upon the table before them. Luchare looked at them with loathing, but Hiero and Brother Aldo with interest, while Gimp's battered face seemed to reflect both attitudes.

The locks themselves were of the curious oily-looking bluish metal which Hiero had noticed the Unclean favored. The heavy neck chains were of some other metal, lighter in weight, though the color was not dissimilar. The mysterious mechanisms lay inside square cases, about three inches around and a half inch thick. There were certain marks like writing incised on them, but no one there, not even old Aldo, could read them. Other decoration there was none. And there were only very faint visible seams and no catch, or opening, on them at all.

"Don't you suppose," said Luchare, looking closely at a fine seam line, "that it would be dangerous to break one? Are they guarded in some way, do you think, so that a person opening it wrong would be hurt?"

"That's possible," said Hiero. He lifted a case and held it to his ear. Was it his imagination or did he hear an almost imperceptible humming inside?

"No, I hear nothing," said Brother Aldo, on being asked, nor did the others. "But I know very little of such things," he continued. "To be quite honest, few of my order do. We have concentrated on developing empathy with all life through our natural mental powers, and again, quite frankly, we dislike mechanical devices of any sort. This may be a mistake. I think myself we may have gone too far in the anti-machine direction. There's no reason that a limited number of machines cannot help the world, if they are controlled and properly designed. And we had better figure out the working of many Unclean devices or we'll be in real trouble. But I'm not the man to do it, I'm afraid. Actually, Hiero, you've had a lot of experience lately with their devices. You should know as much as anyone not actually in their ranks, I would think."

Hiero stared gloomily at the two shining objects on the table. Once more something gnawed faintly at his memory, some random thought, but again it seemed too elusive to come to the surface of his mind.

"The only gadgets I've seen, that is, Unclean devices," he said slowly, "weren't much like this. There was Luchare's lance which is a thought amplifier as well, and that compass thing I also took off S'nerg, way back up North. I had to destroy that; remind me to tell you about it later. Then there was the mind prober they tried to use on me at the Dead Isle. And the machine I call the lightning gun, that blasted me down. I think it shoots charges of static electricity, though God alone knows how. These are mind blocks and they must be miracles of design: they're so *small*."

He sighed. "I can't figure them out at all, and yet something keeps telling me to be awfully careful of them. Maybe Luchare's right; some explosive or poison or something of the sort lies inside for the unwary."

"Well, I better go on deck," said Gimp, rising. "Landfall can't be many hours away, no, nor dawn neither. And I don't want to run on an uncharted rock, not off this coast!"

"I'm going to bed and so is Hiero," said Luchare firmly. "We'll need all our rest tomorrow and only that lazy bear is getting a proper amount of sleep."

"You're right," said Aldo, also rising. "But old men don't need much sleep, princess, so I'll walk the decks with our captain. Perhaps I'll get a message or two."

Hiero yawned and pulled off his boots, sitting on the edge of the bunk. Beside him, Luchare's eyes were already closed. She fell asleep like a child, he had noted, in seconds. *Damn it, what was there about those mind locks that worried him so?* He glared at the things as they lay, still glinting on the table, then blew out the lantern. Whatever it was could wait.

The long, wailing cry "Land - hooooo," woke him up on the instant. Light, the grey light of dawn, was streaming in through an open cabin port-hole. And then as he sat up, he remembered! The memory was of the compass machine he had destroyed weeks ago, far up in the Palood! It had been a tell-tale, an Unclean homing device! And for a dead rat's skin, so too were these damned mind locks!

In an instant, ignoring Luchare's startled cry, he was on deck, bellowing for the captain, yelling for Brother Aldo. Both appeared instantly and watched in horrified fascination as he smashed both locks on the deck, using a handy belaying pin. As he did so, he gasped out the reason and the alarm flew in their eyes. Only when the deadly things were powdered metal did he look

202

up and see to where *Foam Girl* was heading.

The forest of the South! Not a mile away rose a rank of such trees as he had hardly dreamed possible, even though he had been warned what to expect. The actual shore was invisible, screened by rank growth, mostly bushes and shrubs, all of different shades of green. And behind them in turn reared up the giants of the forest: black boles, brown trunks, tan bark, all the hues and per- mutations of brown to black, with reddish glints here and there, rose the mighty trees. The Metz had to almost arch his back to see their incredible tops. Around some of the great trunks and hanging from the lofty branches, there twisted vines and lianas of every hue, some of whose girth looked greater than that of *Foam Girl*'s hull! Splotches of color, mostly blazing reds and yellows, here and there revealed the presence of giant flowering plants, which clung to the trees far up their enormous lengths. Through Gimp's proffered telescope, Hiero could see a mass of intertwined smaller plants festooning every vacant space between the boughs. The smells of the ti- tanic forest reached out across the water to them, a medley of strange scents and musky perfumes. Beside Hiero's head, Klootz suddenly bellowed from his pen, as if in greeting to a wood greater than any he had ever known. The answering call of some strange monster, a thunderous roar, echoed back faintly from the distant shore and a flight of large white birds rose from the foliage directly in front of them. A physical wave of warmth seemed to reach out to them.

"Can you get her in quicker?" The priest turned to Gimp in question. "I'm suddenly horribly afraid. We've given someone a constant clue to our position for over two days. And we're not far from Neeyana, which they control." He ignored Luchare who now came on deck fully dressed and moved up to his side. But she seemed not to mind and bent to adjust her boots.

"Well, Master Hiero, you can see the sails are half brailed," said the little seaman. "I don't dare go ramming in at full speed. We've got three good lookouts in the bows and forepeak. But there may be anything from sunken logs to nice pointed rocks just under the surface. A few moments more should do, though."

In the sun of early morning, the little ship sailed slowly in to the towering green wall of jungle ahead, a light breeze carrying her smoothly over the gentle swells. The hum of a tiny surf beating on the roots and tangled dead- falls of the shore now came to them.

Hiero finished a brief and private prayer session but he was still nervous and inwardly cursing himself. Now he sent out his mind impulses, wishing he had thought to wake up hours before and start doing it to them. Beside him, Brother Aldo stood, eyes shut, seeming to merely breathe in the warm scents of the forest as they grew increasingly strong.

Hiero clutched the old man's brown sleeve suddenly. *Foam Girl* was now only a few hundred yards off the tangle of plants which made up the actual edge where forest met sea.

"There's something coming from the west! I can't probe it! There's a mind guard, a big one, like the one on that Unclean ship you sank! They're coming fast." He felt sudden anguish. What was there he had not failed to do?

Aldo instantly turned and rapped out an order to the captain. "Gimp, put us ashore, the ship too, and get your crew mustered. Hurry, or we're all dead men!" There was no benevolence on his face now, and the high black cheekbones were ramparts of decision. His great eyes blazed with imperious will.

Gimp now volleyed orders in every direction, at the same time aiding in rigging the arrow engine personally. The one-eyed mate, Blutho, took the helm as the two great crescent sails rose and were hauled up full so they filled to the breeze. *Foam Girl* put her nose into a trough, rose on the next long swell, and rushed headlong for the tree-girt shore.

Over the hubbub on deck and the swirl of activity, Hiero became aware of Luchare pressed against his side, buckling on his weapons. *I failed,* he thought to her as he adjusted his battle helmet. It did not occur to him to speak.

Nonsense, came her calm answer. *No one else warned us at all. You've carried all the weight, mostly alone, for weeks.* Even as his brain received the answer, he felt wonder at both the ease of her message and the closeness of their combined mental-physical contact. Being completely male, he could not help his mind going further. *I wonder if we could yet,* he thought, toying with the idea of love-making simultaneously by mind and body, something he had not so far dared attempt.

Probably, came the prompt answer, *but this is no time for it, you clown! Go get Klootz ready. I'll watch the bear.* It was like a (friendly) dash of icewater. He blinked, and came back to the present.

The big morse was wild with excitement and Hiero had to use his own mind hard, like a curb, to quiet him down. Barely was he saddled when they struck.

Foam Girl nosed straight and hard into a solid mass of outthrust roots and stunted mangrove-like trees with a prolonged grating crunch. Many men on

204

deck, who were concentrating on their tasks were jolted off their feet, but nothing worse happened. Fortunately, the sea ran deep here, right up to the shore, and this made their crash landing fairly easy.

"Ashore everyone!" came Gimp's stentorian shouting. He had conferred with Aldo constantly as they raced in, for like any really good gambler, he never hesitated a moment to cut his losses. A squad of hardy rascals hurled themselves off the bowsprit, chopping madly with axes and heavy cutlasses at the packed vegetation. Nothing but a rat or small monkey could have got through that tangle of growth unaided. Behind this gang gathered most of the crew, now armed and loaded with hastily snatched up supplies and emergency gear. Gimp and Blutho led them and behind them in turn were Aldo, the girl, and the priest, who led the morse and the bear, though "led" was not how Gorm saw it. All of the humans save those using the axes were watching down coast to the west. As they looked, the black, slim shape they had grown to dread appeared, nosing around a point not a mile away, white foam curling under the sharp prow.

At the sight, Gimp himself seized a broadaxe and, shoving his men aside, fell upon the green matter before him like a fury, using great hewing strokes which severed foot-thick vines like so much string. Those of the men who could find a footing near him redoubled their own efforts. Brother Aldo noticed the arrow engine crew still stoutly manning the machine on the poop and now ordered them away with the others.

From the Unclean ship, now coming like a storm, a distant screech came down the wind. At the same time a flare of vivid blue light winked from her foredeck.

"The lightning gun!" cried Hiero and Luchare together. A hundred yards off the stern, a column of steam rose suddenly from a white-capped swell.

"Come on now," screamed Gimp not out of sight in the green growth, "We've cut a path for you and it widens. Shake your stumps, you lazy bastard whoresons!" This latter epithet was addressed to his loyal crew, who now scrambled off the bowsprit like so many ants. Behind them, Hiero led and urged Klootz forward, Luchare walking on the other side of the bull's head. Gorm leapt off the deck and followed the men in a second. Brother Aldo, nimble as a cricket, clambered after him.

Klootz trod warily over the tangle of ropes and discarded gear at the bow. The priest and the girl soothed him with soft words as the great brute cautiously examined the jungle ahead. Only Aldo was yet still in sight, beckoning them eagerly on. For some reason, the forest's warmth struck Hiero only

205

now; it was as if they were entering a furnace, though a damp one. Klootz paused, hindquarters bunching.

Whoever was aiming the lightning gun finally got his range. There was a ripping crash, and looking back in horror, the humans saw the after half of the little cabin simply vanish in a cloud of white incandescence. The wave of awful attendant heat almost scorched their back hair.

The bull morse let out a terrified bawl and sprang straight forward off the ship, dragging the two with him, as they clung frantically to the reins. More by luck than anything else, the animal headed straight into the ragged gap cut by the crew in the foliage. Brother Aldo leapt aside just in time to avoid being trampled to death and picking himself quickly up, scuttled in their wake. In a second the empty *Foam Girl,* sails and cordage slatting in the offshore breeze, was the only sign that anyone had been there. The smoke of a brisk fire ascended into the morning sunlight from her blazing cabin and midships. With a sudden rush, the fire ran up the stays to the peak of the main mast and in another instant the peaked sail burst into a flaming blossom of orange light. The crackling bolts of the lightning gun continued to strike through the smoke and haze, but the electric charges simply blasted holes at random in the green curtain of plants on the shore, for the gunners, though now very close, could actually see nothing. At length the order to cease fire was given. The black ship lay hove to, close in, while from her deck sharp eyes tried in vain to discern through the smoke what had become of their prey. It was a patently useless exercise and soon the lean hull turned, the hidden engines started, and the Unclean ship swept away back down the wooded coast to the west. In a few minutes she was out of sight. The now furiously burning *Foam Girl* sent a column of reeking black smoke high in the air, from whence it was bent inland by the wind, over the tops of the enormous trees. Nothing moved on the shore save a few small birds.

Far away, in a crypt deep under the earth and cobbles of old Neeyana, a figure turned away from an instrument board with an exclamation of disgust. "Is this your vaunted efficiency?" The hooded shape hissed to another standing near. "The Yellow Circle would show the Blue, eh? I'll have a word with your Masters in due season!" S'duna of the Blue Circle, enraged and frustrated, left the chamber, his cold rage going before him like a noxious cloud. All who felt it shrank away and hid themselves, but elsewhere in the Unclean citadel, new orders were given and the servants of the Yellow Circle sprang to new action. Another stroke unaccountably had failed, but the chase would not be given up, not while one of the dark brotherhood remained.

206

The camp that night, set deep in the canopy of the great trees, was not a cheerful one. The seamen, long used to the open air, felt the dank heat and the smothering darkness as doubly oppressive and frightening, even though Gimp and Blutho maintained a stern discipline and also continually pointed out that no lives had been lost. Both Hiero and Luchare nursed bad bruises from being dragged through the thickets for a hundred yards in Klootz's initial panic. Two small fires kept some of the gloom away, and a low barrier of fallen logs and branches encircled the camp, providing at least some psychological protection, if nothing more.

But the vast tree trunks rising out of the limit of firelight into the upper dark, the mysterious cries and sounds of the encircling jungle and the blazing eyes which stared out of the night at the fires, all combined to make the men huddle together and talk in low tones or not at all.

"We were lucky to find this clearing," said Hiero, stoically trying to avoid noticing his battered arms and legs. He knew Luchare was equally in pain and also saying nothing, and his heart went out to her. They sat a little apart, with the bear and the morse, the latter now peacefully chewing his cud. Brother Aldo had vanished earlier, only saying that he would be back before moonrise. "Not that it will shed much light down here," he added.

"I guess he went to find that trail, that is if anyone can find it," said the girl. Her dark face was drawn and tired in the light of the flames.

"Listen to that, will you!" said Hiero, springing to his feet, hand on sword. All the others had leapt up too, as a perfectly appalling racket burst out not far away, hideous earthshaking screams of rage rising above a deep hoarse bellowing, as if the father of all cats had attacked the grand uncle of all bovines. The bellowing sound alone made Klootz's loudest efforts sound like a baby's squall. As suddenly as they had begun, the frightful sounds died away, leaving everyone half deafened. The ordinary screeches, yells and howls of the night resumed, aided by the sounds of countless stridulating insects. The men slowly settled down again.

A large beast indeed, came a placid thought from Gorm. *And it was attacked by one almost as large, which it slew. Now it is very angry. I think I would tell the men to be quiet.* Very *quiet.*

Hiero dashed to the nearest group, hissing for silence. One look at his face brought compliance. If the bear warned, he had learned, it was as well to listen. Soon all the men were waiting, weapons drawn, not moving, but simply crouched and staring nervously around and outward.

It comes, was the bear's thought. *Be ready.*

The Metz stood next to Klootz, trying to shield Luchare, who faced the same way into the dark as he did. It was to the south, he noted idly, trying to

207

detect the creature's mind as hard as he could. Presently he thought he had found it. The brain was not too unlike that of the morse, but far, far more stupid, and now filled with insensate rage and much pain as well. Hiero tried to probe it, but the animal was simply too new to him. He had not realized previously how alien the minds of the great herbivores really were, and how much simple affection and long mutual training had to do with his control over the big morse. He tried again, but the brute mind was too full of mad rage for any inexperienced hand to take over its control. And Aldo was absent.

No, I'm back, came a quick, clear thought. *Get out of its mind, Hiero, and leave me alone! I'll try to turn it. Hurry!*

Now everyone could hear the monster. A footfall so ponderous it actually shook the forest floor began to echo, at a steadily increasing beat. Great snorts and grunts sounded.

Get away from the fires! came the old man's thought.

Hastily Hiero passed it on and Gimp and the men began to scurry away to either side. Luchare pulled Klootz's head around and the two tugged him off behind the buttress root of a great tree, clearing the flimsy camp barrier as they did.

Now the incredible steps broke into a crashing run and almost the same time the creature gave voice. Its fight with the slain attacker must have been further away than he realized, thought the priest, as that awful, ringing bellow almost shattered his eardrums.

Out of the dark it came, perhaps just such a titanic bulk as must have peopled the earth for millions of years in the past before the coming of man. Now, due to incredible hard radiation and consequent forced mutation, the same conditions of life had once again given such creatures another, second chance. Its great, brown head, short-trunked on a heavy columnar neck, and carrying upper and lower pairs of ivory tusks, towered up at least twenty feet above the terrified men. The close-furred giant body sloped from pillar-like front legs to shorter ones in the rear, and as it passed the Metz saw its tiny tail, a mere afterthought, flapping in the air. Fresh wounds on its flanks gleamed red in the firelight, and the small ruby eyes gleamed also, as it sought for fresh enemies. But the fires seemed to distract it. It charged straight and hard at the nearest and careened right through it, sending burning logs spinning in every direction. Its voice rising to a new volume, it charged the next fire, and scattered that also. Without ceasing its incredible rush, it blundered across the little clearing through the barrier and into a gap between two monster trees. Even as the light died, it vanished from sight. Everyone stood appalled in the gathering gloom, listening as it lumbered on and away, crashing a course off into the distance, still roaring hideously as the pain of its burnt feet, added to the previous wounds, reached the tiny brain. Almost before one realized it, the sound had died away in the distance and the "normal" noises of the night forest once again resumed.

"All right, men," Brother Aldo's voice came cheerfully. "Let's get those fires going again and build up the barrier. It won't be back, but other things may. Hurry up now, no time for idling." The old Elevener, appearing out of nowhere, stood in the middle of the clearing, helping Gimp and Hiero direct the work, until all was as before, except that the barrier was now chest high at least. When new watches had been set, he told Gimp to turn over command to Blutho and join them. At this point they discovered three men were missing, all ordinary seamen.

"Probably ran off in a panic and got lost or ate by something," said Gimp philosophically. "If people *won't* listen, what can you do? I tell them no-good swipes a thousand times, 'stay here with us', but they know better!"

"I'm afraid you're right," said Aldo. "Let us be glad it's no worse. At least I can detect no Unclean activity, only the Poros, that poor simple beast which blundered into us."

"Poor beast!" burst out Luchare. "That great horror!"

"Well, yes, I think so," was the gentle answer. "This is his forest, you know, Princess, not yours. He had just been in a terrible fight and he thought he saw more enemies in us. I sent him to bathe his burnt feet in the Inland Sea," he added, "and now he'll feel better." His tone was exactly that of a nurse whose spoilt charge had been soothed.

Hiero smiled to himself. The Eleveners were indeed the guardians of all life! He rather approved, he realized, though it would take a long time for him to see the brobdingnagian Poros as the simpleminded child that Brother Aldo obviously did.

"Now that that's over, I think I can keep us from being bothered by any more of the forest people, at least tonight. And I *have* found the trail, you'll be glad to know." The old fellow beamed at them in pleasure, and stroked his curly beard affectionately.

"I'll be glad to know a lot of things," said Gimp aggressively, "such as who's going to pay me for a new ship, not that there's another like old *Foam Girl*, mind. And all her cargo, too, gone in a wink, plus the juicy plunder I claimed from Roke's ship, and hard won that was. All in all, Brother, I could have retired on that lot and my men too. Who's to pay us, eh, and when and also where? Are we going to wander about in this wood until we're all ate by something like that walking mountain we just missed?" Despite his gloomy words, Hiero noted that the little seaman's eye was still bright and his ridiculous pigtail still perky. Though he would have died rather than admit it, Gimp was a pure romantic, actually one of those people who revel in constant excitement and new ventures. He liked pay, of course, if he could get it, but it was only secondary and so was his grumbling. Now he cocked an eye from Hiero to the old man in question.

Brother Aldo knew his man. "Why, captain, can't your hardy men stand a little discomfort? Surely those who've ridden out gales and fought cannibal slavers and angry sea beasts aren't afraid of a few days walk in the woods?"

Luchare and Hiero grinned at each other in silent companionship. "Few days walk in the woods" indeed! But it was the right not to strike with the squat little seaman.

"I've got the toughest crew afloat," he boasted. "Why Roke's men would *all* have run when that big beast come rampaging through here. No, those men'll follow me through hot pitch. But what about our pay? And where are we going now?" His voice was eager on the last question.

"Well," said Aldo, "I have no real right to promise anything like this, but if, mind you, if our Ruling Council agrees with me, all your damages will be paid, including the loss of your ship. After all, you are on Eleventh Commandment business, are you not?"

"Your word's good with me, Brother," said Gimp. "You can't say fairer than that. But what now?"

"I can supply some answers there, Gimp," interjected the Metz. "We're going southeast, the Brother and I, and I guess you and the crew had better come too." He waved his hand around at the monster tree trunks and the shadows at their feet. "I don't imagine your men are going to want to strike off alone, are they? Three are gone already. I've probed the night with my mind and so has Aldo and we detect nothing. I fear they indeed have provided someone a quick dinner. Can you make this danger plain to those who remain? We must stay together."

"Yes," added Aldo, "and tell them Hiero will command the whole expedition from now on. This trip is land work and we need land discipline and experience. I will assist him, of course, and you'll remain in direct command of your own people."

"Suits me," said the sailor. "There won't be no problem about that. I've got thirty men, no, twenty-seven, forgot those scourings that run off.

210

Plus me and Blutho. We have food for two weeks, but only seven big water skins. How's this place for water?"

"I'll find you water and game too," answered Aldo. "We'll leave at dawn. The trail is less than a mile from here, overgrown but still a good road. The beasts use it and so can we, but humans don't seem to have been over it for a long time, at least as well as I can tell in the dark."

As the moon gleamed through the far off branches and the fires died down to orange coals, they talked on, planning as well as possible the next day's march. At intervals, Hiero probed the night for enemy mind sweeps, but encountered nothing suspicious. The high forest teemed with life, but it was natural to it, predators and prey, fur, scale and feather.

Eventually they slept, though with watches set and regular changes of guard.

The next morning Klootz, to his annoyance, was loaded with supplies. *Behave yourself,* Hiero told him, *I'll get to ride you soon enough.* The morse bull was, in fact, trained to carry burdens on occasion, so that his irritation was a matter of pride. He had carried urgently needed supplies to more than one isolated Kandan village in the past. Now he shook his great black antlers and brayed until Luchare's ears rang. The forest answered with a chorus of screams and yells and the day's march began.

First went Hiero and the bear, scouting the path. Next came the mate and his picked crew of axe and cutlass men, ready to cut through any bad obstructions. The main body of seamen under Gimp came next, all armed with swords and pikes. A small group of picked bowmen followed and last of all, the morse, Luchare and the old Elevener. While he disliked being separated from them, Hiero himself had chosen this march order as being the most sensible. It gave them a telepath at each end of the column and danger was more likely to come from in front than the rear.

As Brother Aldo had promised, they soon struck the old trail. Hiero's instinct told him that it ran almost due southeast and although small bushes broke its surface here and there, it was still easy marching. The sailors cheered up and began to sing, songs which Luchare appeared determined to ignore, while carefully memorizing some of the worst to try later on her lover. Part of the cheer, Hiero learnt when they stopped for a noon meal, was due to a crafty rumor of Gimp's that they were in search of a great buried treasure. This artless tale has seldom failed to arouse sailors of any time or nation, nor did it now.

Hiero could not help wishing as he strode along, alert for any movement, that he and Luchare were alone to explore the wonderful green world all

211

about them. The heat had now come to seem normal and in the shadows of the great trees not even very oppressive. Stinging insects were surprisingly few, perhaps because bird life was so abundant and varied.

Monkeys, large and small, chattered overhead and other small beasts, of unknown types to the Metz, scuttled up and down the looping vines and tendrilled growths which shrouded the monster trees. Occasional huge footprints in the earth, none very new, renewed the knowledge that not all the life of the forest was small. And once the bear shied suddenly from what appeared to be a smooth, shallow ditch across the trail itself. Hiero raised a hand to halt the column and summoned Brother Aldo. The great rounded fold in the leaf mold of the road was stunning in its implied message, but the old man confirmed it.

"Yes, my dear boy, a serpent. Let us hope we do not meet it. They are very hard to control mentally and almost invulnerable to any weapon. I should judge this one to be eighty feet." He said no more and walked away. Hiero led off again, considerably shaken, and now even more alert.

Occasionally, due perhaps to outcroppings of poorer soil or perhaps of hidden rock, the forest opened and grassy glades filled with flowers formed sunlit breaks in the green gloom. It was in one of these that a new menace revealed itself.

The priest and his attendant, the bear, were halfway across the glade, which was no more than a hundred yards in extent, when something long and lean, or rather two somethings, erupted from the edge of the wood to their left and raced for the column at a speed so incredible that Hiero never could decide on it afterwards. At first heading for him, the two creatures swerved and plucked the two leading axemen behind Hiero instead, sweeping them off their feet without even breaking stride or hesitating. Before anyone could even raise a weapon, they were gone! A vague visual impression was left on Hiero's forebrain of animals rather like giant distorted foxes on legs like stilts, mottled dark brown on a fawn background, each one with a crewman gripped in great grinning jaws. There had not been time even for the men to scream. Belatedly, he realized, he had used his mind to deflect the attackers from himself, used it subconsciously as a man half asleep raises an arm to defend himself from a blow. He explained this to Aldo when they all halted and also tried to excuse his conduct. But it was Luchare who snapped him out of it.

"Don't be so stupid! I'm sorry those men were killed, too, but you didn't kill them! And how many of us are alive because you have the abilities and courage to use them when you do! Now say a prayer for those

212

two poor souls and go back to being our leader!" She turned on her heel and stamped off to the rear of the line again, Klootz following obediently in her wake.

"We're down to twenty-five lads now, but she's right, Master Hiero, she's right, you know. Without you there wouldn't be none of us. No one blames you, I can tell you that." Gimp had overheard the dialogue and his earnest perspiring face now expressed his feelings.

Brother Aldo patted his shoulder affectionately. "Hiero, why not blame me instead? I am supposed to know these woods and the dwellers in them. Yet I never even noted or felt the minds of those swift creatures which took those two. In fact, to be honest, they are totally new to me, and not yet in our records at the Central Institute, I suspect. So take heart. And remember, we all still rely on you."

"All right. I suppose I couldn't help it. But I feel damned inadequate to serve as leader all the same. Let's go." The seamen marched in silence for a long while after that.

At dusk, they found another campsite between three great trees and built a strong barrier around it. But late that night something large reached over it and simply removed one of the two seamen posted as sentries. The man's fading scream alerted the camp, but his mate had been facing the other way and thus had no real idea what had happened.

"His mind doesn't exist," said Hiero in a low voice after a moment. "He's dead, thank God. What are we going to do, Aldo? We can't go on this way. By odds it ought to be one of us next. These poor devils are getting grabbed because they have no concept of what dangers to expect. Should one of us stand watch, do you think? I'm at my wits end!"

Eventually it was decided that Hiero and Luchare (she insisted on *that*) should keep a waking, if not talking, watch half the night, and Brother Aldo and the bear, who were great friends, the other half. This in addition to two seamen, who would walk guard on roughly each quarter of the night. It seemed to work, since for the next two nights there were no attacks, though Hiero felt that this was due to luck more than anything else.

On the fourth day since leaving the coast, they came at length to a fork in the trail. Both the left and right paths seemed to go roughly in the direction they wanted but one inclined somewhat to the east, the other more to the south.

They called a halt to consider this matter, since in any case it was almost time for the noon break and meal. Hiero's and the girl's crossbows, and their heavy bronze-tipped quarrels had supplied them with plenty of small game, got by ranging only a little wide of the trail. The local wild creatures, though often savage enough, were singularly unwary of men, a fact that Brother Aldo and the priest found encouraging, for it showed few human travelers had used this country.

As they inspected all of the maps, Brother Aldo looked increasingly doubtful.

"No fork shows here at all! Long ago, but mind you, my memory is still fair, I used this road and there was no such fork then. Yet roads made by game, and this trail simply took one over, you know, don't change much over the centuries. Not unless the land itself does, if a river, say, should dry up or a new volcano arise."

He walked over to the fork, and peered down at the actual junction of roads, where a colossal tree, against which he resembled a fly on a wall, towered up at the apex of a broadening triangle of forest. The men were eating silently, watching as their leaders debated. Overhead the unending canopy of green shielded them from the burning sun. The mighty wood lay somnolent under the hush of noon, only an occasional bird song drifting down through the leaves.

Aldo came striding back, his eyes still downcast.

"We'll take the southern fork, I think, unless there's an objection. It would seem to skirt the desert on the map more than the old road did. I never went that far myself, but turned off before the open spaces began. But I am still puzzled as to why a plain fork like this should exist on a road no one human uses, for animals simply don't do such things." Thus they crossed over the border into the realm of Vilah-ree, unknowing.

For some miles, the new road, or rather trail, for it was no different from the one they had been using, marched steadily on, winding around and through the great tree trunks as it had for days. But late in the afternoon, Hiero became conscious of a change and held up a hand to halt the column, and at the same time to summon Luchare, Aldo and Gimp to him.

"So you've noticed too," was the old man's comment. "What do you think?"

"We're going down a very long, gentle slope, into a river valley, I guess. The trees are mostly the same, but there are many more hanging mosses and lichens and great ferns too. The ground isn't wet, but the air's damper. And I hear a lot of new bird calls and songs. What have you noticed, Aldo?"

"That animals are very few, and mostly far up in the trees. No large beasts use this trail at all, no dung, no footmarks, nothing. And yet, I seem to feel, something hovering at the edge of my thought, almost in reach but not quite.

214

Your mind, boy, is more powerful than mine in many ways. Try using it and see what you can pick up. But do be careful!"

Luchare looked anxious for a second, then her ebony face became a mask as she assumed the role of the King's daughter. Gimp looked nervously about them at the leaf-strewn ground. This was out of his sphere of knowledge entirely. Hiero closed his eyes and leaned on his spear, which he had thrust point downward into the soft earth, while he sent his mind abroad.

He touched upon the minds of many small, shy creatures at first: birds high above, lizards on tree limbs, toads and snakes in the mold of the forest floor. Wider and wider he sent his mental net, seeking for any trace of intelligence with every atom of his powerful brain. At length, he was sure that for very many miles in a circle from where they now stood, no mind existed which he could contact on an equal level. He began to withdraw mentally, closing and tightening the mental circumference of his "net," but still watching closely for any trace of an observer, spy or enemy.

Then a strange thing began to happen. He caught no trace of coherent thought, no actual communication, but he knew all the same that someone was there! And in his mind a face commenced to form! The face of a woman!

Or was it? he wondered. The face was long, the chin pointed as were the small ears, just visible under the helmet of hair. And the hair itself? *If it was hair,* he wondered. The tight, almost cap-like covering looked as much like feathers as it did anything else, and seemed to ripple with almost a life of its own. And the eyes! Long and slanted, with vertical yellow pupils, their color was a shifting, opalescent green. No human had such eyes! Green indeed was the overall impression which the face conveyed. The pale, smooth skin and the strange hair seemed to have overtones of green, as if the forest had exuded a mist, which covered the creature who watched him. Yet it was a female presence which observed him.

For he was under observation. That much was clear. The strange and beautiful (for it was both) face saw *him* and although he could detect neither mind speech nor mental contact of any sort he knew, yet he was sure that the entity behind the strange eyes was fully aware of him and his companions. And he knew too that he had been *allowed* to see the face of his watcher. As this thought stirred in his mind, the image vanished, like a burst bubble, one moment clear, the next, utterly gone. But still the watch over them was not relaxed. This also he knew. He brought his mind back to the trail and opened his eyes, to find the others still watching him.

"You have found something," said Aldo instantly. "I can see it in your eyes."

"Something yes, or someone. We are under close observation. But I can

215

feel no mind touch at all, which is strange and frankly makes me nervous. Even the Unclean mind shields are detectable as an impression or shape, though the thoughts they hide are not. But here . . ."

As he tried to explain the picture he had received, he saw a storm of fury begin in his love's eyes and instantly stopped the narrative to take hold of her shoulders and shake her gently.

"Now look, foolish one, a female seen once is no cause for jealousy. I said she was lovely in a way, yes, but I feel not altogether human either. So stop the female anger, eh, and let me go on?" His clear gaze met her eyes and at length she smiled.

"All right, I guess I am jealous. But I don't like beautiful green women whom I can't even see, looking at my man!"

"Quite so," said Brother Aldo impatiently, "but we have other concerns, Princess. Hiero, does this strange creature, who must be one of a group, seem dangerous?"

"I don't know, frankly. But I do feel there is power there, and power of a kind I can't even grasp, behind that face. That in itself is quite enough to make me nervous."

"But what are we to do? Shouldn't we go back, before this invisible witch or whatever casts a spell on us?" What little he could grasp of Hiero's tale made Captain Gimp very nervous. He was a man who could face any physical danger with a bold face, but unseen (to him) green faces and mental warfare were something else again.

You know, he may have a point. This was Aldo's mind speaking direct to Hiero. *Maybe we are being warned and should go back, retrace our path and take the other trail.* But he was interrupted from a strange source.

You cannot go back, came the bear's calm message. *The way is guarded now. You can only go forward, where the*—(his thought was untranslatable, but conveyed an impression of great power) *wish you to.* His mind said nothing more, and he simply sat up on his haunches and sniffed the damp airs drifting down the trail.

Can you hear—whoever is watching us? Do they, or she, talk to you? Do you know their purposes?

I cannot tell you how I know, Hiero, was the answer. *I was told to say what I said, but not by the way you use your mind. It is the same way I know which is the way home. I just KNOW, that's all.* Gorm's thought conveyed the idea that the process he was talking about was quite inexplicable in human terms. As a matter of fact, he was partly wrong, for Hiero's own sense of direction was almost as good as the bear's. But the sub-mental com-

216

munication wave or channel being used was certainly nothing either the old Elevener or the Metz priest had ever dreamt of.

What blocks the return path? was Hiero's next question.

Listen, came the answer.

From far back up the long, gradual slope down which they had lately come, there echoed a cry. The rippling calls of the strange birds above them were hushed and only the cry could be heard, though it came from a long, long way. It was hard to describe. Luchare called it a "cross between a moan and a growl." Hiero thought it sounded more like the howl of an inconceivable wolf in great pain. Brother Aldo kept his own counsel. Whatever it was, it had to be very large and the note of savagery in its voice was unmistakable. One word that subsumed all others in describing the sound might have been "disquieting."

It is a great beast, greater than anything I have ever seen. And it guards the back trail for those who sent it. We must go on. The bear's message was unequivocal.

Hiero looked at Brother Aldo, who shrugged. For the first time since they had met, the priest thought the old fellow looked tired. Again he wondered, how old was Aldo?

"Let's get the men moving, Gimp," said Hiero. "Tell them a big animal's behind us, that's all."

"They know that all right, Master. They can hear that much as good as you!" He turned away and barked an order.

As they marched on, the great clumps of green and brown moss, some of it lovely, others simply grotesque, increased in number. The area to the right and left of the path became obscured, both by the mosses and huge ferns but also by a greenish haze, not a fog, Hiero thought, but more as if the light off the trail had some different properties, which ordinary eyes could not penetrate. He tried probing with his mind, at random intervals, both forward on their route, and back, as well as to both sides, but gained no knowledge. He could not even tap the mind of whatever horrific beast waited behind them. Those who controlled it also shielded its thoughts. *A great feat,* he thought glumly. His own hard won powers seemed those of a child by comparison.

You are needed, suddenly came a thought from Gorm.

Who—me? Hiero was startled.

Yes, I don't know why. Those who speak to me are not clear, perhaps do not wish to be. But you, and no one else in the party, have a task to do. Or else we all are trapped.

Hiero kept marching, crossbow slung loosely over one arm, his spear over

217

his shoulder. Only his helmet was missing, being too heavy for long marches, for him to be instantly battleworthy. *Needed for a task? This grew stranger and stranger. He was wanted, personally, and if he failed, why the whole party perished!* He said a few soldierly words into his mustache, then crossed himself and automatically asked God's pardon for blasphemy. Neither attitude struck him as contradictory. On they went, accompanied only by rippling birdsong.

Just as the light faded, they emerged into a large, moss-floored clearing. The men suddenly shouted as they saw what stood there, but Hiero, Gimp and the one-eyed mate beat them back, cursing and shoving until some semblance of discipline was restored. Still, it was hard to blame them, as Gimp said.

In the center of the clearing were three long, wooden tables. There were no seats, but none were needed. The tables were laden with steaming earthenware platters, all carefully covered against the evening damp and on them too at regular intervals great clay flagons reared up, stoppered in a suggestive manner.

After almost a week of constant danger and a diet of hardtack and tough wild game, it was an incredibly seductive display.

"Wait a minute!" screamed Gimp, waving about the heavy staff he had been carrying. "Suppose it's been dosed, you sorry catamite bastards! D'you all want to choke on poisoned grub, you miserable, rope-yarn, mother-delighters."

Eventually, with even Brother Aldo and Luchare, of both of whom the men were in great awe, helping, things quieted down. When they did, and he got a chance to look more closely at the food, Hiero received another message, again from Gorm.

The food is safe, We can all eat. I tell you, Hiero, the Old One says you are needed! From the bear's mind came a picture of the strange female face! So this was the Old One of whoever held them, the leader of the unknown forest creatures whom they could not even sense!

With Hiero's assurance passed on, all fell to, the majority cautiously at first, but after Hiero had tasted each dish, with more confidence. Indeed, the food was delicious, mostly strange, cooked vegetables and tubers, but also piles of some sweet bread, all very subtly flavored. There was no meat. And the clay flagons contained an odd, herb-flavored wine which managed to grow upon the palate as one drank.

"There's no poison," he told Aldo. "I'm trained to detect it. There's nothing to harm anyone, I'm sure of that. We're being helped,

218

that's all, but why?" He had told the old man of Gorm's message, but it meant nothing to him or to Luchare either, except that she refused to move more than a foot from his side, determined that he was not going anywhere to see anyone without her.

At length, satiated, the seamen stretched out on the soft grass, groaning. Surprisingly, no one was drunk, for the strange wine seemed only to exhilarate. As night fell, under the canopy of the trees, the men were soon asleep, save for the two walking a watch and Hiero and Luchare, who shared the first guard. The bear and Brother Aldo also slept.

It was an utterly still night. No birds called any longer, no animals moved in the undergrowth. Overhead, no life could be detected. The whole forest seemed to lie under some hushed spell. Even the great rounded piles of moss suddenly seemed tense and expectant to Hiero, as if listening in the dark. One small fire was all that could be got to light and it sputtered dismally as the far mists of night closed in.

Hiero first felt his legs growing weak with considerable surprise. *But there was no poison!* his mind cried out, even as he slumped to the mossy ground. His fading sight showed him Luchare lying next to him and beyond her, the two sailors, also fallen. And then into his mind came only a green haze, which swirled in clouds and wreaths across his vision. He felt that some secret lay behind it, but what it was remained unreachable.

Then the mists cleared. He opened his eyes and looked into those of Gorm's "Old One," the strange creature who had watched, guided and finally trapped them all.

He lay in a room, long, narrow and high-ceilinged, which moved under him somehow. He swung his legs over the edge of the bed, for such it was, and looked about him in amazement. In a backless chair before him staring calmly at him, sat the woman, for such she was, whom he had seen in first his own mind and second that of the bear. She was nude, her small firm breasts erect and provocative. Other than a necklace and a slim belt, both of which looked like fine metal mesh, she wore no ornaments. Her greenish-white body was utterly hairless, he noted, and the strange covering on her head seemed a cross between oval, green feathers and tiny brown leaves. Yet it was unmistakably part of her, a natural growth, not a cap.

She was indeed very beautiful, yet even as the manhood in him rose to the sexual challenge of her shape, he was also driven off, repelled by her alienness. For she was not really human at all, and the lovely outward appearance of her body seemed a mask for something utterly different. To his still dazed mind came an unbidden thought *why it's as if a tree or a flower had*

219

tried to be a rabbit or a cat!

Now he could see that the room was lit by candles, fat candles which burned in wall sconces and cast a strange perfume as they burnt. Save for the chair, a small table on which stood some wooden goblets and a jug, and the carved wooden bed on which he now sat, the room was empty. And it swayed! Even as he realized suddenly where he must be and the motion of the wooden floor shook him, a thought came into his mind and he knew that his captress was speaking to him.

We (are) in the trees, high, high above, as you (guessed?) I (can) tell (what) you think but not speak/tell/talk back (?) except by an (effort). We do not speak so/thus/in a manner. Her thought was painfully slow and looking into the green slanted eyes Hiero realized that it was actually physically painful to use her mind this way. She was forcing herself to do it, despite the hurt it caused her.

How do you speak then? Who are you? his mind asked. He was feeling clear of head and he noticed that he still had his sword-knife and dagger. His strange captors had not restrained him in any way apparently and he was becoming intrigued as he lost any fear.

She trilled at him. A string of golden syllables came from her lips, as lovely as the rippling of a woodland waterfall, tinkling over polished stones. Vilah-ree was as close as he could come in speech, and he said it softly, "Vilah-ree." Now he knew one source of the continual bird music they had heard.

At his attempt, she shook her head and sang again. Her teeth were dainty and small. Again he tried to imitate her voice and then gave it up. *Vilah-ree,* he thought, *I can't say your name properly, I fear, not in your language. You'll have to accept my mind speech instead or let Vilah-ree do.*

Then, even as they gazed at one another, the thought of Luchare and his companions came to him. What was he doing, talking like an idiot, while his love and his friends were drugged and helpless, God knew how far away! Were they even alive?

The calm expression vanished from Vilah-ree's face as well, and her full-lipped mouth opened in apparent distress. A stream of golden chiming notes poured forth as she tried to tell him something. Realizing that it was futile, she fell silent, and he felt her thoughts on the edge of his mind again.

No (you are) wrong! We (have) hurt none of the other/untranslatable/(earth-plodders?). Look into/at my mind!

As she became more practiced, the flow of message and pictorial communication between them became easier, just as it once had between himself and the bear, though indeed he always felt the bear to be the less alien of the two. Next she showed him the camp where he had fallen into a drugged dream but now it was guarded by a high fence of some thorny bushes. And around it at intervals stood silent white figures, so like Vilah-ree as to make it plain they were her people. All, he noted absently, were female, and he thought *God help them if the crew ever wakes up!!* Luchare, Brother Aldo and the bear lay apart, on a great bed of leaves and even the bull morse slumbered in an angle of the thorn stockade, looking as if he had been newly slain, save for the rise and fall of his great sides.

We need you, my people and I, thought Vilah-ree, when he had satisfied himself that all of his party were well and unharmed. Her golden pupilled, fathomless, green eyes were close to his as she drew her chair nearer. A faint lovely scent of flowers? bark? honey? came to him and her strangeness seemed to ebb, leaving her both vulnerable and desirable.

What do you want? His counterthought deliberately was harsh, as he strove to break through the glamour, the witchery of her near presence.

She considered him a moment, then rose gracefully to her feet, pale, rounded hips swaying as she walked to the end of the room.

Come—I will show you. She drew aside a long wooden shutter on a track and sunlight poured into the room. She beckoned with one white arm, and he rose and joined her, striving to mask his wonder as he looked out.

They were in the top of one of what must be the tallest trees in the great forest. Below them for miles stretched a green canopy of leaves and branches, some of the latter themselves as immense as normal trees. The room in which they stood was partly hollowed out, partly built into one such, in a way Hiero did not quite fathom, but which seemed to be a graft onto the living tree itself, one which Vilah-ree made plain did not injure it. But he had not been brought just to see the beauty of the daylight on the roof of the forest. She pointed and he looked to the east and saw her enemy.

Far away, fringing the eastern horizon, lay a great, barren expanse of empty sand and rock, its pinnacles and jagged buttes glinting in the morning sun. But closer, between the desert and the forest, part of neither and repelling both, lay something else.

A vast, ugly splotch of color, composed of mauves, dull oranges, oily browns, and sickly yellows, it seemed to have eaten into the green edge of the tree world like a hideous running sore. Without thinking, Hiero reached into his belt pouch and brought out his far-looker. With the eye-piece adjusted, the strange area was brought up close and involuntarily he shuddered. It was indeed an evil landscape.

Even under the sun, the giant puffballs and huge clustering toadstools

221

looked diseased. Other strange fungi, both hanging and dripping foul ichor, covered all the other things in sight. He could see the shrouded shapes of many vast trees, every inch covered with loathsome growth, the trees obviously dead, their tortured skeletons serving as a prop for the bloated life which covered them. All of the colors and shapes were painful to look at, none appearing natural or the work of things that grew by Nature's design. Even as he watched, a bloated bag of some monster puffball sort exploded and the view was momentarily darkened by the billions of tiny spores scattered for hundreds of yards.

Slowly he lowered the spyglass from his eye, then turned to his silent companion.

What can I do about this? The plant world wars against itself? This looks truly evil but why not use fire, unless you fear it of course. Surely this plague of fungi is not invulnerable.

Look again, came her thought. *See if you can see anything moving.*

He did her bidding, sweeping the distant area until at length he caught sign of a movement. Adjusting the focus, he watched carefully until he had located it again, then drew in his breath in a gasp.

Over a bare patch of ground between the forest and the blight there flowed a thing, a monster made of living slime. It had no apparent head or limbs, but innumerable, waving organs rose long and slender from its soft back. Its gross body seemed composed of dark rotted velvet and on the slender rods were tipped with something soft that glowed with a putrid orange fire. Yet it was not without purpose. Its intent, quick movements bespoke intelligence and organized will. Now, as Hiero watched, it suddenly paused and all its long pseudopods or tendrils quivered. Then the whole mass wheeled and slid over the ground in a new direction, toward a clump of bushes at the edge of the still, living forest. From these bushes bounded a creature like a huge, short-eared rabbit, running for its life. It had delayed too long, however. One of the balls of reddish foulness on the end of a slender feeler touched it fleetingly. It gave a convulsive spring and fell dead, as if struck by lightning. The slime creature flowed on until it covered the body, no small one as Hiero could judge. In only a few seconds it moved on again. Where the animal's body had been was nothing, not even grass, only a dampness festering on the bare earth under the rays of the sun.

Again the Metz lowered the far-looker. *Is there more?* his mind asked.

Much more, came the answer. *That thing and (it is) one of many, is only one weapon of the House.* Now into Hiero's mind there came a picture of a strange object, something perhaps like a peculiar building made of brown,

222

still wet, soft mud. It had no truly straight lines, yet somehow it seemed to maintain a basic four-sided structure, which yet shifted from one detail to the next, though only in small ways. A vaguely rectangular wasp's nest, made of soft muck and big enough for many men to live in. But it was alive! Or at least it apparently moved and shifted and ripples seemed to run across its surface.

If the slime thing he had just seen was foul, at least it seemed to answer to the basic laws of life. But this object or creature was repellent beyond belief, repellent because it was utterly unnatural and ab-human in a way like nothing Hiero had ever seen before.

Then, and only then—he remembered the last cast of the symbols on the north shore of the Inland Sea. Here was the House! He looked at its image in Vilah-ree's mind again and shuddered.

11: *THE HOUSE AND THE TREES*

I want my woman and I want the old man with the beard and I want the bear! And I want them now! I need them!

The curious disagreement and discussion had gone on for over an hour. Hiero had learned much about his task but he had not been able to make his own will in the matter felt. Vilah-ree could not, or perhaps would not, see that he wanted at the very least to consult with his partners. To her, he alone was all that was needed. Suppressing as egotistic a thought that her ideas about him had more behind them than a desire to see him defeat the House, he returned to his patient argument.

He had learned that the House—or whatever motivated it; Vilah-ree was not clear on this point—stayed hidden in the center of the fungus blight or infection. It had appeared seemingly from out of the desert beyond some time ago—again, how much was not clear—and at once had attacked the forest edge. Nothing seemed to harm it or its attendant fungi very much except fire, and it, or they, attacked and ate everything remotely organic. The spores raced up and rotted healthy giant trees, the moving slime molds devoured all animal and small plant life, the toadstools grew from decaying plant matter overnight and the great puffballs englobed smaller plants and somehow ingested them. Any organized attempt to interfere was met by bolts of mental? psychic?, at any rate, invisible, force emanating from the House itself. Vilah-ree and her people were not warlike in any case and they were helpless before this foul onslaught. They had no physical weapons beyond small bows and spears and while they could blank out their minds to Hiero, the House somehow could always detect them and hold them paralyzed until a giant slime mold was summoned to feed! And they needed the forest. Without the trees, they would die, Vilah-ree made that plain.

What about that very big animal guarding our trail, which you put there?

224

Why not use that? he asked.

He had noticed Vilah-ree never smiled, but now he detected something like humor in her mind, or at least a thinly-veiled amusement. He was given a picture of one of her white-skinned women swinging a strange flat, wooden device on a long cord, swinging it in great circles around and about her head. He had not seen one for many years, not since his childhood, but he recognized the bull-roarer he had once used to frighten his first girls. Its whirring roar sounded like a hideous monster indeed!

Your friend, whom you call the bear, had a picture of a terrible creature put into his mind. If such a creature truly lived we would be helpless before it ourselves. Thus he convinced you in turn. He laughed, only half bitterly. They had been ensnared by a bluff and a harmless sleep drug!

One other thing had Hiero learned, or rather, deduced. From his memory of the maps they carried, it appeared that the blight of the House covered much the very same area he wished to search! Here a pre-Death city supposedly lay hidden under the edge of the desert. This made him slightly more philosophic about his capture by the tree women of Vilah-ree. It looked as if a struggle, or at least a penetration of the horror caused by the fungus attack would have been necessary in any case.

You attack the House with your mind, your mind which is so strong, came her thought again, reiterating this same simple theme. *While you do so, we will burn the foulness of the House.* Her green eyes revealed no feelings of any kind.

Hiero looked over the balcony again, over the forest roof at the distant splotch of livid colors which was her enemy. He sighed, wondering how he could get through to her. Perhaps, he thought, a new tack would be more useful.

What happens to us if we defeat the House? he sent bluntly. *Will you let us go; help us in our journey?*

For a moment she did not answer. Then her thought somehow seemed hesitant. *Do you wish to go so much?* There was something wistful and puzzled about her mental question, almost like the attitude of a child who cannot understand why it has been told to stay home alone.

The priest studied her as coldly as he was able. She was lovely indeed, whatever she was, but her strangeness increased with acquaintance. The pale ivory body, the calm sculptured face and those emerald eyes were all enchantment. And all, he reflected, seemed less and less to be human! Who was Vilah-ree, or rather what?

Where are your men? On impulse his thought was sharp and quick. *Why*

225

do they not fight for you and help destroy the House? Are they afraid? As he sensed her confusion and alarm at his questions, he continued to probe. But suddenly her mind simply went opaque, "vanished" in fact, as it had when the travelers first had walked the trail far below. Unless she willed it, he could not even detect her thoughts, let alone interpret or control them.

They stared at one another, the very human man and the almost-woman of another race, each entity seeming to make up his or her mind, each one dueling for position. It was Vilah-ree who weakened first, or appeared to do so, at any rate.

Our men are—elsewhere, came her thought suddenly. *They do not fight: no (wrong meaning) they cannot fight. Thus I was desperate/helpless until you came. Now—how soon can you fight the House?*

Hiero leaned back against the wall and matched stare for stare. The question of her strange peoples' absent males had seemed to bother her, but the tree queen, if that were truly her role, recovered quickly.

Pay attention, said his mind. *Listen carefully to what I tell you. Until the three, the woman, the old man and the bear, are brought here and wakened, or I to them, I will do nothing. Do you understand? You know little of mind warfare, Vilah-ree. I need advice and help, help of a kind you cannot give. I will not bargain further. Release the three I named and we will try to aid you. And the others must be guarded and kept safe until the struggle is over in one way or another. They can neither aid nor hinder, but are in our keeping.*

In turn, she debated with herself. Her next thought was cold but her anger nevertheless came through it. *I could slay them all, and you with them. Why should I not?*

Go ahead, I quite agree that you can. But since you need us, I marvel at the stupidity of such a thought.

Again their eyes met. He saw an emotion in the green depths this time which surprised him. It was more like the anger of a woman, almost, he would have said, a jealous anger. But it passed, leaving nothing but gold bars on pellucid emerald.

Yes, she replied. *We will meet at the foot of this tree. Wait, while I go to see to it.* She turned and was gone, flipping right over the side of the balcony in a way that made Hiero's heart catch a beat. He rushed to the rail in time to see her pale shape dropping through the branches along a tangle of great vines at a speed he would have thought impossible. In an instant she was out of sight, but a chorus of golden, chiming notes poured up through myriad leaves. It was answered on all sides, though he could see no one and he knew a host of the tree women must be concealed in attendance all around.

Having descended more slowly, helped by two women to his annoyance, an hour later he was embracing Luchare, while Gorm blinked in the background and Brother Aldo beamed impartially at the score of armed, cold-faced, naked dryads who surrounded them. He seemed actually delighted by the discovery of the tree people, pleased to such an extent that their own mission appeared minor by comparison. He actually patted Vilah-ree on her shapely rump, just a as one might a dog, and stranger still, she did not appear to mind, and even patted him back, her face immobile!

"Lovely, Hiero, just lovely! Imagine, a whole new race of these lovely beings produced by The Death. They must have lived here a long time, to be so adapted to tree life. Remarkable! And aren't they pretty things, too? Vilah-ree, my dear, you must tell me all about your people when we can talk together, eh?"

"I can't stand the way they look at me, especially that one," whispered Luchare against Hiero's chest. She meant Vilah-ree, who was indeed staring at her with uncommon interest.

Tell your woman I wish to speak with her. Alone. Vilah-ree's mind was glacial but utterly clear. Before the priest could even frame a query, she added, *Tell her she will not be harmed in any way. But I* must *talk to her!* The intensity of the last thought was such that Hiero, who was unprepared, was almost stunned by it.

"She wants to speak with you privately. She says its terribly important, though I have no idea why. Are you able yet to keep a closed channel with a strange mind?"

"I think so," said Luchare slowly. Something of the tree woman's passion seemed to have reached her, for with no more ado, she released her lover and followed Vilah-ree, who strode away into the forest. Hiero watched the contrasting light and dark bodies, Luchare's being only minimally covered by her shorts and jerkin, until they were out of sight around a huge tree bole.

"Now what do you think that means?" he asked Aldo. "I have a feeling Vilah-ree is trying to pull something clever. She won't hurt Luchare, will she? If she does, by God . . . !"

"Calm, maintain calm," was the old man's soothing answer. "I cannot read her mind, my boy, but I can read other things, attitudes, faces, eyes, even muscle tension. These curious tree women have no gift for intrigue, I am sure of that. And I think lying almost impossible for them. On whom would they practice it?

"No, this is something female, purely female, if my guess is right. Vilah-ree wants more information about us and decided we stupid males couldn't give it, or perhaps understand exactly what she wanted, that's all."

To Hiero's relief, the two reappeared after not too long a time, and came walking back to the group at a brisk pace. Luchare was actually smiling, though for some odd reason she had trouble meeting her lover's eyes. Vilah-ree paid him no attention, but seemed, to a casual glance, to be more relaxed.

"Oh, she just wanted to talk. Never seen a woman before, I guess. She's not so bad," was Luchare's vague answer to the priest's question. "Goodness how lonely it must be living here in this great woods and never seeing another soul." Her lovely aquiline profile, etched in dusky clarity against a drooping light green frond, seemed pensive. Whatever had happened, thought Hiero, it at least had not frightened her. He wished momentarily he had eavesdropped, but he knew he could not have lived with himself afterward had he done so.

Vilah-ree conversed briefly with some of her attendant women, and now she came up to them again. Puzzled by her new attitude, Hiero watched her stroke Luchare's arm in passing, noting that Luchare seemed in no way annoyed by the caress. Women! Who knew what they were thinking?

"We are to go now and inspect the enemy," said Aldo. "I have been talking to her majesty here, for your guess was right, Hiero. She's the queen and apparently sole ruler. She wants us to eat first, though."

After a delicious but hasty meal of the fruit, vegetables and bread which the tree women served, they were on the way through the aisles of the mighty trees. If they were following a trail, it was apparent only to their guides, a dozen of whom ranged in front, while a similar group brought up the rear. Even Hiero, trained hunter and accustomed as he was to forests and silent movement, had never seen anything like Vilah-ree's people. Like lovely pale ghosts they slipped through the lofty ferns and over the huge, moss-hung logs, never disturbing a leaf and making less sound than a hovering moth.

Twice they paused for brief rest periods. It was around mid-afternoon when the tree women scouting in front began to fall back, joining the main party. Ahead, the humans could see a much brighter light and they knew the edge of the forest must be here at last.

Gorm, to whom the whole situation had been carefully explained, halted, sat up, and then sniffed the breeze. *Dirty air,* came from his mind. *Something long dead, but not-dead, up there in the light.*

Long dead but not-dead! The Metz drew in a deep breath and exhaled long and hard. On his palate now lay a faint film of corruption, an evil stench of some vileness or other. Drifting through the sweet scents of the forest it came, a wavering miasma of rotten life and seething putrescence, unnatural simply *because* it was alive and not dead, as anything so decayed long should have been. The odor of the House!

We dare go very little closer, came Vilah-ree's message. *We have lost many of our people, whom the House somehow caught and held unmoving while they watched from the forest edge. Then, those things you saw came—and fed!*

Now Hiero began to put into effect the plan he previously had worked out with the others. He advanced with caution, his mind probing for any sign of reasoning life, though not neglecting any lesser creatures either. With him the bear went prowling, and the priest could feel his strange mind also reaching out, feeling for alien or inimical contact of any sort.

It had been agreed that this would be the order of their approach, if not of actual battle. Remaining behind them with Vilah-ree, Aldo and Luchare would link minds and prepare to aid if they were needed. But this first move was intended to be a reconnaissance, nothing more.

"Still, we may get drawn in by this thing," said Hiero, when they had discussed the possibilities. "Gorm and I are old veterans now, but we still really know nothing of this House creature, not even what it is, let alone what it actually can do. Remember, it can detect the tree people, by their minds apparently, and we can't! That's enough to make one cautious."

"Then why can't I come too, and help you? I *won't* be left in back!" Luchare was furious.

"Listen, Love, we've been over this a dozen times. You haven't the mental training, although you're learning. You know that Gorm can use his mind better. Brother Aldo has to stay here to help try and anchor our minds, if we need him. And you can help only there, by adding your mental energy store to his." His voice was patient, since he knew the sole reason for her anger was fear of his going into danger without her. Eventually, with Aldo helping, she had been argued into aquiescence, however unwilling. The plan made so much sense that she could really argue no longer.

As man and bear slowly advanced over the moss and through the undergrowth which ringed the great tree bases, the sunlight grew steadily. Hiero paused, seeing for the first time at close range, the shrouded skeleton of a forest giant, bulging with repulsive growths, through a gap in the yet living trees ahead. There were no large animals in the area, not even small ones detectable by his mind. The exceptions were a few enormous greenish flies, their plump bodies shining in the sun with irridescent hues, as they buzzed over the plants about them. Hiero brushed one away, a fluttering pulpy thing almost three inches long, which hovered near his face for a moment.

Still his mind met nothing. Whatever lurked out there in the foul profusion of rot was quiescent. Cautiously, the two went on, their thoughts neatly overlapping as they spread wider and wider, like ripples in a pool.

As they approached the actual border of the living forest, the dead trees, each festooned with horrid growth, became more evident. For some time, the reek of the strange fungi had been growing in their nostrils, and now Hiero switched over the breathing through his mouth alone, so foul and purulent had the odors become. Nor warning of any attacker could penetrate that frightful stench, so why not cut it off at the source? Noses were no good here.

The great flies were still common, indeed seemed to be increasing in number, but nothing else moved. At last, unable to go further, they paused behind the last living tree near them and stared out over the awful panorama spread before them.

Directly in front, a vast puffball, its pocked, white circumference many yards in diameter, reared up in bloated isolation. To the left a forest of monster toadstools, stems brown and broad mottled umbels a sickly orange, stretched out of sight, broken only by the pulp-covered columns of the dead trees rising in their midst. On the right, the dead trees thinned, for here a finger of the outer desert had long ago crept closer to the woods. But now an uneven mound of various smaller fungi, of all shapes and ochreous and bilious colors, extended into the middle distance. There was no normal growth in view, not even grass, nor any bare ground not covered by some slime or smear of leprous muck.

No sound, save for the muted buzzing of the flies, broke the silence. Under the great heat of the afternoon sun, they saw faint steams and moist clouds rise at intervals from the surface of the noxious growths.

Slowly, ever so slowly, they edged closer to the border of crawling horror that was the blight. Still nothing stirred, out in the nightmare world into which they looked and also sent their roving brain impulses.

Then—having lured its prey as close as it could by sheer inaction, the House struck! And it was the man who took the brunt of the blow.

Never in all his varied experience had Hiero felt anything quite like it. An actual chill seemed to settle through his body, paralyzing his will and numbing his nerve endings. Though his personally-devised mind guard had been kept at full strength, the attack passed through his screens as if they were non-existent. Yet not quite. The very last one, the one which guarded the control of his own mind, was untouched. But though he could see and hear, no muscle of his body could so much as twitch. Through eyes which happened to be looking half that way when the sweeping assault came, Hiero could see Gorm frozen, one forefoot raised. He knew that the bear was equally helpless and in so knowing, he despaired.

For with the attack of the House there came knowledge of the attacker. And that knowledge chilled not the body, for that indeed was already numb, but the very soul, the inner being. Steeped in evil and all vileness and cruelty were the adept wizards of the Unclean. But they were nevertheless of human ancestry, and thus, malign though they were, they yet preserved a tincture of humanity.

But the House was other. Somehow after The Death, but in the ancient past, a strange and awful mating had taken place, triune perhaps, between a mycellial spore, an amoeboid slime and somewhere, somehow, an intelligence. Or perhaps the intelligence grew from the slime and gained the spore, then taking a different direction from all other life. Whatever had happened, the result was abnormal, beyond normality in fact. In some ways like the Dweller in the Mist, that seeming embodiment of total evil, yet even further from the upward path to reason and logic was the House.

Fiercely, Hiero strained to free his limbs. At the same time, he tried to link his mind with Brother Aldo and Luchare, back in the forest. Neither effort was successful. He could not move and he seemed enclosed in a curious icy mental shell, so that any outside contact was severed and cut off. His link with Gorm had vanished as soon as the attack began. His brain still clear and unhampered except by the screen, yet he could neither move his body nor communicate with others.

Through the screen about him, now, another attack, if that is what it was, began. The House was revealing itself. As the image of Vilah-ree had first appeared in his mind, despite any real method of communication, so now the misty outline of the thing itself began to build on the beslimed earth fifty yards in front of him. He knew it was not real, but only what he was being willed to see, that the physical body or structure, he did not know what actually, of the House, was nowhere near, but well hidden, somewhere out in the depths of the foul world it had built for itself. But stay—was that world so foul? Even as the wavering shape of the House began to condense and apparently solidify before his eyes, so too a new thought crept into his mind. *The House was alien, different, yes. But was that enough to make it evil? Had it too not a right to live?* The siren message infiltrated his own thoughts very, very subtly. His inner screen was not so much pierced, for the House seemed incapable of doing that, as persuaded, soothed, and his mind was thus ensnared. Yet not quite.

231

For as the glamour of the strange spell grew upon him, his inner being realized two things. First, the House was utterly alien, something which should not *be* and second, that the House was not one entity at all, but many minds of things all swarming like so many maggots in and through the gelid and gelatinous structure. The creatures, whatever they were, were both *in* and *part* of the ghastly thing which now reared itself to a height of many feet in front of him, to the eye as much real as his own hand.

And he was being invited to share, to join! He too could take part of the work to come, the great work of cleansing the surface of the earth, so that only the living House remained, surrounded by the monstrous mutated fungi which were its weapons and its seed. The House's brownish oily structure seemed to shake as he watched, horrified yet fascinated. Strange faces began to appear on its shifting surface, to leer invitingly at him and to vanish again into the mass, only to be replaced by others, equally foul and evanescent. All invited him. *Come,* they seemed to say, *leave your mortal shell and become one with us and live forever.*

Then, in his despair, for though he was not tempted, he was utterly helpless, there came a new factor. It was the bear!

His thought came obliquely somehow through the mental sphere of thought, with which the monster had surrounded the priest. The strong mind was like a draught of cold air.

I am here. It does not understand me at all, I think, and it uses a sending or a force which might indeed hold me if I were only what I seem, a creature of instinct and emotion, as once my people were. It is afraid of you; that I can feel, but not of me. The bear's thought was full of mingled anger and also craft. Yet Gorm was giving away no points, nor counseling hasty action, Hiero realized, only waiting to see what he himself wanted.

They—or rather it, grows impatient, came a fresh message. *There are many very strange minds there, all mixed, but making one, like in an anthill or bees' nest. It will not wait much longer* it added. *It is tired of your refusing whatever it is it wishes. Now—it summons something from outside.* The cool bear mind was calm, detached, as if what were happening had no relation to himself.

The Metz had drawn on his own inner resources at the same time, deducing, analyzing, forming conclusions. Simply knowing that he was not cut off had given him immense strength of purpose. There had even been time for a battle-prayer of split second length, but in due and proper form—God preserve his warrior through all trial. Amen.

Can you reach outside? Get Aldo and above all tell him to bring the weap-

on we have ready. I'm going to keep struggling and focus the attention of this thing on myself. Hurry!

He felt Gorm's mind withdraw and then he renewed his own struggle to escape, trying every level, every method he had taught himself or ever been taught to pierce the web around him and free both his brain and his limbs.

The House now withdrew its sucking blandishments and its horrid appeals for alliance. It still sat before him, or rather, it kept its repulsive, mirage-simulacrum there, but it settled down to watchful waiting. Even as he renewed his apparently fruitless assault, he decided Gorm was right: the House was afraid of him or at leasy wary. He must be something very different from anything it—or they—had ever encountered before. He wondered if the bear were having any success in reaching the Elevener. In a few moments they would know.

Now, through the ground itself, he felt a motion, hardly even a vibration, merely a faint stir, an almost imperceptible tremor. Something was on the move, and he knew, or guessed, what that something was. The slime mold things, or one of them, were coming to feed. His eyes locked on the House, not able to move at all, he saw and suddenly understood the cloud of bloated flies hovering in front of his face and realized then that they were the eyes of the House, and had reported his coming. This then was how the thing penetrated the forest fringe and guarded its borders.

Suddenly the House vanished from his sight. In its place there had appeared the quaking, soft bulk of the slime thing it had summoned. He did not believe its appearance directly before him and the envanishment of its ruler were accidents. Unable to move at all, by a refinement of cruelty he was to be made to see his destroyer coming and know what it was that devoured him alive.

Coldly, never relaxing his struggle to be free, yet to outward eye simply standing still and peering forward, he watched the eyeless bulk glide toward them. The creature was far larger than he had realized when seen at a distance. The soft plush mound towered far above his head and the long rods which sprang from it, each tipped with that poisonous orange glow, were at least four times the length of his own body. It paused and then came on again though more slowly. All the long rods were aquiver, their lengths rigid and yet soft, as soft as the purple pile surface of the unearthly shape. Now it was just in front of him, blotting out the view of all beyond. He breathed a prayer and also continued the struggle without a second's hesitation, wrenching his mind about its strange invisible prison as an eel hurls itself against its woven willow trap, without success perhaps, yet never giving up.

Unflinching thus, he faced his doom and so he saw the horror struck down even as it reared over him.

The blazing crossbow bolt had barely sunk to the feathers deep into the pulpy flesh when another followed, burying itself not a foot away from the first. Slimmer, longer arrows came in a sheet after that, each one with flaming tow tied tightly to the shaft. One of the most ancient devices of man, the fire arrow, was being used against a hell creature spawned out of science-wrought catacylsm and devastation.

Over his head the rain of burning arrows continued and he realized that Luchare and Brother Aldo must have brought the tree women to their aid, conquering somehow their fear of the blight.

The slime mold reared up and shook in its agony and for an instant Hiero thought it would fall upon and slay him in its death throes. Fire ran in coruscuting runnels down its rounded shifting sides and leaped into blazing light on the phosphorescent pseudopod ends, the clean light of honest fire burning out the poisonous phosphorescence by which the thing slew its prey.

At this moment, the mind control vanished. The House, unnerved by this sudden and unexpected onslaught, released its prisoners. No less alert than Hiero, Gorm instantly turned on his own stout length and scuttled for his life, the warrior priest racing hard on his furry heels. In a few seconds they had reached and passed the clean wood's edge. In an instant more, Hiero again was squeezing the life out of his dark love, while to her right and left, Aldo and Vilah-ree directed the dryad archers as they still launched their blazing shafts out into the territory claimed by the House. Gorm promptly sat down and began to lick himself.

Satisfied that Luchare was unharmed (and that so was he), Hiero turned to look back, still keeping one arm firmly about the D'alwah girl's shoulders. It was a wonderful and awful sight.

The ravening molds and fungi of the blight all shared one terrible weakness. How the House had guarded its territory from chance lightning, Hiero could not imagine, but it must have had some method, for now the whole border of the foul infection was ablaze. Fire wrapped the scorched body of the giant predatory slime mold, now writhing feebly in its death agony. But yellow flames raced over the ground, smeared and barren, as well, and bloomed on the mushroom forest, causing the great stalked umbrellas to explode as the heat scorched them. The collossal puffball in the middle foreground exploded as the fire struck it and each tiny spore became an instant coal, a second later a cinder mote. The great murdered trees became living candles of flame as they too burnt, from the caught fire of the shrouding growths which had slain them. Black, greasy smoke, foul and reeking with all the unpleasant scents of the burning fungi, wreathed the scene and began to drift into the forest beyond, where it met and drowned the perfumes of the wood.

Hiero looked at Vilah-ree anxiously. *Is your wood dry? Will the fire spread?*

Better to burn than be killed by that, was her answer. *But the forest is moist. Only two nights ago it rained. And we know how to keep water moving through the ground, my people and I.* She did not elaborate and turned away to watch the holocaust of the blight. He could sense the exhaltation in her almost inhuman mind and spirit as the enemy of her beloved trees and her strange people suffered the flames.

As dusk grew, though occasionally choking and coughing, they still watched the destruction of the foul growth from their vantage point at the forest's edge. When night came, the smoke and filthy vapors hid most of the stars, but at length when the moon rose, there came a breeze out of the north, which drove much of the shroud away before it out into the waste. To their surprise, no fire was now visible in the distance.

"Do you think it raced through the whole area that quickly?" Hiero was frankly puzzled. Aldo looked thoughtful.

"No, I think not, not from what you have told me. And there is the question of the lightning, which we discussed also. I'd judge this House creature had found a way of quenching the fires and has withdrawn, hurt perhaps, but not dead. We won't know until morning how far the fires actually went. So let's wait, or rather rest while we can."

Soon all three humans were wrapped in cloaks and bedded down on the soft moss under a clump of fern. The bear was already snoring a few yards away. As he drifted off into slumber, Hiero's last thought was of Vilah-ree, watching the stars as the smoke cleared. Once, through half-shut lids, he saw her watching him as well, her lovely face seemingly chisselled from alabaster under the moon's rays. Then he fell asleep.

His dreams were vague and formless for a long time, then—slowly they began to take a shape, to tell a story, half still a dream, half lovely reality, but all enchantment. He was awake in the dream, walking through the darkling woods under the pale stars, all alone. Nothing menaced him and he carried no weapons. Indeed, he wore no clothes and seemed to need none. Great fireflies lit his way and patches of pale, luminous blossoms seemed to mark a path for him under the shadow of the vast trees. On and on through the titan forest he seemed to drift. He was going somewhere but where he knew not, save only that journey's ending meant delight. Enticing scents both followed and led him on the breeze.

At length in a moss-hung bower under the arching branches, he caught a glimpse of an ivory form. He sped toward it, calling out only to have it flee. But from a few yards away rang out a rippling chorus of golden notes, questing, calling, mocking.

"Vilah-ree," he called, or seemed to, "Vilah-ree! Don't be afraid! Don't leave me." Again the golden throated notes, the song or speech of some magicked paradise bird, rang out. Driven now by burning desire, Hiero followed down the aisles of the moonlit forest, his feet seeming to have wings, seeking nothing but the maker of the song, oblivious to all else.

Now he glimpsed her poised tiptoe on a low branch, next a marble arm beckoned from a fern thicket, but always when he pursued, she would be gone.

Yet he seemed in the dream to grow in strength, not weaken and at length in a tiny open glade, where short-stemmed flowers made a soft carpet of the floor, the dancing white form seemed to falter and even stumbled as she fled from him. The next instant he had caught and held her. In the strange, green eyes now raised to his, he saw such a storm of passion that almost, for it was but a dream, he woke in fear. Then his own fires flared again and he covered her soft lips with his own, crushing the cold, slim body to him, forgetting everything except the miracle of desire.

And so the dream went and so the dream ended, for Hiero lost the thread and all the lovely images and feelings went swirling and dissolving, down into oblivion.

It was midmorning when he awoke. To his surprise, his first sight on opening his eyes was Captain Gimp, standing and bellowing at some of his men to "look alive there, you binnacle-butted slop-eaters."

Peering around, the priest saw that only a few of the tree women were in sight, standing together against the far side of the clearing. There was no sign of Vilah-ree and he sighed, remembering his dream. But all of the seamen were mustering before him, looking well and hearty as Blutho and Gimp shouted and bullydamned them into place. And Klootz was snorting nearby, tethered to a stump. *Hello, you big clown,* sent his master, eyeing the great polished antlers and sleek hide appreciatively, *have a good rest?* A wave of affection came from the bull's mind in answer, affection and a wordless question which was still very clear to Hiero. When do we leave, when do we go, when do we fight move, get on with the struggle? All these sentiments welled from the mind of the morse and he snorted loudly, pawing the soft earth into great clods.

"I see our big friend wants to leave. Have you had enough sleep, or at least some sweet dreams?" Brother Aldo stood smiling down at him, having quietly come out from the forest behind.

"Where's Luchare, and the bear too?" Hiero got up and stretched, still feeling curiously though not unpleasantly tired despite his long sleep.

"I believe she and Gorm were invited and went for a little visit to Vilah-ree. They should be back soon. As you can see, the seamen and Klootz are in fine fettle. The men think they got drunk and have just waked up, and I have not disillusioned them. I did, however, mention that the tree women were not to be touched, being under a protective spell which would kill anyone who did so. It seems to have proved effective. Curiously, the men appear satiated and uninterested in women. Odd for sailors, wouldn't you say?" Hiero looked suspiciously at the old man, but Aldo met his eyes frankly, his high cheekbones gleaming darkly over the spotless white beard.

"What shall we do now?" went on Aldo, changing the subject. "Would you like to see the waste where the fire killed the fungus plague? I have some ideas about the next move, but I'd like yours as well. Why not have a bite to eat first though?"

The men greeted Hiero boisterously and obscenely as he picked up some cold rations and beckoned Gimp to follow him. They all felt they were living in some strange and incomprehensible world to which he was the only sure guide and they felt fine as long as they could see him and his companions, meaning the girl, the Sage, the bear, and the bull morse, all well and ready for anything.

"What's going on here, Master Hiero?" said Gimp as they picked their way to a burnt over mound where a forest giant had fallen in flames the previous night. From this eminence, whence tiny curls of acrid smoke still rose into the sunlight, they looked out over the late battlefield.

Far away, rolling and undulating, the land stretched, blackened now and scorched by the cleansing flames. But in the remote distance, yet well before the crags and lofty sand dunes of the desert proper, the fire had come to a halt. Even with unaided eyes, they could see that the strident ochres, repellent mauves and sickly orange hues of the House's crop were still in existence. From a quick glance around, Hiero figured that the House somehow had saved about a third of its realm. He pulled out his far-looker and adjusted the lenses. The edge of the fired area was five miles off at least.

The House indeed had possessed a trick in reserve, he soon saw, and as he saw, described it to the others. Gimp had been brought up to date earlier by old Aldo, so that he needed only a limited amount of explanation.

As the fire had raged down upon its lair, the House had somehow forced its brood of fungi (perhaps a special breed) to exude a gummed foam of sticky bile, which hardened on contact with the air. Whatever the stuff was, it must have been completely fireproof. Now a ragged, brownish wall of it, something like congealed glue, glazed over and pitted with holes and bubbles, formed a rampart between the toadstool forest beyond and the burnt lands. Here and there in the latter, smoke curled, mostly from vast, still smouldering logs, but the main fire showed no sign of reviving. Barren though the aspect now was, Hiero felt it to be far more cheerful than the realm of the House when that was flourishing. His mind could detect no sensation of the monster, but he knew from experience that meant nothing.

Now he could see, looking to right and left, that small parties of the tree women, armed with blazing torches, were setting fire to any small bits of the blight which the fire of yesterday had missed, chiefly on the edge of the true forest itself. No seed of that filth was to survive if they could help it!

The day was becoming overcast, with a hint of rain to come, in storm clouds building towers far to the south. As they left the mound, they speculated on the chance of carrying fire further into the territory of the House and what that vileness might do in retaliation if further provoked.

"I don't think it's at the end of its resources, frankly," said Hiero.

"Indeed not, if what you tell of its strength is true, and also what I could feel of the mental barrier it was able to erect between us. How I hate to leave a wicked, unnatural thing like that alive. In a few years, perhaps even less, it will attack again, and we will not be here to save these women and their tree world the next time."

"Have you asked where the tree women's men are?" said Hiero, his mind off on a tangent.

"No, and if I had, I'm sure the answers would have satisfied no one. These strange, lovely creatures have a secret. Perhaps their males are very ugly, perhaps timid, or perhaps the women dominate them so they are never allowed out in public. Why not simply accept it and not waste time on profitless speculation? They seem to be our friends at any rate."

"Yes," sighed Hiero. "But I had a strange dream, strange but beautiful. It was—" He ceased suddenly, for Gimp was looking at him oddly and had stopped walking.

"Did your dream have one of them white-skinned gals in it now, Master Hiero? Just you and her maybe? A *real* nice dream?"

238

"As a matter of fact, yes," Hiero was too old to blush, but he felt embarrassed. "How did you guess that, Gimp?"

"Because me and Blutho and all of the boys, mark you, even old Skelk, who's a bleeding grandfather, we all had the same dream. Each one of us had just one gal, see, and all to ourselves. Nicest dream we ever had, we all agrees. And do you know, none of them naked wenches will even talk to us this morning! How's that for a peculiar situation, eh?" His snub-nosed face looked both pleased and regretful.

As they walked on, Hiero was very thoughtful indeed.

At length, when they were back in the cathedral shade of the great trees, Brother Aldo asked to see the Unclean map again and the three of them bent over it.

"The scale is not quite the same as the Abbey map," said the priest, producing that one also. "But it seems to me that the area I must search is quite close to us." He indicated the symbol marking the site of the ancients. "It must be here, I think, in the angle somewhere between the true desert, the southern corner of the blight caused by the House, and the very end of the forest. I'd put it at a rough guess between twenty-five and thirty-five miles away. You're used to charts, what do you think, Gimp?"

The squat little sailor stared hard at both maps before answering. "That's close to my reckoning also."

"And mine," Brother Aldo folded the maps and returned them to Hiero. "Now comes a time for hard decisions, my boy. Have we fulfilled your agreement with Vilah-ree? The House is wounded and driven off but hardly destroyed. And yet—I feel time presses. There were great waves of mental force used yesterday, both by us, mainly yourself of course, and also by that foul thing out there. In Neeyana and perhaps nearer, too, there are both instruments and evil minds which would take great interest in such phenomena. You have been ruthlessly pursued by the Unclean overlords since you slew that adept far up in the north, Hiero. Do you think they have given up entirely?"

"Not S'duna, at any rate! He swore he'd kill me or die himself and I believe him. You can't lie at that close range and deceive anyone as trained as I am. No, they haven't given up. And S'duna was apparently a person of great power in their councils."

"So I think as well. The main eastern trail to the Lantik Sea lies to our south, perhaps no more than four days good march. If I were the enemy, I would be hurrying eastward along that trail even now, and when I had gone as close as possible to the area, that is, our area, whence came the mental disturbance I had detected, I'd head north. Let us say to be on the safe side that a week from yesterday divides us from our foes. Maybe more or maybe less, but a week seems safe."

Yet while as the old Elevener spoke, his words were being refuted. All that he had said was quite correct, but he, and Hiero too, had gravely underestimated both S'duna's cunning and his malice. An armed and armored host had been collected in the country east of Neeyana and that host had been on the march for four days even as the three took council! But of this development they were ignorant.

As they debated, the clouds overhead grew darker and a moist wind from the south seemed to promise rain would come soon.

Sooner than the rain though, came Luchare. They heard her singing to herself, some song of D'alwah apparently, for Hiero could not understand it. She emerged from a path under the trees and came up to them, her face soft and dreaming. Around her upper arm she wore a lovely twisted torque of gold, with gems, mostly green, carved as leaves, set in its surface, so that the effect was that of a vine.

"Like my present?" she smiled at Hiero and linked her arms around his sinewy neck. "Vilah-ree's farewell gift to me. Gorm's still talking to her. She thinks he's the most interesting of all of us and wants him to come and live here."

"Exactly why should Vilah-ree give you a present?" he mused, fingering the heavy armlet which possessed some of the strange beauty of the giver. "She didn't give *me* anything, did she?"

"Oh—I loaned her something she wanted. And maybe she did give you something." Her face was now pressed into his buckskin shirt and he could not read her eyes. He felt his suspicions growing as the bits and pieces of evidence in his mind fell suddenly into a pattern he had been trying not to see. He straightened up, and held the lovely dark face firmly between his two hands so that she was forced to look at him. The other two tactfully had moved away out of earshot.

"Where are Vilah-ree's menfolk, my little vixen princess?" His voice was half angry, half amused, as he studied the black defiant eyes. There was a silence and then she made up her mind.

"There aren't any. Her people live a long time, though, when they stay in and near their trees. And they *need* men, poor things, to have children. But the children they do have are always more girls. They hope that someday, somehow, a boy will be born. They don't even seem to know how they first appeared here or who or what they are. But they know that human travelers

240

pass south and east of here. And sometimes when a lone traveler or just a few camp for the night, they—well . . ."

"Have a very nice dream?" asked Hiero. But he was smiling at her and encouraged, Luchare somewhat timidly smiled back. "So you made a deal and I got put out to stud. For a bracelet. Well, it's a nice one, I'll say that."

She wrenched herself loose, her breast heaving violently. "Oh—you—man! I suppose you think I *liked* the idea of your making love to her! And I never heard of the bracelet until this morning!" She tore the lovely thing off and threw it at him as hard as she could. He was barely able to get his arms up and catch it to prevent a broken nose. Then he ran to her, for she was weeping bitterly, hands pressed to her eyes, the tumbled corkscrew curls hanging around her face like some odd but beautiful foliage.

Come on, love, he thought. *I was only fooling. You felt sorry for her, didn't you?*

She gulped and buried her face in his chest again, choking back the sobs before she could even use her mind.

Yes, of course I did. Any real woman who was honest would. She's never had a man and she fell in love with you. When she said to me (it was hard to understand her at first, too) that I'd have you always, but could she have just one night, well, I forgot any jealousy. But it was still the hardest thing I've ever done, and don't you forget it!

"Oh, Hiero," she said aloud, her voice sad, "do you know what her last thought this morning was?" *Maybe mine will be the first male. Do not forget me, you who have him for always.* "I almost cried right then."

He patted her back and made encouraging masculine noises. "Don't cry, Love," he said, "I'm not mad. Besides, I *did* have a delightful dream."

She looked up, saw that he was grinning at her, and finally managed a smile. "Look, I don't want to hear any more about it, all right?"

At this point the seamen appeared in marching gear and order, coming out into the open near them, jabbering and craning their necks as they saw the burnt-over waste for the first time. Blutho and Gimp halted them and came over to join the two. Brother Aldo returned as well, leading Klootz, and Gorm emerged from the shadows of a giant tree's base. All were now ready, and Hiero took up his place in the lead again. But though the bear still went with him, the priest now rode upon the bull morse. Klootz's eyes gleamed with pleasure and he bugled, a hoarse bellowing cry which echoed under the cloudy heavens and through the humid air until the echoes died away into silence beneath the arches of the mighty wood.

Hiero looked back, hoping for a glimpse of the wood sprite whose dream he had shared, but he saw nothing. Once from the now silent forest a golden burst of song rang out, but whether it was Vilah-ree or not, he never knew.

They will follow us along the edge of their realm, came Aldo's thought from the rear of the column. *They wish to know if the House is alive and think you can tell them. So the queen told Luchare.*

It's alive, he sent back. *But I hope we can avoid it. I made no impression before. Are we carrying coals?*

Yes, in a clay pot. We can kindle fire in seconds and we have many arrows ready, on my order to Gimp.

Let's hope they won't be needed.

They marched south at a steady pace along the wood edge which towered like a rampart of green, with brown bark only rarely glimpsed. Occasionally, small bursts of flame off to their right showed them where the tree women still set fire to patches of unfired blight, working their way south on a general level with the column. Eventually, even this ceased, however. They stayed a quarter of a mile out in the waste and tramping over the bare burn, which was only gently rolling, the men made very good time.

They halted for a brief meal and then went on. Toward evening, the long-gathered clouds released a torrential bath upon their heads and visibility became so poor and the newly bared earth such a glutinous mud that it was obviously silly to carry on. They made camp under the trees and had trouble even there in getting a fire to light. Eventually one was got going, under a lean-to, and they managed a savory stew for supper. The rain was warm though, and all there were seasoned travelers, to whom a little extra water meant nothing.

It rained most of the night. When dawn came, they knew they were reaching the end of the forest at last. The trees themselves were changing. Palms and acacia-like shrubs began to appear in quantity. The real broad-leafed giants dwindled and soon no longer occurred at all. The heat steadily increased. To the south, wide grassy plains became dimly visible, rolling through thinning copses of trees to the distant horizon. On their left, the out-lying fingers of the eastern desert drew nearer, and with the desert came the all-too-familiar livid colors of the fungus belt. Down here in the south of the forest, the fire had hardly touched anything, for the House had not come so close to the trees, indeed was a number of miles away. Perhaps the absence of the great trees made the area less attractive to it.

However there was plenty of wild game. Beasts resembling deer and creatures like large-horned antelope grazed in herds here and there, only moving slowly out of the men's way. Most were unfamiliar to Hiero. Once they came upon a short-tailed, striped brute half as big as Klootz, which was feeding on the carcass of something fully three times the morse's size. They wisely skirted this scene, and the huge carnivore, which looked a cross between a bear and a ten-times magnified lynx was content, or possibly replete, only growling in tones of thunder. That night they built both large fires and a high stockade, making camp early in order to construct the latter. The bellowings and roarings all about them made this move seem a wise one. This was evidently not a country which either knew, or feared, men.

The next morning dawned clear and hot, the humid air perfumed like a breath of summer. Flowering grasses scented each step as they were bruised. On this day they turned and marched east and all the leaders were in front. The time had come, by all their reckonings, to search for the lost city. Maps were no longer of use.

As they advanced out into the semi-scrub, semi-desert area, the colors of the House drew inexorably nearer. Soon they could distinguish individual growths, gnarled objects like giant, oil-brown shelf fungi mostly and squat puffball things of dirty purplish red and yellow, whose pocked surface exuded some shiny substance equally repellent. They were unlike the northern growths but the hardened muck did not exist here, evidently not having been needed. They had lost all traces of the great fire in fact, for it had never come this far to the south.

Hiero called a halt. "I'm not putting our necks into that damned horrid thing's trap without a very careful search," he said. He indicated the first huge magenta puffballs. "Those things aren't half a mile away. That's quite close enough, judging from my own experience."

Aldo looked thoughtful. "We should, by all that's holy, be almost on the very site you're looking for, Hiero. In fact we may be right on top of it. I can't see anything to indicate this wasn't always a plain, but that's true of many buried cities." He patted the priest's shoulder. "I hope you've also thought that it may be hopelessly buried, son. We'll do our best, but who knows when those symbols were copied on to the maps, and maybe recopied a hundred times over?"

Luchare refused to be discouraged. A curious ally, as unexpected as he often was, was the bear.

"We *can't* have come this far, under such leadership, to find nothing!" cried the girl. Her faith rebuked Hiero's own and he said so out loud.

"We'll need a careful search, but let's look in an expanding arc. Gimp, you and Blutho tell the men we're hunting a city under the ground. Any scrap of human occupation, any sign, anything at all, should be marked down at once."

Gorm's slow thought was as stubborn and cool as ever. *There have been many humans here once. I feel it in my bones. Somewhere, not far away, the human city is hidden.*

Hiero had been afraid the men might panic over the thought of a pre-Death city being uncovered due to the possibility of disease or radiation, but Gimp reassured him.

"They've seen you and Brother Aldo do such wonders, Master, I don't doubt they'd jump into a fire if so be it was you said to." Hiero had been touched, more than he believed possible, by this affirmation of the seamen's trust and liking.

Everyone spread out now, except in the direction of the blight. No one was anxious to get too close to that barrier of evil-looking growth, and the seamen gave it a wide berth.

After some hours, the group had become so widely scattered that Hiero grew nervous about them. Some of the men were little more than dots on the southern horizon. There were few animals in apparent evidence out in this dry scrub area, but who knew what lurked beyond the next bush? He had Gimp sound the ship's bugle in the recall, and felt better when the men straggled back again with no losses in about a half hour. He ordered a rest and meal while he took counsel again with the Elevener, his girl, Gorm and Captain Gimp. The sky was clear but new thunderheads piling up in the south gave warning of more rain to come.

"There's only one conclusion that I can draw," said Hiero reluctantly. "If the maps are correct and the city is *not* a mile beneath us and is even *remotely* accessible—well, we're too far to the west."

"I fear you're right. I am reaching the same unwelcome conclusion out of necessity." Brother Aldo stared at the wall of repulsive fungi rearing itself over the low shrubs and bushes to the east. "We shall have to search more closely that way. And we shall have to be very careful, eh?"

"You're not going without me!" Luchare seized Hiero's arm. "Once was enough."

"You'll do what you're told or be spanked." Hiero's tone was absent, his gaze bent on the distant but menacing barrier. "We will do exactly what we did before, Aldo. You and Luchare will serve as anchors, so to speak, again. Gorm ought to be better at reaching you this time, having had more practice. He and I will penetrate in that direction. Keep the men ready with the fire arrows." He had been keeping the bear in touch by mind as he spoke.

This is the best way, said Gorm. *We have no choice,* he added.

Hiero kissed Luchare gently, repeated a brief orison for both of them and started walking toward the masses of ugly color which walled off the east. Gorm walked about twenty feet to his right, seemingly unconcerned, and sniffing busily. Behind them, the girl held tight on one side to the old man's arm and on the other to Klootz's bridle, and in back of the two, the sailors gathered under their leaders in a dense knot. Smoke curled from firepots they had kept kindled and bowmen were ready in front.

As always when going into danger, Hiero felt the old thrill and the interest of what he was doing rise and suppress any natural fear. Carefully, ignoring the blight as if it did not exist, he searched the ground for any trace of humanity's ancient presence. As he did, he maintained a constant mental link with his four-footed partner. Half an hour passed and always they drew steadily nearer the mold lands of the House.

Wait! The command thrilled Hiero. He saw that Gorm had gone tense and now stood, weak little eyes peering about, emitting great "snoofs" and "woofs" through his twitching nose, as he sought for some elusive scent. *There is metal somewhere,* came his thought again. *It is very faint, though: don't move and I will try to locate it.*

Slowly the bear ambled forward. This part of the scrub and sand area had a few low mounds thrusting up through the flattish surface and eventually Gorm halted before one of these, a rounded tumulus which rose some five feet above the surrounding plain. The thornbushes grew from its summit and tussocks of brown grass sprouted here and there. Gorm sniffed the base of the mound carefully and then began to walk around it. Hiero followed at a little distance, keeping the bear in sight, but not interfering with him in any way.

The eastern side of the mound, that which faced the fungus realm, was steeper and less rounded than that on the west. The light growth itself was now only a few hundred yards away, and Hiero tried to repress a shudder as he thought of it. With an effort he wrenched his mind back to the task at hand.

The bear rooted at a small pile of rock lying at the base of the mound. Still saying nothing, he moved a little farther on and loped down into a place where a long, low depression, still moist from the previous rains of two days back, lay before the now abrupt face of the hillock. Gorm rose on his hind legs and began to paw at the upright slope before him, using his long claws with a curious delicacy. A cascade of sand and small pebbles rattled down into the depression and darker earth was revealed where it had been. Nothing daunted, the bear continued to pick away, as carefully as a woman doing fine embroidery.

Here, came his thought, as calm and unexcited as ever, *here is metal, very, very old human work. I can do no more and you will have to see what it tells you.* He stopped his clawing and dropped down to all fours. Over his head the priest now saw a patch the size of a human face had been cleared of all earth. The smooth, blackened surface of some ancient, metal thing showed through, perhaps a wall, perhaps even though he hardly dared to think this—a door!

The man looked thoughtfully at what Gorm had revealed. The bear sat watching, his task over, waiting for the next step. Hiero marvelled at the fantastic power of scent his ally had displayed. Detecting the ancient, almost odorless metal under a good foot of earth, and at such a distance, was well nigh incredible.

Humans simply have no noses was the bear's answer when he was thanked. *I need your eyes often enough. We make a good team.* But Hiero knew he was pleased all the same.

Next he summoned the others with his mind. Now that he was actually at the site of a vanished civilization, he felt awed and in need of some help. If he and the bear should manage to find a way down into the buried world beneath, they might be utterly cut off. It was time to take a few more risks, despite the House and the nearness of its creatures and creations.

While he waited for the others to arrive, he picked at the earth with the long dagger, his excitement rising. Slowly a long upright surface of dark corroded metal, white underneath when scratched, began to appear, patinated by millenia of time and by secretions in the covering earth. Even as Brother Aldo and Luchare cantered Klootz around the corner of the tumulus, he finished his work. A door stood revealed, unmarked in any way but with the smooth stump of what must once have been a handle on the right side.

"Well, we have a success. But we are very close to the House or at least its minions, aren't we?" Aldo stroked the surface of the door. "Who knows what lies under this ancient thing? But—we are here and we had better make some quick decisions. Gimp and the men are coming on foot and will be here shortly. What are your ideas, Hiero?"

Eventually it was decided to leave the quiescent monster alone, but to maintain a constant watch and guard upon it. But the question of how to do this was more difficult. All four, Luchare, Aldo, Hiero and the bear were absolutely determined to go below if entrance could be gained. Who then would transmit orders to the men at the surface? Suppose trouble were encountered far below, how would any help be summoned?

A compromise was made possible by a suggestion of Luchare's. Her suggestion was simple: why not try and see if any of them, but most especially the bear, could communicate at all with Captain Gimp by using mind speech? This radical but obvious solution had been overlooked.

At once they began to practice, after Gimp had been carefully coached in what was to happen. The tough little skipper was very nervous, but he was no coward. When he was assured by the three humans he had learned to trust that he would suffer no harm, he relaxed and made his mind as receptive as possible.

He flinched visibly when Hiero's thought of a simple "good day" reached his consciousness. Finding it did no harm, he soon rallied and screwing up his face, tried his hardest to send messages of his own. This proved impossible, though the faces he made had Luchare in stitches. But in a very short time really he could "receive" from all four of them. They tested his reception of the bear's thoughts over and over at Hiero's special insistence.

"If we encounter, God forbid, the House or anything else down there, then Gorm may be the only one to get through. I would have been dead (and he also) if he hadn't reached you the last time. His mental channel is so different from a human's it never seems to occur to an enemy it's there at all."

All was in readiness at length and they began to work on the door. It was a sort of white bronze to all appearances. Iron or steel would not have lasted so long they knew, but this metal was new to them. Not even the Metz priest had examined the particular Abbey archives which spoke of aluminum alloys.

Despite their carefully cleaning all the remaining dirt away from the metal frame, the door refused to budge. "Small wonder!" said Luchare. "If I'd stayed shut that long, neither would I."

Two spearheads were broken in attempts to lever the stubborn portal open. Its faceless slab continued to defy them. It was the little mariner who solved the puzzle, using his common sense. Gimp had been peering all along the crack between the door and its jamb, his eye glued to the crevice as he followed it.

"See here," he said suddenly. "That there's a catch of some sort, that is. But it's not on the side near that little knob, but down here on the bottom!"

A quick glance showed them the sailor was right. A heavy shadow showed where a bolt had been rammed into the hole in the metal jamb. And better yet, the jamb seemed slightly warped there. Another hastily requisitioned spear was jammed into the slot. The tough ash stem bent and creaked, but slowly, groaning and protesting, the door began to rise in the air! No one spoke as Hiero and Gimp got their hands under it and continued to force it up. As it rose, previously invisible lines formed across it and it began to buckle. It was a folding door, of a kind none of them had ever seen before and as it rose it bent at regular intervals and then slid back into a recess just above its own top. Fortunately, no dirt had sifted into the narrow storage space above, a tribute to its ancient builders.

A last shove pushed the door up and as far in as it could be made to go. The two men stepped back, perspiring and breathing hard, for the effort required had been a strong one.

Before them all, as they stood in silence under the hot afternoon sun, a dark opening yawned. From it came a breath of cool air, not unpleasant, but vaguely stale, like that of a suddenly opened and long-unused attic or closet. More to their interest were the broad metal steps which could be seen gently curving down to whatever lay below. One seaman started a half-hearted cheer, but he was hushed by his fellows. Who knew what they had opened? They felt the moment was too solemn for any cheering.

"What about light?" said Luchare practically. No one had thought of it, of course, and they looked dismayed. But common sense triumphed. Two of the earthenware firepots were produced, which left three more in reserve. Luchare took one unlit, and Brother Aldo the lighted other. The extended wicks gave about as much light as a candle, which was deemed enough. At any rate, it was the best they could do.

Gorm went first, his small eyes gleaming with excitement for once. Then came the old man, clutching a light and his heavy staff. Hiero, sword ready, followed close. Last came Luchare with the reserve light and her spear ready, the one which Hiero had taken from S'nerg so long before and so many miles distant.

As they descended, the light from behind grew dim until it vanished altogether. Soon they were relying entirely on the pottery lamp. Luchare carried a small skin of oil, hopefully to replenish these, but no one knew how long their quest would last.

The stair wound downward for an apparently interminable distance. Gorm's nose could detect no sign of life and Hiero's periodic mind sweeps caught nothing either. They paused at intervals to make sure they could still reach Gimp and his men and each time the contact with the sailor's mind proved easy. He was not alarmed, having been warned they would attempt this.

248

Eventually, after what seemed hours, the stair emerged from its tunnel onto a broad surface. The fleeting shadows showed that they were in a large open space of some kind and their very footfalls seemed to echo in the distance. Both Hiero and Gorm detected movement at the same time, high up and far away. A ghostly chittering and squeaking came ever so faintly to their ears.

"Bats!" said Brother Aldo. "This place communicates with the outside air somehow." The implications were disquieting. Where did the other entrance to this buried realm lie? And who or what had access to it?

Luchare had been examining something she had noticed while the others talked. Now she called them over to see it. On a sheer wall were set a large group of switches, each one numbered in some archaic script.

"I'm frankly scared to touch these," said the priest. "What do you think?"

"So am I," said the old man after some debate. "But I think we must. Our oil may not last long, even if we husband it. There must be other sources of light down here and we desperately need them. I feel we must take a chance. Our whole venture is a terrible risk. This is only another such."

Hiero smothered his doubts and pressed the first switch. For a second nothing happened. Then to their gasps of wonder, around them grew a dim glow of light. It grew steadily brighter by degrees until it finally stopped, well short of direct sunlight, but casting an effulgence perhaps equal to that of a very overcast day.

They were standing on a platform set high on one wall of an immense cavern.

12: *AN END AND A BEGINNING*

The view of the mighty cave of the ancients was one to make a first sight a quiet and reflective one. How far below the earth they were, they could not imagine, but it must be a very long way indeed. Yet this giant's delving was apparently artificial! The long, dimly glowing bars of pale light hanging far above from the invisible roof (reminding Hiero of the blue lights on Manoon) which now illumined the whole great space showed that clearly, though there were obvious dark gaps where they had failed.

The walls, stretching out of sight almost, were geometric and regular, sharply cut in the shape of a pentagon from the bedrock of the planet. Above a certain height they were unfinished stone, but below that, to a distance of some thirty feet above the floor, they were smoothed and polished. The glint of metal showed where many of them were actually paneled. A wide circular space ran all around the structures in the center, separating them from the walls.

"Look at those things, will you!" Hiero's voice was low and reverent. The many great shrouded shapes, standing about the floor, covered with the dust of countless centuries, were vast, almost beyond the comprehension of men of a later day. There was spiritual fear both in his voice and in his mind. These must be the actual devices of the legendary pre-Death era. Perhaps they themselves had helped loose The Death upon the cowering world above! Ingrained in every reasoning human, save for the Unclean of course, was such a horror of The Death, that gazing upon things such as this was very like a glimpse of Hell itself. Brother Aldo's face was rigidly controlled and might have been carved of jet, but the repulsion in his eyes was clear. Luchare had actually fallen to her knees. At only seventeen, even after all she had been through, an actual glimpse of the titan engines of the legendary and horrific past weakened her legs as perhaps nothing else could.

Hiero bent and helped her up and as they moved together to the heavy metal rail of the platform for a better look, he kept an arm about her.

As they looked up, they also saw a spider's maze of slender catwalks and beams, strung from wires and metal cables, but so far off in the upper gloom that many of them looked suspended on nothingness. The hush of many centuries brooded over them. Above them, higher yet, glowed the lights, in turn hiding the ceiling from which they hung.

"You could put a regiment, ten regiments, of Metz Frontier Guards in here and lose them," was Hiero's awed comment, half to himself. His mind was staggered by the immensity of the place. And more than that. He knew what he was supposed to be looking for—the computers, if they still existed. But how to find them? Or anything else, in a place so huge and alien? True, he knew certain names, certain symbols in the dead languages, but would they be obvious, would they even be legible? His task, now that he had actually arrived at one of the ancient sites, suddenly seemed impossible.

Luchare left him and she and the white-bearded Elevener were now examining something on the far side of their platform, where a metallic box-like structure thrust itself out on the floor. As he was about to join them, he felt Gorm's sudden thought.

The bats have all gone. Where did they go? There is something I don't like about this place, Hiero. Bad air is entering far off on the other side. I smell, very faintly again, the sort of deadness which yet moves.

Hiero used his far-looker while sweeping the area with his mind as well. There was no real sentience in the aether, but the small minds of a few of the bats were revealed, far away and getting further still. They had left by an invisible ceiling hole, some natural crevice perhaps, and were impossible to read for direction. The far-looker showed not one opening indeed, but several, black tunnel entrances, two, perhaps a half mile off, on the opposite, eastern side of the man-made grotto. As he looked, he saw yet another far off to the left, on the south side of the cavern. And around one of those on the west were things which did not appear artificially constructed. There seemed to be dark stains, perhaps pools of moisture there, as well as he could see from that distance, and in the poor light, the upright objects arranged in clumps. He had been in caves and seen stalagmites and stalactites before, but these appeared different somehow. Was there not a dim glow about them? However he forgot them as Aldo spoke.

"Hiero, come here," said the old man. "I think we have a way to get down, if we can still trust the incredible mechanics of a long-dead age. I have seen drawings of things like this. This box thing goes up or down on this track set against the wall. That is why the stairs, which I imagine were only an emergency exit, go no further. Come and look."

He explained to the three of them, using his mind, how an elevator worked. He and Luchare had been cleaning off the control switchboard of its accumulation of dust and the three buttons were now easy to see. He next tested them by reaching around and in, while himself remaining on the platform and with a creak, the ancient thing began to move slowly down. He stopped it quickly.

"I thought so! I know the words. The bottom black button is 'down', the top 'up'. The red one I don't know, but red was often used for danger, so we will ignore it. Let's get in. Hiero, what are you doing now?"

"Maintaining communication with the surface. Gimp and his crew are still all right. They're camped now and set up for the night. I wanted a last mind check before we got into that thing."

Despite the pleased certainty in his voice, Aldo would not have been human if he had not been nervous as they all climbed aboard the elevator. The layers of dust were over six inches thick on its floor, and they had already learnt to move slowly, to avoid stirring it up any more than necessary. Fortunately, the dust must have contained much powdered rock, for it both rose slowly and settled quickly.

The elevator ran on two metal tracks set deep in the cavern's wall, and these had allowed only a little deposit of any kind to adhere. But of course the machine was old, old beyond the concept of even its designers. It creaked and groaned ominously as it started down, and the noises did not decrease as they sank lower. Some long-ruptured circuit made them stop at each level and it took an almost physical effort of Hiero's part to push the button and restart the contrivance afresh. There were five similar appearing platform levels and even the bear, who had been shielding his thoughts, let out an audible "whoof" of relief as they settled at last to the base of the shaft. They all felt the same. But their relief was to be short-lived.

As they left, farsighted old Aldo, who was the last one out of the metal cage, reached back and touched the 'up' button. He had decided to find out if they could return again in a pinch. Now, his cry of dismay alerted them all. The elevator would not move. For ten minutes they poked, prodded and fiddled with the mechanism and tried to at least locate the power source. The latter must have been buried deep under the floor, for they could find nothing. Thus they were five stories lower now with no known way back to the surface.

"I would wager we must be at least half a mile down altogether," said

Aldo soberly, putting their common thought into words.

We will have to find another way out, came Gorm's cool thought. *At least we are on our own feet, not in that thing which moves.* The alien mechanism had rasped the ursine nerves more than he cared to admit.

Around them now, in the much dimmer light of the cavern floor, loomed the dust-covered shapes of what had to be the great machines and devices of the past. From the platform far above many of these things had looked to be of modest size. Now it was seen that all were large and many were absolutely monstrous.

Hiero walked over to the nearest, intrigued by something puzzling in its shape. He used the shuffling walk which they had learned stirred up the least floor dust and he gently brushed the coating of inches thick grime away from the surface of the shrouded object, while the others waited.

"I thought it looked odd!" His laugh stirred remote echoes in the dusty aisles and corridors between the silent bulks and rebounded from cornices and projections far above.

"This is a cover! All these things are protected. Look, you can lift it and see what is underneath." He raised a corner of the heavy plastic wrapping, still moving slowly so as to avoid raising any more dust that necessary. The soft gleam of a metal base, untouched for thousands of years, met their eyes, which by now were accustomed to the dim light.

Excited, the soldier priest ran to the next great object and then the next. All were covered with thick plastic sheeting, a substance which mocked the centuries, and the metal underneath appeared untouched by any corrosion or other of time's ravages. Hiero drew his dagger and began to cut pieces of the plastic away, for the huge sheets were far too large to be pulled off by their puny efforts; many of the devices they covered being as high as a two-story building and half an acre in extent.

"Hiero," came the Elevener's strong voice. "I think we had better be told what we are seeking, don't you think? I have no wish to pry, but . . ."

"Of course. I meant to tell you earlier, honestly. There's been so much on my mind, I simply forgot."

While they stood about, or leaned on the buttresses of the incredible machines, he gave them a mental, closed-circuit recapitulation of the Abbey mission, describing the lost computers, or at least their purposes, as well as he could, and explaining carefully why the Abbeys felt they were so important.

"If what Demero told me is true, and I believe every word," he concluded, "we need one of these things desperately. The attacks against us are mounting and co-ordinated. Our defense and any counter attack won't have a prayer unless they are also."

Aldo had no more questions. Now that he knew what to look for, he began at once to examine the nearest mechanisms, seeking labels or identity marks of any kind. The others joined in, the bear helping him to lift the plastic covers, the girl aiding her lover in the same task.

An hour later, they paused in their work, looked at one another and laughed. Sweat and disturbed layers of dust had covered them all with a pale mantle and even the bear looked a furry ghost of his former self.

"Let's see," said Brother Aldo, who had been writing in a small book he had produced, "we have found nothing so far about computers, Hiero." The priest wiped a grimy forehead with an even dirtier hand and tried to concentrate. Brother Aldo's knowledge of the ancient languages was vital now, since Hiero himself only had been able to memorize a few simple words and phrases before setting forth.

"We have found 'engines,' that is, machine," Aldo continued, "and we have found other things, controls apparently. What these engines ran on, their power source, by the way, baffles me. Unless," and he looked very grave, "it is the lost power of the atom itself, which caused most of The Death when misused. But I prefer not to even think about that." Hiero did not see fit to mention that he felt the Unclean well might have rediscovered that particular power source. It was only a suspicion but he had never ceased wondering what silent engines drove their dark, sailless ships.

"We have found 'air-conditioning' and 'thermal control'," put in Luchare.

"Yes, but these are things, as I said, which occur in other sites I have visited. They mean fresh air and artificial heat, that's all. We have no idea how they did these things, but we know they are neither weapons nor computers."

"We're poking around out on one edge of this place," said Hiero, after a moment's thought. "How about heading for the middle? If there is an information storage-center, it might be there, logically. I am trying to recall how the place looked from up top, and I think there was a circular space, with things set about on it in some regular pattern."

This plan was adopted and they began a circuitous approach toward the center. Time and again they would find a pathway or aisle blocked by some rearing hulk or other and would have to go around or even retrace their steps. Hiero felt they were all minute creatures trapped in some vast and incomprehensible maze.

Eventually, all coughing and sneezing by now, they emerged from a corridor between two long lines of machinery into the open space which Hiero had glimpsed from far above. For some time they had been moving up a very gentle slope and it was now apparent that this radial point in the center was set higher than the rest of the cavern. "Probably a system of drains buried under all this dust, so they could flush the place down when it needed cleaning," said Hiero.

They could see things of interest at once. Before them stood a vast semicircular control board, its function very clear since all of the things they had seen, it alone was not covered by plastic. Yet it had been, that was evident. For piles of plastic sheeting, *minus any dust,* lay here and there as if each section had been ripped from the control board and cast aside at random. The thirty or so seats which were set in the floor in front of the board were not uncovered however, and still retained their plastic shrouds.

On the board's center, several small, unwinking lights, three amber and one red, glowed in what was obviously the main panel, since it lay in the center of the great board's gentle arc. The three humans stared for a moment, only realizing by degrees what was indicated by all this.

"Someone's been here," breathed the girl. "Who could it have been? How long ago? Look, those lights must have been turned on." She spun around suddenly as if to catch someone or something stealing up behind them. Yet nothing moved save for themselves. The dusty relics of the most ancient past towered up in forgotten majesty around them, only the three tiny lights of the board the sole indication that life was not extinct in the relics of a vanished age.

The bear moved slowly forward and began to sniff. *Come here,* said his mind. *Something has been here and it has left a track. Something we know,* was his grim afterthought.

Stepping forward, Hiero looked down and saw what Gorm had found. A broad, grooved mark, its greasy path only slightly tinged by dust, came from off to their left out of yet another aisle in the bulking engines. This trace went along the front of the control board, occasionally broadening into a wide smear where the plastic sheets had been flung aside, and then vanished again, down into the gloom of still another canyon in the forest of silent machines. The message was clear. Something had come, uncovered and examined the board, and then gone away again. Had it turned on the lights somehow? Where was it now and when would it return? Hiero shivered. Whatever had

255

made that strange mark was certainly not human and even before the bear's next message he felt he knew what it was.

That House thing or one of its creatures has been here, came Gorm's calm thought. *Can't you smell it yet?* In his four-footed friend's mind, Hiero caught the irritation at his duller senses, but he paid no attention.

Swiftly now he relayed a warning to the other two. At the same time, he bade Luchare relight the lamp she had extinguished when they had managed to get the cavern lighting system activated. Fire had been their only weapon against the House before and it might still save them should the monster reappear, or should it send its servants.

"See here!" Aldo had been examining the portion of the board where the three small lights gleamed. "I can read these signs or some of them. Some words such as 'gantry' and 'silo' are new to me, but here are 'missile launch' and a long series of numbers. We have found something terrible here, Hiero. This is a place which sent out into the air the flying Death itself, the great machines which travelled over and above the whole world, shedding foul poison and radioactive destruction." He was shaken to the core as he looked down at the silent board. "Perhaps," he added in a low voice, "perhaps some of those things are still waiting, waiting to spread more death, even after five thousand years." No one spoke, even the bear's mind, perhaps appalled at the thought that they might be able to somehow, by mistake, again loose such a horror on the world.

It was Hiero who recovered first. His active brain simply could not mull over the past for too long. He had come here to find something, a weapon in fact, and instead he had found a deadly enemy, which if not actually present, was certainly not too far off. These matters transcended any brooding over vanished tragedies.

"What are those lights?" he asked, his voice deliberately brusque. He wanted to shake Aldo out of his present mood and stir him to new activity. Tough as he was, the Elevener was a very old man, and he was facing in the flesh, so to speak, things he had thought of only as the abstract components of a nightmare. But now it was a living, revived nightmare, whose return to the world he dreaded more than any mere bodily peril to himself.

With an effort, Brother Aldo returned to the present.

"Those lights? All of them are marked with one word underneath. The two yellow ones say 'standby' which I believe means 'wait'." He peered closely at the red bead on the smooth black panel. "This one says 'alert', which means 'be on guard'. A moment though! A line of inlaid silver leads

256

away to another area, over here to the right." Muttering to himself, he stepped around two of the chairs, still tracing the line of bright metal with his eye. The others followed in his wake, waiting for a translation. The line wandered about for a distance along the board, at last coming to rest on a black ovoid projection. Under this bulge were more letters.

"Let's see now," the old man said, " 'lift cover for total-self-destruct.' " He turned and faced them. "Did you by any chance understand that?"

I did, said Gorm unexpectedly. *You are becoming very careless with your minds down here, all of you. You radiate even while using your human speech. You have found an old thing which will destroy all of this whole place, and us too, I gather.* His mind was quiet and amused again. One would have thought he was describing his last meal.

"I'm going to lift that cover," went on Brother Aldo in steely tones, ignoring the bear. "The best thing I know about this awful place now is that we may be able to destroy it. I frankly regret having aided you to come here." His passionate hatred of the pre-Death artifacts around him rang in every syllable of his voice.

"Let me," said Hiero quietly. "Don't forget, I'm more used to machines than you are. You look over my shoulder and tell me what you read there. I won't do anything without permission, I promise." So strained and taut had both Aldo's brain waves and speech become, Hiero was beginning to fear the old man would do something irrational.

The Elevener closed his eyes for an instant. When he opened them he suddenly looked more at peace, and a faint smile touched his mouth.

"I caught a fragment of your thought, boy," he said. "You are quite right. I must not give way to emotion and I was very close there. You go ahead and I'll try to supervise if I can."

The Metz examined the almost conical black projection. He saw that it had a knurled edge, obviously designed for fingertips and he began to turn it. A screw mechanism slowly revolved and as it lifted he saw both what lay underneath and the wisdom of such a cover. With sudden death for the whole area in one control, a screw opening allowed time to circumvent a madman or an enemy bent on self-destruction. A simple hinged affair would have been too easy.

Under the cap, which he laid carefully aside, was a thing like an uncovered dial. A row of thirty numbers, engraved in the archaic system of the ancients bordered a curved slot. At one end, set sideways in a smaller slot, was a pointer. Studying the mechanism, Hiero saw that the pointer could be pulled up, out of its own slot and moved down the larger to any of the numbers desired.

"Those are hours, or hour symbols, I feel sure," Aldo peered over his shoulder. "It must be that one can set the thing for up to thirty hours and then—the whole place goes."

"Suppose they're minutes, not hours, or some other unit of time, we don't even use any longer?" asked Hiero dryly. Luchare gasped behind them.

"It says 'hours' here," Aldo pointed to a pair of tiny letters which Hiero had not even seen, at the base of the slot. "This is an abbreviation, but one I have seen many times."

"Sorry," said the priest. "I'm getting jumpy. What do you say we have a meal? It must be well into the night up above and I imagine we all could use some food."

Once their stomachs had been called to their attention all were indeed hungry and Gorm protested bitterly that he was being slighted when Luchare gave out each agreed-upon ration.

You're so fat you could live for a week on nothing at all, said she, poking his plump sides. *Do you good to go without for awhile.*

Hiero wondered to himself, as he ate the dried meat and biscuit, whether the water would last until they got out. He said nothing to disturb the others. They only had brought one large waterskin with them and when all had drunk it was only a bit more than half full. The all-pervasive dust had made everyone very thirsty.

Barely had they finished, when the bear suddenly rose to his feet, apparently sniffing, head erect.

Nothing comes, was his thought. *It is the mind of Gimp* (here a pictorial composite of the little captain was made clear). *He tried to reach us. There is trouble up above.*

Instantly both Hiero and Aldo shut their eyes in an effort to tap the sailor's mind far over their heads, up on the surface of the dark plain. It was full night now, on the portion of the world's surface nearest them.

Gimp felt them at once and they could gather the relief in his mind as he did. He was not, of course, used to sending messages this way, but they persisted, probing and questioning, until out of jumbled images, emotions and attempts to communicate, they got his story or at least the gist of it. This was the tale:

A lone guard, for the others were asleep, had heard something moving in the brush and had the sense to keep quiet and awaken Gimp. That worthy had found two more men accustomed to move quietly and had awakened one-eyed Blutho and put him in command, with orders to arouse the camp and get under arms in silence. Gimp and his two trusties sneaked out and presently heard a man, they thought, moving, off to the south. They stole closer and were able to see, in the moonlight presumably, a number of mounted men on hoppers *(on what?*—Hiero; *Never mind, I'll tell you later*—Aldo), Gimp cleverly ambushed one such person, killing the mount and capturing the rider without noise. This man, for it was a man, had been taken back to their camp and hastily interrogated. What they had learnt was disquieting. A small, hand-picked army of the Unclean, both men and Leemutes, were coming from the south (the rider had been one of an outer screen of scouts) and were heading for a 'buried world,' one to which they had a 'door'. They were led by master adepts (Gimp called them 'magicians') and they were hunting a terrible man from the far north, a dangerous enemy who had to be slain at all costs. The Captain wanted advice fast, for he now could hear the approach of the army itself. That was all.

Hiero wasted no time. The prisoner was to be decently killed at once. The seamen were to take Klootz on a lead and move north as fast and as quietly as possible. The prisoner's death was necessary since he might otherwise be mind-traced by the enemy. His total absence would probably be ascribed to wild beasts or to accident. As usual, Hiero wasted no sentiment on the Unclean and their vassals.

His task done, he turned to the others and explained. Aldo had heard everything but Luchare and Gorm had to be filled in. The girl pointed out the obvious clue, though the others had already guessed.

"They're heading for a 'buried world'. It must be this one! Hiero, Gorm told us we were using our minds too loudly. They must have been listening somehow. There has to be another entrance and they know it. We're trapped!"

Gorm was less excited by the news and even a bit smug. *I've been telling you for some time that you were using your minds too much, but it can't be helped now. We must find a way out somehow. We have before.* He seemed unafraid and not even interested very much. He added: *Tell me when you want to start.*

Brother Aldo patted Hiero's shoulder in his kindly way. "The clue, Hiero, I'm quite sure, lay in our battle with the House. The waves of mental power that struggle gave off must have been easy to detect. Don't blame yourself, my dear fellow. The Unclean were a bit smarter for once than we gave them credit for being. Also, they must have been a good deal closer than we thought, must have been well on their way to reach us, from out of Neeyana. No one's fault, but we have to really think now."

"It's S'duna," said Hiero bitterly. "He's sworn to kill me or die trying. He must have done some brilliant calculating all the same to estimate where we were heading so well." He looked about at the dimly lit vastness around them. "How in God's name we can either fight or escape is beyond me." His shoulders sagged visibly.

"Think!" thundered Aldo, no longer sounding kind. "You are the warrior, as well as the priest, and this is no time for resignation. One thing even I can point out. They are still terribly afraid of you. Why else have they not used their minds, located and captured Gimp? They are using mind shields, those mechanical things they hide behind. For fear of *you,* that's why! Now take that fear of the enemies' and use it!"

Luchare said nothing. She came close and put her hands on his shoulders and looked at him, just looked, her eyes full of love and trust. Then she patted his cheek once, lightly, and moved away, humming softly to herself. Her man was there, and he would find a way out. How was only a detail!

The twin appeal was sufficient to galvanize Hiero out of his momentary despair. The strange, huge vault in which they were apparently incarcerated lost its brief terrors. Once again he was able to reason, to plan, to look at all sides of the problem. Brother Aldo saw the changed expression and the tightened jaw and waited, content. Their leader was back with them again.

The moment he began to think ahead once more, two factors occurred to him. The House was one and his unfulfilled mission the other.

"Spread out, but mark your path in the dust so you don't get lost, you two. *Gorm, go with Luchare. Give warning of the House or any enemy.* Brother Aldo, look for signs, names, I guess, of computers, if the damned things ever were kept in a place like this."

"They were," was the answer. "We read that it was the computers which somehow sent these terrible weapons out into the world and told them where to go and whom to kill. Certainly there is one here at least." He turned and strode off, swinging his staff and clutching his own small knife, with which to cut any enshrouding plastic. Luchare and Gorm were already poking about away down in another direction. The bear was so sensitive to danger that he was a superb sentinel, and she had forgotten she did not understand the ancient languages and thus could be of little real help.

260

Hiero badly wanted to be alone. He had some mental probing to do and once that was done some very careful planning. Already the germ of an extremely grim idea had come to him, an idea fraught with horrible risks, but also one which might be of tremendous benefit.

His mind he sent roving ahead, seeking out the enemy. In a moment he found him, or rather them, and he was somewhat shaken as a result. He had forgotten to ask Gimp if his prisoner had worn a mind shield. For *all* the minds he now encountered had them and he could not even make an estimate of how many there were. All he could do was estimate the physical distance from himself to an oncoming conjoint aura of defensive screens. Like a great blob of energy it was advancing from the south and above, at hazard, no more than a mile away. It was a real feat, he ruefully acknowledged, to shield so many in such a short time.

Coldly he assessed his own and his companions' chances. One thing was clear, the Unclean somehow had acquired a good knowledge of this place and thus were coming on without hesitation. Did this mean they had been here before? He considered this. It seemed doubtful, on reflection, that they had. Only the central switchboard, of the entire complex, had been disturbed and that recently. And he knew who, or what, had done that!

No, the Unclean Masters must have ransacked their own accumulated files and records, just as the Abbey Council had done before sending him out on his own quest. The place was well marked on the enemy map he had looted from the dead adept's body. No doubt the enemy had other charts as well, with more detailed directions. This cavern would have been one of a large number of places indicated for eventual examination, when time and manpower permitted.

But that plan had been changed when S'duna and his allies had determined to follow him, now their single greatest fear and enemy, to his doom! And they had found him somehow, half by guess and half by detecting his mind's energy bursts when he fought the House, that is if Brother Aldo were right. He probably was. That struggle indeed must have registered a long way off, to those who were watching and aware.

All this went through Hiero's mind in no more than an instant. He was standing, leaning actually, on the central control panel, as he thought, and he now made a sudden gesture and freed the cap on the destruct device. And as he did, he began to consider the House. From this thought his decision hardened. His hand moved.

The Metz next replaced the cap and then walked quickly away, in the direction of the eastern tunnels or openings he had glimpsed from the platform. There was a relatively clear path and he moved fast although with caution. Meanwhile, he contacted the bear and Aldo on a wavelength Luchare could not yet follow and told them briefly where he was going and why. He had not forgotten the House and its method of mental ambuscade. Should he not communicate at regular intervals they would come after him.

At this point he suddenly saw the slimy track of whatever creature the House had sent out, approaching the same corridor he was on from the left. He could see that ahead of him it continued on down the very aisle he had chosen. He instantly chose the next gap to the right and placed himself in a parallel alleyway between other lines of mechanical collossi. *No sense in going to the thing's front door.* He had seated a quarrel in his crossbow and now lighted the spare firepot as well. The crossbow bolt had oil-soaked cloth wrapped around it and he could light it in an instant were it necessary. *And if I'm given an instant,* he added to himself.

Now a new sensation came to Hiero. Over the musty, stale smell of the whole place, there came to his nostrils a familiar whiff of organized corruption. The bear must have detected this all along, he realized, even if it were far fainter here than up on the surface. Sickly sweet and abhorrent, it came to him, the stench of the living rot which was the hallmark of both the House and its realm.

He stooped under and rounded a lofty corner of some ageless mechanism and then quickly ducked back again. Before him was the work of the monster!

Here, far underground, the fungi were stranger even than those on the surface. It was as if the House saved its more delicate and cherished outgrowths for this hidden realm. And it was obvious that they needed no light, for many of them glowed with an evil light of their own making.

A broad, dark pool, full of floating scum, had formed where the floor had actually sunk or collapsed near the east wall of the great cave. Water trickled steadily over and down a broad area of slimy rock, for this wall was unfinished, indeed hardly even smoothed down by the craftsmen of long ago. An underground spring must have burst forth in ages past and still flowed into the pool, leaving by some hidden outlet.

Around this sinister tarn, which was many yards in extent, there grew a forest of tall, gently tapering, spires of soft, living matter. Several men's height they were, colored with pallid and crepuscular shades, ugly faded violets, insipid yellows, and debauched, bleached oranges. On top of some of them glowed round areas of foxfire and dim phosphoresence. This was the

262

light, the priest realized, which he had glimpsed far off when they first entered the cavern.

As he watched this buried obscene parody of a living wood, Hiero was moved by its allure as well as by its horror. Totally alien and awful were the purposes of the House but it could still create an eldritch beauty. He checked his mind sharply at this thought and examined his own reasoning, fearing a mental trap, an allurement into which the entity called the House might be subtly trying to draw him.

But there was no contact and he knew he was truly free. Besides, somehow he had the feeling that this was a place of utter privacy to the House, a hidden chamber of repose which the monster deemed inaccessible and utterly safe. How he knew this, he could not have said, but perhaps his terrible struggle with the lord of the fungi had allowed him to fathom, if only unconsciously, its emotions and thought processes; he had thus established a strange rapport with his enemy.

At first he thought nothing moved and he was about to emerge himself when he caught a flickering shadow out of the corner of his eye and instantly froze. The forest of fungoid spires was truly alive!

The things' movements were so slow and rhythmic he had almost missed them, but now that he watched carefully, he could see it all. The unnatural forms were not rooted or fixed, not even as much as a mushroom, but were moving, ever so slowly about on their broad bases. As he watched, fascinated, he saw that it was like a mockery or simulacrum of some stately dance, or even a solemn religious service. The weird beings, plants or whatever they were, would approach one another slowly until their sides touched, then, a rippling motion seemed to run up and down their entire length. Those whose crowns glowed with the pale phosphorus seemed to deepen that glow in these encounters. Too as they approached each other, a clot of slime or soft bulging flesh developed at their bases and then dissolved as they retreated in the same almost imperceptible fashion, to begin their peculiar gyrations anew with a fresh partner.

The ghastly things were sentient in some way, of this he felt sure. Just as the great slime molds he had met far above were able to sense enemies or their food, so too were these living fungi able to feel, to react, perhaps even to *know*. Had he revealed himself, he was sure that he would have been detected, if not even captured and slain. He drew back further into the shadows of whatever vast machine was giving him shelter.

The living cones or fungus candles, for they were thinner than a normal cone shape, partially masked the black rift of the tunnel, which opened on the far side of the water. For it was a tunnel, of that he was sure. Its sides were regular and smooth, too rounded to have occurred naturally. Once in remote ages it might have been a major entrance to the underground hiding place of the great missiles. But the slime and muck which coated the lips of the entrance proved that nothing human had passed that way for many long years.

Well, he had learned all he could. He quietly slid further back away from the stagnant water and the evil, living spires of mold. When once out of sight, he began to run, always angling toward the south. One portion of his brain meanwhile had kept a ceaseless watch on the inchoate but collected mental force which he knew represented the Unclean horde. Since they had steadily advanced, there was only one place from which they could be coming, and that was one of the tunnels in the southern wall. A fairly clear road must exist to it from the surface and the Unclean leaders would be moving into and down it as rapidly as possible.

He paused and calculated various times for a moment. No trace of his mind or that of the others could the enemy now detect. This he felt sure of, for his powers had become such that he could have kept a protective shield over many more than just four minds, even if Aldo were not on guard. In any case, defense was always far less effort than attack, for it could be maintained with and by an unconscious effort of mind. No, he could check on the enemy's progress, but not the reverse. Aldo had been right. Their fear of him was such that they were relying on physical strength and hiding under their mechanical mind screens.

Now he sent messages to his companions to join him, whether they had found anything worth taking or not. He simply stood still and waited, until they came. In a few minutes the white beard of the aged Aldo appeared around a corner and the other two came only a little bit behind. The priest was so wrought up, he noticed nothing of the small package Luchare carried.

"Look," said Hiero stooping. He traced a design in the dust of an engine's buttress next to him. It was hard to see in the dim light but there was just enough when he added that of his little lamp.

"Here's where we are. Here's a pool of water over on the east side. The House has an exit here. I'll tell you about that later. Over here," his finger drew yet another circle, "is the southern entrance. S'duna and the Unclean must be coming this way. That elevator machine is broken and we can't go back. All right, we're going *out* the way the enemy comes *in,* to the south. But you'll have to do exactly what I tell you." He paused and grinned, his face quickly looking years younger on the instant. "Even then, there's a good chance it may not work. It depends on two things. One, S'duna's so eager to get me, he'll stop at nothing, and, hopefully, not think straight. Two, so will somebody else, not think straight, I mean. Oh yes, and neither of them knows or is aware of the other at all. That's the equation and it has to be perfect to work."

Brother Aldo laughed, honest chuckling laughter. "I see your plan, I think. It may work out totally, but if not, well, there's still a great load off my spirit. Tell me what you want us to do."

Gorm, who had been kept informed simultaneously, sent a quick thought. *A terrible idea. Let's hope it works.* Luchare simply pressed herself close to him.

"Here's what we do," the priest went on. "You go this way, over to the southwest wall and hide the best way you know how. I'll find you. I have to go back where I came from. Now hurry!" He kissed the velvet cheek gently and then spun on his heel, erasing every thought but those needed for the task ahead. The Unclean army was very close!

Returning to the evil pool of water was easy, for his own marks in the untrodden dust of centuries were simple to follow. In a matter of minutes he was peering around the corner of another machine at the dark water and the moving nightmare garden (if such it was) of the House. In the dim light, the living candles still moved and stank.

He took a careful aim with his crossbow, lowered it, having once got the range, and raised it again. In the interval he had lighted the oily rags bound around the quarrel from the rekindled firepot. He released the trigger and with a hiss, the now blazing dart shot across the water and deep into the pulpy substance of the tallest of the moving towers of putrescence.

The reaction was instantaneous. As he had prayed, the horrid things were every bit as inflammable as their fellow fungi far above, up on the earth's surface. The fire raced over the tall writhing shape in seconds and the sudden whipping movements and frenzied gyrations of the mold beast touched and set fire to a half dozen of its fellows in hardly less time. Hiero had been readying another bolt, but so speedy was the awful destruction he had wrought with only one that he stayed his hand.

At the same time there came into his brain a terrible shrilling, a piercing vibrato, on an incredibly *high* wave length, which rose and fell like the skirling of some demoniac orchestra. He knew he was hearing the death agony of the foul things and being a kindly man felt momentarily sorrow even for these.

Then he remembered his mission and stepped into the open!

The moving spires, such as were not already alight and writhing in their fiery death throes, were aware of him at once. He had been right he realized, the creatures were indeed sentient! Immediately they knew him to be the author of their misery. The tall columns bent as one in his direction. He could feel an almost material wave of venomous hatred emanating from them as their fellows blazed and shook all around them. The very slime with which their movements had coated the naked rock was itself a pyrotic and fresh runnels and gutters of moving fire sought sought out many of those who were nowhere near their burning fellows.

The splendor and horror of the sight almost made him a victim himself. One of the awful spires whose top was as yet aglow only with its own poisonous foxfire bent until it pointed in his exact direction. Then from its crown a dully-glowing series of blobs were launched in Hiero's direction. So unexpected was the attack that he barely had the presence of mind to leap aside as the first ball of glowing slime raced his way. Even so, it splattered almost at his feet and one minute fragment struck his right hand. The pain was savage and only the instant application of the oil-soaked rag he still clutched made it die down. He hastily backed away, keeping on his toes, so that the next poisonous missiles came nowhere near. Actually, if one stayed alert, he realized, they were easy to avoid.

All the while he was praying for something else. He had provoked the ruler of this foul realm, carefully and deliberately. *Where was it? Had he guessed wrong?* Mind and body keyed up to the highest degree, he backed slowly away from the inferno of the dying fungi. The stench of the corrupt and burning bodies, and the thick, greasy smoke made even this close proximity almost unbearable. *Where are you, House, damn you?* And even as he bent his thought upon it, it came.

He had been watching the gaping mouth of the tunnel beyond the pool, a task made increasingly difficult because of the swirling smoke wreaths and nauseating reek, for he was sure this was the entrance to the creature's lair. Perhaps it was, but there were others.

Almost before he had time to realize it, a surge of filthy liquid overflowed the near edge of the buried underground pool and sent a wave of fluid corruption racing over the floor in his direction, and the bulging, gelatinous horror of the House began to emerge *out of the water*. As it grew in size, it sent one bolt after another of mental force at the lone man.

It was well that Hiero had armored himself against this very time. In odd, waking moments, ever since his first encounter with the monster he had carefully analyzed his medusa-like power of paralysis, and he had deduced that its true strength lay in an attack on the psyche, rather than the actual brain. The emotional centers of the body were its targets, not the reasoning process and in the subconscious alone could it establish its unearthly stranglehold.

One remote corner of his mind registered mild surprise at the relatively modest size of the alien monstrosity. Its brownish, slimy bulk was not too much higher than his own head and scarcely more than five or six yards in total width. It still preserved the odd, four-cornered shape which had made Vilah-ree name it, but the lines moved and shook, the angles continually reformed in peculiar abhorrent and sickening ways. Hiero saw also that it could move on its blobby base, just as the horrible candle things did and that it could move fast. Also now, long glistening tendrils or pseudopods sprouted from its upper parts and waved hungrily as it slid rapidly in his direction over the floor. And all the while its ravening hatred and power beat upon his mind. His own rapport with the alien growth had become so strong that he understood why it laired so deep here and what actually he had done when he had attacked the fungoid spires. The pool was the center of not so much a garden but more (though not entirely) a harem!

The seal which he had painstakingly set upon his inner being held. Even so, he prayed for strength as he backed away from the water and into the aisle in the machinery from which he had first come. After him flowed the monster and behind it, in turn, came the remaining spires.

No more did the House use its vile blandishments to make of him an ally, and thus attempt to lure him within its reach. For it recognized him. Its hatred of the one being who had ever broken its power and had helped destroy much of its awful kingdom overcame it, until its strange composite mind could think of nothing else but to obliterate the impudent minikin before it. What— did the very inner parts of its buried realm, its hidden mates' playground hold no safety from this feared and dreaded enemy? On, on and slay! Its speed increased and its groping vibrissal pseudopods failed the dead air as it sought to rend him.

Carefully, judging his speed to a nicety, Hiero fled from the thing and its pack of followers. The assaults on his mind he repelled, content merely to ward off the House's attack and not to try to retaliate. Any such trial on his part might serve instead to open new corners of his own brain to fresh and unknown assaults. Who knew of what else the monster was capable if allowed, even for an instant, to forget its mad rage?

Down the silent, dust-laden corridors, under the dim illumination of the glowing bars of millennia-old light, the strange chase continued. The human fled, the living lord of the slime sought to overtake him and extinguish its bitterest foe from the earth. Save for the light footfalls and breathing of the man and the sucking, slithering noise of the fungoid pack's progress, there was utter quiet. The deadly race to an observer would have appeared some strange and voiceless charade or shadow show. The squat House and the tall dozen remaining mold pillars sped on; the man ran; the shrouded ancient machines were backdrop.

Always, the priest led his pursuers south, shifting a little back and forth so that it would not be too obvious and straight a road, but never going very far from the line he had chosen. And now, at length, there fell upon his ear a sound for which he had yearned. It was the distant vibration of a legion of people moving, the faint but distinct echo of many feet! The Unclean host was upon them and must even now be debouching into the great cavern!

Still, husbanding his strength, Hiero ran on, and implacable as ever, the alien master of the mold things and its last minions followed on his track, centuries-old dust by now coloring them all the same pallid grey.

At a certain intersection of two opposing aisles, Hiero suddenly increased his speed. His careful appearance of fatigue was suddenly shed, as quickly as that of a parent bird whose apparently broken wing has led the searcher far from its huddled young.

Now, he turned and darted away at full speed, taking the House by surprise as he did so. He flashed away toward the south wall and then—barely before leaving the shelter of the machines—darted into a narrow gap between two huge engines and was gone. One instant the House thought it had him trapped, the next he was utterly vanished!

Ravening, the unstable, shifting bulk increased its speed, layers of filth and dust flying as it sped forward in the manner of some Brobdingnagian snail on its rippling base, its slender mates coming on in its wake.

Hiero, now two hundred yards off and well to the left of his former track, peered cautiously out toward the open, the southern end of the ancient cave. What he saw made him draw breath in exhultation.

Pouring into the cave, rank upon rank, file upon file, came the massed forces of the Unclean. Even as he watched, the last ones entered the great cave and the tunnel gaped empty behind them. At least two hundred creatures were already streaming across the open, some of them men in dark uniform clothes armed with pikes, others Leemutes in their own skins. He recognized red Hairy Howlers, brown Man-rats, and far off to one side, a clump of the new things he had first encountered on the ship, the Gliths, their grey scaly hides glistening. Not far from the entrance itself, marshalling their forces, were a group of men in dark cloaks and hoods. The adepts were preparing for a master stroke and he smiled grimly as he thought that only one man was the cause of all this preparation! Truly, the enemy had not been properly challenged for a long time.

And then it happened. The first part of his desperate scheme came to fruition, just as he had planned it and willed it, but (down inside) never dared believe it would.

Out into the open from the central passageway, charging along in its blind rage, seeking the hated human and oblivious of all else, came the House!

From his vantage point, Hiero could see it all, every stage of the weird ensuing drama. All movement ceased instantly out on the quarter mile of open, between the machines and the cavern wall. Not a man, not an Unclean mutant stirred. The little group of hooded masters of evil were frozen, standing with their heads together, as if turned to ice in the middle of their plots.

He spared a glance for the House. It too had checked and come to a halt, and for once its own unstable, wobbly outlines were not moving. A little way out in the open from the street he had just quit, it halted, its acolytes motionless also. Its pursuit was forgotten as it strove to adjust to a new situation with all the power at its command.

I'm right! the priest exulted. The strange mesmeric power of the House was unaffected by the Unclean mechanical screens, screens which Hiero himself had been unable to penetrate. It, the House, really did not operate on the brain at all, and the blocking power the Unclean scientists had devised was therefore useless against it.

Around him, surging in a way which to his sensitive mind was practically physical, Hiero could feel the ferocious wills of the Unclean overlords struggling to be free. But the only free brain in the House's environs now were his own and those under his protection. The monster's pressure upon his had ceased as it grappled with its new and unexpected foes. It had never had so many creatures to control before and it was having a hard time holding them immobile. Hiero, observing from the "outside," so to speak, could actually feel with his mind, the House's efforts to maintain its screen as the swarm of enemy beings tried to break the hold it had laid on their bodies.

But now the priest was himself in motion again, running hard to the left along the southern tier of silent engines. He kept in the shadows and neither the House nor the Unclean army seemed aware of his flitting shape, engrossed as they were in their silent grapple.

In a few moments he spied tracks in the dust ahead of him, coming from the center of the mechanical maze, and followed them to an alcove between two canopied buttresses. Here, Brother Aldo, the girl and the bear were waiting, the humans' faces strained and intent and even Gorm shaking with excitement and shifting nervously from one paw to another.

Come on! sent Hiero. *Don't even think from now on if you can help it. I'm going to keep covering your minds. Aldo—build a reserve shield under mine, if you can. Now, let's go—fast!*

"Hiero," cried Luchare, trying to say something, but the blazing glance he spared her made whatever message she had die unspoken.

They were only a few steps from the open space on the south and he led them quickly out into it. He felt Luchare, whom he was actually leading by the hand, tremble at her first sight of the massed enemy off to their right, but she never faltered. Behind them the other two trotted in their wake, raising yet more dust. *By now,* thought Hiero, *we must be visible. God help us if my screen drops!*

The House did indeed sense their motion somehow. Despite the efforts it was putting forth to hold the Unclean ranks imprisoned, it spared another bolt for them. Hiero warded it off, using his new technique, with almost contemptuous ease. Once one knew how the House operated, its traps were not all that clever, and besides, now it could only spare a fraction of its strength.

But to the other enemy, who had never met it before, its methods were deadly indeed. Strain as they might, the Unclean army, masters and slaves, Leemute and human, could not move a muscle. Two evil forces worked to allow the good freedom!

Soon Hiero was compelled to pass close to a squad of black-clad soldiers, with dark metal helmets and long spears. They had been racing toward the northern section and the House had caught and held them in mid-stride. Their eyes gleamed with deadly hatred as the four loped by, but they could not twitch so much as a finger to impede their progress.

Another such group and another they passed, living yet locked like statues in the foul embrace of the fungoid horror.

Next they passed what had been a crouching bounding crew of the giant Man-rats, creatures Hiero knew well from the past as devilish foes, huge mutated rodents with all of human reasoning ability and clawed hands as capable as any man's. Their fists now clutched sharp knives, clubs and long lances, while their brown-furred bodies bore elaborate harness and equipment. But no more than their human allies could they break the grip of the House on muscle and nerve. Only the red eyes glared with hate.

Next, close to the mouth of the tunnel itself, the fleeing four came to the half-dozen hooded shapes of the enemy commanders. Of those looking his way, Hiero could see the knowledge and hatred flare in their eyes as his little group passed by. But though they would, he did not doubt, cheerfully die in order that he too might be slain, they were as helpless as the stupidest and least of the evil servitors in their forces. For it was obvious that they did not understand the House's power and methods any more than had the warrior priest himself when he first encountered it.

His crossbow slung, he carried his sword-knife in his right hand as he ran, leading the panting Luchare with his left. But his fear that one or more of the Unclean would free himself proved groundless. On past the last of them, a pair of Howlers whose acrid stench supervened even over the drifting reek of the House, he sped, the others close behind. They were actually into the tunnel now and he saw at once why the enemy had chosen and used it.

Before them, still clear in the remaining light of the cavern's glowing rods, stretched a smooth, level ramp, thirty feet across, curving up in a gentle spiral sweep into the gloom ahead. Many heavy feet had beaten a path down the dusty floor, indeed, the dust had hardly had time to settle, but the way ahead seemed clear enough.

The priest stopped and relit the firepot to which he had stubbornly clung ever since he had shot his flaming arrow into the living towers of the fungi. They would need some light ahead, for they were leaving the artificial glow of the lost cavern.

He released Luchare's hand, pushed her on and waved the others past. In silence they moved obedient to his orders. Alone, Hiero watched the scene below for a last fascinated instant. About his head he had never stopped feeling the surging currents and giant forces in contest, as the Unclean tried to free themselves and the counter-grip of the House still stubbornly kept them trapped in its invisible mesh. One look only he spared, seeing for the last time, the slime-bedewed greyish shape, its attendant pale cones towering over it, and between it and himself the equally silent, motionless legions which had come to destroy him.

The Metz turned and ran, holding his lamp high as he caught up to the others. Indeed, they had not gone far, but were waiting for him only a little above. Aldo held the other lamp and Luchare was just filling it from the now depleted oilskin which she cast away. They did not light it but fell in behind Hiero and began their upward journey. He set a sharp pace and no one questioned it, but they were all too exhausted to run and a brisk walk was the best they could do.

"How long can it hold them, do you suppose?" gasped Luchare at length.

"Long enough," said Hiero curtly. "For god's sake, darling, save your breath! We're not out of danger yet. The ancients had exact time devices and I don't! Just keep walking and try to keep your mind a blank."

She did not flare up in anger, for she recognized by now that his orders had reason, and they trudged on in silence. The light showed the ramp to be almost featureless, a great tube lined with some age-defying substance, which had been cut into the earth and rock with micrometer precision by its long dead makers. Once or twice they passed a sealed opening in the walls, but they did not stop. There were no lights visible and only the flicker of their little lamp lit the way.

This must have been the main path, reflected the priest, driving his weary legs forward and upward. They had been walking a long time, at least it felt like forever, but he dared not rest. The forces trapped in that place behind them were too awful to take any chances with. But talking might ease the strain.

"Did you find any computers?" he asked at length.

"No," was Aldo's answer. "Such a search might take a week, or a month. But Luchare found something. She is carrying it. Do you think the Unclean can free themselves? They have the man, and beast power, to find anything there. And what about the House. It is so *powerful,* Hiero. What might it not do with the knowledge of the past?"

"The House cares nothing about the past or machines or weapons. I know what it thinks or feels as well as anyone, human, that is now alive. It has no use for mechanical devices, but only what it makes or grows itself." He forgot Luchare's find as his worry reasserted itself.

"Yet it, or perhaps one of its creatures was looking around at the control board. Don't forget that."

"I know," Hiero's laugh was grim. "And it had no idea what it was doing, I'm sure of that too. Yet it may have given us a way out by its action. How long have we been walking, do you suppose?"

"At least an hour, I should think. Are we safe yet?"

"No. Keep walking. We've got to keep on till we drop if necessary. I can still feel the pressure behind me. And the House is weakening!"

"Can they kill it and follow us? Maybe we can block this tunnel then." Luchare's tone was defiant, her attitude that of the princess she was. Hiero's heart warmed to her.

"Maybe we can," he said more cheerfully." But it hasn't quite let go yet. It never had to control so many powerful minds before, all alien to it and all trying to break loose. It hasn't dared move, I can feel that all right. Perhaps it's summoning some of its carnivorous slime molds. And the Unclean are still there too. I can feel all their minds even under their screens, like one big ball of force."

"I also," Aldo admitted. "What an amazing creature the House is. How I would like to know it, to learn what it thinks, feels and wants from life." His tone was wistful.

Hiero glanced at his aged ally in amazement. The Eleventh Commandment really embraced everything, it seemed!

We are close to the good air. Gorm had been waddling unhappily along, his pink tongue hanging out and his fur an inch deep in grey film. Now he scented escape from this underground world he disliked and his spirits lifted.

Hiero momentarily covered the lamp with the edge of his cloak, and they all strained their eyes. Was there a faint lessening of the blackness ahead? The very thought revived their flagging energy.

Soon it was a reality. As the light grew, Hiero slowed his pace. "There may be a rearguard," he said. "They'd be fools if there weren't something of the kind. Let me probe a bit while you three rest and catch your breath."

His mind sped forward ahead of them, seeking any intelligence that might be lurking above at the tunnel's mouth. But he could detect nothing, not even the shrouded energy which he had learnt meant an Unclean mind shield. Unbelievable as it seemed, the whole force of the enemy had apparently plunged into the bowels of the earth, so overconfident of his destruction they had left nothing behind.

He told the others this and they went cautiously on. Three more great curves and the light was quite strong enough to make the guttering lamp unnecessary.

The faint calling and piping of birds came to their ears now, and even the human noses could catch the sweet scent of the air which poured down the shaft.

"Let me go first," Hiero took the lead again and soon saw the great opened doors ahead. He absently noted the shattered hinges and when he stepped outside the cleverness of the device amazed him. For the two huge doors were made of something on the outside which imitated weathered grey rock and yet which must have been far more impervious than any granite. The Unclean had been indeed cunning to penetrate their secret and so quickly follow on his traces.

All this raced through his mind as he drank in the cool air of the tropic dawn, but he urged the others on as before.

"Hurry," he said, "Hurry! We can't delay yet! We may not be safe for hours!" He gave Luchare, who was stumbling, his arm again. He was oblivious to the small packet to which she clung with her other hand, for her telescoped spear was now tucked through her belt.

The four set off away south over the boulder strewn waste onto which the huge tunnel had opened. Limping and staggering they went on, no one questioning Hiero's iron determination or right to thus drive them. Aldo now frankly leaned on his heavy staff, something no one had seen him do before.

Still, they staggered on, their breath coming in painful gasps, their muscles twitching and burning. The ground was semi-desert, tall weeds and thornbush growing up through patches of rock and scree. The cool air of dawn gave way to the burning heat of morning and (very slowly now) they hobbled forward. Time seemed to pass with terrible slowness.

Then it happened. Hiero, who had been listening, both with his mind and his other senses, felt it first.

"Down!" he shouted and falling, pulled Luchare close to him. Aldo too, fell prone while the bear simply collapsed.

First came a gentle tremor of the earth, so slight it might have deceived them into thinking it was a muscle spasm of their own over-used bodies.

Then the earth began to shake and heave, rising and falling in a great wave, as if the tiny atoms of flesh which clung to it were being tossed in some inconceivable blanket. For the first time, Gorm let out a howl of sheer terror.

A distant muffled roar filled the air. Slowly the heaving of the troubled earth died away. A ringing in their ears also ceased. They raised their heads and looked at one another. Hiero was the first to grin, his white teeth flashing in a countenance so dirty it looked like pure mud. Then Aldo laughed, a deep-throated ringing sound. Hard on his heels a bird began to sing nearby, tentative at first, then bursting into its full series of rippling cadences.

Luchare kissed Hiero. When she pulled her lips away, she murmured drowsily, for she was almost asleep from sheer exhaustion, "What was that?"

"That," answered Brother Aldo as he helped them both up, "was the button marked 'self-destruct' on the central control board. Right, my boy?"

"Yes, I gave it four hours. What a race of men! After five thousand years their death still works! At least the Unclean got nothing from them. Nothing but destruction. The House too. And yet—if it hadn't held them I couldn't have done it."

274

They looked north in silence. Where there once had been a wide level plain, a vast shallow bowl had now appeared, its sides and rim of raw, tumbled earth and chunks of riven rock. The low trees and scrubby bushes had vanished, lost in the rubble caused by the great explosion.

"We'd better move," said the priest. "Klootz and the men are apt to be way up north by now and we need to push on as soon as possible."

"Your road should be easier henceforward," said Aldo, the sun highlighting the grey dust in his once snowy mane and beard.

"I hope so," said Hiero wearily. "But I still haven't found a computer. And this army of theirs wasn't a real percentage of what the Unclean could put into the field if they wanted.

"Besides," he added, "S'duna's not dead. I would have known somehow if he'd been down there. He wasn't. We have an appointment to keep somewhere, he and I."

"You may not have found a computer," said the old man, "but look what Luchare is carrying. She found a stack of these things on an apparently abandoned desk. Possibly someone's study area. I could read the title. Try it yourself."

Half numb from what he had been through, Hiero scanned the title of the small flat book which Luchare had handed him with one finger. *"Principles of a Basic Analog Computer,"* he read in halting English, the lost language. Inside were plastic page after plastic page of diagrams and close-printed text. He could say nothing and felt choked. Here was how a computer could be built, perhaps by anyone! The other two smiled at the look on his dirty, sweat-streaked face.

"Look," said Aldo, using his finger in turn," it says *"Volume I.* Luchare found a stack of them. And she has the other two, Volumes II and III as well. She called me over and I read off the titles. But I think she knew, somehow, even without me!"

Wordless, Hiero pulled Luchare's arm around his waist and the three humans and the bear began to retrace their steps, moving north like cripples over the barren and shattered landscape. Gorm tried to have the last word, or rather thought.

No one ought to move so fast he grumbled. *From now on, let's try to move at a calmer speed.*

The world moves at a certain speed answered Aldo, after a bit. *We all must learn to move with it.*

GLOSSARY

Abbeys, the: Theocratic structure of the Kandan Confederacy, comprising the Metz Republic in the west and the Otwah League in the east. Each Abbey has a military-political infrastructure, and the Abbey Council functions much as the House of Lords in 18th Century England, with all science and religion also as its prerogatives.

Batwah: Trade *Lingua franca;* an artificial language used throughout the areas bordering the Inland Sea, and well beyond in some places.

Buffer: Giant bovines, probably mutated bison, which migrate in vast herds through the western Kandan regions on an annual basis.

Chespek: Small kingdom on the Lantik Sea, often allied to D'alwah and equally often at war with its immediate neighbor.

Circles: Administrative areas, named by color, of the Unclean and its masters of the Dark Brotherhood. Hiero passed through three, the Red, Blue and Yellow as he went south and east. Until his journey, their existence was unknown.

D'alwah: Largest and most developed of the east coast states on the Lantik Sea. A kingdom, organized as a benevolent despotism, but where commoners have few rights. A debased branch of the Universal Church exists.

Dam People: Aquatic rodents, of human intelligence and more than human bulk, which live on artificial lakes in the Metz Republic, under terms of mutual toleration; probably mutated beaver.

Dark Brotherhood: Their own name for the Masters of the Unclean. The fact that they use the word "dark", indicates that they sought universal conquest and, more important, gloried in it and realized that they were, in fact, basically evil. Modern Satanism, in its real sense, is a parallel. *(See Circles; Unclean.)*

Death, The: The atomic and biologic blight which destroyed the major population centers and most of humanity, some thousand years in the past. Still a name of dread and ultimate menace in Hiero's day. "All evil came with The Death" is a proverb.

Deserts of The Death: Patches of ancient atomic blight, where there is little or no water and scant or no vegetation. Yet life exists in these horrible places, though most of it is inimical and strange, bred from hard radiation and a ferocious struggle to survive. Some of the deserts are hundreds of square miles in size, and in Hiero's day, avoided like The Death itself. They are rare in Kanda, but many exist in the south. Blue, radioactive glows mark the worst of them at night.

Eleveners: The Brotherhood of the "Eleventh Commandment" ("Thou shalt not destroy the Earth nor the life thereon.") A group of social scientists who banded together after The Death, to preserve human culture and also love for *all* life, and knowledge thereof. This group permeates all human societal life and though opposing violence, battles the Unclean, often in hidden ways.

Forty Symbols: The tiny wooden signs that a trained priest-exorcist carries on his person. By putting himself (or herself; there are priestesses of great power) in a trance state, the priest can "forelook", or to some extent see the future, using the symbols.

Frontier Guard: The army, or embodied forces of the Metz Republic. The Otwah League has a similar group. There are sixteen "legions," self-contained units, in the Metz Republic. They are under, *not* the Republic's orders, but those of the Abbey Council, which in turn, reports to the Lower House (Assembly) on its decisions, which are always approved. Priests usually lead and direct the Frontier Guard.

Glith: A recent form of Leemute, possible bred from a reptile, by the Unclean. A humanoid, scaled and very strong physically, utterly the slave of the Dark Masters.

Grokon: Giant descendants of our present day hogs, which roam the northern forests. They are much sought for as meat but are very dangerous to hunt, being clever and the size of extant oxen, when adult.

Hairy Howlers: One of the commonest and most dangerous varieties of Leemute. They are great fur-covered, tailless primates, highly intelligent and used as soldiery by the Unclean. They hate all humans save their dark masters. They resemble huge, upright baboons as much as anything.

Inland Sea, the: The great freshwater sea formed by the ancient merger of the Great Lakes, and covering roughly an area of all their present outermost boundaries. Many islands exist and much of the Inland Sea is uncharted. Ruins of ancient cities dot the shores and much commerce, interrupted by piracy, moves on the waters.

Kanda: The area of the ancient Dominion of Canada has kept its old name, almost unchanged, though much of it is unknown in Hiero's day, save for the central parts of the Metz Republic and the Otwah League, in west and east, respectively.

Kandan Universal Church: The state religion of the Metz Republic and the Otwah League. An amalgam of most current Christian beliefs, with a strong core of traditional Roman Catholicism, though there has been no contact with Rome for millenia. Celibacy is long gone as are many other beliefs and attitudes held by the ancient churches. A related sect, though much corrupted and debase, is the state religion of the east coast kingdoms and states, such as D'alwah.

Kaw: A beast of burden used south of the Inland Sea, both for agriculture and raising, as is the Korean ox of today. A large bovine, probably an almost unaltered member of some ancient stock of domestic cattle.

Killman: A highly trained warrior of the Metz Republic, who has taken intensive training, much of it psychological, in warfare and the use of all known weapons. Killmen are officers of the Frontier Guard automatically, but also rangers of the forest and special agents of the Abbey hierarchy. Hiero is unusual, though not exceptional, in also being a priest and exorcist. This combination of talents is highly approved but rare.

278

Glossary

Lantik Sea, the: The Atlantic Ocean, though with much altered western shoreline. No records exist of any trans-Atlantic contacts for over three thousand years.

Leemute: A word meaning an animal, or other non-human creature of human intelligence, which serves the Unclean. Gorm, the bear, would never be described as a Leemute, nor would the Dam People. The word is a corruption of the phrase "lethal mutation," meaning an animal which cannot survive to replicate under natural conditions, but its meaning is now altered to mean "inimical to normal humanity," and even normal life of all kinds. New varieties (such as the frog creatures Hiero found) are continually appearing as discoveries spread. Not all such new finds are Leemutes, however.

Lowan: A species of incredibly large, flightless waterbird, fish eaters and divers, which are found in remote areas of the Inland Sea. Though very shy, Lowan have few enemies, since an adult can reach 80 feet in length, with weight in proportion. They are uncommon, and thought by many to be a legend.

Lucinage: An Abbey drug, used to enhance the spiritual powers of its adepts and priests, especially when they are seeking mind contact. Also a relaxant and in small amount, sleep-inducing.

Manoon (the Dead Isle): A rocky island in the north central Inland Sea, the place of Hiero's captivity. One of the main headquarters of the Dark Brotherhood's Blue Circle.

Man-Rats: Giant, man-sized rodents of high intelligence, a ferocious type of Leemute, much used as warriors by the Unclean. Probably mutated *Rattus norvegicus,* which they resemble in all but brains and bulk.

Metz: The dominant race of Kanda. A corruption of the ancient word *Metis,* a term used for a racial stock of mixed Caucasian and Amerindian strains. The Spanish word *mestizo* has the same root and means the same thing. The Metz survived The Death in an undue proportion to other races, mainly due to rural isolation and the fact that they existed in small, somewhat isolated groups in more remote areas. Atomic and bacteriological blights thus slew relatively few. The Otwah League Metz tend to be lighter in color, due to more Caucasian genes.

Morse: The basic riding and plough animal (though only scrub stock is used for the latter) of the Metz Republic, which first bred them, and to a lesser degree the Otwah League. A very large and intelligent variety of the present-day moose, the largest member of the deer family. (Moose have been tamed for riding and carriage pulling in modern Scandinavia, though not often.)

Neeyana: The largest port in the southeastern area of the Inland Sea. Though legitimate trade passes through it, the Unclean actually rule, through a merchants' council dominated by their appointees. In fact, the main headquarters of the Yellow Circle of the Dark Brotherhood is buried *under* the town. No one untouched by evil lingers in Neeyana. (Possibly a corruption of "Indiana.")

Otwah League: The eastern sister state of the Metz Republic. The League, which takes its name from ancient Ottowah, is smaller than the Republic, from which it is separated by a vast expanse of wild land and Taig, through which run few roads. But close contact is maintained as well as possible and the Abbeys are a unified structure in both, serving the League government in the same capacity as in the Republic.

Palood, the: Greatest of all the northern marshes, the Palood stretches for hundreds of miles along the northern edge of the Inland Sea. It is avoided even by the Unclean and many strange forms of life not found elsewhere exist in its trackless fastnesses. Terrible fevers often wrack those who venture in, and its boundaries are largely uncharted.

Per: Corruption of "Father." Title of respect for a priest of the Kandan Universal Church.

Poros: Monstrous, four-tusked herbivore of the great southern forest, perhaps twenty feet tall at the shoulder. Its ancestry is unknown.

Snake-heads: Giant, omnivorous reptiles, found in small herds in the depths of the southern forests. Primarily eaters of soft herbage and fruit, they will also devour carrion and anything else slow enough to be caught. Something very like a bipedal dinosaur, though bred from some smaller reptile of the pre-Death days.

Snapper: Seemingly the living snapping turtle, grown to the size of a small car. A universal pest of any large body of water, being ferocious and almost invulnerable.

Taig, the: The great coniferous forest of Kanda, not too unlike that of today, but containing many more deciduous trees and even a few palms. The trees run larger on the average than those of today, though nowhere near the size of those in the far south.

Unclean, the: A general term meaning the Dark Brotherhood and all its servants and allies, as well as other life forms which seek, through intelligent direction to destroy normal humanity and to subvert natural law for evil purposes.

Were-bears: A little-known variety of Leemute: Not truly bears at all, but a sort of grisly, night-prowling monsters, short-furred and possessed of strange mental powers, by which they lure victims to their doom. The things have only been glimpsed once or twice. Though *of* the Unclean, they seem to be allies rather than servants. Their origin is unknown. Fortunately, they seem rare.